Ab

Sophie Pembroke writing about rom Mills & Boon as p at Lancaster Unive fiction for a living really is a dream con Abu Dhabi, Sophie grew up in Wales and now lives in a little Hertfordshire market town with her scientist husband, her incredibly imaginative and creative daughter and her adventurous, adorable little boy. In Sophie's world, happy is for ever after, everything stops for tea, and there's always time for one more page...

Scarlet Wilson wrote her first story aged eight and has never stopped. She's worked in the health service for twenty years, trained as a nurse and a health visitor. Scarlet now works in public health and lives on the West Coast of Scotland with her fiancée and their two sons. Writing medical romances and contemporary romances is a dream come true for her.

Martha Kennerson has enjoyed a successful career in executive management for over twenty years; of which twelve years have been in marketing and outreach. Her love of reading and writing is a significant part of who she is. Martha lives with her family in League City, Texas. She believes her current blessings are only matched by the struggle it took to achieve such happiness.

Affairs of the Heart

Affairs of the Heart:
Daring to Win

SOPHIE PEMBROKE

SCARLET WILSON

MARTHA KENNERSON

MILLS & BOON

First Published in Great Britain 2021
By Mills & Boon, an imprint of HarperCollins*Publishers,* Ltd
1 London Bridge Street, London, SE1 9GF

www.harpercollins.co.uk

HarperCollins*Publishers*
1st Floor, Watermarque Building,
Ringsend Road, Dublin 4, Ireland

AFFAIRS OF THE HEART: DARING TO WIN © 2021 Harlequin Books S.A.

Heiress on the Run © 2014 Sophie Pembroke
The Heir of the Castle © 2014 Scarlet Wilson
The Heiress's Secret Romance © 2018 Martha Kennerson

ISBN: 978-0-263-30039-0

MIX
Paper from
responsible sources
FSC™ C007454

This book is produced from independently certified FSC™ paper
to ensure responsible forest management.

For more information visit: www.harpercollins.co.uk/green

Printed and bound in Spain
by CPI, Barcelona

HEIRESS ON
THE RUN

SOPHIE PEMBROKE

For Mum & Dad
for always believing I could

CHAPTER ONE

'I DON'T UNDERSTAND,' Faith said, fingers gripping the fabric of her uniform too tightly. The body-hugging grey pencil skirt didn't have a lot of give, but she needed something solid and real in her hands. Something that definitely existed. Unlike the plane that was supposed to be taking her and her latest tour group back to London. 'How can there not be a plane?'

The airport official had the air of a man who'd had this conversation far more times than he'd like today, and in more languages than he was really comfortable with. It was in no way reassuring. 'There is no plane, *signorina*, because there is no company any longer. It's been declared bankrupt. All customers of the Roman Holiday Tour Company are being asked to contact their insurance companies and—'

'But I'm not a customer!' Faith interrupted, her patience exhausted. She'd been in the airport for three hours now, and she really needed a cup of coffee. Or an explanation for what the hell had happened to trash her immediate future overnight. 'I'm an employee. I'm the tour guide.'

The official's gaze turned pitying. Faith guessed that meant she wasn't likely to get paid this month. Or ever. Great. Just when her bank account could really have done with the help. 'Then I suggest you call your employer. If you are able to find him.'

Oh, that really didn't sound good.

Turning away, Faith gave what she hoped was a reassuring smile in the direction of the huddle of tourists waiting for her to report back on their journey home. Holding up her index finger in the universal 'just one minute' gesture, she fished in her capacious bag for her phone. Time to find out what the hell was going on.

'Marco?' she asked, the moment the phone stopped ringing. 'What the hell—'

There was a click on the other end of the line. *Thank you for calling the Roman Holiday Tour Company! There is no one available to take your call right now...*

Her own voice on the voicemail message.

Faith hung up.

Around her, Leonardo da Vinci Airport buzzed with life. The sounds of crackly announcements and suitcase wheels on smooth flooring. The chatter of excited holiday-goers. The smell of fast food and strong coffee. The twelve British tourists standing around their suitcases, looking at her hopefully.

Faith took a deep breath, and approached. 'Okay, guys, here's the situation. I'll be honest, it's not great, but I'm still here and I will help you sort everything out, okay?' Maybe she wasn't getting paid any more, and maybe her boss had disappeared off the face of the earth, but she'd spent the last two weeks showing these people the sights and sounds of Italy. They trusted her. She owed it to them to at least make sure they got home safely. Maybe, that way, their memories of this holiday wouldn't just be of a total disaster.

No one actually relaxed at her words, but at least they looked slightly less terrified, which Faith figured was the best she could hope for, given the circumstances. *Now for the hard bit.*

'So, let's start at the top. Does everybody have travel insurance?'

It took a full two and a half hours, four cups of coffee, twenty phone calls, and plenty of sweet-talking, but eventually Faith had everyone either rebooked on other flights or safely ensconced in a hotel room until their insurance could organise their return home.

Everyone, that was, except for her.

Dropping down to sit on one of the airport benches, ignoring the guy asleep with his head on his backpack next to her, Faith pulled out her phone and tried Marco's number again.

Thank you for calling the Roman Holiday Tour Company! There is no one available to take your call right now...

She jabbed the end call button, dropped her phone into her lap, and closed her eyes. Okay, so, time to review the situation. Where was she?

She was in Rome! Centre of history, romance and really great pizza. She knew her way around, she had, ooh, twenty euros in her purse, she...was unemployed, homeless and stuck.

Faith sighed, and opened her eyes again, looking around the busy terminal. Everybody there seemed to know exactly where they were going, and how they were going to get there. She didn't even know where she was going to sleep tonight.

She could call Antonio, she supposed. Except for the part where she really, really couldn't. Ex-boyfriends weren't generally inclined to be hugely helpful when her life fell apart, she'd learnt the hard way, and the one she'd left in a fit of anger only two weeks earlier would probably throw her out on her ear. Or worse.

And since everyone else she knew in Rome was either part of Antonio's ridiculously extended family or related to her missing employer, or both, that pretty much exhausted the local options.

Which left her with…home. She should be back in London by now, ready to pick up her next group and embark on a tour of the Italian lakes. She guessed that was off, too. She'd barely seen more of the homeland than the cheapest airport hotel at Heathrow since she left Britain a year and a half ago, and even if she hadn't cut all ties with the friends she'd had before that, how could she just call up and say, *Hey, I'm kinda stranded. Want to buy me a plane ticket?*

No, the only people anyone could do that to were family. And she really didn't want to have to call them, either.

She had no doubt that dear old Mum and Dad, the Lord and Lady Fowlmere, would welcome her back into the bosom of the family in no time. After all, the publicity of the wild child heiress returned to the Fowlmere estate would make great copy, and her father always loved anything that made him look good in the press.

Faith had left home three years ago, ready to be herself for once, not an aristocratic relic to be trotted out for charity galas and other occasions, or a standing joke in the society pages. Going home now would undo all that hard work. Not to mention bring up the reasons she'd had to leave in the first place.

But it didn't look like she had an awful lot of choice.

Rubbing a hand across her forehead, Faith straightened her white blouse, then ripped off the hideous orange and red necktie that Marco insisted on his guides wearing and shoved it in her bag. It meant that the neckline of her blouse was a little more revealing than was entirely appropriate, but she didn't care. If she was going to have to call her family, she needed a drink first. And perhaps flashing a little cleavage as she walked into the airport bar would mean that she didn't have to waste any of her precious twenty euros buying it herself.

'Explain to me again how this happened.' Lord Dominic Beresford looked at the icy-cold bottle of Italian beer sitting on the bar in front of him with longing. He'd spent all day in meetings, worked in the cab all the way to the airport, and was just ready to switch off and relax before his late-night flight back to London, when Kevin, the Temp from Hell, called.

Dominic's beer would have to wait until he'd fixed whatever Kevin had screwed up now.

On the other end of the phone line, he could hear Kevin frantically turning pages in one of the many files Dominic was sure he had stacked on his desk. Stupid Shelley and her stupid maternity leave anyway. Wasn't keeping him sane a higher calling than a baby?

Dominic swept a finger down the beads of water on the neck of his beer bottle. Even he had to admit, probably not.

'Um, best I can tell, sir, your secretary booked in the tour guide with your usual company some months ago. And then…' Kevin trailed off nervously.

And then, Dominic filled in mentally, the owner of that usual company, Lady Katarina Forrester, also known at the time as his fiancée, had been caught on camera in a rather compromising position, leading to a media storm that had threatened his family's reputation.

So he'd called off the engagement. And in retaliation she'd cancelled their professional relationship, too.

Which left him with six American businessmen and -women flying into London tonight, expecting entertainment and tourism to go with their meetings. And probably, now he thought about it, hotel rooms, too. Kat had always taken care of the accommodation for his business guests.

The fact that this was almost entirely his own fault for getting involved with a business contact in the first place didn't make Dominic want that beer any less. He should have known better.

'I think I can remember what happened next,' he told Kevin drily. 'But I'm more interested in what happens now. Here's what I need you to do. First—'

'Um…' Kevin said, the way he always did when he was about to ruin Dominic's day. Surely Shelley didn't need a full year off with the baby. What if she didn't come back at all?

'What?' Dominic bit out.

'The thing is, it's nearly eight o'clock, sir. I'm supposed to finish work at five-thirty.' Kevin sounded more whiny than apologetic about the fact. How had Shelley ever thought he'd be a fitting replacement for her? Unless her mothering instinct had kicked in early. Kevin certainly needed taking care of.

'Add the hours onto your time sheet,' Dominic said, attempting reason. 'I'll make sure you're compensated for your time.'

'Thank you, sir. Only it's not just that. I've got a… commitment tonight I can't break.'

'A date?' Dominic tried to imagine the lanky, spotty Kevin with an actual woman, and failed.

'No!' The squeak in Kevin's voice suggested he had similar problems with the idea. 'Just a group I belong to. It's an important meeting.'

The thing with temps, Dominic had found, was you couldn't just threaten them with the sack. They always had something new to move onto, and no incentive to stay.

And, it was worth remembering, Kevin had screwed up almost every simple job Dominic had asked him to do in the last week. Sometimes, if you wanted a job done properly...

'Fine. Go. I'll fix it.'

The scrambling on the other end of the line suggested Kevin was already halfway out of the door. 'Yes, sir. Thank you.' He hung up.

Dominic gave the beer another wistful look. And then he called Shelley.

The wailing child in the background wasn't a good sign. 'Dominic, I am on maternity leave. I do not work for you right now.'

'I know that. But—'

'Are you sure? Because this is the fifth time you've called me this week.'

'In my defence, you weren't supposed to go on maternity leave for another two weeks.'

'I am very sorry that my son arrived early and disrupted your busy schedule.' She didn't sound very sorry, Dominic thought. She sounded sarcastic. 'Now, what do you want? And quickly.'

'The Americans. Kat cancelled all our bookings and—'

'Told you not to sleep with her.'

'And I need to find them somewhere to stay and someone to look after them while they're in London.'

'Yes,' Shelley said. 'You do.'

'Can you help?' He hated begging. Hated admitting he needed the assistance. But Shelley had been with him for five years. She knew how he worked, what he needed. She was part of the company.

Or she had been, until she left him.

She obviously still had more loyalty than Kevin, though. Sighing, she said, 'I'll check my contacts and text you some hotel names and tour companies you can try. But you'll have to wait until I've got Micah back off to sleep.'

'Thank you.'

'And this is the last time, Dominic. You're going to have to learn to work with Kevin.'

'I could just hire someone else,' Dominic mused. The thought of a whole year with Kevin was untenable.

'Fine. Whatever. I don't care. Just stop calling me!' Shelley hung up.

Placing his phone on the bar, Dominic looked at the bottle of beer. How long did it take to get a child off to sleep, anyway? He might as well have a drink while he was waiting. But, as he reached for the bottle, a woman boosted herself up onto the stool next to him and smiled.

Raising the bottle to his lips, Dominic took in the low-cut blouse, too-tight skirt and wild dark hair framing large hazel eyes. The smile on her wide lips was knowing, and he wondered if she'd recognised him. What she wanted from him. A drink. A night. A story to sell. She wouldn't be the first, whatever it was.

And whatever it was, she wouldn't get it. He'd made a mistake, letting Kat close enough to damage his reputation. It wasn't one he intended to make again—certainly not for one night with a pretty girl with an agenda.

But, to his surprise, the first words she said were, 'Sounds like you have a problem, my friend. And I think I can help you out.'

It wasn't the way she normally got work, but there was a lot to be said for serendipity, Faith decided. Walking into an airport bar, jobless and broke, and hearing a guy talk about how he needed a London tour guide and hotel rooms? That was an opportunity that was meant to be.

'And how, exactly, do you intend to do that?' the guy asked. He didn't look quite as convinced by coincidence as she was.

Faith held out a hand. 'I'm Faith. I'm a tour guide. I know London even better than I know Italy and Rome, and I've been running tours here for a year and a half. And it just so happens that I've finished one tour today, and I have a break before my next one.' She didn't mention the slight hiccup in her heartbeat at the idea of going home to London. Probably it would be fine. She could be in and out in a week or so, heading off on a plane to sunnier, less panic-inducing climes.

Besides, at this point, it wasn't as if she had a lot of other options.

'Dominic,' the guy said, taking her hand. He looked familiar, she realised. But then, after a while, all men in grey suits looked the same, didn't they? Maybe not quite as attractive as this one, though. His gaze was cool and evaluating. The high-end suit said 'successful businessman', the loosened tie said 'workaholic' and the beer said 'long day'. She could work with all of those. 'And how, exactly, do you know I need a tour guide?'

'I eavesdropped.' Faith shrugged, then realised the move strained her struggling blouse a little more than was wise in a professional environment. Maybe she should have left the necktie on.

'Not exactly the key quality I look for in an employee.' He frowned down at her cleavage with more distaste than she was used to seeing in a man.

'Really?' Faith asked. 'Someone who listens even when they're not required to and anticipates your needs? I've always found that rather useful.'

It was funny, Faith thought, the way you could watch someone re-evaluate you, and see the change in their attitude as a result. When she'd first sat down, she'd known all he saw was boobs and hair. Then she'd offered to help him, and his expression had changed from dismissive to interested. And now…now he was really intrigued.

'Okay, so, we've established I need a tour guide. I also need seven luxury hotel rooms in a central London five-star hotel.'

Thank goodness for airport Wi-Fi.

Logging into her browser from her smartphone, Faith scrolled through to the late booking accommodation site Marco always used, and set her search parameters. 'For tomorrow?'

Dominic nodded. 'Staying six nights.'

There weren't a lot of options, so Faith just presented him with the best one. 'How about the Greyfriars?' She turned the screen for him to see the eye-watering price, next to the photo of a hotel suite larger than the flat she'd shared with Antonio in Rome.

A slight widening of the eyes, a tight smile, and Faith knew he was re-evaluating her again. Good. She could be useful to him, and he could be even more useful to her. Time he realised that.

'The Greyfriars should work.'

Faith tapped a few more buttons on her tiny screen. 'I've reserved the rooms. Do you want to trust me with your credit card information, or call and speak with them directly?'

He raised his eyebrows, even as he pulled his wallet from his jacket pocket. For a moment, Faith thought he might actually hand it over, but then he picked up his phone, too. 'Give me the number.'

Grabbing her well used red notebook from her bag, Faith scribbled down both the phone number of the hotel and the reservation reference, and pushed the page across to him.

While he spoke with the receptionist, Faith ordered herself a glass of wine, hoping that Dominic would be impressed enough by her efficiency that she wouldn't have to rely on her last twenty euros for much longer.

So. She'd got the man his hotel rooms; surely he had to offer her the tour guide job now, right? Which meant his next question would be 'What do you want?' She needed to formulate an answer—one that didn't let on exactly how much more she needed his help than he needed hers.

What did she want? For Antonio never to have found out who she really was. For Marco not to have done a bunk. For her parents to be normal middle-class people. Teachers, perhaps. People who fitted in, which her parents certainly did not. She wanted to not have to worry that every camera or phone she saw might be about to send her picture soaring around the realms of social media, ready to be identified as Lady Faith, the Missing Heiress.

She wanted to have never been caught on camera leaving that hotel room, three years ago. That was a big one.

But right now, she'd settle for a ride back to London, a hotel room for the week, meals and drinks included, and maybe a small salary at the end of the job. Enough to tide her over until she found her next gig. It wouldn't take long; she was good at her job, she enjoyed it, and people liked her. That was important in the events and tourism industry.

'Thank you for your assistance,' Dominic said, and put down his phone. Faith looked up with a bright smile. Okay, she didn't really know who this guy was, or what business he was in, but he could afford seven rooms at the Greyfriars, so he could get her out of Rome without having to call her family, which was the most important thing.

'Let me tell you a little bit more about what I need,' he said, and Faith nodded, her best attentive face on. 'My name is Lord Dominic Beresford, and I run a number of businesses from my family's estates.' Faith's stomach clenched at the name. Of course he looked familiar. She'd probably seen him on the society pages a dozen times when she lived in London, usually next to photos of her mother looking tipsy behind her fake smile, or her father charming another man's wife. Or even of Faith herself, leaving the current London hotspot on the arm of someone very unsuitable. Lord Beresford, on the other hand, was always immaculately dressed and frowning.

'I have six American businessmen and -women arriving in London tomorrow morning,' Dominic went on, oblivious to the way her stomach was rolling. 'I need you to meet and greet them, plan entertainment for the hours they're not going to be in meetings, and accompany them on tours, the theatre, whatever you come up with.' He gave her a sharp look. 'Can you do it?'

Spend a week in the company of a man who could at any moment realise exactly who she was and expose her, all while avoiding anyone she knew in London, and working at the same time?

'Of course I can.'

Dominic nodded. 'Then we'll talk salary on the plane. Finish your drink; we'll go get you a ticket. But first…' He picked up his phone again, tapped a speed-dial number, and waited.

Was that crying Faith could hear in the background?

'Shelley?' Dominic said, almost shouting to be heard. 'Don't worry. I've fixed it.'

CHAPTER TWO

HE'D ASKED THE wrong question, Dominic realised, later that evening. He shouldn't have asked Faith if she could do the job. He should have asked her if she knew how to be quiet.

The answer was now startlingly obvious: no.

She'd chattered through the ticket line. All through security. Yammered on in the first-class lounge. And kept talking all the way to the gate and onto the plane.

And now they were cruising at thirty-two thousand feet, the cabin lights were dimmed, and she was still asking questions.

'Have you taken clients on the London Eye before? What about up the Shard? I haven't done that yet, but I've read reports…'

Grabbing another file from his briefcase, in the vain hope that the growing stack of them on the table in front of him might suddenly make her realise he was trying to work here, Dominic tried to tune out the chatter from the seat beside him. It wasn't as if she took a breath long enough for him to answer anyway.

Why did she have to sit next to him? First class was practically empty. There were plenty of places for her to stretch out, watch a movie, sleep. Not talk.

'Do you know if they're theatre buffs? I can do some

research on what's the hottest show in town when we land. Or maybe the opera?'

Of course, there were plenty of other questions he should have asked, too. Like why she was so eager to come work for a total stranger for over a week. Did she need to get out of Rome? Or was she just homesick? Jobless? He should have asked for credentials, for references, for anything that proved who she was. He hadn't even managed a glimpse of her passport as she handed it over to the ticket clerk.

It wasn't like him to be so impulsive. Yes, he'd been in a corner and needed a quick fix. And okay, he'd wanted to prove to Shelley and Kevin that he could manage quite well without them, thank you. He was still the boss, after all.

But if he was honest with himself, he knew the real reason he'd hired Faith was because of her attitude. It took guts to walk up to a stranger in an airport and tell them to give you a job. Guts and desperation, probably. But if she had a reason for needing this job, she hadn't let on. She'd focused entirely on what she could do for him, and it had worked.

Coupled with her curvaceous, striking appearance, that courage and determination meant she'd probably go far, in whatever she decided to do—if her blunt, frank manner didn't get her into trouble first. She was the exact opposite of anything he'd look for in a woman normally, but Faith wasn't a woman. Not to him, anyway. She was an employee, and that was a completely different thing.

Of course, she wasn't exactly like his other employees, either. Shelley, outspoken as she could be now, hadn't started that way. For the first year she hadn't questioned anything, hadn't complained, hadn't offered an opinion. And she'd still never be seen dead in a skirt as tight as Faith's. No, Shelley was beige suits and pastel blouses, where Faith was red lipstick and high heels.

Dominic didn't even waste time on a mental comparison between Faith and Kevin.

'And, uh, actually…I should have asked…'

Good grief, was there a question she hadn't blurted out already?

With a sigh, Dominic looked up at her, only to find her plump lower lip caught between white teeth, and an uncertainty in her eyes for the first time since they met.

'Yes?' he asked, surprised by her sudden change in demeanour.

'Will you want me to stay at the hotel with your guests?'

He blinked. 'Well, yes. That would be easiest.' He'd need to get an extra room, he realised. Efficient as she seemed to be, he could hardly leave his most important clients with a stranger for the next week. No, he'd need to stay there too, that much was obvious. But if Faith was staying in the hotel, at least he could delegate their more mundane requirements to her. 'Unless you have a pressing need to stay somewhere else?'

'No, no, it's not that.' She gave him a smile, an understated, nothing to worry about here smile. One he didn't entirely trust. His mother had smiled like that, in the weeks before she left. 'It's just that I've been living in Rome for the last year and a half. I don't actually *have* anywhere to stay in London.'

It was only when the muscles in his shoulders relaxed that Dominic realised they'd tensed at all. Of course she didn't have anywhere to stay. That made perfect sense.

It didn't entirely explain why she'd been so eager to leave Rome on a moment's notice, with only a pull-along suitcase for company, but Dominic was sure he could persuade her to tell him that story, in time. He was a very persuasive man when he put his mind to it. And he *really* wanted to know what Faith was running away from. Just in case it was something he needed to defend his reputation against.

'You'll have a room at the hotel,' he promised, before realising something else. 'But we'll need to see if we can get one for tonight, too.'

Faith glanced down at her watch, and he knew what she was thinking. By the time they got into London it would be the early hours. Anyone checking in last minute to a hotel at that kind of time wasn't usually there on business. Not the legitimate sort, anyway.

'Maybe it would be best if I checked into one of the airport hotels?' she suggested. 'That way, I'll be on hand ready to meet your clients there in the morning.'

It made perfect sense. And suddenly Dominic couldn't face the drive into London, all the way to his penthouse apartment, just in time to wake up and pack ready to move into a hotel for the week. 'Good plan,' he said. 'As soon as we land you can book us both in.'

She flashed him a smile, this one more confident, more teasing. 'Does that mean you're trusting me with your credit card at last?'

He'd have to, he realised. She'd need a method of payment for all the things he'd asked her to do, to set up. Even if it was just having some petty cash to make sure she could buy the Americans a coffee if they needed it.

'I'll call the bank in the morning, get you set up with a card linked to my expenses account.' The bank knew him well, and he certainly gave them enough business to request a favour. They could monitor the activity on that card. 'In the meantime, I'll provide you with some petty cash. A thousand should do it.'

'Right.' Her eyes were wide, he realised. She hadn't expected him to actually hand over his money. She had to realise, from the way he'd casually paid for her incredibly expensive last-minute seat in first class, that money wasn't much of an object to him these days. But it obviously was to her.

As was trust. Interesting.

Dominic had a feeling he had a lot still to learn about his latest employee.

But that could wait until London. 'And now, if you don't mind, I've got some work I'd like to finish before we land.'

She nodded, silent, and he turned back to his file, enjoying the peace and quiet. Who knew that all he had to do to stop Faith talking was offer her money and trust? If he'd have guessed, he would have tried it hours ago.

She couldn't just sit there. Apart from anything else, it was boring. What was in those files that Dominic found so fascinating?

Faith wasn't a sitting still and waiting kind of girl. She got fidgety.

Besides, the longer she sat there, staring out of the aeroplane window at the night skies, the more she imagined, in detail, every possible way this whole plan could go wrong. It wasn't a pretty list.

He wanted to get her a credit card. Which meant he'd need her full name. She'd managed to avoid him seeing her passport information, just, but he'd have to have it for the bank. What did she do? If she gave him a fake name, the bank might not authorise the card and she'd have to explain everything anyway. No, the only option was to give him her real name, minus the assorted titles, and hope he didn't recognise it.

At least Dominic didn't seem like the sort to spend his mornings reading the society pages, however often he appeared in them.

She needed to know more about him, Faith decided. If she knew who he was, what mattered to him, she might be able to predict his response if he figured out who she was. Would he drag her back to her parents by her hair, as her great-uncle had threatened? Or would he out her to the media, like Antonio had said he would? Or would he let her slip back out of the country, quiet and safe, to carry on living her own life?

If only she could be sure.

Faith sighed and, beside her, Dominic made a small irritated sound. One thing was clear: she wasn't going to find out all about her new employer by asking him questions when he was trying to work. No, she'd have to do this the modern way—Internet stalking. Surely the airport hotel would have free Wi-Fi?

'Do you have to think so loudly?' Dominic asked, reordering his papers again so half of them crept over the edge of the table, almost onto her lap.

'I'm pretty sure thinking is, by definition, a fairly quiet activity,' Faith said, shoving the papers back up onto the table.

'Not the way you do it.'

Right. Well, if she couldn't talk *or* think, maybe it was time to go and find something more interesting to do. Somewhere Dominic wasn't.

'Okay, let me out.' She nudged her elbow against his side, and he looked up in surprise.

'Where are you going?' he asked.

'Somewhere I can think without disturbing your hypersensitive hearing.' Yes, he was difficult and crazy, but he was at least paying for her to get back home. Best not to totally annoy him this early in the game.

Shuffling his papers back into a neat stack, Dominic slid out of his seat, into the wide, wide aisle. God, she'd missed first class.

'Don't get into any trouble,' he said, looking disturbingly like Great-Uncle Nigel.

Faith gave him her most winning, most innocent smile. 'Me? I never get into trouble.'

And then, leaving him looking utterly unconvinced, she sashayed through towards business class to find some more interesting people to annoy with her questions and her thinking.

He was being ridiculous. How could it be harder to concentrate without Faith beside him, fidgeting, talking and *thinking*, than it was when she was there?

But somehow, it was.

Pushing his files across the table, since he clearly wasn't going to be able to concentrate on them tonight, Dominic leant back in his seat and considered. Where would she have gone? They were on a plane, for heaven's sake. It wasn't as if she could have run away. If they'd been sitting in any other area of the aircraft, he'd have suspected her of running off to first class to try and win over the affections of a wealthy businessman.

He glanced around the small section of seats on his side of the curtain. No sign of her. The only other occupants—an elderly gentleman in a suit and a woman with a pashmina wrapped around her, almost covering her face—were both asleep.

Maybe she'd gone back to business class to find a new friend there. Maybe the promise of a job with him wasn't enough. Maybe she just needed him for the flight home, and now she'd moved onto looking for her next opportunity...

Dominic forced himself to stop that line of thought. Just because certain women behaved that way, taking what they wanted then running, leaving destruction in their path, didn't mean that Faith would. He should give her the benefit of the doubt. Hadn't he just told her he trusted her enough to hand over a significant amount of money? Of course, money came easy to him, these days. Reputation was much harder won.

On the other hand, she was his employee. His responsibility.

The only responsible thing to do, really, was go find her.

To Dominic's surprise, there was no sign of Faith in business class. He got some funny looks as he peered across darkened seats, trying to spot a dark, curly head, but he ignored them. Maybe she'd found a steward or something to talk to? At least she hadn't been heading the right way to try and bother the pilot...

Pushing through the curtain, business class gave way to economy, where the occasional empty seats ended, replaced by cramped and crowded rows of people. Many were sleeping—it was the middle of the night, after all—but there were more screens and lights on than in either of the other sections. Dominic supposed it was harder to get some shut-eye when you were crammed in like cattle.

Faith must have disappeared into the bathroom, he decided. He just hoped that she was alone—the last thing his reputation needed was an article in the press about him and his employee being banned from an airline for joining the mile-high club. It wouldn't matter to a reporter that Dominic hadn't been the man with Faith at the time. Those sort of details never did, he'd found.

But then, as he turned back to try and get some more work done before landing, he spotted her and stopped, just to watch.

She was crouched down at the front of the economy section, just beside the seats with the space for a baby's bassinet against the wall; he must have walked right past her on his way through. Her dark head was bent over a bundle in her arms, and when she looked up at the parents of the child she was holding, her face glowed. Smiling, she whispered away in rapid Italian, all while tucking in blankets and stroking the baby's fine, downy hair.

This wasn't what he'd expected. In fact, this wasn't even recognisable as the woman he'd hired. Except… As he got closer, he caught a few English words scattered in her conversation. Big Ben. Madame Tussauds. The Tube.

A smile tugged at the corner of Dominic's mouth. She was offering them tourist advice. Planning their trip to London with them.

Without drawing attention to himself, Dominic slipped past, back through the curtain to where his files were waiting.

Perhaps he had hired the right woman, after all.

CHAPTER THREE

IT TOOK FAITH a moment to remember where she was when she woke up the next morning. Smooth white cotton sheets, rain battering the window, the glow of a reading lamp she obviously hadn't managed to turn off before she passed out the night before. Definitely not the flat she'd shared with Antonio and, given the rain, probably not even Rome.

No, Faith knew that rain. Knew that cold splatter and relentless fall.

She was in England. London.

Exactly where she shouldn't be, ever again.

Faith buried her head deeper into the pillow, as if she could block out the grey and the rain and the sheer London-ness of it all. She hadn't had a choice, she reminded herself. She'd made the best decision she could in a difficult situation.

But she couldn't help but wonder about all the people she'd left behind when she ditched the city she loved the first time. Were they still there? What would she do if she saw one of them on the street? Turn and walk the other way, or brazen it out?

She guessed she wouldn't know unless it happened.

Hopefully it wouldn't. In and out, that was the key. Do the job, take the money and run.

So, back to the job. And her employer.

Dominic had chosen the most expensive of the airport hotels once they'd landed in Heathrow, which hadn't really surprised her at that point. To be honest, she could have slept in a chair in the terminal, she was so tired. But the blissfully soft pillows and firm mattress of the hotel room were a definite improvement.

Reluctantly pushing herself up into a seated position, shoulders resting against the headboard, she tried to wake up enough to get a handle on the day ahead. Dominic had said the Americans were arriving around eleven, and it was only eight-thirty. So she had plenty of time to shower, dress…wait. What was she going to wear? She had her uniforms from the Roman Holiday Tour Company, she had her going-out-for-dinner dress and she had some jeans and plain T-shirts. She hadn't exactly packed for corporate events when she'd left Rome. She'd packed for an overnight in London and then another tour.

It would have to be the uniforms, she supposed, for now at least. Maybe she could ask Dominic about an advance on her wages, or even a clothing allowance. Given the disapproving look he'd given her outfit in the bar the night before, she suspected he might be amenable.

A knock on the door dragged her thoughts away from her wardrobe and onto her growling stomach. Was that room service? Had she remembered to leave the breakfast card out the night before? She really hoped so. She was useless without a decent meal in the morning.

Swinging her legs out of bed, she glanced down at her rather skimpy red nightgown—a present from Antonio, of course. He never did have any concept of subtle. Still, she supposed that room service had probably seen much worse.

Except, when she yanked open the door with a smile, it wasn't room service.

Dominic's eyes travelled down over her body at an offensively quick speed. Any other man, Faith knew, would have lingered over her curves, outlined in red silk. Any other man would have enjoyed the view of her bare legs.

Her new employer, however, merely catalogued her attire and raised an eyebrow at her. 'Do you always open your door dressed like a lingerie model?'

Faith felt the heat flush to her face. 'I thought you were room service with breakfast.'

'I'm afraid if you want breakfast you'll have to get dressed. Assuming you have something more suitable to wear...' His eyes flicked over her shoulder to where her skirt and blouse from the day before lay draped over a chair. Faith winced when she noticed the pale pink lace bra lying on top of them.

'Actually, that was something I wanted to talk to you about...'

Dominic glanced at his watch. 'No time. Get dressed and we'll talk over coffee, before we head over to arrivals.'

'I thought your clients didn't get in until eleven?' Faith asked, confused.

'They don't.' Dominic was already walking away down the corridor. 'But you need a briefing before they arrive.'

He turned a corner and was gone. Apparently busy executives didn't have time to finish conversations properly. Or tell people where to meet them when they were decently dressed.

An elderly couple appeared at the end of the corridor and Faith realised, a little belatedly, that she was standing in the open in her really inappropriate nightie. Stepping back inside her room, she shut the door firmly behind her and headed for the shower.

Time to prove to Lord Dominic Beresford that she was capable of doing any job he needed doing, whatever she was wearing.

Good God, did she sleep in that every night? Even when she was alone and exhausted and straight off a plane, Faith managed to slip into a sexy little number for bed. Dominic shook his head. What kind of a devil temptress had he hired?

Unless, of course, she'd put it on especially for him that morning. Unless she planned to seduce and ruin him, just like Katarina had tried to do. Just like his mother had done to his father.

It was all still a little too neat. Dominic didn't believe in coincidences, or serendipity, or any of the other things Faith had chattered about on the plane, her smile too wide, her lips too tempting. She'd been in exactly the right place at exactly the right time and, in his experience, that sort of thing didn't happen without some forward planning.

Still, he did need a tour guide, and she seemed to be an adequate one. All he had to do was stay out of her way while she worked, and she'd never get the chance to put any sort of plans into action. It would be fine.

As soon as he could erase that image of her in fiery red silk from his brain.

Figuring she'd take an insane amount of time to shower and dress, Dominic headed down to the restaurant and ordered coffee while he perused the papers. He wasn't much for breakfast, but he'd grab a piece of toast or some fruit when Faith joined him. They had too much to discuss to waste time on food.

However she'd come into his life, and whatever she hoped to get out of it, the only thing that mattered to Dominic was that she did the job he hired her to do: take care of his clients. He knew his strengths weren't always in the socialising side of things—he'd generally rather be in his office. That was why his arrangement with Katarina had worked so well. She'd taken care of the smiling, small talk and looking interested side of things. He took care of the business.

Bloody Katarina. She was right up there with Shelley on his list of women determined to thwart him right now. He just hoped that Faith wouldn't be added to it before she and the Americans left at the end of next week.

Sooner than he'd expected, Faith appeared at the entrance to the hotel restaurant. She waved a hand in his direction but, instead of heading for his table, she made for the breakfast buffet.

Holding in a sigh, Dominic watched as she bypassed the platters of fruit and the glass containers full of cereal. Instead, she loaded up her plate with eggs, bacon, sausage, beans, fried bread…and grabbed a side plate for a couple of mini pastries, too.

Apparently those curves were made entirely of breakfast.

'Hungry?' he asked, eyebrow raised, as she finally made it to the table.

Depositing her plates, Faith ripped off a bite of *pain au chocolat* as she dropped into her seat. 'Starving. Do you think they'll bring me some tea?'

His mother's lessons in etiquette and good manners towards women were deeply ingrained, and Dominic found himself motioning over a waiter to request a pot

of tea and more coffee for himself before he even realised he was doing it.

'You've eaten already?' Faith asked, after swallowing an enormous forkful of eggs and toast.

'I don't usually eat breakfast,' he replied, folding
his paper neatly across the middle and placing it on
the empty table beside them. 'Especially when I've an
important day ahead.'

'That's just when you need it,' Faith said, sounding
eerily like a nanny he'd had when he was eight.

'I've made it this far. I think I'll survive. Now. To
business.' Casting his gaze over her outfit, he was relieved to find it less revealing than the day before, and
certainly less fantasy-inducing than the silk concoction
she'd had on first thing. The skirt, he realised, was the
same as yesterday, but paired with a plain white T-shirt.
Still, while the higher neckline hid the very tempting
cleavage the blouse had displayed, it emphasised her
curves even more.

I'm not thinking about this. I am not *thinking about
this.*

Of any man alive, surely he knew better than most
the perils of giving in to temptation and forgetting obligations. Faith was here to work, and that was all. He
had to remember that.

'Yes. Work,' Faith said, bringing his attention back to
the topic at hand. 'I wanted to run through a few things
with you, actually.' To his surprise, she whipped a small
notebook from her bag, uncapped a pen and sat poised
to write down his answers. 'First, can your office send
me an itinerary for the week so I know exactly what
you've got planned for your guests, and I can work
around it? Also, it means I can make myself available
if anyone has any questions between meetings.'

'I'll ask Kevin to fax one over,' he said, trying to remember if Kevin even knew how to work the fax machine.

'Great. Once I have that, I'll put together a tentative itinerary and email it to you for your approval.'

'You'll need a laptop,' Dominic realised, belatedly.

'No need.' Pulling a tablet computer from her bag, she waved it at him. 'I use this.'

He blinked at her. 'Well, great. Okay then.'

'Next, do you have any background details on the clients themselves? Their lives, their families, their businesses, anything that I can use to get to know them?'

'You do realise you're a tour guide, not a dating service, right? You don't need to find them their perfect match.'

Her face turned stony, and he regretted the joke. She was trying to do a good job, after all. He should be encouraging her, not ridiculing her.

'These people are a long way from home for almost two whole weeks. It's my job to make sure they enjoy themselves and feel comfortable here. Knowing a little about them makes that easier. I'll talk to them myself when they arrive, of course, but a little forward knowledge would mean I can get going sooner.'

'Of course,' Dominic said contritely. 'Well, their businesses I can tell you about. But, as for the rest of it…' He spread his hands out. 'Katarina used to handle that sort of thing, I'm afraid.'

Faith paused with her mini cinnamon swirl halfway to her mouth. Katarina. That was a new name. 'Is Katarina your secretary?' If so, she could call and ask her for all the gossip.

'No. Not my secretary.' Dominic shifted in his chair,

looking sorry he'd ever mentioned the woman. Not a secretary. Then…

'Your wife?'

He sighed, and reached for the coffee. 'My ex-fiancée, actually. But, more pertinently, she runs the company we usually use for this sort of thing.'

'But not this time,' Faith said.

'No. Not this time.'

'Because you split up.'

Dominic gave her an exasperated look. 'Can't you ever take a hint to stop asking questions?'

Faith shrugged unapologetically. 'I like to know exactly where I stand with things. Makes life a lot less complicated.'

'Well, she doesn't matter any more. She's gone. You're here now to take her place,' Dominic said, entirely matter-of-fact.

Faith felt a peculiar squirming feeling in her stomach. 'As a tour guide. Not as your fiancée.'

Dominic looked up, appalled. 'That goes without saying!'

Faith flushed. 'You don't have to be quite so horrified at the prospect,' she muttered.

'Right. No. I just meant…' He sighed. 'This is a business arrangement, for both of us. Katarina…she's out of the picture now, and I'm afraid you can't really call her for insights on our guests.'

Now, that was interesting. Surely the woman would have an assistant or something that Faith could call for some notes. For Dominic to be so certain she wouldn't help, something pretty dramatic had to have happened between them.

'Bad break up?' she asked.

'The worst,' Dominic groaned, and for the first

time since she'd met him in that airport bar he seemed human. Normal. As if he had actual emotions and feelings, rather than a sensor that told him when to be disapproving of something.

'Want to talk about it?' she asked.

'Not even a little bit.' He didn't leave any room for discussion.

Oh well. Human moment over.

'Okay, well, if you can't tell me about them as people, you must be able to tell me why they're here. What's the very important business you have with them?'

Dominic leaned back in his chair. 'I'm looking to expand the activities and operations we have running on the Beresford estate. We're considering buying up some neighbouring land to build on, as well as utilising the Beresford family's London properties.'

In which case, Faith thought, they'd be one of the only aristocratic families to actually *increase* their family estates in generations. 'So these guys are your investors?'

Dominic nodded. 'Potential investors. But also potential clients. They want to see what we have on offer, and possibly use Beresford Hall in the future for international corporate retreats.'

'Okay, that helps. Now, they've visited London before, right? I don't suppose you've got a record of what they've seen and done…?' Dominic winced. 'No. Of course not.'

Faith sighed. Looked as if she was doing this the hard way. In which case, she really needed a kick-ass outfit to give her confidence.

'Okay, since you can't actually give me any practical help to do my job—'

'I gave you the job itself, didn't I?' Dominic's words

came out almost as a growl, and Faith decided to change tack.

'And in order that I can do it to the best of my ability and present the right impression of your company to your clients…I was wondering if there might be some sort of clothing allowance involved…'

His eyes did that quick flash over her body again, and Faith gave thanks she hadn't put the other, scoop neck, T-shirt on that morning. Not that he'd have noticed, of course. All he seemed to care about was that she wasn't wearing some boring suit.

'You're right,' Dominic said. 'I do need you to make the right impression.'

Faith perked up a bit. 'So you'll give me money to go shopping?'

Dominic shook his head, and the smile that spread across his face was positively devilish. 'No. I'll take you shopping to find something suitable.'

Something suitable. Faith slumped down into her chair a little.

Why did she suspect that Dominic's idea of 'suitable' would translate into something she'd never usually wear in a million years?

CHAPTER FOUR

'I'M NOT WEARING THAT.'

Dominic sighed and turned towards his newest employee with his best 'I'm the boss' face in place. Faith stared back at him, unaffected.

He hadn't expected the airport to be a shopping Mecca—he was normally more concerned with finding a quiet spot in the first-class lounge to work when he passed through. Still, he knew that there were plenty of shops, and that people enjoyed taking advantage of them.

Sadly, it hadn't occurred to him that most of them would be selling holiday apparel, especially at this time of year. Options for professional attire were somewhat limited.

'It's a suit, Faith. An inoffensive grey suit. It's perfectly respectable. What's wrong with it?'

'What's wrong with it?' Eyebrows raised, she parroted his words back at him. 'It's a suit. A perfectly respectable, inoffensive suit. Do I look like the sort of woman who likes to appear respectable and inoffensive?'

'Well, you don't look like a Beresford employee yet, if that's what you mean.' Hooking the clothes hanger back onto the rail, he smiled apologetically at the shop assistant and followed Faith back out of the shop, into the crowded terminal. A large clock, hanging somewhere overhead like a countdown, told him his clients would be arriving in less than an hour, and Faith still looked like a waitress in a university bar.

'Look, here's the deal,' he said, waiting until she stopped walking and turned to face him before continuing. 'If you want to work for me, you have to look like a professional, grown-up woman.'

'As opposed to?' Faith asked, eyebrows raised.

How to put it… In the end, Dominic decided to err on the side of caution. 'This is a bigger, more important job. You can't just look like a tour guide.'

Faith's mouth tightened, and Dominic prepared himself for an onslaught of objections. But instead, eyes narrowed, she held out a hand. 'Give me the money.'

'What?'

She rubbed her fingers together. 'Hand over the cash you would have spent on that hideous suit. Then go and get yourself a coffee.'

'And what are you going to do?' Against his better judgement, Dominic was already pulling the notes from his wallet. It hadn't been a cheap suit.

'I'm going to show you that you don't have to spend a fortune on something that looks the same as what everyone else is wearing to look professional.' She took the money and tucked it into her bag. 'I'll meet you over there in forty-five minutes.' Then, waving her hand in the direction of a coffee shop, she walked off, leaving him a few hundred pounds lighter, and minus one employee.

Apparently, she'd taken the trust he'd promised her, and run with it.

If there was one thing Faith knew, it was how to shop for clothes. Growing up, her mother had instilled in her the need to look polished, appropriate and, above all, expensive. In the years when her father had spent most of the estate income on a horse that didn't come in or a woman who visited far too frequently, wearing something new and fabulous to every occasion could be something of a problem. And once her parents had finally admitted that the money was gone, and Faith said goodbye to her boarding school blazer, trying to fit in at the local secondary school, even in the same polyester skirt as everyone else, had been a whole new challenge.

There, clothes had been the least of her worries. There, she'd been the rich kid with no money, the posh kid who swore like a sailor, the girl who thought she was too good for them, even if she didn't. There'd been no place for her at all, no little corner to fit in, and the loneliness of it still burned if she thought about it too much. She'd spent lessons daydreaming about being someone else. About leaving home, her parents and her title behind her. Of being Just Faith, instead of Lady Faith.

She'd thought she'd managed it, once she left school and moved to London. Thought she was her own person for once. Except it was so easy to fall in with people who she realised, too late, only wanted her for her title. Women who had closets of spare outfits to dress her up in, dresses and skirts that cost a fortune but barely had the structural integrity to survive a night of dancing and drinking at whatever club they used her name to get into.

They definitely weren't the sort of clothes Dominic wanted her wearing on this job.

Later, living abroad, alone and with only her seasonal tour earnings to keep her, clothing hadn't been a priority. She'd been her own person for the first time ever, and she hadn't had to dress a certain way to prove it.

The sense of freedom, of relief, was enough. So she had uniforms for work and a small, flexible, casual wardrobe for the rest of the time.

Dominic had been right about one thing—not that she'd admit it to him—this new job required new clothes.

But she'd be damned if she was spending the next week and a half in one plain, boring suit.

She didn't have long, so she worked a strike attack formula, identifying the three closest mid-range high street stores most likely to stock the sort of thing she needed. In the first, she picked up two skirts—one grey, one black—and a couple of bright cardigans. In the next, a jacket, three blouses and a lightweight scarf. The last shop took the largest chunk of her money, but in return provided her with a pair of low heels that looked professional, but that she could walk miles in. When she mixed in the plain T-shirts, underwear, bag, dress, make-up and jewellery she'd brought with her from Rome, she thought she was pretty much prepared for anything Lord Dominic Beresford could throw at her that week.

Stepping out of the last shop, laden with bags, she checked her watch. Five minutes left. Just enough time to change.

It was strangely gratifying to walk into the coffee shop and realise that Dominic hadn't even recognised her. He glanced up when she walked in, but his gaze flicked quickly away from her and back to the clock on the wall. He expected her to be late.

Dumping her bags on an empty chair, she dropped into the seat opposite him and grinned as his eyes widened. This time, he studied her carefully, taking in the jacket and blouse—worn over her white T-shirt to en-

sure maximum modesty in the cleavage department—
and the way she'd pinned her hair back from her face.

She gave him a minute to appreciate the transformation, then said, 'This works for you?'

Dominic nodded.

'Great.' Grabbing his coffee from in front of him, she drained the last inch of caffeine. 'Then let's go meet your clients.'

He had to stop looking at her. What kind of a professional impression did it make if he couldn't stop staring at his employee? It was just…a transformation. Faith looked respectable, efficient, and yet still utterly herself. And he still didn't quite understand how she'd managed to make his money stretch to the bags and bags of shopping he'd had to send back to the hotel before they headed to arrivals.

Now, while his driver loaded up their suitcases and Faith's shopping at the hotel, they were waiting in the arrivals hall for the next flight in from JFK. He could have sent a driver to meet them, Dominic supposed, but Kat had always hammered home the importance of the personal touch. And since she wasn't here to be personal any longer, that just left him. And Faith.

His gaze slid left again, taking in the way she gripped her fingers tightly in her other hand. Was she nervous? Did Faith really get nervous? It seemed unlikely.

'They're a nice bunch,' he said awkwardly, in an attempt to set her mind at ease.

'I'm sure.'

'They'll like you.'

She rolled her eyes at him. 'Of course they will. Being likeable is part of my job description.'

'Really?' Dominic glanced at her again. 'You don't seem to be trying that hard with me.'

Faith flapped a hand at him. 'Don't lie, you adore me. Besides, you matter less.'

'I am the boss,' he reminded her. Just in case she'd forgotten. He was starting to wonder...

'Yeah. So you'll be taking care of them in meetings and things, right? I'll be with them the rest of the time. When they're having fun. So it's important they think I'm a fun person to be around. You'll probably be back in the office by then anyway, so what do you care?'

It should set his mind at ease, Dominic thought, knowing that she wasn't expecting him to be around all the time, holding her hand through this job. She obviously believed she was capable enough to get on with it alone. And, against the odds, he was starting to believe that too.

So why was he mentally reshuffling his calendar to figure out which evenings he could join them on their tours and outings?

'You're right,' he said, shaking away the uncomfortable thought. 'As long as you keep them entertained and happy, that's all that matters.'

'Good.' Faith nodded, then sucked in a breath as the words and numbers on the display board changed again. 'Because they're here.'

She was not afraid. She *was* not afraid. She was *not* afraid.

She'd done this a million times before. The meet and greet was the most important part, sure—people tended to stick with their first impressions, even when they claimed not to. But she was good at this. Good at smiling and welcoming and helping and making people feel at home.

So why were her hands clammy?

Maybe it was the clothes. Maybe she should have gone with the stupid suit...

'That's them,' Dominic said, and then it was too late to worry about any of it anyway, because they were surging forward into handshakes and smiles and polite greetings. Faith beckoned over the driver who'd met them in the arrivals hall to start collecting bags onto a trolley, glad of something real and useful to do. Something she knew and understood. How could she have thought that looking after a group of high-powered businesspeople in London would be the same as shepherding holidaying Brits around Italy? They were already launching into conversations with Dominic that she couldn't even begin to follow. The three letter acronyms alone were baffling.

The drive into London, in a spacious limo complete with high-end coffee machine, at least gave her a chance to get her latest charges straight in her head. There was Henry, large and jocular—easy to remember, as long as she kept picturing Henry VIII when she looked at him. Next was Bud, skinnier in the face but a little rotund around the middle. Like a bottle of beer. Perfect.

The first two names fixed, she turned to the next pair. Both in navy suits, both dark-haired, both serious-looking. Thank God one of them wore glasses or she'd be getting them confused all week. Their names, however, were even easier—an improbable ice cream concoction of Ben and Jerry. As long as she remembered that Jerry had the glasses, she was golden.

The last two of Dominic's clients were easy, too. The blonde woman in the fantastic red suit was Marie, which made Faith think of Marilyn, which made her think of Monroe. And the brunette in the more severe black trouser suit with spectacular heels was Terri, who could just be the one she couldn't think of a great mnemonic for. Five out of six wasn't bad.

With everyone straight in her head, Faith settled back in her seat to nurse her espresso, and try to make some sort of sense of the conversation. She followed the discussion about land purchase and architects all right, until they started throwing out figures and referencing forms. She sighed to herself and decided she needed to have attended at least six months of previous meetings to even begin to understand.

'I'm guessing this is kinda dull for you,' Ben—no, glasses! Jerry—said, leaning in to whisper close to her ear.

'Not dull,' Faith objected. 'Just…not my area of expertise.'

Jerry's eyes flashed down to her blouse. 'And what exactly is that? Dominic didn't say.'

'Faith is your tour guide for the week,' Dominic said sharply, from the other end of the car. Faith looked up in surprise; she hadn't realised he was paying any attention to her. And how had he even heard Jerry from there?

Suddenly all attention was on her. Plastering on her best social smile, Faith said, 'That's right. So if you've any thoughts on places you'd like to go, things you'd like to see, just let me know!'

'Oh, I can think of a couple,' Jerry murmured, still looking at her breasts. Faith shuffled a little further away, until her leg pressed up against the car door.

Looking up, she saw Dominic glaring at her. He couldn't have heard Jerry's latest comment, but surely he had to know this wasn't her idea?

Or not. Turning his attention back to his clients, Dominic launched into another highly dense and baffling business conversation. Faith listened for a moment until she spotted Marie giving her a sympathetic smile. Then, tuning out the figures and the jargon, she pulled her tablet from her bag and started planning the week ahead.

She might not understand Dominic's job, but she was damn good at her own, thank you.

Dominic needed to get out of cars and hotels and into the office. How was he expected to concentrate on the finer details of the outstanding contract when one of his clients was hitting on Faith?

She'd handled it well, professionally even, but he was under no illusions that she wouldn't let rip if the guy pushed his luck. And quite rightly, too. Perhaps he should have a little word with Jerry…

The Greyfriars Hotel was a hit with his guests, proving Faith's knowledge of the luxury hotel market spot on. Procuring an extra room for himself wasn't difficult—although booking the penthouse suite seemed a little excessive even to him, given he had his own apartment just across town. Still, it looked as if it would be a long week. He'd probably need a luxurious space to relax at night.

'So,' Faith said as she handed out keycards, 'I know you've got meetings planned this afternoon, but what would you like to do this evening? Sleep off your jet lag, or go out and party?'

Dominic was secretly hoping for the sleeping option, but the Americans all seemed to be up for a party.

Faith clapped her hands together. 'Great! I'll make sure to come up with something really special.'

Maybe he didn't have to go. After all the meetings in Rome, plus this afternoon to get through, he could really use the time in the office. Surely Faith would be okay without him?

But then he saw Jerry sidling up to Faith with his spare keycard in hand.

Stepping closer, he heard her say, 'Oh, I wouldn't worry. If you lose it, the hotel can make you another one.' She pushed the card back into Jerry's hand, and Dominic gave a mental cheer.

As Jerry stalked off towards his room, not looking particularly beaten, Dominic leant in towards Faith. 'Count me in for whatever tonight's activity is.'

She turned to him and scowled. 'Don't think I can handle it by myself?'

He grinned. 'Oh, I'm certain that you can. I just want to watch the show.'

The smile she gave him in return was positively devilish, and he didn't even try not to watch as she walked towards the lifts, hips swinging.

Maybe he wouldn't have that word with Jerry. It might be far more satisfying to watch Faith cut him down herself.

He'd just make sure he was on hand in case she needed any assistance.

CHAPTER FIVE

HER HOTEL ROOM was bigger than most of the apartments she'd lived in since leaving home, but somehow Faith still found herself down in the hotel coffee bar, just off the lobby, as she planned out the week's entertainment. She told herself it was because the Wi-Fi connection was faster, or because she'd be able to see the clients and Dominic arriving back at the hotel after their meetings. But actually, it was just a whole lot less lonely than sitting upstairs on her own.

She missed Antonio. Well, actually, that wasn't true. She didn't miss *him* exactly. More the idea of him. What she'd thought he was. A future, a family, a proper place in the world. A life that revolved around who she really was, who she wanted to be—not what other people expected of her.

Well, now she'd just have to find her own new place to belong. Wasn't as if she hadn't done it before. Maybe, if she did a good enough job, Dominic would take her on full-time, replacing the infamous Katarina on a more long-term basis.

Except that would put her closer to her old life than she was comfortable with. No, better to get the job done then move on. Again.

Faith's finger hovered over the touch screen of her

tablet, ready to type in her search for availability at London tourist hot spots that evening. But instead she found herself typing in the name Dominic Beresford.

She shouldn't feel guilty about this, she told herself, as page after page of results scrolled up. She was researching a new employer—standard procedure. Dominic would probably have done the same to her, although hopefully using the name Faith Fowler, one she'd made her own on the Continent. The only stories of interest about her were tall tales of the Italian landscape, and reviews of popular tourist destinations. Nothing to alarm him, and absolutely no photos.

There were lots of photos of Dominic, though. Photos of him glowering at the camera, as flashbulbs went off around him. Photos of him with an icy-cool blonde on his arm, almost as tall as he was, perfect pout in place for the paparazzi. That must be Katarina, she supposed.

Lady Katarina Forrester, in fact, according to the caption. Faith didn't know her, she didn't think, but that wasn't hugely surprising. She'd never been particularly enthusiastic about socialising with the aristocratic set—at least, not the respectable ones—whatever her mother's dreams of her finding a perfect, financially supportive match amongst them. There hadn't been a space for her there. Her place at boarding school hadn't been the only thing she lost when the money was gone.

Her finger paused over another link. This one was harder to justify. This one, if she was honest, was just Faith being incurably nosy. As usual. It really wasn't any of her business what Katarina Forrester got up to, or why she'd split up with Dominic.

Of course, she pressed it anyway.

And was instantly glad that she'd turned off the sound on the tablet. The video that sprang to life was really not one to be watching in public. Eyes wide, she paused it, then stared for a moment longer before closing the window down. That had to be Katarina, with that long blonde hair let loose from the chignon it had been contained by in every other photo. But the naked guy there with her? Definitely not Dominic.

Well, she supposed that answered the question of why they'd broken up. And it kind of made her wonder exactly what she'd find if she Googled her own name. Possibly best not to know.

Except…she was back in Britain, working the kind of job that might get her spotted at any minute. Wasn't it better to know what was out there waiting for her if she was recognised?

Before she could change her mind, Faith tapped out her real name in the search bar and waited to see what popped up, apprehension stirring in her chest.

At the top of the page, a row of photos loaded. Two of her looking bleary-eyed in a too-short dress, blinking at the camera as she left some nightclub. The rest…all from that night. Or, rather, the morning after.

God, was it really even her? She barely recognised the woman she was now in the girl on the screen. She'd thrown away the clothes she wore in the photos—the tight black jeans and the corset top, moulding her curves and pushing up her breasts. Her hair was shorter than it was now, just curling around her jawbone. The hotel name, high end and far more expensive than she'd have been able to afford on her own, was clearly visible in the back of the shots.

And on her arm, Jared Hawkes, a little too pale and scowling, but otherwise giving no indication of the hellish night before. Or that he was about to go home and beg his wife for another chance.

No, the photo looked exactly like what everyone had believed it was—a money-grabbing girl stealing a famous, and famously troubled, rock star away from his patient, wonderful wife and adoring kids.

The guilt had faded over the years. She'd made a lot of mistakes when she was younger, sure, but who hadn't? And this one, that one time, she really hadn't done anything wrong, as much as the world's media had tried to convince her—and everyone else—otherwise. It had taken her a while to accept that and forgive herself, after she dropped out of the public eye. But she was done with guilt. All she had left now was the resentment, and the pain of the injustice.

Faith clicked the browser closed. She didn't need to see any more.

She took a large gulp of coffee and tried to clear her head. Time to get back to the matter at hand—finding somewhere to take the Americans that evening.

She took her time perusing the usual websites, and also reading the best London blogs, to get some more unusual ideas. She'd forgotten how much there was to do and see in London, how much she loved being there. Sure, Rome was romantic as hell and had plenty to offer, but London…it was more of a patchwork. More bits and pieces and scraps from all across history, and across humanity. She liked that in a city.

By the time the hotel lobby doors opened to reveal chattering Americans, she'd worked up a decent plan for the week and got some provisional bookings in place. The name 'Lord Beresford' had opened plenty of doors she suspected might have stayed closed to Faith Fowler, Event Planner and Tour Guide, and while she'd vowed not to use her own title for the purpose of getting ahead, she had no qualms about using Dominic's.

Pushing aside her empty coffee cup—the third of the afternoon—she packed up her notes and tablet and headed out to greet the Americans before they disappeared up to their rooms to change.

'How did the meetings go?' she asked Dominic as his clients got in the lift on the other side of the lobby.

He shrugged. 'As well as I could hope, I suppose.'

Which sounded rather Eeyore-ish to her. Maybe he was depressed. After all, he'd just lost his fiancée to a muscly premiership footballer in a YouTube video. Hardly surprising if he felt a bit down about things. 'Well, I'm sure they'll all be on board with anything you propose after the evening I've got in store for them.'

He raised his eyebrows at her, and his forehead crinkled up. 'Really? Do I get to know the plan in advance?'

'You kinda have to,' Faith replied. 'I need you to pay for it. They're holding the reservation for another hour.'

Dominic fished in his jacket pocket and pulled out his wallet. Opening it, he pulled out a shiny silver card with the name 'Beresford Estate Expense Account' emblazoned on it, and handed it to her.

Faith stared at the card, even as she noticed the slip of paper with it. 'Memorise the PIN and destroy that paper,' he said. Then, when she just kept looking at it, he added, 'Go on. Don't you have a reservation to confirm?'

Faith swallowed. 'Don't you want to know what I've got planned for the evening?'

Dominic's smile was wicked. 'I trust you. Surprise me.'

Later that evening, as Dominic stared at the limited wardrobe he'd brought to the hotel, he regretted not asking Faith to share the plan for the evening. At least then he'd know if he needed the dinner jacket or if an ordinary suit would suffice. Or if whatever she had arranged would be more comfortable in jeans… Surely she'd have mentioned if they needed any sort of special outfits, though. Right?

Why hadn't he let her tell him?

Sighing, Dominic dropped to sit on the edge of the bed, tie in hand. The reason, if he was honest with himself, was simply that she'd looked so excited about her plans. Standing there in her bright red blouse, with her hair tied back, she'd bobbed excitedly up and down on her toes. And just the idea that she was trying so hard to get this right, to do a good job…he wanted her to have a moment of glory when she pulled it off.

If she pulled it off.

He should have checked. He should be approving all the plans for the week. He would with any other new supplier or contractor. So why was it different with Faith?

Because Faith was different, he answered himself. Faith was so many worlds away from Kat and the way she worked. Faith, for whatever reason, needed this job, and needed to do it well. And he was going to trust her and let her get on with it.

Even if she could be using his credit card for anything right now. She could be on her way to the airport and back to Italy. Or anywhere.

No. Faith wanted this job; that much he was sure of. Still, they'd only talked vaguely about budgets on the plane, and Faith didn't seem the sort to be constrained by vague limits when the perfect opportunity for fun showed up. Although she'd been pretty canny with his money when she went clothes shopping.

He should have more faith.

Groaning at the unintentional mental pun, Dominic lay back on the bed and wished it was eight o'clock and time to meet in the lobby already.

In the end, he was twenty minutes early, dressed in a suit and clean shirt, no tie—although he had one in his pocket in case of emergency. Compromise, he'd decided, was the name of the game. Something the Americans could stand to learn at the negotiating table, actually.

He was early, but Faith was earlier, already standing in the lobby, dressed in a black dress that skimmed her knees, and with a red cardigan over it that hid the neckline. Respectable, but not too formal. Maybe he could ditch the tie at reception...

'You're early,' she said, smiling at him as he approached. 'Too impatient to wait any longer?'

'Something like that,' Dominic admitted. Up close, he could see the red lipstick that made her mouth even wider and more tempting than normal. And he was studiously ignoring the way her black heels made her legs look endless.

Rifling through her oversized handbag, Faith said, 'I've got receipts and confirmations here—printed them out at the business centre. Do you want them as we go along, or shall I put them together in a full report at the end of the week?'

Dominic let his shoulders relax. 'It can wait. Just give me the full accounting when we're done. Including your hours and salary.'

Her eyes widened again as she looked at him. 'Okay. Will do.'

What was it that made it so hard for her to let people trust her? he wondered. Was it just that the scope of this job was a little outside her normal remit? Or was it something more?

Maybe he'd ask her, one day. If he got the chance.

'So, is it time for me to know where we're going yet?'

Faith gave him a mysterious smile. 'Soon,' she promised.

The Americans obviously hadn't been given any hints, either. They arrived in the lobby in dribs and drabs, dressed in the same cautious smart/casual attire Dominic had opted for. As soon as they were all assembled, Faith clapped her hands to get everyone's attention and said, 'Okay, ladies and gentlemen. Time for your first, proper London experience of the trip.'

Leading them out of the lobby, she kept talking. 'I know you've all been to London before, and I know that you've probably experienced a lot of the standard tourist attractions. But there are some things that are so quintessentially London, it would be wrong to miss them out this week. I promise there'll be some more unusual outings in your future but, just for tonight, I went for the classics.'

She certainly had. Dominic blinked at the sight of an old-fashioned Routemaster double-decker bus parked outside the Greyfriars Hotel. It looked utterly incongruous, like a penguin in the desert. Glancing over at Faith, he saw she was biting her lip, nervously awaiting his reaction. The Americans were already jostling to get on board, chattering and joking excitedly. But she was waiting to see what *he* thought. His opinion mattered to her. He liked that.

'Can't wait to see where it's taking us,' he said, and offered her his arm.

Grinning, she took it, tucking her hand into the crook of his elbow, and he realised that it must be the first time they'd touched. Because if he'd felt that electric shock at contact before, he'd have remembered. The touch, the scent, the closeness of her filled his senses, and he had to concentrate on putting one foot in front of the other to reach the bus and help her up the steps.

Note to self, he thought as he followed her. *Do not touch Faith Fowler again. That way lies madness.*

Faith held her breath as she stepped onto the bus, praying it was everything Julian had promised. She'd called in favours from every person she knew in the tourist trade in London to find the best options for the week ahead, and sent up thankful prayers when Julian told her that his latest venture, Big Red Tours, had a last-minute cancellation for that night. The photos and testimonials had been great, but you never knew for sure until you were there…

With the last step, she looked around and let out a relieved sigh. It was perfect.

Ben and Jerry were already seated at the table at the back, and a waiter in black tie dress was offering them a drink. The original bus seats had been torn out, replaced by wooden tables for two and four, bolted to the ground, as were the mismatched chairs around them. Red, white and blue cotton bunting hung from the ceiling, and the adverts were all replaced by vintage wartime posters.

Terri and Marie ventured upstairs and Faith followed, wondering at the sight of more bunting and an honest-to-God rooftop garden, with more seating areas dotted about.

'This is incredible, Faith!' Marie said, beaming as she took a glass of champagne from the upstairs waiter. 'Where on earth did you find such a thing?'

Faith smiled. 'Trade secret.'

She waited until everyone had explored the bus and chosen a seat before instructing the driver to start the tour. Period music, the sort that would have played on the American bases during the war, sang out from the speakers as they drove along the river, through the heart of London. The waiters served canapés and topped up champagne flutes as they went, the lights of the city sparkling outside the windows.

And all Faith could focus on was the fact that Dominic was sitting opposite her, smiling.

'Do I want to know how much this is costing me?' he asked, holding out his glass for a refill.

Faith shrugged. 'They had a last-minute cancellation, so I got a good deal.'

'I had no idea you could do this sort of thing. I mean, in general, not you personally.'

Quite honestly, Faith hadn't been sure of either. But, since everything seemed to be going okay, she decided not to mention it.

'The guy who started up the business—Julian—used to work with me last time I was doing tours in London. I thought it might be a fun start to the trip.'

'It is,' Dominic said, and he sounded as if he meant it. Faith felt something inside her start to relax and she reached for a glass of champagne.

'I just hope the next part of the evening is as big a success.'

'What is next?' Dominic asked.

Faith smiled. 'Dinner.'

Dinner, it turned out, was a bit of an understatement. Dominic hadn't known you could have canapés and champagne and roof gardens on buses, but he also hadn't realised you could actually eat dinner on Tower Bridge. Or, rather, inside it.

'Has this always been here?' he asked, staring out over the River Thames.

'They opened it for catering years ago,' Faith told him. 'We got lucky with a spare table tonight.'

They'd been getting lucky a lot, it seemed to Dominic. 'Another last-minute cancellation?'

Faith squirmed a little. 'Not exactly.'

Dominic raised an eyebrow. 'Let me guess; you used my name?'

'Wouldn't you?' Faith asked. 'To get a table at a restaurant, or a better seat on a flight, or tickets to some play?'

He wouldn't, but he couldn't deny that Shelley sometimes did. It just made him feel a little uncomfortable. 'I suppose. So, what happens to the poor saps we kicked out of this place tonight?'

Faith shook her head. 'I wouldn't do that. I just... persuaded them to rearrange things a little. That's all.'

'Can you talk anyone into anything?' he asked. After all, she'd done all this over the phone in the course of an afternoon. He couldn't even blame the mind-boggling effects of touching her, or even just looking at her, for the world falling at her feet. Or was that just him? Was everyone else immune, and it was just Dominic Beresford who found himself handing over jobs, money, credit cards and trust to this woman without a second thought?

Faith gave him a rueful smile. 'I wish I could. Do you know how many places I had to call, how many people I had to talk to, and how much research I put in to pulling all this together? A lot of places just said no upfront. Some I'm still in negotiations with to fit us in later in the week. I lucked out tonight, but I've still got a lot of hard work to put in to pull off the rest of the trip.'

She stopped, as if she hadn't meant to say so much.

'I'm sorry,' he said. 'I didn't mean to suggest you hadn't been working hard.'

'That's okay.' Faith's gaze darted away, out of the window. 'I mean, it's supposed to look effortless, isn't it? That old swan metaphor. Swimming smoothly along, paddling like mad underneath.'

Ridiculously, all he could think of at her words was Faith in a bikini. He cleared his throat, buying time for the image to dissipate. 'Well, it all seems like, uh, very smooth swimming so far.'

She gave him a curious look. 'Good. I'm glad you're enjoying it.' She glanced over his shoulder. 'Looks like our table's ready. I'd better gather the others from the bar.'

She strode off towards the Americans, who were all ordering cocktails. Apparently the champagne had put them in an excellent mood. If only he could get them to sign the contracts now...except that would be unethical. And his lawyers would kill him.

Sighing, Dominic headed for the large round table directly overlooking the river. Usually this sort of an evening was nothing but a chore, time away from the office he could ill afford. But Faith had managed to make it fun, different.

He couldn't wait to see what she had planned for the rest of the week.

CHAPTER SIX

IT WAS NEARLY midnight by the time the group climbed onto the Routemaster bus again and headed back to the hotel. And as they pulled up outside the Greyfriars, Faith silently thanked Dominic for quashing Henry's suggestion that they carry on to a club after dinner. She needed sleep and, before that, she needed to check her emails and reply to any confirming spaces for events over the next few days. And, as Dominic had pointed out, the Americans had a lot of meetings to fit in before their trip to the Beresford country estate later in the week. He needed them alert in the morning.

Fortunately, everyone except Henry had agreed. And when she'd promised to take him dancing another night—something else to add to her never-ending list of requests—even he'd been mostly appeased.

As the others headed for the lifts, waving tiredly behind them, Faith hung back with Dominic.

'Bed?' he asked, and for one moment, before she remembered that this was Dominic Beresford, more automaton than man, she thought he meant together and her eyes widened.

He noticed. Damned observant man. 'Are you going to yours now, I meant,' he said, not looking at all flustered at the misunderstanding. 'Rather than any sort of inappropriate proposition.'

'I knew that,' Faith said quickly. 'And yes. Bed. After I finish up some emails and such.'

Dominic nodded. 'Come on. We can work in the office of my suite. Keep each other awake while we finish up for the day. I've got some things I need to go over with you, anyway.'

She shouldn't. All she really wanted to do was take off her make-up, curl up in her bed with the late-night TV on low, and answer her emails until she passed out from exhaustion. Working in Dominic's room meant keeping on her high heels and actually making coherent conversation, both of which seemed like they might be beyond her until she'd got some sleep.

And yet…

'We can have a nightcap,' he said, striding off in the direction of the lift. 'Come on.'

She followed. He was her boss, after all, and she was obliged to bow to his requests. At least, that was what she was telling herself. She was too tired to think about the part of her that wasn't ready to say goodnight to him just yet.

Dominic's suite was twice the size of her, already impressive, accommodation. It had a kitchen area, a full dining table, a lounge filled with an oversized corner sofa and a glass coffee table and, tucked away in a corner by the bedroom door, the office.

There was only one desk, but two chairs, and another low table between them. Dominic took the desk chair, flipping open his laptop as he sat, so Faith settled into the visitor's chair—lower, more comfortable, and far too likely to send her to sleep.

Wearily, she reached into her bag for her tablet, contemplating just kicking her shoes off regardless. It was late. He'd understand. And her feet couldn't smell that much, could they?

Hmm. Maybe better not to risk it.

'Drink?' Dominic asked, and when she looked up she saw that he'd taken off his jacket, his shirt collar lying open beneath it. Her gaze fixed on the hollow at his neck, just above his collarbone, and she wondered, in what could only be a sleep-deprived daze, what it would be like to kiss him there. How his skin would feel under her lips, under her fingertips. 'I've got brandy, whisky, probably some rum…'

Faith blinked, and brought her attention back to the real world. 'Um, a whisky would be great. Thanks.'

Work. She was here to work. She really had to remember that.

She swiped a finger across the screen to bring it to life, and brought up her email program. Thirty-seven new emails. And since this was a new account Dominic had set up for her to do the job at hand, chances were that very few of them were spam. She suppressed a groan. She was never going to get to sleep tonight.

Dominic returned from the bar in the kitchen area with two tumblers, filled with ice and topped with what she imagined would probably be the finest whisky. Did she even remember what that tasted like? she wondered. Her father had only ever drunk the best, most expensive Scotch whiskies, and he'd tried to ensure that she grew up with a taste for the finer things, too.

'Here.' Dominic bent down to hand her the glass, and Faith's mouth moistened as that hollow at his neck grew closer.

This was ridiculous. She needed to go to bed.

As soon as she'd finished work.

Leaning back in the swivel chair at the desk, Dominic stretched his legs out in front of him, arms folded across his chest, and studied her.

'What?' Faith asked after a few long moments of scrutiny.

'You did a really great job tonight,' he said.

A warm glow flushed across her skin. 'Thank you. I knew it was important to you that your clients start the trip off with a bang.'

'And you certainly did that. The bus was a masterstroke.' And yet still he kept staring at her.

'Is there a *But...* here?' Faith didn't care if she was being blunt. It was far too late at night for subtle.

Dominic shook his head, unfolding his arms to push himself up into a straighter seated position. 'No buts. Just a few questions.'

Questions. Possibly her least favourite things. 'Such as?'

'Well, I never got to see your full résumé. We didn't even have a proper interview.'

'And you want to do that now?' Was the man crazy? 'You realise I'm already doing the job, right? And doing it well, according to you.'

'I know.' Dominic sounded completely unruffled. 'Like I say, I just want to know a little bit about your background.'

Her work background, Faith reminded herself, as her heart started to beat double time. All Dominic cared about was the job he'd hired her to do. Even if he did start developing suspicions about who she really was, he probably wouldn't care unless it interfered with one of his meetings. All she needed to do was keep things professional. How hard could that be?

'Well, I started working in events in London,' she

said, carefully editing out that part about how, as Lady Faith Fowlmere, she'd mostly been attending the events. Or, at most, throwing epic parties at her famous friends' houses. 'Then moved more into the tour guide side of things for a while.' After she ran away from home and became Faith Fowler. 'That's where I met my previous employer, who hired me to run his tours in Italy, where I've been for the last year and a half.' After Great-Uncle Nigel spotted her at an event in London and almost dragged her home and she realised that another country would be much easier to hide in. 'That's about it,' she finished with a shrug.

Dominic gazed at her, his eyes still assessing. But finally he nodded. 'Well, you obviously learned a lot in your time. Like I said, you're doing a great job. I trust you'll find more wonderful experiences to entertain us over the next few days. And you're coming to Beresford Hall with us later in the week, of course?'

Faith froze, the pleased smile she'd had at his words fixing into place as she realised what he was asking. Beresford Hall. Family seat. Full of people who knew the aristocracy, knew the families, kept up with the news.

Full of people who might recognise her.

'Actually, I was thinking that perhaps I should stay here and get the last couple of nights' entertainment sorted out?'

Dominic raised his eyebrows. 'We have Wi-Fi at the Hall these days, you know. You can work there.'

'Right. Of course.' Maybe she could hide on the bus. Or in a deserted corner bedroom. Or a cupboard. Anywhere. 'Only, I was thinking—' she started, but Dominic spoke over her.

'Then that's settled.' He tilted his head as he studied her. 'I'll be interested to see what you make of the old place.'

'Oh?' What did it matter what she thought? She was only the hired help.

But Dominic nodded. 'I want Beresford Hall to be an all-inclusive events location. It's more than a piece of history now, more than heritage. There are a lot of opportunities there—at our conference facility for a start. If you wanted me to introduce you to the head of events there...'

'No,' Faith said, too loudly. 'I mean, thank you. But really, this job is just a one-off. In between tours, like I said. I'm not looking for a permanent conference and events job here in the UK.' Especially not at Beresford Hall, where someone was bound to recognise her on her first day. No, thank you.

'So you'll be going back to Italy, after this week?' Dominic's gaze was sharp, and Faith got the impression that this was the real question he'd wanted to ask all along.

'Um, probably not Italy, no,' she admitted.

'So, you don't actually have another job lined up there?'

'Not exactly.' Faith plastered on a sparkling smile. 'I like to keep moving, you see. Don't want to be tied down to just one country.'

'I see.' Dominic leant back in his chair again. 'You never did tell me exactly why you had to leave Italy.'

Because my ex-boyfriend was threatening to bring the international media down on me, and the company I was working for went bust.

Neither of those facts were really going to put Dominic's mind at rest, were they? When in doubt, lie and run.

Faith gave a high, tinkling laugh. 'Well, you know,

after a while even pizza gets a bit boring. Besides, I wasn't sure my hips could take any more pasta!'

Before he had a chance to respond, Faith gathered up her tablet and notebook and shoved them into her bag.

'And I know how lucky I am to have this great job,' she added, getting to her feet. 'Which is why I need to get some sleep, ready to do my best work again tomorrow. Goodnight!'

She kept smiling until the door closed behind her, well aware that Dominic was still staring after her. But her heart didn't stop racing until she was back in her room.

She needed to make sure that Dominic didn't have any more chances to ask her questions about her previous life. It was far too tempting to tell him the truth.

She was lying to him, Dominic thought for the hundredth time as he took his seat on the executive coach taking the group to Beresford Hall three days later. Faith had been the perfect employee so far, arranging dinners and tours with such finesse that Dominic would have felt entirely comfortable letting her take charge of everything alone, except for one thing: he knew she was lying to him.

He had absolutely no idea why, but Dominic hadn't got where he was without developing the ability to spot when he was being lied to. The only question was, what on earth could Faith Fowler have to lie about?

Even if her career history had been embellished—although, given how little she'd actually told him, it seemed unlikely—she was doing a good enough job that he wouldn't care. She clearly didn't want to visit Beresford Hall—she'd come up with half a dozen excuses over the past few days to try and get out of it. But he'd stayed firm. He wanted her there, if only to find out why she didn't want to go. But it still didn't seem like something to lie about. Which meant it had to be something to do with why she was in such a hurry to leave Italy.

The last of his clients climbed aboard and took their seats, followed by Faith, in full professional mode. Shading her eyes from the sun streaming in through the coach window, she did a quick head count and nodded to the driver, barely sparing a glance and a tight smile for Dominic as she chose her own seat—as far away from his as was possible in the circumstances.

He'd lain awake for far too long after she'd left the other night, dreaming up elaborate falsehoods and scandalous pasts she could be hiding. Associations with the Mafia, drug trafficking, murder. Just the fact he was having to think about these things meant he should probably fire her and minimise whatever risk her lies represented.

But he didn't. Partly because he couldn't believe it was actually that bad. But mostly because she was Faith, and he wanted to give her a chance. He wanted her to stick around.

Which didn't mean he was going to stop trying to find out what she was hiding.

Beresford Hall lay less than two hours' drive outside London. Dominic spent the journey catching up on some reading, chatting with Ben, Henry and Marie about his next trip over to the States, and trying not to stare at the back of Faith's seat.

It was just the mystery, he told himself. Strange woman walks into his life, just when he needs her, and proceeds to do a perfectly good job while lying to him the whole time. Of course he was intrigued. Of course he'd been thinking about her. He needed to know the truth to protect himself, even if he suspected it would turn out to be nothing. A row with a boyfriend, perhaps. Nothing more.

And, whatever her reasons for leaving Italy, she didn't want to come to Beresford Hall either, that much was clear. But maybe she'd open up to him there. Maybe he could get her to talk.

Seeing the estate he'd saved from ruin and built up into a multi-million-pound business often made women feel fondly towards him. No reason to suppose a little imposing grandeur wouldn't do the same for Faith.

The coach pulled up the long driveway, curving through the landscaped gardens, past the fountains and up to the front of the Hall. In the past, all you'd have seen from the road was woodlands and immaculately trimmed hedges. These days, Dominic got a thrill from spotting a gang of archers heading off to the archery range, and a group of men in suits making their way towards the conference facilities. No weddings today, he supposed, with it being a Wednesday, but there were at least two stag dos booked in for the weekend, taking over the rally track and go-carting on the outer edges of the estate.

Dominic didn't try to dampen down the surge of pride he always felt when he saw the Hall, and especially when he saw the reaction of his clients to the magnificent building. Yes, he'd been born into a privileged family. But it had taken every ounce of his own determination and ability to make his family name, and estate, what it was today.

Maybe the people looking on only saw the money made, the clever business decisions he'd taken. But he, at least, knew that it was more than that. He'd done his time feeling ashamed as a boy—of his mother, his name, his life. But he'd grown up since then. He'd taken on the challenge and surpassed it. He'd reclaimed his heritage, his self-respect, his future.

And he had every right to be proud of that.

But when he finally caught Faith's eye, as she stood to guide everyone back off the bus, he didn't see the expected awe or appreciation in her gaze. Instead, she was frowning at the Hall as if it personally offended her.

His most likely reason for her reluctance to come with them that day rose up in the back of his mind again. Perhaps she just resented the aristocracy, and perceived privilege. Hadn't she been happy enough to use his name to get what she wanted from their suppliers that week, though? If there was one thing he couldn't stand, it was a hypocrite.

Dominic clenched a fist against the back of the seat beside him as he stood. He'd make sure Faith Fowler got a full tour of Beresford Hall. He wanted her to understand exactly what he'd achieved here, although he couldn't have said why it mattered to him so much.

Beresford Hall was beautiful, magnificent, a shining example of some sort of architecture or another, and everything else the guidebook said it would be. But all Faith could see was the shadow of Fowlmere Manor hanging over it, reminding her how hard she'd worked to get away from places like this. People like this.

Sure, Fowlmere was maybe half the size of Beresford Hall, and there were far fewer people hanging around it these days, but the similarities caught her everywhere she turned, and she couldn't shake the shiver that crept over her shoulders when she thought how close she'd come to being trapped somewhere like this her whole life.

Dominic led them up the stone steps to the imposing front doors, hauling them open and holding one to let them pass into the main hall. It was early on a weekday, but there had been several coaches parked in the car park when they arrived and the hall already boasted three lines for tickets. This, Faith supposed, was where Fowlmere really differed. Even if her father had let them, what tourists would want to pay to visit a crumbling manor that had sold most of its heirlooms to pay gambling debts?

Beresford Hall was often held up as an example of heritage done right. Open most days to the public, save one wing that was kept as family quarters, Dominic had put history on display for all to share and he'd done it in style.

'Come on through, guys,' he said, lifting a red tasselled rope to let them skip the queue. 'I'll give you the house tour myself, before we get a better look at the newer additions to the property.'

Faith followed, remembering the horrible attempts to open Fowlmere to the public when she was a child. Only two days a year, her father had decreed, and he'd give the tours himself. Except, when it came down to it, it turned out he didn't know much about the history of the house, or the family. And when her mother had stepped in to take over, Faith had realised she was already slurring her words at ten in the morning.

Faith had learned everything she could about the Manor and her ancestry, to be ready for the next open day. But, in the end, her father had declared it a waste of time and shut the gates again.

Not so at Beresford Hall.

'This is the chamber prepared for Queen Victoria, when she visited the Hall.' Dominic waited as they all took in the room, with its rich red walls and imposing four-poster bed. Gold accents glittered on everything, adding a shine to the faded history. 'Beresford Hall has been host to five British monarchs, and we have memorabilia from each of their visits.'

He was obviously proud of his family and his history, Faith thought. She wondered what that would be like. Whether she'd have stayed if her own family hadn't been such a shambles. Who would she be if she'd grown up somewhere like Beresford, where her future was neatly mapped out for success, rather than finding buckets to catch drips from leaking roofs, or hiding bottles from her mother and lying to debt-collectors when they came looking for her father?

But she wasn't that girl. She was Faith Fowler now, and that was all she ever intended to be.

With a sigh for things lost, Faith followed Dominic through the next doorway to a magnificent dining room, staring out of the window instead of listening to him talk. She was his employee, not his girlfriend. She didn't have to hang on his every word. She didn't have to care about this house, or its history. She didn't have to learn which king stayed when.

Because this wasn't her world any more. And it never would be again.

CHAPTER SEVEN

'WHAT ARE YOU frowning at?' Sylvia asked.

Dominic looked down at his sister, taking in her wrinkled up nose and exasperated eyes, and tried very hard to shake his bad mood. 'Nothing. It's all perfect. Thanks for setting this up for me.'

Sylvia shrugged. 'Just an ordinary day's work. You do realise I do this for paying customers every day.'

It showed, Dominic thought. When they'd first opened the tea rooms in the old stables, he'd been doubtful. They already had the restaurant, over in the Orangery, offering fine dining to the visitors, and the café over on the other side of the yard, serving sandwiches and drinks. A third eating area seemed like overkill.

But Sylvia had wanted it. Sylvia, who never really asked for anything, only went along with his plans and said, 'If that's what we need to do.' So when she'd said, 'No, Dominic. You're wrong. This will be a really good thing,' he'd listened.

He was glad he had, now. Sylvia had taken on all the planning and running of the tea rooms, picking out the perfect curtains and matching tablecloths, light and airy without being too chintzy. She'd tasted every baker's cakes from Beresford to London, and finally hired a young man called Russell to bake the scones, cakes and biscuits for the afternoon teas. People flocked to them—not just the senior citizens on their day trips, which he'd sort of expected, but everyone. Hard-nosed businessmen on a break from their conference schedule over at the events suite. Lovers checking out the Hall as a possible wedding venue. Hungover stag parties. Everyone.

For once, Dominic was actually pleased to be proved wrong.

The Americans certainly seemed to be enjoying it, too. He'd originally asked Sylvia to find them a private room somewhere, but she'd refused, saying half the charm of the tea rooms was the atmosphere. And she'd been right again. They were chatting away with the tourists on the next table, exclaiming over the scones and clotted cream and the cucumber sandwiches.

Even Faith looked as if she might be enjoying herself for the first time that day.

'You're staring at her again,' Sylvia commented, and he could hear the smirk in her voice.

Diverting his gaze towards the tower of cakes on the counter, Dominic said, 'Staring at whom?'

'Your event planner. Tour guide. Kat's replacement. Whoever she is.'

'Merely a last-minute employee for the week,' Dominic said, ignoring the tiny part of his brain that screamed at him that she should be more. 'Kat cancelled on us.'

'Understandably.' She gave him a sideways look. 'After that video.'

Just hearing the words made the shame rise up again, stinging in his throat. The memory of the moment he'd first seen it sharp and constant in his brain. And the swift realisation that what hurt most wasn't the personal betrayal, wasn't the fact that Kat had slept with another man. It was the humiliation. The way it sent him right back to his childhood, and those unbearable days after his mother left, when all anybody seemed able to talk or write or think about was his family's shame.

He'd promised himself he'd never be in that position again, and Kat had made him break that promise. Maybe he couldn't have changed what happened with his mother, but he should have been able to control Kat. And he could sure as hell make sure it never happened again. Which meant finding out what Faith was hiding.

Sylvia was still watching him carefully, as if waiting to see if he might explode at the very mention of the video. Dominic closed his eyes and wished very hard he'd never heard of YouTube. 'Just tell me you haven't watched it.'

'I don't think there's a person we know that hasn't seen at least a glimpse of it.' Sylvia shook her head. 'You think you know a person.'

'It's wildly unsuitable and inappropriate for you to even mention it.'

'I don't know why you're so bothered. It's not like you're in it.' Dominic looked at her, and she winced. 'Of course, I suppose that might not actually make things any better.'

'I'd like to stop talking about this now, please.'

Sylvia gave a quick nod. 'Absolutely. Good idea. You can tell me about your latest employee instead.'

As if that was any safer a topic. 'What do you want to know?'

'Her name would be a good start. Where you met. What she's like. That kind of thing.'

'You realise you'll probably never see her again after today, right?'

'Oh, I don't know,' Sylvia said airily. 'At the very

least, there's the theatre trip you promised faithfully to let me come along on…'

Damn it. He'd forgotten that. He'd have to ask Faith to try and score an extra ticket.

'You forgot. Didn't you?'

'Of course not,' Dominic lied. 'I just need to ask Faith something…'

'Aha! So her name is Faith. We're getting somewhere.'

Dominic rolled his eyes. Apparently she wasn't giving up on this one any time soon. 'Her name is Faith Fowler, she's a tour guide I met in Italy and hired to come over and run this tour, and she doesn't like stately homes. That's about all I know.'

Sylvia's brow furrowed. 'Except this one. She likes this stately home. Don't you, Faith?'

Glancing up, Dominic saw Faith approaching, too late to steer her away from his sister's insatiable curiosity.

'I love these tea rooms,' Faith said, not really answering the question. 'And the scones are to die for.'

'I'll introduce you to Russell before you go,' Sylvia replied, suitably distracted. 'He's a marvel in the kitchen.'

'Faith, we're going to need an extra ticket for the theatre tomorrow,' Dominic said. For some reason, the idea of Faith and Sylvia getting chummy made him nervous.

'Not a problem.' Faith whipped out her tablet and made a note. 'We're in the box anyway, and I think there are a couple of extra seats at the very back. Or I can always just skip it.'

'No. I need you there.' The words came out too firm, even to Dominic's ears, and both women looked at him in surprise.

'I'll still be around to get you all there and home again,' Faith said.

'Still, you don't want to miss the play,' Sylvia said, but she was looking at Dominic. He tried to keep his face blank. The last thing he needed was his little sister questioning his motives for hiring Faith. And he didn't want to explain that he needed to keep Faith close until he discovered what secrets she was keeping.

'I'm not much of a theatre person,' Faith said with a tight smile.

She was lying again, Dominic thought, wondering when he'd got so adept at spotting even her little fibs. But why? Why wouldn't she want to go to the opening night of the play she'd been so excited to score them tickets for?

'Is this another wardrobe issue?' he guessed, and Sylvia started staring at him again.

Faith flushed, the pink colour clashing with her scarlet cardigan. 'Not entirely. I could always wear my black dress again.'

'You've worn that dress every evening this week,' he pointed out. 'It's going to fall apart if you dry clean it once more.'

Faith blinked at him. 'I didn't think you'd notice.'

'I didn't think he could tell one dress from another,' Sylvia added, glancing between them. 'It must be a very special dress.'

'It's really not,' Faith told her.

'So go buy a new one,' Dominic said. 'You can go shopping while we're in meetings tomorrow. Just put it on the card.'

'I really don't need—'

'I'll come with you!' Sylvia clapped her hands together with excitement. 'It'll be great! I'm in town anyway for that evening, and I love a good shopping trip…'

Faith glanced between them, and suddenly Dominic felt just a little sorry for her. Not enough to get her out of a shopping trip with his sister, though.

'Well, that would be…' Faith started.

'Expensive,' Dominic finished for her. 'That's the word you're looking for. Expensive and exhausting.'

'Oh, shush,' Sylvia said. 'You want her to look her best, don't you?'

He didn't care, Dominic realised. He didn't care what she wore, what she looked like. He just wanted her there with him. And not just so he could uncover her lies.

He was in trouble.

Faith spent the coach ride back to the hotel sulking. Not that anyone could tell; she was cheery and chatty enough to the clients. Maybe Dominic might have noticed but, since it was his fault anyway, she didn't care.

How had this happened? She'd known all along the theatre trip was a risk, but not much more than anything else she'd agreed to that week. The theatre was one of her mother's passions; her circle of friends liked to patronise up-and-coming directors, playwrights, actors. Tomorrow, the opening night of a well-hyped show, directed by London's next big thing…no way they'd miss it. Maybe her mum wouldn't be there, but someone who would know Faith on sight would be, she had no doubt.

She'd planned on hiding out in the coach. She could get them all in and settled easy enough, then slip out and hide. Mum's gang were bound to be the last in so, as long as she got the rest of them there early, she'd be fine. When Dominic had said about needing a seat for

Sylvia, things got even easier. They'd never even notice she'd gone.

But now, suddenly, not only was she attending the bloody thing, she was buying a new frock, just for the occasion.

And the absolute worst thing was, she didn't even mind. Because it meant an evening with Dominic, dressed up and looking her best, and as close to off-duty as she could get this week.

Faith sighed, and slouched down in her seat. Falling for her employer. How cliché. And just the sort of man her mother would love her to marry, too. Perfect.

After the long day trip, Faith had planned a quiet dinner at a restaurant not far from the hotel. With only an hour to answer emails, catch up on work and get changed for dinner, she didn't have much choice but to pull on the hated black dress again. She'd thought it was versatile enough to see her through the week, but then she hadn't fully anticipated having to accompany the group on every single one of their evenings out. And she hadn't counted on Dominic being there, watching her, either.

Taking in her reflection in the hotel room mirror, she pulled a face. And then she grabbed her red shoes, red cardigan and brightest red lipstick. Worn right, he might not even notice the dress underneath.

'Nice dress,' Dominic said ten minutes later when they met in the lobby. Faith pulled a face at him, and he laughed.

Dinner, Faith thought, would have been more or less perfect if it wasn't for two things. One, the heel of her shoe breaking as she returned from the bathrooms after dessert. And two, Jerry insisting on accompanying her back to the hotel when she decided to leave while the others had coffee. After four days of fending off his advances, she was running out of excuses.

Even then, it might have been salvaged if Jerry hadn't followed her up to her room, staring intently down her cleavage as she rooted through her bag for her keycard.

'Thanks for helping me home,' she said, smiling falsely up at him. 'I think I can manage from here.' She waved her keycard, just to prove the point.

'What kind of a gentleman would I be if I didn't see you safely into your room?' He gave her a smile that made her want to shudder. 'I can check for monsters under your bed, if you like.'

I'm much more concerned about what you want to do in *my bed.* 'I'm a big girl now, Jerry. I think I can manage.'

His gaze dropped down to her breasts again. 'You certainly are.'

Okay, that was enough. 'Jerry, I'm tired. I'm going to bed. I suggest you do the same.' How much wine had he drunk with dinner? His eyes weren't entirely focused when he finally managed to look up at her face.

'Aw, come on. Just a quick nightcap. After all, we missed out on after-dinner drinks.'

'I really don't think that's a good idea,' Faith said, slipping her keycard into the door. 'Early start and all tomorrow. Goodnight, Jerry.'

A hand appeared above hers on the door, pushing it open, and the first pangs of panic stabbed in Faith's chest. Focusing on her breathing, she grabbed the handle and yanked it closed again, almost catching Jerry's fingers in the door as she did so.

'I said goodnight, Jerry.' The words came out much

calmer than she felt. Her heart pounded against her rib-cage and she wanted to kick out, stamp on his feet in her one remaining red heel, the way the self-defence classes had taught her.

But he was Dominic's client. And he hadn't actually done anything yet, except make her feel desperately uncomfortable.

Of course, if his hands moved from the door to her body, she was taking him down.

Fingers, hot and sweaty, landed on her hip and Faith didn't waste time thinking any more. Stamping down with her right foot, she tried not to smile in satisfaction as Jerry let go and howled.

'Oh, I'm so sorry. Was that your foot?' she asked, her voice syrupy sweet.

'You bitch! You wait until I tell your boss about this.' Jerry was practically curled up over his foot, his face shining red, his eyes furious.

Faith managed one moment of relief before a figure appeared at the edge of her vision, coming around the corridor from the lift. And, before she could even look, she heard Dominic say, 'Tell her boss about what?' and her heart plummeted.

CHAPTER EIGHT

JERRY HAD SCAMPERED back to his room before Dominic could get any coherent account of what had happened, which he supposed meant he'd have to trust Faith's version of the story to be fully accurate. Normally, he hated only hearing one side. But on this occasion…he trusted Faith a hell of a lot more than the man he'd been doing business with for nearly three years.

'Tell me what happened,' he said as Faith let them both into her room, kicked off her ruined shoes and headed straight for the minibar.

'Pretty much exactly what you think happened.' She pulled out a small bottle of Scotch and reached for the glasses on the counter above.

'I don't know what happened,' he said reasonably as he took a seat in the armchair. 'All I saw was my client on the floor, practically crying in pain.'

Faith shrugged. 'I stood on his foot.'

Dominic's gaze dropped to the ridiculously high heels she'd discarded in the corner. The one with the intact heel certainly looked as if it could do some damage. 'Why?'

'Would you believe me if I said it was an accident?' Faith poured the whisky evenly between the two glasses and handed one to him.

'No,' he said, taking a sip. Not as good as his, but not bad.

With a sigh, Faith dropped onto the sofa, curling her legs up under her. 'He was drunk. He got...ideas. And he didn't appear able to comprehend the word *no*.'

Dominic stopped, stared, his blood heating up. He'd kill him. How could he even think for a moment that Faith—Faith!—would want to...?

'You don't believe me.' Glancing over, he saw Faith's wide eyes looking at him with disappointment.

'Oh I believe you,' he said, the words scratchy in his throat. 'And that bastard is on the next flight home.' Pushing himself to his feet, he let his anger carry him towards the door, but Faith stopped him before he got there, her small hand on his arm, a touch he hadn't expected.

'He was drunk,' she repeated. 'And stupid. Very, very stupid. But I took care of it.'

'You shouldn't have had to.'

'No, I shouldn't. But, trust me, it's not the first time it's happened. Guys get ideas in hotels, for some reason. But I learnt to look after myself, and no one has ever got any further than a hand on my waist unless I wanted them to, I promise.'

She sounded so calm, so certain, that Dominic's blood started to cool, just a little. 'I still want to punish him.'

'Oh, by all means,' Faith said, giving him a lopsided smile. 'Just find something more subtle than getting yourself arrested for grievous bodily harm, yeah?'

Dropping back down onto the couch, Dominic realised that he would have done. He'd have gone to that bastard's room and pounded him to a pulp, without caring what the police would do, or what the press would say, what damage it would do to the business, to these negotiations. Three years of strategising down the drain, and the Beresford name on the front of every paper for all the wrong reasons again.

He couldn't risk that.

He wanted to believe that he'd have done it anyway because he was a noble man who knew right from wrong. But, as Faith sat down beside him, her thigh close enough to touch his, he knew that gentlemanly behaviour had nothing to do with it.

He'd have hurt that man for touching Faith. Any other woman…he'd have reported it to Jerry's superiors, to the police if it had gone far enough. But Faith… was different.

'You okay?' she asked, bumping her arm against his.

He gave a humourless laugh. 'Shouldn't I be asking you that?'

'Probably. But I'm clearly fine.'

Dominic studied her, taking in her pale skin, and the spots of pink on her cheeks that were probably the fault of the whisky. 'Are you?'

She gave a half-shrug, and took another sip. 'Just a little shaken. I should have known better than to let him walk me back, really.'

'This is in no way your fault,' Dominic said firmly.

'Oh, I know that. Trust me, I blame him entirely.'

'Good.' Leaning back against the sofa, Dominic began to imagine ways of making Jerry pay. At the very least, he was going to get every meeting request for every video conference until the end of time, whether he needed to be there or not.

'You're thinking of torture techniques, aren't you?' Faith curled her feet up under her again, twisting to face him on the sofa, and he couldn't help but notice the way the skirt of that bloody black dress rode up her thighs. God, he was as bad as Jerry.

'Corporate torture,' he promised. 'Entirely legal.'

'Well, that's okay then. Wouldn't want my boss getting into trouble.'

Her boss. Of course that was all he was to her. And he wouldn't even be that much longer. Once the Americans were on the plane home, she'd be gone. Onto the next job, the next adventure. He couldn't even plan on calling her back next time he had guests in town; God only knew where she'd be by then.

Unless…

'I meant to talk to you about that, actually.' Or he would have, if he'd thought of it before now.

Faith's eyebrows drew together. 'About what?'

Dominic took a deep breath, and made his play. 'About whether you'd like to make the boss thing a more permanent arrangement.'

Faith stared at him long enough that he started to go out of focus, then snapped her gaze away. Of course he was so impressed by her professional abilities that he wanted to keep her around. Nothing to do with her more personal attributes. She had to remember that.

But still…he did want to keep her around. Just the idea gave her a warm glow greater than anything she'd got from the alcohol in her glass.

Except, she couldn't stay. The realisation made her wince into her whisky as she looked down so she didn't have to see his face as she answered.

'That's…very kind…' She scouted around her poor scrambled brain to find the right words, but Dominic was already talking again before she got to them.

'It makes sense, right? I mean, I need a new tour

company, one way or another, and I got to thinking that it would be easier if I just had someone on staff to take care of these things. Obviously we'd need to come to a more formal arrangement—you'd need an office in my building, and we'd have to discuss salary, relocation expenses and all of that.'

She wanted to say yes. It was a fantastic offer, something that would really let her build up her life as Faith Fowler. But how could she do it in the shadow of her family name? How could she risk living in London again, knowing that any moment they could find her and thrust her back into the limelight?

Dominic gave her an encouraging smile and she tried to return it.

Would it really be so bad, even if they did find her? She was a grown woman. They couldn't make her go home. And with a stable job with Dominic, she'd never be reliant on them for money, or anything else again. This could be her chance at true independence.

Until Dominic found out the truth. No way he'd hang onto an employee who brought the paparazzi down on him for harbouring a missing heiress. And once they'd found her, all the stories would start up again, and the pictures of her leaving that damn hotel room would be back in circulation, and the rumours about her relationship with a married drug addict rock star…no. Dominic wouldn't stand for any of that. Even if she could make him believe that the papers had it all wrong.

No. She couldn't stay. There was no place for her in Dominic's world any more, if there ever really had been. Getting close to Dominic…it was a mistake. One she was very afraid she might have already made. But there had to be a line, a point she couldn't cross. She couldn't fall in love. And so she couldn't risk staying.

Besides, she told herself, she didn't want to stay in London anyway. She wanted to see more of the world, more than just Italy.

Even if she'd rather see more of Dominic.

'You're going to say no, aren't you?'

Faith gave him an apologetic smile, and he shook his head.

'Is this because of the Lord thing?'

She blinked. 'The Lord thing?'

Shifting to face her, Dominic's expression was serious. 'Yeah. I saw the way you were at Beresford Hall today. You hated every minute of it. So, what's the problem? You hate the aristocracy?'

I was the aristocracy. 'Of course not.'

'So, what, then? Trust me, whatever it is, I've heard it before. That I'm an over-privileged, spoilt brat who only got where I am because of my family. That I'm stealing from the mouths of others by having so much. That—'

'Dominic.' Faith spoke as calmly as she could, placing her hand against his arm again. 'I didn't say any of those things.'

He sighed. 'But you did hate being there today.'

No point lying about that one. 'Yeah.'

'So, why?'

Faith drew in a deep breath while she considered her answer. Obviously she couldn't tell him the truth— that it reminded her too much of her own home. But he clearly wasn't going to be fobbed off with a blatant lie, either. Besides, even if she couldn't stay, she wanted him to think well of her when she was gone.

'I guess I…I don't know how to explain it, really. It made me feel uncomfortable. All that history and opulence.'

Dominic frowned. 'Uncomfortable? Why? I mean,

I've had people be angry about the privilege, had people be jealous or bitter. But why uncomfortable?'

'Does it really matter?'

'It does to me.'

He was very close now, closer than even Jerry had been before she maimed him. When had she shifted so close? When had the hand on his arm become a gentle caress rather than a calming gesture? When had his thigh pressed so closely against her legs, his arm along the back of the sofa just behind her?

She didn't ask why it mattered to him; it was enough that it did. And she wanted him to know the truth, to have one moment of honesty from her before she left, taking all her lies and secrets with her.

'It made me feel trapped. Like all that history, tradition, expectation were weighing down on me, instead of you. Like there was no room for you to be yourself or explore what you wanted. Because the family name, upholding what that means, would always make you follow a certain course. That's why it made me uncomfortable.'

Dominic stared at her, realising too late that he was close enough now to see every fleck of green and brown in her hazel eyes. He could kiss her without moving more than a few centimetres.

But he wouldn't. Because of Jerry, because she was leaving, and because the very basis of his life made her 'uncomfortable'.

'That's not how it is.' Sitting back, he slid his arm back along the sofa, tucking his elbow in at his side, keeping his hands far away from her tempting skin. 'What I've done at Beresford Hall…that's all me. When my father died, he left things in a less than ideal condition.' Had she ever heard the story? he wondered. Everyone he met in society knew; he could see it in their eyes when he was introduced. After all, it was such a good story—the Lady of the Manor who went wild, running off to the Med with a billionaire tycoon, leaving behind two children and a distraught husband. A husband who barely got over the loss enough to look after the children, let alone the estate. Who could blame people for telling it over and over again?

Of course, they didn't see beyond the pictures in the society pages. His mother, living it up on some yacht, flaunting her adultery, her betrayal. And his mother never had to see what it did to the family she left behind. How Sylvia cried and screamed and then went silent for two long months. How the husband she left behind faded to a shadow of a man.

Or how Dominic dealt, every day, with the photographers and the journalists, at the door and on the phone. And with the constant humiliation of every single person in his life knowing how little he meant to his own mother.

It came up less in the business world, at least—one reason he preferred to keep his focus on building up the business and the brand, rather than attending the compulsory charity galas and events that he'd inherited with the title. But did ordinary people really care? Did Faith?

She raised her eyebrows at him. 'Less than ideal? What does that mean?'

Did it matter any more? The shame he burned with at the memories? Had he done enough, finally, to set it all behind him? Would he ever?

Faith was still waiting for an answer, though. He swallowed down the last gulp of his whisky, enjoying the slight burn in his throat. 'After my mother left…my father checked out of life,' he said bluntly. 'He didn't care about anything any more. Not even the scandal my mother left behind. The estate suffered.' He shrugged. 'When he died, he left us with nothing but our name.'

'And you fought back from that.' Faith's eyes were wide as she watched him. 'You built up the estate, the business…'

'I saved the family name,' he corrected her. 'The rest was incidental.'

'It meant that much to you. The name, I mean.'

'Yes.' He glanced away. 'It was all I had left, after all.'

She was silent for a long moment, but when he looked back her gaze was still fixed on him. Her teeth bit down on her lip, a flash of white in the dim lamplight of the darkening hotel room, and he wondered what it was she wanted to say. And whether she'd decide to say it.

'My father,' she said finally. 'He was—is—the world's most charming man. But…he gambled. Still does, I imagine. He…lost. A lot. Even if he'd never admit it. Life had to go on as if everything was normal, like we were as good as—better than—everyone else. Even if we couldn't afford to buy my school uniform. That's one of the reasons I moved away. I didn't want to watch him destroy himself, or our family.'

The words caught him in the chest, and it took him a moment to identify why. That was, he realised, the first real thing she'd ever told him about herself. He knew about the tours she'd led, the people she'd met. He knew her opinion on subjects as varied as clothes and theatre and London traffic.

And now he knew something of her. A small token, before she left him.

It wasn't enough.

'Didn't you ever want to just give up?' Faith asked. 'Just walk away from it all and start a new life?'

Had he? He couldn't remember. It had never seemed an option. From the moment he'd inherited the title, he knew exactly what he needed to do and he just got on with it. Besides… 'How could I? Sylvia was only ten, and we had nothing…I couldn't leave.'

Faith's smile was sad. 'No. No, of course you couldn't.'

Tipping the last drops of whisky down her throat, she placed her glass on the coffee table. Dominic stared at her lips and the way her tongue darted out to catch the last drop of liquid from them. He wanted to kiss her. And he knew, just knew, from the way she leant into him, close enough to touch, that she wouldn't pull away. She wouldn't say no, wouldn't pull any of her self-defence moves on him. She'd let him kiss her, and then what? He'd take her to bed, just to let her leave him in a few days' time? She wasn't going to stay. And he was already in too deep. He couldn't risk falling any further. Not after Kat.

'You never did tell me the real reason you left Italy,' he said. Maybe now she knew some of his secrets, his truths, she'd be willing to share some of her own. Let him in enough that he could stop worrying about her lies.

Faith pulled back, wrapping her arms around her knees. Suddenly, even though she still sat on the same sofa, she felt miles further away. How bad was her truth that she couldn't let it near him?

'That day we met, at the airport,' she said, her voice slow.

'I remember,' he said drily. As if he would ever forget.

'I'd just found out that the company I worked for had gone bankrupt. I got everyone in my tour group sorted out with flights and hotels but I...I was stranded. Until you offered me this job.'

'Until you demanded it, you mean.' She was telling the truth, he was sure. But he was equally certain that there was more, something she was still hiding.

'Hey, I'm doing a good job, aren't I?'

'You're doing an incredible job,' he said, and she looked up, wide eyes surprised. 'I just wish you'd stop lying to me and let me see the real you.' He got to his feet, ignoring her alarmed stare. 'You should get some sleep. Goodnight, Faith.'

CHAPTER NINE

'How about this one?' Sylvia asked, and Faith glanced up from the racks of overpriced, over-decorated dresses to shake her head at Dominic's sister for the tenth time that morning. And they were only on the second shop. Faith sighed. Dominic hadn't been kidding when he'd said this would be exhausting.

Sylvia hung the dress back on the rail with a clatter of metal on metal. 'You know, this would be a lot easier if you could tell me what you're looking for.'

Faith flicked past another few dresses. 'I told you, I'm not sure. I'll know it when I see it.'

'Utterly unhelpful.' Flinging herself into a cream leather armchair outside the fitting rooms, Sylvia pulled out a small pink suede notepad and a sparkly pen. 'Come on. Let's figure this out. First question: cocktail or ballgown?'

'Cocktail, definitely. No one wears floor-length to the theatre any more, do they?'

Sylvia shrugged her slim shoulders and made a note on the pad. 'Not anyone your age, anyway. Okay, black or colour?'

'Colour,' Faith replied. 'I'm sick to death of black after a week in that one dress.'

'Plain or decorated?'

'Plain. It'll go with more accessories that way.' If she was getting to buy a dress on Dominic's card, it might as well be something she could wear again and again.

She turned her attention back to the rack and was only half paying attention when Sylvia spoke again.

'Okay, most important question, then—how do you want my brother to look when he sees you in it?'

'Awed,' she said without thinking, then smacked a hand over her mouth. 'I didn't say that,' she muttered through her fingers.

Sylvia gave a gleeful grin. 'Oh, you did. You most certainly did.'

'Well, I shouldn't have.' Faith studied the dresses again with unwarranted attention, since they were all exactly what she didn't want, but did at least distract from the way her cheeks were burning. 'He's my boss.'

'Only for a few more days,' Sylvia pointed out.

'At which point I'll be leaving. Hardly a winning argument.'

'You could stay,' Sylvia suggested. 'Maybe Dominic could offer you a permanent job.'

'At which point he'd be my boss again.' Faith shook her head. 'Besides, he already did. I think he's much more interested in keeping me as an employee than anything else.'

'Given the way he was staring at you yesterday, I'd take that as a compliment,' Sylvia said, her tone dry. 'You must be incredibly good at your job.'

'I am.' Faith pushed the dresses back along the rail. 'Which is why we're going to try the next shop in the hope of finding a perfectly work appropriate dress for tonight, so I can go out and do what I'm being paid for. Nothing more, nothing less.'

'Are you sure?' Sylvia asked, holding the shop door

open for her. 'Because I have to tell you, Dominic never looked at Kat that way.'

Something froze inside her, and Faith was awfully afraid it might be her heart. Like it had been shocked into stillness by the idea that Dominic wanted her more than she'd ever dared to imagine.

He'd almost kissed her the night before; she'd seen it in his face. She still wasn't sure what had stopped him, although she could list a dozen perfectly reasonable options off the top of her head. Probably it was Jerry, she'd decided. Dominic would never try anything so soon after she'd had to fend off the attentions of another man. It wouldn't be Proper.

And Dominic was all about Proper.

Which was exactly why she couldn't let herself have him. She had given up any chance of a place in Dominic's world when she ran away, and that was a decision she had to stick by.

Besides, if they started something, anything real, the truth would come out. It always did. And she couldn't bear the thought of the disgust and disappointment on Dominic's face when he found out.

She ignored the small part of her brain that said she only had a few more days. Maybe she could have that, at least. Surely she could keep her secret that long…

It all came down to one simple fact. If Dominic knew who she really was, what she'd done, he wouldn't want her. And on the infinitesimally small off chance he did, if she wanted a real chance with Dominic, she'd never get to be Faith Fowler again.

Lose-lose.

Kind of like the shopping expedition so far.

She sighed as Sylvia dragged her into the next boutique, another tiny, expensive shop filled with incredible dresses Faith's mother would have loved.

'Do you really think we're going to find anything in here?' she asked.

'We won't know until we look,' Sylvia replied, already scouring through the individual dress hangers on the walls to find the perfect outfit.

Faith was pretty sure that not one of the dresses Sylvia was looking at would fit over her not exactly model-shaped frame. The women these dresses were intended for didn't have curves. She couldn't even swear they had hips, looking at the narrow cuts.

Still, Sylvia seemed happy browsing through the fabrics, so Faith let her attention wander, imagining what the evening ahead might be like if she did let herself be talked into some glamorous, fabulous dress that showcased all her best assets.

Would Dominic notice? Would he look her over in that way of his and take in her figure, rather than her inappropriate clothes? Would he sit beside her in the theatre, transfixed by the plunging neckline of her dress?

Probably not.

The bell over the shop door chimed and Faith looked up absently, then froze. Lady Ginny Gale. Her mother's best friend.

Her head felt fuzzy, as if every thought she'd ever had was buzzing in there, all at the same time. She couldn't let Ginny see her, recognise her. This was just what she'd been afraid would happen at the theatre that night.

Getting to her feet as casually as she could—jerky movements would only draw attention to her—Faith turned her body away from the door, where Ginny was talking to the assistant. Then, grabbing the first dress she came to, she murmured to Sylvia, 'I'm just going to try this on.'

Sylvia's eyebrows rose in surprise, probably because the dress was everything Faith had said she didn't want—full length, black and decorated with crystals in a fan pattern on the skirt—but Faith ignored her, moving serenely towards the safety of the fitting room.

Of course, once safely behind the heavy locked door, she collapsed onto the velvet padded seat and buried her head in her hands.

This was why she couldn't stay in London. This was why she couldn't consider trying to seduce Dominic that night. As if she needed the reminder. She wanted out of his world, not back in. She'd been crazy to even take the job, once she'd figured out who he was.

Still, she'd see it through now, of course. Which meant finding something utterly un-Faith-like to wear that night. She needed to be so unrecognisable even her own mother would walk past her in the lobby if she showed up. And she wasn't going to find that in any of the shops Sylvia was dragging her to.

'Faith? Are you okay?' Sylvia's voice rang through the fitting room, and Faith winced. Why hadn't she lied about her first name, too? Would have made things much easier. Except she'd always been Faith, and she hadn't wanted to lose that too, when she was letting go of everything else.

She'd probably forget to answer to another name, anyway.

'Fine,' she called back, her voice low. 'I don't think this is the one for me.'

'Well, I think we could have predicted that before you came in here,' Sylvia said drily. 'Lady Gale has left, by the way. She was just placing an order for a new jacket.'

Was she that obvious? 'Who?' Faith tried innocently but, as she unlocked the door to the changing room, Sylvia was standing on the other side, arms folded and eyebrows raised.

'Want to explain to me what just happened?' she asked.

Faith shook her head. 'Not really. It's old news now, anyway.' Which didn't mean anyone had forgotten about it. Certainly not the Internet.

'Former employer?' Sylvia guessed.

'Something like that.'

'I won't tell Dominic, you know. Not if you don't want me to.'

'There's nothing to tell,' Faith lied. Then, leaving the hideous black dress hanging on the rail, she headed back out into the shop and straight for the door. 'Come on; I think I've got a better idea of what I'm looking for now.'

Dominic was a busy man. He'd had important meetings all day, emails and calls to deal with, not to mention some valuable forward planning with Marie and Henry that afternoon. They'd made some real headway on the expansion plans, and Dominic could almost see his dreams coming to life.

Which was why it was particularly embarrassing to admit, even to himself, that he'd spent most of the day wondering what sort of dress Sylvia would persuade Faith to buy for the theatre that evening.

He hadn't had a chance to see Faith all day, despite his attempt to catch her at breakfast. He had, however, seen Jerry, which had been entertaining enough in itself.

The man had turned white, then slightly green, then run in the opposite direction down the corridor away from him. Okay, maybe it was more of a power walk than a run, but when Dominic told the story to Faith he expected to make it more of a sprint.

When he finally saw Faith, of course.

Maybe he'd pushed her too far last night, letting on that he knew she was lying to him. Faith was like a small frightened animal at times, behind her confident exterior. Whatever she was hiding, it scared her, which in turn worried Dominic even more.

Two and a half days. That was all the time he had left to uncover Faith's secret. To find out if it was something he could live with. Something they could deal with together.

And if it wasn't…then he had two and a half days before he never saw Faith again.

The thought made him shudder.

By the time he made it back to the hotel that evening, he had a scant half hour to shower and change, but he still managed to make it to the lobby before anyone else, ready for their evening of theatre.

Faith was next down, as he'd expected. He'd come to value the brief, quiet ten minutes before they left for the evening's entertainment. Ten minutes when it was just them and they had a chance to catch up on the day, and the plans for the next one. It was work, of course, but somehow it felt more like play when Faith was there.

The lift pinged, and Dominic turned to see if Faith was on board, sucking in a breath as the doors opened. Would it be backless? he wondered. And surely not black. Whatever it was, she'd look fantastic. And he'd get to spend the whole evening looking at her. Almost as good as if it were really just them going out together for the evening.

But then Faith stepped out of the lift, into the lobby, and Dominic's breath slowly released in disappointment.

'Sylvia let you buy that?' he asked as she strode across the lobby in plain flat navy shoes. What happened to the glorious red heels of last night? Oh yeah. Broken, even before she stamped on Jerry.

'What's wrong with it?' Faith asked, looking down at herself.

Dominic searched for the right words. In lots of ways, it was perfect. Navy dress, cream cardigan and handbag. Nothing too revealing or showy, but smart enough for the occasion. Maybe Sylvia *had* chosen it. He had a hard time believing Faith would because, despite everything that was right with it...

'It's just...boring.'

Faith beamed. 'Thank you. That's just what I was going for.'

Dominic shook his head. He was beginning to believe that he didn't stand a chance of ever understanding what went on in Faith's brain. Especially if he only had two days left to learn.

The others arrived shortly after, and they piled into pre-ordered taxis to take them to the theatre. There'd be food at the after-show party later, so he'd told Faith not to bother with booking a dinner.

The press were out in force for the occasion, and he lost sight of Faith in the melee as they were shepherded through the crowds into the theatre. Inside, the place was crowded with half familiar faces, and Dominic quickly lost track of who he actually knew and who he just recognised from TV.

'I've arranged drinks with the barman over in the balcony bar,' Faith said, suddenly at his side. She was shorter without her heels, and had to stand on tiptoe and shout into his ear to be heard over the crowd. Someone brushed past her and knocked her balance and, without even thinking about it, Dominic wrapped an arm around her waist to keep her upright.

'Lord Beresford?' Dominic looked up to see the official photographer for the evening brandishing a camera at him. 'A photo, if you please?'

He hated this. Hated that his attending a play was the cause for photographs and reports. Hated that anyone cared.

Still, it was part of the deal. He knew this. And, even if he hadn't, his father had made it perfectly clear when he was growing up. Whatever else was going on, you played the part.

One of the many things his father forgot after his mother left. Including his children.

He gave the photographer a swift nod and let his arm fall from Faith's waist.

'With your friend?' the photographer asked hopefully.

Of course. 'Do you mind?' he asked, turning to where Faith had been standing, only to find that she'd gone. He caught a brief glimpse of navy disappearing into the sea of people, but didn't bother calling after her. 'Apparently not,' he told the photographer, who looked disappointed, but snapped away at a couple of shots anyway.

He eventually found Faith, along with Sylvia and his clients, in the upper balcony bar. 'What happened to you?' he asked, taking a glass of champagne from her hand.

'Just doing my job,' she said, smiling innocently. 'Your guests were thirsty.'

She was lying again. He almost wished he couldn't tell. The number of casual lies she told him in a day was honestly disturbing.

'So, what's this show about, anyway?' he asked, to distract himself from the fact that not only was the woman he'd fallen for leaving him in two days, but she'd been lying to him the whole time he'd known her and it was getting increasingly likely that he'd never get to know the truth.

'You don't know?' she asked. 'But you specifically asked me to arrange for us to see it.'

He covered a yawn with his hand. Apparently late nights and long days weren't compatible with theatre visits. 'Sylvia said it was the biggest show opening this week. Although I think she just told me that so I'd get her a ticket, too.'

She stared at him. 'You're going to sleep through the whole thing, aren't you? The lights will go down, the theatre will be warm, the seats will be cosy, and I'll spend the entire evening trying to pretend you're not snoring.'

Actually, that didn't sound all that bad. 'I'm sure I'll wake up for the interval drinks.'

Faith rolled her eyes, but then he felt her body tense beside his.

'Lord Beresford? Perhaps I could get that shot of you with your friend now?'

Photographers. Knowing his luck, they'd get one of him fast asleep halfway through the first act. And now worrying about that was going to keep him awake.

'Faith? Is that okay?' He turned to where she'd been standing just moments ago, but the space was empty.

Where the hell had she gone now? And why?

'Sorry,' he told the photographer unapologetically. 'She's camera shy.'

And then he set about finding Faith, and some answers.

CHAPTER TEN

FAITH HAD FIGURED that the tiny alcove on the back stairs leading up to the Upper Circle was a decent enough place to hide. Plenty of people passing by, none of them likely to recognise a used-to-be-notorious girl in a boring navy dress.

She hadn't counted on Lord Dominic Beresford's tenacity, though.

'What the hell are you hiding from?' He planted himself outside her hiding place, hands on his hips.

'I'm not hiding,' Faith lied. 'I just got a bit claustrophobic. You know, with all the crowds up there. Thought I'd get some air.'

A group of theatre-goers trying to reach their seats forced Dominic off the staircase and into her alcove, and suddenly Faith really couldn't breathe. He was too solid, too attractive—and too close! How was she supposed to keep her story straight when she was surrounded by the scent of his aftershave, when she could feel the heat of his skin through his shirt?

'Claustrophobic.' Disbelief coloured Dominic's words. 'So you hid here. In a ridiculously small alcove with hundreds of people walking past.'

'I was *trying* to get outside,' Faith said, knowing he didn't believe her. 'I just got a little turned around.'

'Then let's go.' Grabbing her hand, Dominic led her down the staircase and out through a side door. Faith sucked in the cool evening air, letting it fill her lungs and calm her.

That had been close. Too close. If that photographer had got her photo and run it with a caption about Lord Beresford…it wouldn't matter where she went next, Dominic would still have to deal with the fallout when someone realised who she was.

He'd still end up hating her.

'Feeling any better?' Dominic asked as the side door slammed shut behind them.

Faith nodded. 'But I don't think we're getting back in that way,' she said, motioning at the handleless door. 'And I left our tickets in my bag, upstairs in the bar.'

'I'm fairly sure they'll let us back in.' Dominic leant back against the brick wall of the theatre, arms folded over his chest. 'If I ask them to.'

He was watching her too carefully and his words from the night before flooded her brain.

I just wish you'd stop lying to me and let me see the real you.

How did he know? And how much did he suspect?

'Are you going to?' she asked.

'That depends,' Dominic said.

'On what?'

'On if you're going to tell me the truth.'

Fear crawled through her middle. 'I told you. I just needed some air—'

'Not about tonight. Well, not just about tonight,' he amended. 'You've been lying to me since the moment we met, and I want to know why.'

Faith stilled, and looked up into his dark eyes.

'No,' she said. 'You really don't.'

* * *

Her words hit him in the gut. That was it then. Whatever her secret was, it was too big for them to move past. Too huge for her to even trust him with.

It was over, before it ever really started.

He should walk away now. Head back into the theatre and his clients and his sister. Let Faith work out the rest of the trip, without letting her any closer to his heart. Then he should put her on a plane and resign himself to never seeing her again.

He knew exactly what he should do.

But instead he said, 'Then we're not going back inside.'

She looked desperate now, her eyes wide and pleading. 'Dominic, don't be ridiculous. We've got your clients to sort out; my handbag is in there…'

'I'll text Sylvia. She can deal with everything.' In fact, he rather thought his sister might cheer approvingly.

'So what are we going to do?' Faith asked.

It wasn't a plan, wasn't something he'd thought out or weighed up and decided on. And it might be the most un-Lord-Beresford-like thing he'd done in his entire life.

But somehow Dominic knew it was the only thing to do.

'We're going to take a night off.'

'A night off?' Faith's forehead crinkled up.

He nodded. 'One night. Just one night, where I'm not Lord Beresford and you're not my employee. One night to just be Dominic and Faith.'

She wanted it, he could tell. Her eyes were wider than ever, filled with amazement, and the slight flush on her cheeks told him she hadn't missed any of the possibilities of the suggestion.

'For just this one night,' he said, moving closer, 'it doesn't matter about the truth. Doesn't matter about our pasts, or our futures. For tonight, all that matters is us.'

He took her hand, rubbing circles on her palm with his thumb, and held his breath when she looked up at him, her lower lip caught between her teeth.

'Just one night?'

'Just one night,' he echoed.

'What will we do?' she asked, and Dominic's mind filled with possibilities, most including getting her out of that ugly dress as soon as possible.

No. Too quick. If he only had one night with her, he needed to do this properly.

'First, I'm going to take you out for dinner. Anywhere you choose.'

Some of the tension dropped from her stance at that, and she smiled. 'I know just the place.'

The crowds were still gathered out front, but by keeping close to the side of the building they managed to avoid them as they dashed across the street behind the theatre, the warm evening air smelling of freedom and possibility.

One night. Just one night. That was what he'd said. And even though Faith knew she shouldn't, knew that this could end in disaster, or at least a broken heart, she couldn't resist that kind of temptation. Surely she could keep her secret for just one night?

Covent Garden buzzed with life, filled to overflowing with tourists, buskers, after-work socialisers, people wanting to sell something and people looking to buy. Faith let the sights and sounds warm her, make her feel at home again. She hadn't realised she'd felt so out of place in her own London that week, until now.

'So, where do you want to go?' Dominic asked. 'Somewhere around here?' He cast an arm around him at the market piazza, almost hitting a tourist in shorts and a Bermuda shirt as he did so. 'Looks like there's plenty of places to choose from.' Seeing Faith's horrified look, he added, 'What? I know it's not exactly up there with the meals you've been organising this week—'

'That's not it,' Faith interrupted. 'Just...Covent Garden's for the tourists. It's the equivalent of eating pizza right next door to the Coliseum in Rome. You'll get perfectly ordinary pizza at three times the price.'

They'd stopped walking, Faith realised, and were standing still in a sea of people, swelling and ebbing around them. Dominic's hand came down to rest at her waist, pulling her in closer, anchoring her against the tide. Heat spread out through her body from the place where they touched, and she swallowed, hard.

'Follow me,' she said, and grabbed his hand with her own.

It was easy to get trapped in the slow-moving crowds if you didn't know what you were doing. Dominic would have been far too polite to do the essential barging through if she'd left him to his own devices. That was the only reason she held his hand, she reasoned.

Of course, once they'd escaped the market and were walking more casually away along Long Acre, she didn't let go. By that point, it felt far too natural.

'Where are we going?' Dominic asked, his thumb rubbing the back of her hand in a relaxing rhythm.

'A little Italian I know.' Marco had taken her there, back when he was trying to hire her for his fledgling tour company. He said it would give her a real taste of Rome.

Dominic's thumb stopped its comforting movements. 'Missing Italy already?'

'Not really,' Faith said, giving him a smile. 'Mostly just the pasta.'

He returned the smile and started stroking her hand again.

Faith suddenly found herself wishing that she'd bought the dress Sylvia wanted her to have, the backless, wine-red dress that cascaded down her legs and showed off every single curve, instead of the boring navy shift she'd chosen.

Tugging on his hand, she led him down a hidden backstreet into the cooler shadows where the sun never reached, even at noon on midsummer. Halfway down the alley, a tattered red sign hung above a dirty window, and read simply, 'Lola's'. No one would recognise them there.

'This is it?' Dominic asked, looking dubious.

'Trust me,' Faith said, and he sighed.

'Seems to me, trusting you could get me into a lot of trouble.'

Faith smiled brightly to try and pretend that didn't hurt, just a little. After all, he was right. 'Oh, I don't know. You're doing okay so far.'

'This is true.' He pushed against the door and a bell clattered tinnily. 'Come on, then.'

Inside, the restaurant was even darker than Faith remembered. But then, most of her memories were of the picture Marco had painted of Rome in the summer, and of the Italian lakes. Well, that and the fantastic walnut pasta and red wine that went down like water.

A waiter in jeans and a T-shirt led them to a table at the back, and Faith watched in amusement as Dominic realised nearly every other table in the place was already occupied.

'Am I the only person who doesn't know about this place?' he murmured as they took their seats.

Faith slipped her cardigan from her shoulders and placed it on the back of her chair. White cashmere didn't go well with red wine. 'There are a lot of people in London,' she pointed out. 'Not everyone can afford to eat at the finest restaurants every night. Besides, the food's better here.'

'Can we see a menu, please?' Dominic asked, as if looking for proof, but the waiter shook his head.

'No menus,' he said, his rich Italian accent adding extra amusement to his tone. 'We'll bring you the best we have.'

As he spoke, a younger girl appeared, also in jeans, and filled their glasses with red wine. Dominic raised his eyebrows, but lifted the glass to his lips anyway.

'Not bad,' he said as the servers disappeared.

Faith tried her own. 'Liar. It's gorgeous.'

The smile Dominic gave her was warm and intimate, and suddenly Faith knew it didn't matter if the food had gone drastically downhill since the last time she was there; this would still be a better evening than the one with Marco. Apparently all she needed for a fantastic evening was the presence of Lord Dominic Beresford.

She wondered if that worked for everyone. She could use him on all her tours…

'What are you thinking?' Dominic asked, and Faith shook herself back into the real world. He wasn't Lord Beresford right now, anyway. He was just Dominic. Maybe even *her* Dominic, just for the night.

'Absolute nonsense,' she admitted. 'And worrying a little about abandoning my post.' Getting out of the theatre had seemed like the best plan, given that dodging every single camera was probably impossible. But, on the other hand, she'd been hired to do a job and she wasn't currently fulfilling those obligations.

'I'm the boss,' Dominic pointed out. 'You can look on this as…a mid-project appraisal.'

'Is that so?' Faith leant back in her chair and watched as he nodded. 'In that case, how am I doing?'

'Fantastically.'

Faith hoped the candlelight was forgiving enough to hide her blush. 'Anyone would think you were biased.'

Dominic's eyes turned dark. 'Oh, but I am.' Reaching across the table, he took her hand again. 'Utterly, utterly biased. Because I want you to stay in London with me.'

Maybe it was the wine, but suddenly Faith felt reckless. They weren't at the hotel, or at an event. There were no clients around. There was no chance of bumping into anyone who might recognise Lady Faith Fowlmere at Lola's. This was their one night. There was nothing at all to stop her asking for the truth.

'Because you want me to work for you?'

His smile was slow. 'Faith. I promise you that, for once, work is the furthest thing from my mind tonight.'

It wasn't quite a lie, Dominic reasoned and, even if it was, she'd told enough of her own. He'd offered her a night off, a night away from who they really were, because he couldn't bear the idea of her leaving without doing *something* about whatever compulsion it was that burned between them.

It wasn't easy, though. Business, sure. He could forget about contracts and meetings in a heartbeat. But the title, the heritage, they were scored deep into him in a way she couldn't understand. You had to be born to that kind of obligation. Still, just being with Faith made it easier. It was impossible not to relax around her, harder still not to lean into her, touch her, flirt and caress, however much he'd planned to take things slow.

Around the third glass of wine, he stopped even trying.

The servers, for all they looked as if they'd been yanked in off the streets, knew what they were doing. Dominic barely noticed when they topped up his glass or cleared away their empty plates. The food—incredible-tasting food on plates for sample-sized portions—just kept on coming, course after course. Antipasti, pastas—three kinds—fish, meat, and then, when they were almost fit to busting, a sorbet so sharp it almost cut the mouth. The tiramisu to finish would have been beyond him, but Faith grabbed her own spoon and dug into the shared plate, and the expression on her face as she tried it made him want to know what made her look like that. If he could replicate the experience for her in other ways…

'Oh, that is good,' he admitted, taking his own bite.

Faith gave him a smug smile. 'I knew you'd enjoy letting go for once.'

Suddenly, his head was filled with all the ways he could make her let go. How she would look if he kissed her breathless. How he could touch her until she forgot who she was, never mind him.

He swallowed down the last of his wine. Too much, too soon. 'So, what do you want to do next?' he asked, as the waiter brought over two tiny glasses of Limoncello, along with the bill.

Faith picked up her glass, took a sip, then licked her sticky fingers. Dominic felt something tighten in his chest at the sight. 'Well, that depends on you,' she said.

'On me? How?'

'Do you think you've managed to suitably forget who you are for the night?'

Watching her across the table in the candlelight, Dominic thought he might actually be a whole new person, after all. 'I think I've managed it, yes.'

'In that case,' she said, pushing his liquor glass towards him with two fingers, 'drink up. Because I want to show you *my* London.'

CHAPTER ELEVEN

SHE STARTED ON the South Bank, because she loved the way it lit up and came to life at night. They crossed at Waterloo Bridge, with a crush of other people heading the same way, and walked west along the river, towards the London Eye.

'I've been on that, at least,' Dominic said, looping her hand through his arm. 'Does that earn me any points?'

Faith considered. 'Depends. Did you go on an ordinary day with ordinary people? Or were there champagne, strawberries and schmoozing involved?'

'The latter,' Dominic admitted. 'Does that mean I have to go on it again?'

'Probably. But not tonight.'

They walked further, staring back across the river at the lights of Westminster, watching Big Ben as it chimed the hour. It was already getting late, Faith realised. She wondered how Dominic would feel about getting the night bus back... She shook her head. A step too far for this trip, she decided. Besides, if the evening went the way she hoped, she didn't want to waste time on buses.

'You know, I don't think I've ever done this,' Dominic said as they paused at the railings, just taking in the skyline.

'Done what?'

'Just…wandered around the city with a beautiful girl on my arm.' He tugged her a little closer at his words, and Faith felt the warmth of him seeping through her dress. He thought she was beautiful. No one had ever called her that before. Sexy, yes. Gorgeous, yes. Beautiful? No.

'How long have you lived here?' she asked, hoping to distract from her blush. 'How is that even possible?'

Dominic shrugged, and shifted again, drawing her into the circle of his arms, making her feel warm and safe. 'I grew up on the country estate. Trips to London were always for a purpose. I went from car to hotel to venue or event, back to hotel then car and home again. I wasn't exactly encouraged to explore.'

Faith leant back against his chest, remembering how that felt, that being shuffled from one place to the next, more of an accessory than a person. Surely Dominic, of all people, could understand why she'd run?

'What about when you grew up?' she asked.

'It didn't occur to me,' Dominic said, amused honesty in his voice. 'I don't know why. No, I do. There was just so much else to do. I had an entire family name to save. Every single thing I did, for years, was about building up the estate, making new connections, finding new ways to use the land, the influence, the money that started coming in. I didn't have time for anything else.'

'Not even people?' He sounded so lonely. How could she leave him when he sounded so terribly alone?

'Just Sylvia, really. Until Kat came along.'

Ah, of course. Maybe he had a reason for wanting to be alone. 'I don't like to pry…'

'You love to pry. You're officially nosy.'

'Okay, yes, I am.' How had he got to know her so well, so fast? 'I saw the YouTube video.'

'You and every other person in the country with eyes.' There was a bitterness to his words Faith didn't like. Was he still in love with Kat?

She tilted her head round to see his face. 'Want to tell me what happened?'

'You want a blow-by-blow account?' he asked, eyebrows raised. 'I thought you saw the video.'

'Not that,' she said. 'Between the two of you. A woman doesn't just go off and betray her fiancé on the Internet for no reason.'

He sighed, and she could feel the air leaving his chest, leaving him smaller, sunken. 'She didn't know she was being filmed, apparently. Not that it's much of an excuse.'

'It really, really isn't.'

There was a pause, and for a moment she thought that was all he would say on the matter. Then he spoke again. 'She was unhappy. With me, mostly. She…she wanted me to let her in, she said. She never felt like she was a real part of my life.'

Faith winced. She could see that, could see Dominic defending everything he held dear, holding it so tight that there was no room for anything else. Until tonight.

'You loved her, though?'

Dominic shrugged. 'She seemed like a good fit. Similar background, similar ambitions. She'd have been a great lady of the manor.'

Faith frowned. 'You make it sound like you were marrying her to enhance your brand, not because you loved her.'

'Maybe I was,' Dominic admitted, and Faith's eyes widened. 'Not intentionally, of course. I thought it was the real thing. But now, I wonder… Maybe she's right. Maybe I never let her in.'

'Because then she couldn't really leave you.'

She'd turned almost completely round in his arms now, Faith realised too late. His grip had tightened too, and anyone seeing them would surely have no doubt that they were lovers, held close in a lovers' embrace. Her body pressed up against his chest, her hands at his back. Would he kiss her this time? Would she let him?

Somewhere, a car horn blared, a crowd of guys laughed out loud and music played. Dominic ignored all of it, staring straight into her eyes. Then, without giving any indication of what had changed between them, he said, 'So, what's next on this tour of yours?'

Faith blinked, trying to break out of the moment. And then she realised that there was still one very special place she wanted to show him. 'Let's go see the pelicans.'

'Are you going to make me break into a zoo?' Dominic asked as they crossed back over Westminster Bridge, the Thames gleaming with lights below them. 'Because I think not being Lord Beresford for the night stops at criminal behaviour.'

Faith rolled her eyes, then tugged on his hand to make him keep moving. 'Have you honestly never seen the pelicans in St James's Park before?'

'Didn't even know we had any.' How many times had he walked through that park, on the way to somewhere? A few, at least. Wouldn't he have noticed big white birds swooping overhead?

The gates to the park were still open, thankfully, which meant it couldn't be too late, even if it felt like some magical witching hour. That was probably just Faith's influence.

'What time does the park close?' he asked as they headed into trees and lush grasses, just moments from the busy city centre.

'Midnight,' Faith replied, her tour guide brain still working.

'Do you know everything about London?' He'd lived in the city most of his adult life, and apparently missed everything of any importance. He had to spend more time exploring. If he ever got the chance.

'I know that the park has been home to pelicans since 1664, when the Russian Ambassador gave the first ones as a gift. And I know that the city of Prague gave the park three new ones last year, and I haven't met them yet.'

She talked about them like friends or relatives, he realised. 'You like the pelicans?'

'They're my favourite part of the city,' she admitted, stumbling to a stop on the lakeside path. 'Look!'

Dominic's gaze followed where her finger was pointing, into a clump of reeds at the edge of the lake. It took him a moment to spot the white feathers in the moonlight. 'It's asleep.'

Faith gave him a scathing look. 'Of course he is. It's late.'

Glancing at his watch, Dominic realised she was right. 'Eleven-thirty. Cars should be picking up from the theatre around now. Heading to the after-show party.'

'Want to head back and catch up with them?' Faith asked.

Dominic didn't even need to think about his answer. 'No.'

'So what do you want to do?' She was close again,

too close. Closer even than she'd been as they'd looked out over the river, talking about Kat. Close enough to make him crazy. 'It's your turn to choose.'

'I want to spend tonight with you.'

So close he could see her eyes darkening, even in the faint moonlight under the trees. 'I thought that's what we've been doing.'

He shook his head. 'This was just the evening. I want the whole night.'

And he did. He wanted it so badly he ached. And he didn't care if she couldn't stay, didn't care if it could never go anywhere. Didn't care what the risk was. He just wanted her.

'Are you sure?' Faith asked, her lower lip caught between her teeth.

'Absolutely.'

'I'm leaving—'

'I know. We both know what this is, and what it isn't. What it can't be. I don't know what you're hiding from me, but I trust you it's better that way. And I can't let you leave without…' He stopped, trying to find the words. Wrapping his hands around her waist, he pulled her closer, close enough that she had to be able to feel every line of his body through that hideous dress. 'You've shown me your world tonight. All the things you love about a city I've lived in for years and never got to see.' No, that wasn't right. 'Or, worse, all the things I've seen every day and never felt the way you do. I want one night to see everything through your eyes. Just one night.'

Rising up on tiptoe, Faith pressed her lips against his and his whole body almost sagged with relief. Then his brain caught up and he hauled her closer again, practically lifting her off the floor as he kissed her properly, thoroughly. The way a woman like Faith deserved to be kissed.

'Back to the hotel?' Faith asked when he finally pulled away.

Dominic nodded. It was past time to take Faith home to bed.

They caught a cab back to the hotel, Dominic's hand at her waist the whole way, and Faith could feel the blood thrumming through her veins too fast, driving her on. He was Lord Beresford again now, she could tell, so there was no inappropriate behaviour in the taxi, much as she considered just climbing into his lap and kissing him speechless.

Or maybe she'd be the one without words. But the man could kiss! One touch of his lips and she'd forgotten anything she ever knew about any city in the world. If someone had asked her where she was right then, she'd have struggled to answer.

In a way, she was almost glad of the reprieve his propriety gave her. She needed a moment to gather her thoughts, to enjoy the anticipation of what was ahead. And besides, with only one night to enjoy with him, she wouldn't have wanted him to be pretending to be anyone else.

No, against the odds, and despite everything, it was Lord Dominic Beresford she'd fallen for, and Faith didn't want to even pretend otherwise.

The taxi pulled up outside the hotel, and Dominic handed over a couple of notes to the driver—too much, probably, not that Faith cared right then. She glanced around to check before getting out of the car, but there was no sign of the service she'd arranged to collect the clients from the theatre. She checked her phone quickly; no one had called, so hopefully that meant they were all still having fun at the after-show party, somewhere they wouldn't see her and Dominic heading up to his suite together.

Perfect.

Dominic took her arm as they headed into the hotel, and she felt a certain relief that he wasn't hiding this. Wasn't hiding her. She'd worried he might be…embarrassed, if not ashamed. After all, as far as he was concerned she wasn't in his social strata and besides, she was his employee. Dominic wasn't the sort to blur the lines of propriety that way, even without the secrets he knew she was keeping.

The doorman at the hotel foyer gave no sign of anything out of the ordinary when they walked in. The concierge nodded politely, but otherwise kept a blank face. The receptionist barely even looked up. Faith held her breath. This might really happen. One night: one perfect night. She'd earned this much over the last few years of voluntary exile, surely? He never had to know who she was. What she'd done.

They were silent in the lift, a respectable few inches between them. She wondered if Dominic really felt so keenly about keeping up appearances and respectability that he wouldn't even touch her in an empty lift. Or was he just afraid, as she was, that if they touched again they wouldn't be able to stop…?

She got her answer the moment the door to the hotel suite swung shut behind them.

'Faith…' His hands were on her waist in a moment, pulling her closer into him, his lips descending before she could even think, even comprehend what they were doing here.

He reached for the zip at the back of her dress, tugging it down with impatient fingers, and Faith breathed with relief to be out of the stupid thing. What had she been thinking, trying to be anyone but herself around this man? He might not know her true name or identity, but he saw exactly who she was. He'd found her, under the disguise, and wanted her anyway.

Kisses ran across her neck, her shoulders, and she realised Dominic was whispering between each one, murmuring words of affection and longing and desire. She bit her lip, tilting her head to give him better access, and wondered if she'd ever stop being surprised by this man. This man who had looked at her body with distaste when they met, but was now admitting exactly how much he wanted it. This man who appeared every inch the respectable aristocrat every moment of the day, but was currently whispering exactly what he wanted to do to her in enough detail to make her whole body pulse.

He was so much more than she'd ever imagined that night in Rome, and she wanted him more than she could have dreamt.

Reaching up, she trailed her own kisses across his jaw, to his ear, his hands gripping her tighter as she went. Then she whispered, 'Take me to bed,' and felt the floor disappear under her feet as he lifted her and turned them round, covering the space between them and the bed in a very few steps.

Faith's back hit the mattress and her greedy hands pulled him down on top of her, not wanting their bodies to be separated for a moment. This was it. Her one night with Dominic Beresford. One night to be entirely herself, whatever name she used. And she was definitely going to make the most of it.

Afterwards, in the dim light of the darkened room, Faith curled closer into Dominic's side and tried to control her breathing. 'We definitely have to do that again,' she said without thinking, then winced. 'Before I leave, I mean.'

'We really, really do,' Dominic said, and she relaxed. But then he added, 'You have to leave?'

She nodded against his chest, pressing a kiss against his breastbone as an apology. 'I do.'

'Why?'

It was easier, admitting things in the dark. 'I can't be who I need to be, here.'

'With me?'

'In London,' she corrected him.

He sighed. 'And I can't leave. Not for ever, anyway.'

If he were anyone else, he could, Faith knew. Anyone but Lord Dominic Beresford, defender of reputation and honour across the British Isles.

'The estate.'

'My family.'

'Your name.' She hadn't meant it to sound bitter, but it did.

Dominic shifted, turning onto his side and pulling her closer against him. She could only just see his eyes in the darkness, but she could feel his heartbeat against hers. 'It's not just the name. It's who I am. Who I was born to be.'

'You were someone else tonight,' she reminded him.

'Just for tonight. I wish…' He shook his head. 'I know you don't get it, Faith. And maybe it is just the way I was brought up, or my heritage. But…these things matter to me. Responsibility. Trust. Duty. Reputation. They do, and I can't change that. My mother…she didn't take those things seriously. She put her own desires ahead of her responsibilities and it almost destroyed us. She betrayed all of us when she ran away, but the family name most of all. I couldn't do that. And then Kat…'

Faith's heart grew heavy at the other woman's name. 'She betrayed your trust.'

'She did. But more than that… It wasn't just that she cheated on me. It was that she did it in a way calculated to cause the most damage to everything I hold dear. My family, my reputation. She hurt them. And she hurt me.'

He spoke simply, stating the facts, but the iron weight that had settled in Faith's chest in place of her heart pulled her down further at his words. Wasn't she doing the same? Whichever way things went. She was a runaway, a betrayer just like his mother. And she was making him take a risk of scandal and embarrassment, without even letting him know the danger was there, just like Kat. She should have told him, and now it was too late.

But if she'd told him…they'd never have had this night. And Faith couldn't give that up, even for honour's sake. Maybe that was the true difference between them.

A sharp ringing noise jerked her out of her thoughts, and Dominic reached across her body to grab the hotel room phone.

'Yes?' he said, then as he listened to the voice on the line his body stilled. 'We'll be right down.'

Hanging up, he pulled away from Faith, sitting with his back to her on the edge of the bed.

'What's happened?' she asked, her heavy heart beating too hard now.

Dominic's voice was calm and steady as he replied. Unfeeling. 'They need us in the lobby. There's someone down there asking for you. Apparently he's causing quite a scene.'

Oh no. Faith swallowed, reaching for her dress. 'Right, of course. I don't…I can't…' How could she explain that she didn't know who it was, because there were too many options to choose from? Her father. Antonio. Great-Uncle Nigel. Who'd found her? And who had such awfully bad timing as to ruin this night?

'I suppose we'll find out what this is about when we get downstairs,' Dominic said, and Faith nodded, a sick feeling rising up in her throat.

She didn't bother with her bra or tights, just pulled the dress over her head and shoved her feet into her shoes. She probably looked a state but, well, wasn't that just what people would expect anyway? Even Dominic, in trousers and an untucked shirt, looked less respectable than normal. Not as free and abandoned as he'd been half an hour before, but Faith knew, in her heart, that she'd never get to see that side of Dominic again. Whoever was waiting for her in the lobby had ruined that for her.

The lift ride down was silent again, but this time the tension between them was filled with questions rather than anticipation. Faith kept her eyes on the toes of her shoes and prayed that she'd be able to talk her way out of whatever this was.

But then the lift door opened and before they could even step out she heard her name being yelled across the lobby.

'Faith!'

She froze. The accent was wrong for Antonio, or her father, and Great-Uncle Nigel sounded like the fifty-a-day smoker he was, so...

'Lady Faith Fowlmere.'

Dominic froze beside her, and Faith made herself look across the lobby to see who it was that had unmasked her. Who had ruined her one night.

She closed her eyes against the horror as she recognised the photographer from the theatre striding across the lobby towards her. Then her brain processed what she was seeing and her eyelids flew open again. He had his camera. He had his camera out and pointed at them.

'We need to go,' Dominic said, grabbing her hand, but Faith knew it was already too late. The flash of the camera lit up the subdued lobby, light reflecting off the marble tiles and the mirrors on the stairs. There was no hiding this now.

'You need to come with me. Now!' Dominic's words fought their way out from between clenched teeth and Faith ducked her head, turning and following him towards the lift.

'Lady Faith! Would you like to make a comment on your whereabouts for the last couple of years?' the photographer called after them, still snapping away.

'Do not say a single word.' He sounded furious. She'd known he would be. She'd just hoped he'd never have to find out. Or at least that she'd be many, many miles away when he did.

'Or perhaps what made you want to come back?'

Faith couldn't resist a glance over her shoulder at that, even as Dominic stabbed the call lift button repeatedly. The reporter was smirking, obviously assuming he knew exactly why she was there: Dominic. Just as they'd been so, so sure they knew what she was doing in that hotel room with Jared three years ago.

They were wrong again.

She hadn't come back to London for Dominic, and there wasn't a chance in hell he'd let her stay now he knew the truth.

The lift pinged and the doors opened at last. Dominic hauled her inside, holding down the close doors button before she was even through. All Faith could see was the reporter's smile, even after the lift started to move.

And then she realised she was alone with Dominic. Again.

'My room,' he said, the words clipped. 'We don't talk about this until we are safely behind a locked door.'

CHAPTER TWELVE

THIS WASN'T QUITE how he'd imagined having her in his room tonight.

Faith stood against the wall by the bathroom, arms folded over her chest, looking like a schoolgirl caught smoking. Like she was just anyone. Like she was still his Faith, only guiltier.

Lady Faith Fowlmere. How had he not known? Okay, so he didn't exactly study the social pages, but even he'd heard the story of the missing heiress, and the scandals she left behind. There must have been a clue, something that he'd missed. Probably because he was too busy being swayed by her curves and her enthusiasm for life.

A life away from the one he lived.

'Were you planning on telling me?' he asked, his eyes landing on her bra, still tossed across the arm of the chair. Just how had this gone so wrong so quickly?

Faith's head jerked up and she met his gaze head-on, her eyes wide but steady. 'No.'

Hope drained out of him. If she'd said anything else—that she was scared, that she hadn't known how, that she wanted to know how he felt first…anything else at all—maybe they could have worked it out. He could have understood, perhaps.

But she'd never wanted him to know who she was. Ever.

'Why?'

A half-shrug, one hunched shoulder raised. 'We agreed one night. Come on. You knew I wasn't going to stay, and you knew there was a reason. Look me up on the Internet and you'll see why. I'm a scandal; everyone knows it. And I know you. You'd have fired me if you found out. Too much of a risk. And, more than that, you'd have wanted me to talk to my parents, to reconcile, for the good of the family name. You know you would.'

She was right. She did know him. Better than he'd ever been allowed to know her. 'And you won't.' Not a question. He knew her that well, at least.

'I don't ever want to go back there.' The vehemence in her voice surprised him. He didn't know the Fowlmeres personally, but they were her family.

'You might have to. We need to put a respectable face on this, and "runaway heiress returns home" sounds a hell of a lot better than "runaway heiress found in high-priced love nest".' He reached for his phone, trying to keep his temper under control. He needed to think, not react. And he needed to ignore the part of his brain that was telling him that the secrets were out now. He knew the worst of it. Maybe he could salvage something from this.

But first he had to fix it.

'Here's what's going to happen now,' he said, scrolling through his contacts. 'I'm going to call my PR people, get them down here. I'll sit down with them, come up with a plan. Maybe we can talk to the reporter, or more likely the newspaper owner. Maybe we can get an injunction. I don't know. But I am *not* going to let your past ruin my future.'

Faith hadn't even moved from her position by the door. 'And what am I going to be doing, while you set about fixing my mistakes?' Her voice was cool, calm—everything he didn't feel right then.

'You are going to be sitting in your hotel room, not talking to anyone, not seeing anyone, not even *thinking* about anyone. Do you understand me?'

Her eyes were sad as she spoke. 'Oh, I understand. You're going to rewrite not just my history, but our entire past.'

'I've known you a week, Faith. I don't think what we had qualifies as a past.'

'We had tonight.'

'And now we don't.'

Faith felt very cold, as if someone had left a window open in winter and the icy wind was chilling her through, layer by layer. Was this how it felt to freeze to death? And, in the absence of both winter and wind, was Dominic's coldness enough to finish the job?

'You're treating me like a child,' she said, the words hard lumps in her throat.

'I'm treating you like what you are,' he replied. 'A scandal and a flight risk.'

Just like his mother, Faith realised. But knowing why he was mad, expecting it even, didn't make it any easier.

And it didn't mean he got to take over her life.

'I understand,' she said again, wrapping her arms tighter around her. 'You'd better make your phone call.'

Dominic gave a sharp nod. 'Go straight to your room. I wouldn't put it past that photographer to have snuck back in, assuming security kicked him out by now. He could be anywhere. I'll call you in the morning,' he said, and she nodded as she collected her belongings and headed back towards the door, away from him, thinking hard.

He wanted her to stay hidden. Wanted her to let him fix her life for her. Wanted her to be a good, obedient Lady Faith.

It was as if he'd never known her at all.

This would be all over the Internet by the morning, however hot Dominic's PR team were supposed to be. And if she were going to be a story again, a scandal even, she was doing it on her own terms. She couldn't stay with someone who was embarrassed by her, ashamed of her.

Not even Dominic.

The story was out now, and that changed everything. What was the point of hiding when everyone knew where she was? This job had been her last chance. Without it—and without her salary for the week—she was out of options. She couldn't just hop on a flight to another country this time. Chances were, she'd be spotted at the airport, anyway.

No, Faith knew what she needed to do next. Even if it was the last thing she wanted.

Back in her hotel room, Faith packed quickly and economically. Three years as a tour guide had taught her the best way to roll clothes, as well as what was essential, and what wasn't.

She stripped off the hideous dress she'd bought for the theatre and left it folded on the chair. She wouldn't need it again. Instead, she pulled on an old pair of jeans, a T-shirt and a cardigan, loading her case with the rest of her clothes. She removed her make-up before packing her cosmetics bag, shoved her feet in her trainers and headed for the door.

As one final thought, she left Dominic's expenses credit card on top of the dress. He already thought badly enough of her. She didn't want him thinking she was a thief, too.

She kept the money in her purse though, the last remains of the petty cash he'd given her at the start of the week, to buy a train ticket back to the only place she had left.

Home.

Dominic was up early the next day, after a night spent liaising with his PR team and barely sleeping. He could still smell Faith on the bed sheets, and knowing she was only a few rooms away, awaiting his decision on her future, didn't help. He knew he couldn't really have handled it differently, under the circumstances. But knowing that didn't make him feel any better about it.

Now he just had to break the plan to Faith.

'We'll sell it as a rehabilitation,' Matthew the PR guy had said once they'd established there was no way to keep the news that the runaway heiress was back in town from breaking. 'You met in Rome and brought her back to try and reconcile her with her parents. There'll still be a lot of talk about her past, I'm sure, but as long as we present it right, get in early with the story, you should both come out okay.'

The first step, they'd agreed, was to get Faith to give an interview, with Dominic at her side as a sort of mentor. Then they'd stage the reunion with her parents, build it up carefully. After that, Matthew said, Dominic could wash his hands of her altogether, if he wanted.

It was a plan. It wasn't perfect, but it should at least

minimise the damage. Once he convinced Faith to play along.

Showered and dressed, he headed to her room, annoyed when she didn't answer his knock. He banged louder, and this time the door opened—only there was nobody on the other side. Anger and frustration started to build. The room was empty, with no sign that anyone had even slept in the bed last night.

Dominic swore. The runaway heiress had run again.

'I'm not staying,' Faith said, the moment her mother opened the door. Time was, there'd have been the butler to do that, but after Jenkins died when Faith was seven, there'd never been the money to hire another one.

Her mother raised her eyebrows at her, gestured inside with her glass and said, 'Then I assume you want money. There isn't any, you know.'

'Trust me,' Faith said, lugging her suitcase over the threshold, 'I know.'

Her father, at least, seemed pleased to see her.

'We missed you around here, you know,' he said, kissing her cheek and taking her arm as if she'd been away on holiday, not missing for three years. 'Nobody to laugh at my jokes!'

'I can't imagine that's true.' There had always been someone to laugh at the right time, to sparkle and smile when he wanted it. Lord Fowlmere had never needed his daughter—or even his wife—for that.

He laughed. 'Dahlia! Fix this girl a cocktail. She's probably been travelling for days to return to the bosom of her family.'

In fact, Faith had caught the first train north from King's Cross, studiously avoiding all the papers at the station and refusing to log into the train Wi-Fi. Instead, she'd slept all the way, then walked the three miles from the nearest station and arrived at Fowlmere late morning. Also known as cocktail hour to her mother and father.

While her mother fixed her drink, Faith took herself and her suitcase back up to her old room.

Now she was back, it almost felt as if she'd never left, except for the aching loss in her middle where thoughts of Dominic used to reside. If she thought about him, about the disappointment on his face or the feel of his body against hers, she'd cry. And if she started, she might not stop. So, no crying.

But, seriously, why was it she cared so much about his disappointment? She'd let down every single member of her family, scandalised the society in which they lived…why would she care about disappointing one man who she'd known for less than a week? Especially one who'd wanted her to stay put and stay quiet while he managed her life.

The answer whispered around her mind, but Faith refused to acknowledge it. That way lay madness, and probably a lot more cocktails than was advisable.

She managed to avoid most of her parents' questions by hiding in her room until dinner, ostensibly napping. Her father blamed jet lag and let her be, which was a blessing. But Faith knew she'd never sleep until she faced things head-on. So she pulled out her tablet, took a deep breath and checked out the damage.

The blogs and the websites had the news first, as always. The photo of her and Dominic in the lobby of the Greyfriars, looking as if they'd just rolled out of bed, was plastered everywhere. Faith scrolled past, wishing that every glimpse of the picture didn't make her remember exactly what they had been doing just before

it was taken. How his body had felt pressed against
hers. How perfect everything had been, for one fleeting moment.

The text below tended to be scant. Nobody knew
anything except that she had been seen in London with
Lord Dominic Beresford. Which was, she supposed,
all there really was to know—especially if Dominic's
PR team had got to work. There was speculation about
where she'd been, and whether she was still holed up at
the Greyfriars, but that was it for new news.

So, of course, they rehashed the old news instead.
Faith buried the tablet under a pile of blankets on the
trunk at the end of the bed when she reached that part.

Dinner with her parents was a stilted affair. Dad
would try to make jokes, telling anecdotes that grew
more obscure and confused with every glass of wine,
but neither her mum nor Faith laughed. When he pulled
out the whisky after dinner, Faith thought of Dominic
and declined.

'I need an early night,' she said.

Her mother frowned. 'You slept all afternoon.'

'Jet lag, Dahlia,' Dad said, and Faith didn't disagree.

She wandered through the halls of the manor towards
the main staircase, her gaze alighting on the holes in
the carpet, the empty spaces on the shelves where expensive trinkets once sat. In some ways, it was hard not
to compare Fowlmere with Beresford Hall. In others…
there just was no comparison.

Fowlmere was decaying, ruined. Over. Just like her
relationship with Dominic.

Tucked up in her childhood bed, the old feelings of
isolation and hopelessness pressed in on her, but she
willed them away. She'd escaped from this place once.
She'd do it again. This was merely a temporary stop,

until everything blew over and she was employable again. That was all.

She would never have to be that Lady Faith again. The girl with no place in the world, whose very home was falling apart around her, whose parents couldn't see past their own problems to see her misery. She was an adult now, and she got to choose her own life.

And nobody in their right mind would choose this.

The next morning, Faith pulled her tablet out from its cocoon and braved the news sites again. Nothing much new, except a note that Dominic had checked out of the Greyfriars, but with no sign of her. There was a new photo, showing Dominic stalking out of the hotel, dark eyes hard, ignoring every single reporter and photographer waiting for him. Something pulled at Faith's insides at the sight of him.

How he must hate her right now.

She shook her head. She had more practical matters to worry about. The news would have made it from the Internet to the papers this morning, which meant that her father would read it. And if the world knew she was no longer at the Greyfriars, the paparazzi would be coming here next. She needed to warn her parents, see if they were willing to stick with a 'no comment' rule until the reporters got bored. After all, none of them were very likely to want to sit in a field outside a crumbling mansion for more than a day or two, even if it meant getting a photo of the Runaway Heiress.

But before she got further than pulling on her dressing gown against the pervasive chill of Fowlmere Manor there was a sharp rap on the door and a mug of tea poked into the room, followed by her father.

'Am I allowed in?'

'Of course.' Faith took the drink and sipped. Milk and two sugars. She hadn't taken sugar for years.

Entering, he moved to the bed and sat, bouncing a little on the mattress. 'I haven't been in here for a while,' he admitted. 'Your mother, she'd come and sit in here whenever she missed you, but I found it easier just to stay away. Much like yourself.'

Faith blinked. 'She missed me?'

'Oh, very much. We both did. Not just for the laughing at jokes thing.' He gave her his trademark lopsided smile. 'And then when I saw that business in the papers this morning…I understood. No jet lag then, I suppose?' A blush heated Faith's cheeks. 'Shame you couldn't bring Lord Beresford with you, really. I wouldn't mind picking his brain on a few subjects.'

'It's not…we're not…' Faith swallowed. 'It wasn't how I imagine they made it look. Not really. And anyway, it didn't end well.'

'But it is ended?' her father asked. 'That's a pity. He's done incredibly well, really, given what he started with.'

Faith rather thought that Dominic had done incredibly well for anyone, but that wasn't her main concern. She could see her father calculating what he could do with access to a fortune like the Beresfords'. How there might be the chance of a little loan, something between friends. She'd seen it before. But not again.

'No. It's definitely over,' she said.

'Ah, well.' He shifted on the bed, kicking up his feet. 'Your mother tells me you're not planning on staying.'

'That's right.' Faith sat down on the dressing table stool and took a sip of her too sweet tea. 'I've just finished a job down in London. I should be able to pick up another one fairly quickly.' As long as they didn't want references from Dominic. Or Marco… 'Once I'm sorted, I'll move out again. But I might be able to send some money home, to help out.' It would just go onto the gin budget, she knew, but at least she might feel a little less guilty.

'What sort of a job?' her father asked, curiosity in his gaze. When she gave him a look, he threw up his hands to protest his innocence. 'It's not like we have any idea what you've been doing for the last few years. Or even where you've been, except for the news that you apparently somehow fell in with Beresford.'

Guilt pinged at her middle again. Okay, so they'd been lousy parents for the most part, and it hadn't really occurred to her that they might be worried about her whereabouts, but she could have at least dropped them a postcard, or something.

Except they'd have dragged her back. Although, right now, she wasn't sure if that might not have been a good thing. She'd never have met Dominic. Never ended up in this hideous mess.

But she could never really wish not to have met Dominic.

'I've been working as a tour guide,' she said, reaching for her mug again. 'In London, and in Italy.'

'A tour guide?' Her father looked fascinated. The idea of work had always been interesting to him. Just a shame he'd never had the desire to actually do any himself. 'Showing people around things?'

'And organising their hotels, their travel, looking after their needs, their trips and so forth. Yes.'

'Sounds like being a servant,' her father said, and laughed. 'Did you have to wear a uniform?'

Faith nodded. Who was he to suggest that her job was below her station? At least she was doing more than sitting around drinking in a decaying relic of an earlier era. 'I did. And actually it was fun. I liked it, and I'm good at it. So I'll find another job doing the same sort of thing, uniform and all if required, and send some money home for the drinks cabinet. Okay?'

'Whatever makes you happy, buttercup,' he said, instantly making her feel bad for acting so defensive. It really was just like old times. 'Only I was just thinking that it might be you don't have to go all that far to find that new job of yours.'

Faith felt her parental sixth sense tingle. This wasn't going to be good. 'I was thinking London…close enough to visit, right?' Not that she intended to. But if she could borrow the car to get to the station, she could commute from Fowlmere until she had enough cash to find a place of her own.

Her father shook his head. 'I've got a better idea. You want to be a tour guide? You can do that right here. At Fowlmere!'

Faith thought of the entrance hall, with its dingy lighting and faded and fraying curtains in the windows. So different to the bright open halls and lovingly restored features at Beresford Hall. 'Dad, I really don't think anyone is going to want to tour Fowlmere at the moment.' The whole house was in the same state. Who paid money to see mould and decay?

'Not yet, maybe, but I've got a plan.' He tapped the side of his nose.

Faith bit her lip to hold in a sigh. Just what she needed. Another one of Dad's plans.

'Perhaps, in the meantime, it might be better if I—'

'You want to go to London; I understand that.' Dad waved a hand around. 'That's fine. I need you in London. You can come to my meetings with me.'

'Meetings?' Dad's meetings only usually took place

in the pub, with men who knew exactly which horse was going to come in, really this time, honest.

He nodded. 'I've met with a young guy who is helping me save this place—for a cut, of course. Still, it might fill the old coffers again.'

Because that was what it was all about for her dad, wasn't it? Living the life he truly believed he was entitled to, even if they couldn't afford it. 'What does he intend to do?' she asked, as neutrally as she could manage.

'Do this place up. Use the land for corporate activities, events, the whole deal. Like Beresford did down at his place. I'll introduce you tomorrow; he can tell you all about it.'

The image of Beresford Hall, all clean and crisp facilities, clashed horribly with Fowlmere in Faith's memory. 'I think it might take a bit more work than you're anticipating, Dad. I've been to Beresford Hall. It's pretty spectacular.'

Her father smiled a beatific smile. 'That's why it's so wonderful that you're home to help me. Serendipity, don't you think?'

Fate was playing with her, just like it had at that airport bar in Rome. Her father looked so excited, so full of self-belief. But all Faith could feel was her escape routes closing in on her with every word.

CHAPTER THIRTEEN

THREE WEEKS LATER and still the world didn't seem ready to let him forget about Faith and move on.

The first week had been the worst. Once the picture of Dominic and Faith looking dishevelled together at the Greyfriars hit the Internet it was in every single paper by the evening editions. And then came worse—the photographer who'd caught them leaving the theatre hand in hand. Footage of Westminster Bridge that evening where someone's camera phone just happened to catch them embracing in the back of a photo. An anonymous source—Dominic suspected Jerry—who detailed how long Faith had worked for him and claimed 'they always seemed like they had some big secret. Like they were laughing at us behind our backs.'

There were more stories after that. Someone—presumably a friend Faith had spoken to when setting up the events that week—told the story of Faith talking her way into the job over drinks at the airport. It read as far more sordid than Dominic remembered the reality being, and even Sylvia had called him up and squealed at him, demanding to know if that was really what had happened.

And then Faith's apparently numerous ex-boyfriends

had started getting in on the act, and Dominic had stopped reading the stories.

But he couldn't avoid the headlines. Ridiculous puns and alliterations that no one showed any sign of getting bored with. 'Runaway Heiress, Runaway Bride?' was the latest one. Dominic hadn't quite managed to restrain himself from reading the entire speculative article that followed that one, suggesting that Faith had left him just after he'd proposed marriage.

The worst of it was, with every article he learned something new about Faith—although he'd probably never know for sure what was truth and what was pure fabrication.

He'd learned about her family, finally making sense of the bits and pieces she'd told him. No wonder she'd hated being at Beresford Hall. By all accounts, her father had spent his way through the Fowlmere fortune in record time. He must have been a constant reminder of what she'd lost.

He'd followed the story of her misspent youth, too. The media had happily mined the photo archive with every article, although Dominic had barely recognised his Faith in the scantily clad, drunken society girl falling out of nightclubs and being caught on camera with the hot young celebs of the day.

His Faith. That was one thing she'd never been, not really.

In fact, if the papers had it right, if she was anyone's Faith it was Jared Hawkes's, the married rock star with a notorious drug problem who had, apparently, left his wife and kids for Faith, before she skipped the country.

She looked more like he remembered her in the photos of her leaving the hotel with Hawkes, which somehow made things worse.

He'd tried to keep his head down and focus on work, wait for it all to blow over like Matthew the PR guy advised. But even if Sylvia was reporting record numbers of visitors to Beresford Hall, the Americans had returned home leaving the contracts unsigned, after many awkward conversations and superior looks from Jerry. So now he was waiting. Waiting to see if his professional life could move past this scandal. Waiting to see when the next comparison piece between his mother and Faith would appear in the papers. Waiting, against reason, for Faith to suddenly appear in his life again, the way she had the first time.

Because, the truth was, London wasn't the same without Faith. She'd already been gone longer than she'd been with him, but in three weeks that feeling of something being missing hadn't faded. In the office, he missed her snarky emails pinging through every so often. In his apartment, he missed the idea of her sprawled across his sofa, tablet on her lap, sipping whisky. And in the city…well, that was the worst.

It seemed that everywhere he went there were reminders of her. A poster for a show she'd wanted to see. A view of Tower Bridge and the memory of the dress she'd worn to dinner that night. A tiny backstreet Italian restaurant that was never Lola's, but often looked close. A pelican staring balefully at him in St James's Park.

He seemed to be, inexplicably, spending a lot of time walking through St James's Park these days. He couldn't even remember how he used to get from one place to another, before Faith introduced him to the pelicans.

The most embarrassing part was that he kept thinking he saw her. All across London, any time he spotted a woman in a red cardigan, or wild dark hair, his brain screamed 'Faith!' Several times, he'd found himself halfway to accosting a curvy stranger before he re-alised that, even if it was her, she'd betrayed him, she'd run away from him, and they were done.

He had a list of things he wanted to say to her, though. A mental list he added to each night when he couldn't sleep, remembering the feel of her body against his, under his.

It started with the obvious. *Why couldn't you just do as I asked you for once?* If she'd just stayed, he could have fixed things. She knew that, surely? How desperate must she have been to get away from him that she ran anyway?

Just one night. That had been the agreement. Which led to the second item on his list. *Why didn't you want to stay?*

Except that sounded too desperate, as if there were a hole in his life waiting for her to fill it, even after all that she'd done, so he always mentally scratched that one off again.

The list went on and on, through anger, pain, loss and outright fury. But the last question was always the same. *Why couldn't you have just left me alone in that airport bar?*

Because if he'd never met Faith, his life wouldn't be so disordered, so confused. And people wouldn't be discussing his private life again, the way they had after the revelations about his mother's affair.

And that, he had to admit, was the part that made him angriest of all.

But the dark-haired woman across the street, or the park, or the shop was never Faith, so he never got to ask her any of the things on his list.

No one seemed to know where she was, but Dominic assumed she'd skipped abroad again. The reporters had staked out Fowlmere for a few days after he checked out of the Greyfriars and it became clear she was no longer there with him. He'd read a brief statement from Lord Fowlmere saying that his daughter was just fine, thank you, but taking a little time off. No hint on where she might be doing that. Dominic couldn't even be sure that the man really did know where Faith was.

The search for the runaway heiress had reached a dead end.

Until, unexpectedly, one evening, at a charity ball Sylvia had insisted he attend, the woman across the room really was Faith, and he didn't even recognise her.

'Look!' Sylvia nudged him in the ribs, hard, just in case he'd missed her not-at-all-discreet attempt at a stage whisper.

Dominic straightened his dinner jacket. 'Where, exactly, am I looking?'

'Over there! Cream dress. Gorgeous skin. Hair pinned back.'

He followed her also-not-discreet pointing finger with his gaze. 'Still not getting it,' he said. Except he was. There was something. Not in the polite expression of interest on the woman's face as she listened to some bore drone on. And not in the high-cut evening dress, complete with pearls. But underneath all that…

'It's Faith, you idiot!' Sylvia prodded him in the ribs again. 'You need to go and talk to her.'

Around him, the room was already starting to buzz. Whispers of his name and hers. Those looks he thought he'd left behind years ago, the ones that said: *We know your secrets.*

What was she doing here? Shouldn't she be in Italy or Australia or anywhere by now? Not standing next to her father at the most glamorous, most publicised and photographed charity ball of the year.

Had she really gone home? The journalists must have grown bored of staking out a crumbling estate in the middle of nowhere pretty quickly not to have noticed. But if her big plan was to go home anyway, why couldn't she have just stayed long enough for him to fix things?

He had to leave. He'd drop a large enough donation to the charity to excuse his absence at the ball, and he'd be gone. No way he was providing entertainment to a room full of gossip hounds by actually talking to Faith.

'People are starting to stare,' Sylvia pointed out, as if he hadn't noticed.

'Let them.' Dominic slammed his champagne flute onto a passing waiter's tray. 'I'm leaving.'

'Dominic, no.' Sylvia grabbed the sleeve of his jacket and held on, her brightly polished nails digging into his arm through the fabric. 'Look, the only way this blows over is if you and Faith act like it doesn't matter. You can't be all affronted and embarrassed. You have to bore them out of it.'

'I'm not talking to her.' Just looking at her, acting the perfect heiress she'd never been before, had made it perfectly clear she couldn't be for him… It made his teeth ache his jaw was clenched so hard.

'Well, if you won't, I will,' Sylvia said, marching off across the room before Dominic could react.

Any eyes that weren't on him before swivelled round to catch the scene.

Bore them, she'd said. Somehow, Dominic suspected that wasn't the most likely outcome of this situation.

'Of course, I've always found…' Lord Hassleton said, and Faith tuned out again, secure in the knowledge that the peer liked the sound of his own voice far too much to ever expect her to comment on what he was actually saying. As long as she nodded occasionally and kept a polite smile on her lips, she'd be fine. And maybe one day, if she was really lucky, one of those waiters with the trays of champagne would come her way and give her another glass. Or brain Lord Hassleton with the silver tray. She wasn't fussy.

This was her role, for now. She'd got her parents to keep quiet about her return, hiding out in her room until the photographers outside Fowlmere Manor grew bored. But it seemed her father was deadly serious about them working together on the regeneration. She couldn't hide for ever, not if they were going to save the Manor, he said. They needed to get out there, meet people, start making new connections, new networks. And no one pulled a guilt trip quite like her father, so here she was, shaking hands, smiling politely and wishing she was anywhere else in the world.

It was only until her father got everything up and running, she told herself. After the intense interest about her return in the media, she needed this new boring Faith to make people forget her past. Then she could get on with fixing her future.

'Faith!' The bright voice to her left made Faith freeze. She didn't relax one iota when she realised who it was.

'Oh, Lord Hassleton,' Sylvia said, her tone light and happy and lots of other things Faith wouldn't really expect from Dominic's sister. 'I'm *so* sorry to interrupt. But you don't mind if I steal Lady Faith away from you for just a moment or two, do you? It's been an *age* since I saw her, and I'm *dying* to catch up.'

Lord Hassleton looked down at Sylvia's petite hand on his chubby arm and said, 'No, no, of course not. You gels go and…talk, or whatever.' He turned to Faith, and she quickly twisted her lips back into the fake smile she'd perfected in the mirror. 'We'll continue this another time, Lady Faith.'

'I look forward to it,' Faith lied.

But as she turned away from Lord Hassleton and let Sylvia lead her across the room, she started to think she might have had a better time listening to another hour's rambling on sewage works near his estate, or whatever it was the man had been going on about.

Just steps away stood Dominic, watching her with wary eyes. How had she not noticed him come in? Too busy trying to stay awake while listening to Lord Hassleton drone on, she supposed. But now… Now she could feel the stares on her back, the anticipation in the room. Everyone knew they'd been together. Everyone knew she hadn't been seen again since, until tonight. And everyone was waiting to see what would happen next.

'I don't think this is a good idea, Sylvia,' she said, slowing to a halt.

'Trust me, it is.' Sylvia tucked a hand through Faith's arm and dragged her forward, smiling like a politician. 'Like I told him, the only way this ends is if you two act like it doesn't matter.'

But it does matter, Faith didn't say.

'Faith,' Dominic said as they reached him, his voice cold and clipped. 'I wouldn't have expected to see you here.'

'I lost a bet,' Faith joked, and watched as Dominic's eyebrows sank into a frown.

Sylvia glanced between them, eyes wide. 'You know what? I think maybe I'd better leave you two to this.'

'Probably safest,' Faith agreed with a nod. Then,

glancing around the room, she watched as every person there suddenly pretended not to be staring at them.

'Actually,' Faith said, turning away so most people couldn't see her face, 'why don't we take this conversation out onto the balcony, Lord Beresford? Fewer witnesses that way.'

Sylvia's eyes grew wider still, but Dominic just gave a sharp nod and took her arm. 'Let's go.'

CHAPTER FOURTEEN

WITNESSES. SHE WAS worried about witnesses. Dominic supposed that he should be grateful she wanted to take the conversation out of the public domain, but instead all he could think about was what on earth she had planned she didn't want witnesses for.

Or perhaps she was more afraid of what he might do. His list of questions rose up in the back of his mind but, in the end, the moment the balcony door swung shut, the first thing he said was simply, 'Why?'

Leaning back against the balcony rails, too high up above ground for Dominic to really feel comfortable with her lounging over them, Faith raised an eyebrow. 'Why what? Why did I leave? Why did I lie? Why am I here?'

'Yes,' he said. He wanted answers to all of them. He also wanted to know how he could be so furious with her and yet so desperate to kiss her at the same time, but he suspected she wouldn't have the answer for that one.

Besides, fury was winning by a comfortable margin.

'You ran away,' he said, the words hard in his mouth. 'I was going to fix this. I could have stopped all of... this.' He waved an arm at the expanse of windows between them and the ballroom, where a host of well-connected people in evening dress were barely even pretending not to be watching them any more. 'All you had to do was stay put and—'

'And let you fix my life?' Faith's voice was cool, colder than he thought he'd heard it before. As if she thought she had some right to be angry with him, after everything that had happened. 'No thank you. My life, my problems, my solutions.'

'Solutions? Since when did running away solve anything?'

Faith tilted her head as she looked at him, and Dominic couldn't tear his eyes away from the lovely line of her neck above her dress. 'That's what this is really about, isn't it? You're mad at me for leaving you.'

His gaze jerked back to her face. 'No! I'm furious because you lied to me. You risked my reputation and you ruined a deal I've been working on for years.'

She stilled, and for a brief moment he thought he saw something like guilt in her face. 'The Americans didn't sign?'

'Not yet. They want to see where we are when things have "settled down".'

Faith winced. 'I'm sorry.'

'*That's* the thing you're sorry for?' He laughed, even though it wasn't funny. 'Of course. The job always meant more to you than I did.'

'No.' Her eyes jumped up to meet his and for a second he almost believed her. 'I'm sorry I couldn't tell you the truth. But I knew how you'd react, what would happen if it got out. I couldn't risk it.'

'Because you needed me. You needed the job.'

'Yes.' Her gaze dropped to her shoes. 'I didn't know who you were either, when I met you. Not when I first asked for the job. And even then…it wasn't until later that I realised what me being, well, me, could do to you. And by then, things between us had become…more.'

Dominic pushed away from the wall and paced across to the edge of the balcony. From there, he could see all over London, all the places he'd never again be able to look at without thinking of her. But it was still better than looking at her face. 'It was never more. The first sign of trouble you ran away, like you always do.'

'I went home.'

'I know.' He shook his head, leaning against the rails as he stared down at the street below. 'Letting me help you was such a terrible prospect that you ran straight to the place you'd been trying to get away from all along.'

'I didn't have a lot of options.' There was an edge in her voice now. Good. She should be angry too. Between them, they'd messed this up good and proper. And even if it was all her fault, he wanted her angry. Wanted her to hate the way their one night had ended.

He shouldn't be the only one being eaten up by the fury.

He couldn't show it anywhere else. To the rest of the world, he needed to be the same in control Lord Beresford he'd always been. This couldn't be seen as more than a tiny blip on his life radar.

But to her…she knew. And so she was the only person he could tear apart.

'You had my credit card,' he pointed out. 'You could have gone anywhere in the world if you'd really wanted.'

Faith gave him a scornful glare. 'You think I'm a common thief, now? Gosh, you really don't have any respect for people outside your social sphere, do you?'

'But you're not outside it. You're Lady Faith.' He spat out the last two words. 'And I've learned a lot about what that means in the last three weeks.'

'Don't believe everything you read in the papers,' she said, as if it were a joke. As if it were even the slightest bit funny.

He turned to face her. He needed to see her reacting to this one. 'Maybe not. But a picture is worth a thousand words, don't they say?'

There. A tremor of something, under the bravado. But still, she tried to excuse herself. 'Like the picture of us?'

'We can't deny what happened just before it, however much we might want to,' he said. 'And it seems like it wasn't your first time in that particular situation.'

That was it. That was the line that got to her. Her whole body, usually so kinetic and full of energy, stopped cold. The only time he'd ever seen her so still was in his hotel room, just before she ran.

Dominic half hoped she might just run again. But she didn't.

'You mean Jared,' Faith said, proud that she could even find her voice. Did he truly think this was the same? That she had some habit of causing scandals for guys and then skipping town?

She'd hoped he knew her better than that. Apparently her real name wasn't the only thing he hadn't realised.

'I heard the poor guy left his wife and kids for you, before you ran. Guess I should be grateful that all I had to lose was my reputation.'

'Funny. I always thought that was all you cared about anyway. If it wasn't, maybe you'd have the wife and kids already and would never have to have worried about me at all.' Ouch, that hurt. It hurt her, and she was the one saying it. But if he honestly believed everything they printed about her…well, a little insult was nothing, surely.

And Dominic wouldn't let her see, even if it did sting. His expression was back to that robot look of the early days, the one that didn't let anything show. The one that had almost convinced her that he wasn't interested in her, didn't want her the way she wanted him.

But she knew better now. She knew him, even if he'd never really known her.

He drew back, leaning away from her against the railings. He wasn't going to rise to the bait. Of course not. As much as she'd love a knock-down drag-out fight with the guy, just to get it all out, to clear the air, maybe even let them start afresh…Dominic would never let go like that. And he'd certainly never do it where they had an audience. Through it all, he'd kept his voice low, his hands clenched at his sides or holding the railings. No outward sign of the fury burning in him.

Well, the crowd behind the glass might not be able to tell, but Faith knew. She knew he was every bit as angry as she was. And she knew he'd never let himself show it.

'So. What are your plans now? Will you stay at Fowlmere as the happy heiress?'

'You mean, will we be required to make polite conversation at every social function until the end of time?' Faith shook her head. 'Thankfully for both of us, no. Dad needs a little help setting up a new project, something to get the estate running properly again, and then I'll be on my way. Fowlmere is only ever a temporary stop for me.'

'You'll be running away again, then. Of course.'

Faith bristled at that. 'I'm not running *from* anything. I'm running *to* something new. My new life. A life where I don't have to answer to people like you.'

He raised an eyebrow. 'People like me?'

'Yes, people like you. And them!' Faith swept an arm out to encompass their audience, just a window pane away. He was the only one on that balcony who cared if they knew they were talking about them. 'All you care about is what other people think about you, what they say. Your precious reputation.'

'What's left of it now you're done with it,' Dominic muttered and grabbed her arm, trying to keep her calm, undemonstrative. Docile.

Ha!

Faith wrenched her arm away. 'Why does it matter to you so much what people think? So your mother left. That's her story, not yours! So you slept with a scandalous runaway heiress. Who cares? And what makes it any of their business anyway?'

'You cared,' he pointed out. 'Or are you trying to tell me that when you ran away the first time it wasn't because of what people were saying about you and Hawkes?' He shook his head. 'All that time I wasted trying to figure out what dreadful secret had made you leave Italy, when all the time I should have been trying to find out why you left Britain in the first place.'

'It wasn't because of Jared,' Faith said, remembering how it had felt, then, to be on the receiving end of that media fever. At least this time she'd actually slept with the guy. 'Not entirely, anyway. I just wanted to be somewhere—someone—else. I wanted people to not care what I did, to be able to live my own life.'

'Without caring what you left behind.'

'That's not true,' she said, but she knew he was never going to understand. 'And you never answered my question. Why does your reputation matter so much to you?'

His lips curved into a cruel smile. 'Didn't you say it yourself? It's all I have.'

'No, it's not.' She looked up at him, willing him to understand this one thing, even if everything else between them would forever be a battleground. 'You have so much more. I saw it, that night in London. The real you. You're more than just Lord Beresford. You're Dominic, too. And you're denying the real you just to keep up a façade in front of people who don't even matter!'

'Whereas you don't even bother with the façade,' he snapped back. 'You just run away when things get hard. You pretend to be anyone except the person you really are. Don't talk to me about denying my true self, *Lady Faith*. I doubt even you know who you really are any more. But it sure as hell isn't this woman in pearls and evening dress.'

Faith's skin burned pink above the fabric of her gown, and Dominic took a perverse pleasure in knowing he could still affect her that way. 'Maybe not. But I know something else I'm not. I'm not going to be your scapegoat any longer. I'm not taking the blame for this. Life is risk. You fail. People leave. And until you take that chance, you'll never be happy. You wanted one night with me, and you got it.'

'And you always told me you were going to leave,' Dominic said. 'At least that was one thing you didn't lie to me about.'

'What, you expected me to stay? As your events co-ordinator, right? No thanks.'

'I might have wanted more if—'

'If I weren't such a scandal? An embarrassment?'

'That's not it,' he said, but even he knew he was lying.

'Yes. Yes it is.' Faith shook her head and reached for

the balcony door. The buzz and noise of the ballroom filled his ears again as she stepped through. They were talking about them again. It seemed to Dominic they might never stop.

'Goodbye, Dominic,' Faith said, and he had to grip onto the railings to stop himself hauling her back, from making her finish this. He needed her to understand what she'd done to him, what it meant...

He watched as she made her way back into the crowd. Saw her put on her smile, the one that looked completely different to the quick, bright grins he'd seen when she was just Faith Fowler. And nothing at all like the slow, secret smiles she'd given him between kisses, on that last night.

He studied her a little closer. The tension in her shoulders, the slant of her head. The desperation in her eyes. All things he'd never seen before she became Lady Faith again.

She looked as if the walls were closing in on her, bricking her up alive. How hadn't he seen that before? This life, here, was killing her. And he didn't know how to live anything different.

No wonder she'd only ever wanted one night.

'You know,' Sylvia said, sidling up to him, 'that wasn't entirely what I meant when I said "be boring".'

'Faith doesn't know how to be boring,' Dominic said.

'No,' Sylvia agreed, staring out across the ballroom at Lady Faith Fowlmere, too. 'I always liked that about her.'

'Me too,' Dominic admitted.

CHAPTER FIFTEEN

'So. That was an interesting little show you and Lord Beresford put on for us all.' Faith scowled out of the taxi window at her father's words. Bad enough that the whole of London society had been watching through the glass. She didn't need to deconstruct the misery with her father, too.

'It wasn't meant to be for public consumption.' It should have just been her and Dominic, working things out. Making sense of everything that had happened between them. Not just trying to hurt each other without anyone else noticing.

'Wrong venue then, buttercup.' He patted her knee. 'Come on. You know people are fascinated by you. By all of us, really. But especially by you.'

'Maybe that's why I left.'

'And here I thought you didn't care what people thought about you. Wasn't that always what you used to say, when your mother would complain about another photo of you showing your knickers outside a nightclub?' He spoke the words lightly, as always, but Faith thought perhaps there was something harder underneath this time.

'I'm not that girl any more.'

'No, you're not.' Her father smiled at her. 'After all,

you came home this time.' He stretched out his legs as far as the taxi seats would allow and folded his hands behind his head. 'So, are you ready to tell me why you did leave? Really, this time?'

Faith shrugged. 'Nothing complicated. I wanted to be myself, and I felt I couldn't be that with the title round my neck and everyone watching my every screw-up.'

Except Dominic had been right about one thing. She would always be Lady Faith, however much she pretended otherwise. Maybe she really was no better than him. Hiding from her true name wasn't very different from hiding behind a reputation.

'And now?' her dad asked. 'Now you're back. What do you want to be now?'

'Still myself,' Faith replied, because that was always, always going to be true. But... 'Lady Faith, I guess. Whoever she turns out to be.'

'Well, if you really want to find out, seems to me the best place to learn is Fowlmere Manor.'

'I suppose it is.' Could she stay? Should she? Not just for a quick pit stop, but long enough to figure out what it really meant to be Lady Faith Fowlmere, here and now.

'I've got a meeting with Jack tomorrow. We're going to be talking about some of the plans for the estate. You should come with me.'

Was she ready? Getting involved with Dad's scheme...that wasn't something she could just run away from. If she committed to it, she'd have to see it through. Not doing so would mean leaving her parents in the lurch, more than ever before.

Was she ready to take on the responsibility she'd always avoided? Yes, maybe her parents had been responsible for running down the estate. But did that mean she shouldn't help build it back up?

'There'll need to be some changes...' she said.

'I know, I know.' He gave her a self-deprecating smile. 'I know I haven't always done right by you. Or your mother. But we've been trying, you know. When you left...things were bad for a while. But we've turned a corner, I think. And having you home...maybe we can all make it work. Together.'

She'd heard it before, plenty of times. But something in her wanted to believe it was true this time. 'How do I know you won't gamble it away, or get bored and find something better to do?'

'You don't.' He took her hand and squeezed it lightly. 'But, buttercup, what you do know is that it's a lot more likely I'll make a mess of it without you.'

That was true.

Maybe this was something she could do. Something she could be good at.

Maybe, against the odds, the place in the world she'd been searching for, the space she needed to feel at home was, actually, home.

Faith bit her lip. Then she said, 'Give me the guy's number. I'll call and tell him I'm running the project with you now.'

Her father beamed, and Faith hoped she wasn't making a colossal mistake.

'You really should talk to her,' Sylvia said, and Dominic sighed into his paperwork. Was even the office not safe now?

'I can't help but feel we've had this conversation before,' he said, shifting a pile of folders to the middle of his desk, making a wall of filing. 'Don't you have a tea room to run, or something?'

'Russell is taking care of it for the day.' Sylvia

dropped into his client chair and kicked her feet up on his filing wall. 'Which leaves me free to bother you.'

'How wonderful and special.' Dominic reached for the next folder in the stack. He had no idea what it contained, or what he might need it for, but if it meant not talking to Sylvia, he was all for it.

Except she was still sitting there. Watching him. Waiting for him to crack.

'What do I have to do to get rid of you?' he asked.

'Talk to Faith,' she replied promptly.

He sighed and put down the file. 'What on earth could I possibly have to say to her that wasn't already covered, in excruciating public detail, at the event last month?' And in the gossip rags the next day. Everyone was speculating about their mythical on-again, off-again romance. Some even dared to speculate that Faith had spent the last three years in their private love nest on the Continent.

If only they knew the truth, he thought. They'd be so disappointed. Not unlike him.

'That doesn't count,' Sylvia said, which made no sense at all.

'Trust me. It was the most honest conversation we've ever had. Possibly the only honest one.' He shook his head. 'I don't think there's anything left for Faith and I to say to each other.'

'Except that you're in love with her.'

For a moment it seemed so obvious, so profound a truth, that Dominic couldn't speak. Then reality reasserted itself.

'Of course I'm not,' he said, grabbing another handful of files. Where did all these bits of paper even come from? And what happened to them normally, when he wasn't using them to help him ignore his sister?

'Oh, Dominic.' When he looked up, Sylvia was shaking her head sadly. 'Are you really *that* stupid? I mean, I always knew I got the brains in the family. But really?'

'Hey,' he said, a little sharper than he intended.

'Well, right now you are being officially stupid!' Leaning forward to rest her wrists on her knees, Sylvia stared at him so intently he felt obliged to put down the files. 'Listen. She's great. She's honest—fake identity notwithstanding—bright, efficient, gorgeous. She's everything you've ever wanted in a woman.'

'She's a liability,' he countered because he couldn't exactly claim that any of the above weren't true. 'She'd ruin us.' Just like their mother almost had.

'How? By speaking her mind?' Sylvia shook her head. 'You wouldn't want a docile miss who never said what she was really thinking. It would drive you crazy, trying to figure out what she wanted.'

'She's a scandal,' he offered. 'She was caught having an affair with a married man. A drug addict. No one knows where she was for three years. There are all sorts of stories...'

'You know where she was,' Sylvia pointed out. 'Does any of it bother you?'

Yes, Dominic wanted to say. The idea of Faith being with another man, living with him. Loving someone who wasn't him. But he couldn't help but think that might bolster Sylvia's argument more than his own.

Which only left him with the truth.

'She'd leave, Syl. It's what she does.'

Sylvia's face fell, her eyes suddenly very wide. 'Oh, Dominic. You can't possibly think that's true.'

'I don't need to think,' he said, shuffling his files again. 'I know. And she's already done it once! You saw her at the gala last month. She hates that sort of thing.

She hates our whole world. Why else do you think she ran away?'

'But she came back,' Sylvia pointed out. 'She's at Fowlmere right now. It's been weeks and she hasn't left. So maybe she changed her mind?'

He shook his head. If only it were that easy. 'She told me herself, Syl. As soon as she sorts out the mess her father's made of the estate, she's out of there. She'll be back in Florence, or India, or Australia before you can speak. She's not the staying kind.'

'Maybe she just hasn't found something worth staying for yet,' Sylvia suggested in a small, quiet voice.

He gave her a lopsided smile. 'Yeah, well. I think she's made it pretty clear that's not me. Don't you?'

'Faith? It's Sylvia.'

Faith didn't bother asking how Sylvia had got her number—she just assumed she'd stolen it from Dominic's phone. It seemed like a Sylvia thing to do. So, instead, she motioned to Jack to keep walking the hedgerow between the lower and upper fields without her. He knew what they were looking at, and looking for, far better than she did anyway.

'Sylvia. What can I do for you?'

'Oh, I was checking in, see how you're getting on. You're still at the old homestead, I understand?' Sylvia spoke airily, as if it was a matter of no consequence, but Faith knew that if she'd spoken to her brother at all, she had to know that it was.

And yes, she was still at Fowlmere. And, against the odds, actually enjoying being there for the first time she could remember. Which wasn't to say that her parents weren't still capable of driving her crazy at times, but working towards something, as a family, seemed to be making a difference. Even her mother was hard at work pulling out long lost heirlooms and trying to restore them to their possible former glory. Maybe all they'd needed all along was a shared goal.

Maybe that was all she had needed, too.

'I'm still here,' she told Sylvia. 'Actually, it looks like I'll be staying for a while.'

'Helping your father with the estate, I understand?' Faith wondered where she'd heard that. Well, news got around, she supposed. Even when it was a lot more boring than scandalous nights in hotels and missing heiresses.

'Trust me, he needs the help,' she joked.

It was never going to be Beresford, but Faith was discovering that Fowlmere had its own charms, and its own opportunities to shine. To her surprise, she was even excited about them, far more so than planning a tour of some foreign land. This was her home, her heritage, at last. And, for the first time, she wanted to share that with other people.

'So…you think you'll be staying, then?' Sylvia asked.

Suspicion started to prickle at the back of Faith's neck. 'Yeah, it seems like it. Look, Sylvia, not that it's not lovely to hear from you, but was there something that you actually wanted?'

Sylvia sighed down the phone line. 'He's miserable without you.'

'No. He's safe without me. Respectable. Just like he wanted.'

'He was wrong.' Hope tugged at her heart at Sylvia's words, but Faith stamped it back down.

'I can't imagine him saying that.' Or even admitting it to himself.

'Maybe not. But I'm his sister. I know these things. So, you know, bear it in mind.'

Bear it in mind? What did that even mean?

But then a car pulled up on the driveway, just across from the field where she stood, and Faith knew, even before he got out of the car, exactly who the driver was.

CHAPTER SIXTEEN

'BETWEEN YOU AND your sister, this is all starting to feel a little stalkery,' Faith said, folding her arms over her chest as she reached the car.

'My sister?' Dominic asked, cursing Sylvia mentally in his head. This was all her fault, somehow. If it hadn't been for her with her insinuations and questions the day before, he'd never have felt the strange compulsion that led him to check up on Faith. Just to make sure she was okay. And maybe, a little bit, to find out what was making her stay at Fowlmere. 'What did she do?'

'She called. Apparently to check I was still here.'

'And you thought I'd asked her to do that?' Dominic asked.

Faith raised her eyebrows and indicated his presence. 'Not looking entirely far-fetched. Except that I'd have expected it to take you longer to get here.'

'I didn't ask her to call. I imagine she was just concerned for your wellbeing and wanted to see how you are. She's nice like that.' Which sounded much better than, *She's overly invested in our non-existent relationship.*

'Which still doesn't explain what you're doing here.'

'You wouldn't believe the same?' She raised her eyebrows at him. He got the message. 'Fine. I heard you were still here at Fowlmere. And I didn't want to leave things between us as they were. The papers seem to have lost interest, so—'

'So it was safe to come see me. I get it.' There didn't seem much point denying that one.

'I thought maybe you might need some help.' He hadn't been able to get the image of her, confined by evening wear, desperation in her eyes, out of his head. He needed to know she was still here because she wanted to be. Not because she didn't have any other options. 'Word is that you're trying to renovate the Fowlmere estate. Open it for business, like Beresford.'

'I'm not *trying* to do anything. I *am* doing.'

'Right. I just…I didn't expect you to stay this long.' Not voluntarily, anyway.

'You mean you didn't expect me to stay at all.' She looked away, staring out across the fields at some guy with a tape measure. 'Maybe something of what you said stuck. Maybe I'm done with running away.'

'Really.' Stood to reason she wouldn't decide to stay somewhere until *after* she'd run away from him.

'You don't believe me.' She didn't give him time to answer. 'Well, it doesn't matter what you believe. You, or your sister, or the papers, or my parents' friends. I'm back and I'm staying.'

'Why?' Dominic asked, just like he had on the balcony. Would this woman ever stop making him question things?

'Because I found something to stay for,' she said simply, and Dominic stared at the open truth in her face.

She'd found a reason to stay. But it wasn't him. It was never him.

'You were right about one thing,' Faith said. 'Pretending to be someone else, living in hiding, that wasn't

being me. I'm Lady Faith Fowlmere, and nothing I do
or say will change that. And nobody can take it away
from me, either. So I'm here, where I belong. I'm making my own place in the world, not looking for it everywhere else.'

His heart weighed heavy in his chest. He wanted
to be happy to see her so free, so alive again. But he
couldn't help wish she could have found that happiness with him.

'That's great,' he said. 'And really, I can...I can help.
If you want. I've got contacts, been through a lot of the
stuff you're going to come up against...'

'Thank you, but no.' She smiled as she spoke, but
the words still stung.

'Why not? Because you're too stubborn?'

She shook her head. 'Because I can't have someone in my life who is ashamed of me. I'm done being
ashamed of myself. I've made mistakes, sure, but...'
She took a breath. 'That's not who I am any more. And
I can't have you reminding me at every turn what an
embarrassment I am.'

He winced at the reminder. 'When I said...I didn't
mean to...'

'Yes. You did.'

'You weren't exactly complimentary to me, either,'
he pointed out, and she sighed.

'Look, Dominic, it's okay. Really. We knew each
other for, what, a week? It's crazy to think it was anything more than a flirtation. We barely even made it to
fling status. It was a one-night stand. Yes, things ended
badly, but it's over. You don't have to check up on me,
try to help me. You don't even have to feel guilty about
the things you said. It's over. We just...move on.'

It was all perfectly reasonable. Almost as if she did

this sort of thing all the time. Rational, even. The sort of sensible argument he'd normally be the one putting forward, not her.

The only problem was, it was a lie.

Whatever had been between them in that week, it was more than a flirtation. More than a fling, even if they never made it past one night together before everything fell apart. And it meant more to him than she could possibly know.

But the most untrue part of all was something he'd been lying to himself about, right up until the moment he saw that tilted chin, the pride in her warm hazel eyes.

He couldn't move on. He needed her in his life. No matter what her past, or who she was. No matter what the papers would say, or his mother's friends, or anyone else.

He needed her. Even more than he wanted her.

Now he just had to convince her of that.

'Dominic?' she asked, and he realised he was staring at her.

'Sorry. Just…thinking.'

She shook her head. 'You think too much. Look, I mean it. You can go.'

He didn't want to. But he needed time. He needed a plan.

Across the field, the burly guy with the tape measure beckoned to her.

'That's Jack,' she said. 'He's helping me with the estate. I've got to go. Thanks, though. For coming and talking to me. It's good to…' she let out a breath '…I don't know. Have closure, maybe.'

'Closure is good,' Dominic agreed. If she wanted to think that this was it, that this was the end for them, fine. It would make it all the more fun to prove her wrong.

Faith bit her lip, then jerked forward suddenly, wrapping her arms around him for a very brief moment. Her body felt stiff, unsure—so unlike the way she'd melted against him in the park at almost midnight, or the way she'd come apart in his arms in bed that night.

A clear sign that this was just not the way it was meant to be.

'Take care of yourself,' she said, stepping back. 'And…I don't know. Try not to overthink things. And loosen up, sometimes, yeah?' She sounded as if she thought she'd never see him again.

'I will,' he promised, watching her walk backwards away from him. His heart hurt just to watch her go, but he held firm. He had to do this properly. He had to find a way to convince her that it didn't matter who she was, where she'd been, what she'd done, or how she might ever embarrass or humiliate him in the future. He loved her. And none of the rest was worth anything, without her.

'Faith?'

She paused. 'Yeah?'

'One more thing. What really happened? With you and that rock star?'

'Jared?' Her eyebrows shot up. 'Didn't you learn everything you needed to about that from the papers?'

He shook his head. 'I don't believe them. You wouldn't do that.'

She bit her lip and he wanted to kiss her, so very badly. 'You're right,' she said. 'It wasn't what it looked like. His wife had just walked out on him, taken the kids, and he'd got himself into a hell of a state at some club. He called me—we were friends, before everything that happened. I picked him up, got him back to his hotel and spent the night sobering him up and listening to him wail about his life. I was taking him home to call his wife and beg her for another chance when they took the photos.' She looked up at him. 'Satisfied?'

'Yes,' he said. He should have known. Should have trusted her. She thought she was a scandal, but really... she was just his Faith. And, for the first time, it didn't matter what anyone else believed about her. 'And thank you. For telling me the truth.'

She shrugged. 'It's a new thing I'm trying. And tell your sister to stop checking up on me, yeah?' Faith added with a grin as she walked away. 'I'm fine.'

Sylvia. She'd help him fix this. Of course she'd also tease and probably hit him, but he could take it.

'Trust me,' he said, smiling at Faith as he climbed back into his car. 'I'm going to go have a long talk with my sister. Right now.'

Faith turned, halfway across the field, and watched his car as it pulled away, trying to ignore the emptiness that threatened to fill her. She'd see him again, she knew. If she was staying at Fowlmere, in society, it was inevitable. But they'd never be just Dominic and Faith again. She'd never get to take him to see the pelicans or eat at Lola's. She'd never feel his lips against hers, or his body over her.

She'd never get to tell him that she loved him. And she'd given up any chance of ever hearing him say it back.

Loss coursed over her in waves, as if she'd lost her whole life, her whole future, instead of just one man.

It was for the best, she reminded herself, wiping away the tears that dampened her cheeks. She didn't even know if he wanted more—certainly not after everything that had happened. How could she possibly work alongside him, day after day, without giving into the desperate desire for him? And how could she let him help her when she knew he'd be putting his professional and personal reputation on the line to do so?

There was a chance that her plan to save Fowlmere would fail. She wasn't stupid; she knew that. And she couldn't let everything that Dominic had worked for at Beresford be dragged down with it.

Besides, like she'd told him, she was done being ashamed. Done with seeking a place in a world that didn't fit her. She was making her own place, and Dominic Beresford could never understand something like that.

No, this was the perfect ending. A little bittersweet, sure. But they both knew it was the right thing, they had closure, they'd said goodbye.

Now she could move on with her life.

Without the man she loved.

With a shuddering breath, Faith called out to Jack. 'Okay. What's next?'

'You want to do what?' Sylvia screeched to a halt in the middle of the pavement when Dominic announced his intention. He smiled apologetically at the irritated pedestrians who crashed into them.

'Marry Faith,' he said again, his voice calm. It was strange how, once you figured out what needed to be done, the doubt and the worry faded away. All that mattered now was the plan. The right steps he needed to take to make her say yes. 'I'm pretty sure it was your suggestion, actually.'

'I said you were in love with her! I figured you'd date her first. Like a sane person.'

Dominic shook his head. 'It has to be all or nothing.'

'Why?'

'Because she won't say yes to anything else. Actually, she probably won't say yes to this. Which is why I have to get it exactly right.'

Sylvia stared at him, sighed, then started walking again. 'You know, when you said we should go shopping, I was hoping for something more in a shoe line.'

'You don't want to help me choose a ring?'

That changed her mood. 'Yes. Absolutely I do. You're bound to get it wrong without me.'

'So you are in favour of my plan.'

Sylvia lifted a hand and wobbled it from side to side. 'Maybe.'

'How can I convince you?'

Halting in front of the first jewellers shop on the row, Sylvia paused with her finger on the doorbell. 'Tell me why you're doing this.'

Dominic considered. It was one thing to know it was the right move in his head, another to articulate exactly why. Finally, when it became clear they weren't going anywhere until he answered, he said, 'I love her. I'm pretty sure she loves me. I know, in my heart, we belong together.'

'So ask her out. Go for dinner. Take it slow.'

Dominic shook his head. 'Won't cut it. Slow means… it means her worrying I'm going to end things if she does something I find embarrassing. It means leaving an escape route, a way out if she leaves me. A way to pretend it didn't matter. And it means leaving open the chance that we can walk away if things get hard. It means stories and rumours and whispers designed to try and split us up. And it doesn't show her how I feel. That it doesn't matter who she is, what she does, any of it. As long as she's with me. I'll take any risk—even the risk of her leaving—if she'll give me a chance.'

'A lot of those things can still happen, even if you're married,' Sylvia pointed out. 'In fact, there'll probably be more talk if you just rush in like this.'

'I don't care,' Dominic said. 'It won't matter.'

'Because you'll have your ring on her finger.'

'Because she'll be my wife,' Dominic amended. 'Exactly.'

Sylvia rang the bell. 'Then we'd better go choose you one.'

'Thank you,' Dominic said, grinning. 'For helping.'

'Oh, you're going to need my help with a lot more than this,' Sylvia said as the jeweller came and opened the door. 'Have you even thought about how you're going to propose?'

Dominic smiled. 'Trust me. That part I've got covered.'

CHAPTER SEVENTEEN

IT HAD BEEN a week. One whole long, boring week since they said goodbye. Faith had tried to keep busy, knowing that the only way she was going to get over Dominic was by stopping thinking about him. When she was knee-deep in dusters, polish and tarnished brass, it was harder to remember nights in luxury hotel suites, working together, both watching for a sign of something more…

No. Work was the thing. She couldn't daydream when she was discussing the estate plans with Jack, or working with her parents to clear decades' worth of junk from the attics. Jack had the first round of potential investors visiting at the end of the month—and she had tons of work to do before then.

Work was the way forward. Not worrying about her parents, who seemed a little saner every day. Not thinking about Dominic, who was gone. Not even wondering why Sylvia kept ringing. Faith ignored the calls. She'd moved on. She had closure. No point ruining all that now.

Except it seemed Sylvia wasn't very good at taking a hint.

'Sylvia!' Faith said, hopping down the steps of Fowlmere Manor to meet the car. 'I wasn't expecting you.'

'That's because you don't answer your phone any more. I've come to take you down to town for the day.'

Faith groaned inside. 'That's very kind of you, but I've got a lot on here at the moment...'

'Exactly why you need a day off! Come on, we can go shopping again.'

Faith didn't have especially fond memories of their last shopping trip, but she did like Sylvia and she really didn't want to hurt her feelings. Besides, she did need a new suit for the investors meeting...

'I've got Dominic's credit card,' Sylvia said, waving the card temptingly.

'I don't need that.' Faith was pretty sure there was a little bit of room left on her own.

'Just jump in,' Sylvia urged, and Faith gave up the fight.

'Okay. Let me just settle up a few things here...'

With hindsight, she should have been more suspicious from the start. If not then, certainly when Sylvia drove them straight to the Greyfriars Hotel for their lunch. But Sylvia kept chatting about nothing and keeping everything light and unimportant, so Faith's suspicions only really started to grow when they stepped outside at the exact same moment a red double-decker tour bus pulled up.

'What fun! A tour!' Even Sylvia didn't manage to not sound fake at that one.

'What's going on?' Faith said, rounding on Dominic's sister.

'I've always wanted to take a London bus tour,' Sylvia said, obviously lying. 'Come on, you can be my tour guide! You can stand up front with the microphone and everything.'

'They normally hire someone in to do that,' Faith

said as Sylvia dragged her up the bus steps and grabbed the microphone from its stand, handing it to her. 'Besides, it's been years since I did a bus tour. I've probably forgotten everything…'

She trailed off. She wasn't suspicious any more. Because she knew beyond a shadow of a doubt that she'd been set up.

Lord Dominic Beresford sat in the bus driver's seat.

'What are you—' The words echoed around the bus and she fumbled for the off switch on the microphone. 'What are you doing here?' she whispered.

Dominic grinned at her. 'Sylvia's always wanted to take one of these tours. So I commandeered a tour bus. We figured you could do the guide bit for old times' sake.' As if that were the most normal thing in the world.

Faith glanced back. A bus full of tourists stared at her, cameras and guidebooks at the ready. 'For the love of… You stole a tour bus? You? Lord Beresford?'

'Borrowed,' Dominic corrected. Starting the engine, he checked his mirrors and put the bus in gear. 'You remember that night you showed me your London?'

As if she could ever forget. 'Yes.'

'Well, today I'm going to show you mine.' The bus pulled away from the kerb. 'Come on, tour guide, aren't you supposed to be talking into that thing?'

Faith stared at the microphone in her hand. 'I don't know where we're going.'

'Yes you do,' Dominic said, and started to drive.

Dominic wiped the palm of his hand against his trousers before grabbing the steering wheel again. In his pocket, the hard lump of the ring box dug into him, a sharp-edged reminder of exactly what craziness he was pursuing. Oh, not the proposal, exactly. That, he was certain about. But the method… How had he thought this was a good idea?

Maybe it wasn't. But it was the only chance he had of convincing Faith he was serious. If nothing else, she couldn't worry about his fear of embarrassment any longer. Nothing she could ever do could humiliate him more than what he was about to do. Especially since he suspected his sister would be secretly filming the whole thing to share with the Internet.

Beside him, Faith had begun her tour, talking in only a slightly wobbly voice about the landmarks they passed. He'd decided to start off with the usual tour route, down past St Paul's and Fleet Street before he detoured over the river after the Tower of London. Faith still knew this route backwards, she'd told him on their tour of her London, and, for now, he was happy to let her talk, feel comfortable. As if this really was an official tour with an unusual driver.

'The Tower of London has a long and varied history,' Faith said, and Dominic risked a glance out of his window at the landmark. Maybe he'd take her there one day, just to listen to her get excited about the stories the building could tell. 'Most notably, of course, it's known as the site of the murder of the princes in the tower…'

Not romantic enough, Dominic decided. Time to start the plan properly.

Swinging the bus over to the other lane, he headed for the bridge over the Thames, ignoring Faith's murmured protest. Then, as they crossed over the water, she put her hand over the microphone. 'You're going the wrong way.'

'I'm really not.'

'They usually go along to Big Ben and the Houses of Parliament next,' she argued.

Dominic flashed her a smile. 'Trust me. I know exactly where we're going. Now, give me the microphone.'

'What?' She grabbed it closer to her chest at his request.

'Put it on the stand there so I can talk into it,' he said, nodding towards the steering wheel.

'What are you going to say?' she asked, but she did install the microphone as he'd asked.

'I'm not a hundred per cent sure yet,' Dominic admitted. 'But I'm sure I'll figure it out as I go along.'

Figure it out as he went along. Faith was pretty sure Dominic had never figured out anything as he went along. The man liked to have a plan. A fixed, unchanging, reputation-saving plan. So what on earth was he doing?

Sinking down into the guide's chair at the front of the bus, hands gripping the arm rests too tightly, she waited to find out.

'Hello, everyone. I'm your driver, Dominic. I'm afraid that today's tour is going to be taking a little bit of a detour. You see, not very long ago, your tour guide, Faith, introduced me to a side of London—and a side of myself—I'd never seen before. Then, for reasons we really don't need to get into, but suffice to say it was mostly my fault, she left me here alone in this big city. And now I want to show her my London, and how it looks without her.'

Faith's cheeks burned at his words. She couldn't look at him, couldn't even acknowledge what he was saying. Was he trying to humiliate her? Was this some sort of ridiculous revenge? No. This was Dominic. Whatever might have happened between them, he wouldn't do that to her.

'And, Faith?' he said. 'Trust me, this is going to be far more embarrassing for me than it is for you.'

Somehow, she wasn't entirely convinced.

'On your right, you can just about still see the River Thames.' Dominic's voice automatically took on the cadence she'd heard when he was presenting at meetings, or holding court over debate at the dinner table. 'We're now officially on the South Bank. Coming up, you'll see the back of Shakespeare's Globe Theatre, amongst other things. We can't really get close enough to the river in this big old thing, but that's okay. All you really need to know is that every single time I walk along this river, I think about Faith. I remember walking along the South Bank with her, practically in the middle of the night, looking out over the London skyline.'

Faith was pretty sure that wasn't all he remembered. Whenever she thought of it, her body remembered his arms around her, his chest under her cheek, the way he'd kissed her as if she were the air he needed to breathe...

'As we swing around here,' Dominic said as the bus lurched around the corner, 'we can head back over the river. From here you can see the London Eye, and across the way the Houses of Parliament. But what really matters is, if you look back along the river the way we came, you can see Tower Bridge in the sunshine.'

Tower Bridge. The place they'd first had dinner with all his clients. What on earth did he remember about that night? Behind her, the tour group were all whispering, chatting and giggling. About her, Faith assumed. Well, at least they were having fun. And it wasn't as if she hadn't had more embarrassing moments in her life. Even if she wasn't exactly sure what this one was lead-

ing up to. Another way to convince her to let him help
with Fowlmere? A really weird first date?

'Tower Bridge was where I first realised how incredibly smart, intelligent, organised and good at her
job Faith is. How she could take on my job in a second if she wanted. Anything she sets her mind to, this
woman can do.'

Faith tilted her head to stare at the ceiling, trying to
ignore the blush burning her cheeks.

'Is it working, love?' the old woman sitting behind
her asked. 'Have you forgiven him?'

'It's not about forgiveness,' Faith muttered, sitting
up straight again. 'We agreed this was a bad idea, is all.
I'm not going to work with him.'

'I don't think that's what he's asking, dear,' the
woman said. 'Besides, I don't think he's finished yet.'

As Dominic steered the bus back across the river,
he pointed out the spot where they first kissed, giving
her a lingering look as he spoke that nearly resulted in
them crashing into a bollard.

'Eyes on the road,' Faith screeched.

Dominic laughed and, before they'd gone very much
further, pulled into a bus stop and pulled on the brake.
'Okay, ladies and gentlemen. This is where we need to
continue our tour on foot, I'm afraid.'

'Dominic!' Faith said, even as the tourists started
gathering their bags and cameras. 'These people have
paid for a bus tour, not a walking tour. That's what
they expect.'

'They'll like this more,' Dominic promised her,
planting a swift kiss on her lips. 'And I hope you will
too. Come on!'

She couldn't help but jump down off the bus after

him, her lips still tingling from his kiss. But then she stopped on the pavement.

'Wait. Just… Dominic. Wait.'

Twenty paces up ahead, at the front of the gaggle of tourists in their cagoules, cameras at the ready, Dominic stopped, turned and looked at her.

'I just…I don't understand what's going on. I don't know what you want.' Tears burned at the back of her eyes, and Faith blinked them away. 'Why are you doing this? We agreed…'

'We were wrong.' Dominic walked back towards her, and held out his hand. 'We were stupid to think we could just put this away in a box and ignore it. I'm never going to be able to walk through St James's Park without thinking of you. Without wanting you in my life. It's not possible.'

A small, sharp flare of hope burst into life in her chest. 'So, you want…'

'I want you to come with me to see the pelicans,' Dominic said.

'Okay.' Faith nodded. She could do that.

CHAPTER EIGHTEEN

GETTING THE WHOLE group of them across the road and into the park was quite an operation. Dominic would happily have left them to find their own way there—they all knew their jobs, after all—but Faith was in full tour guide mode again, shepherding them all across and stopping traffic just by standing in the middle of the road. It made Dominic's heart clench just to watch.

But finally they were all through the gates of St James's Park and the last, most important part of the plan was in motion. Maybe the first part hadn't gone quite as well as he'd intended when he'd described his plans to Sylvia; her storyboard for the afternoon—which Dominic fully intended to frame and give to Faith on their first anniversary—had included Faith swooning into his lap with delight before he'd even started driving.

This part, though, he had faith in. How could she resist pelicans, the perfect ring, and the most romantic, embarrassing proposal of all time?

This was weird. This was officially the weirdest thing any man had ever done for her. And she still wasn't entirely sure what exactly was going on. All she knew was that she was walking around St James's Park with the man she loved, and fifty total strangers, looking for pelicans.

Totally normal.

'There's one!' one of the tourists yelled out, and suddenly everyone was crowded around the edge of the lake, staring at it. Faith hung back, Dominic beside her, and watched. Then, without warning or any obvious sign, the whole group turned back to face them, grinning manically.

'What's going—' Faith started, then stopped as she heard music. Impossible, lilting music coming from some sort of sound system somewhere. She looked around, trying to spot where it was coming from, to figure out what everyone was looking at—

'It had to be you,' Dominic sang, his voice strong and sure and only slightly off-key.

Faith froze, even as he smiled at her. And then he started to dance. Faith clapped a hand to her mouth as Dominic foxtrotted around her with an imaginary partner as he sang. It was, by far, the most surreal moment of her life.

Around her, the tour group picked up the tune to the classic song and supported Dominic as he dropped to one knee. And then, like some sort of crazy dream, they started to move, stepping in perfect unison to the side, then into pairs, clearly rehearsed and planned and anticipated by everyone who wasn't her.

Their dance, choreographed to the last step, swirled around them, the words coming clean and strong in sopranos, altos, tenors and basses. Faith blinked with disbelief, even as she watched. Crowds were forming on the paths beyond, staring as the bus of people she'd tried to tell about the Tower of London foxtrotted in perfect time through the park, singing as they went.

Bystanders were joining in now, and right by the lake Faith spotted Sylvia, hand to her mouth with excitement. Even the pelicans seemed to be enjoying themselves.

And there, at her feet, was Dominic, holding out a ring box.

'Too much?' he asked.

'Um…'

'Only I wanted you to know. You're worth any embarrassment. Any story in any paper. I can ignore any of it if I have you with me.' He sounded so earnest, so open. Faith couldn't remember ever seeing him like that, except in this place. And one precious night when he'd let himself go, only to have everything ruined.

'Even if I'm a scandal?' Because she was. And probably always would be. If he wanted her, he had to want all of her, even the parts that were too brash, or showed off too much cleavage, or walked up to strangers in airport bars and demanded a job.

'I don't care,' he said, so swiftly she couldn't help but believe him.

'I suppose no one is going to ever find anything to laugh at you for more than this,' Faith mused as the performers reached the climax of the song.

'Unless you say no,' Dominic pointed out.

'I should, you know,' Faith said. 'Just to be sure you can really take the humiliation.'

Dominic flipped open the ring box, letting the sunshine sparkle off a diamond that could probably fix the roof of the west wing at Fowlmere. 'Are you going to?'

Faith looked down at him, into his warm eyes, his raised eyebrow, and thought, *How I love this man.* He was, by turn, ridiculously stiff and unyielding, then hilariously open and embarrassing. She might never get a handle on him completely. On how to make him open up when he needed to, and how to know when something was too much.

She'd probably embarrass him a thousand times over, and he'd probably drive her crazy at least once a day. The society pages would talk of nothing else for weeks. He'd want to interfere in everything she did at Fowlmere, then forget to ask her advice at Beresford.

But they'd sneak off to Lola's once a month, and book a suite at the Greyfriars when they needed to get away from it all. She'd get to be herself, not Lady Faith, not Faith Fowler, just her. Because she knew, beyond anything else, that was who he loved most.

There was a lot they'd need to figure out. But they'd get there. She had faith.

'You're not afraid I'll run away?'

He shook his head. 'I'll take the chance. Besides, I don't care where you go, as long as you always come back to me.'

The song finished and the dancers crowded round them, panting slightly, not adding anything at all to the romance.

'So. What's your answer? Are you going to say no to test my humiliation level?'

'Yes,' Faith said.

Dominic's brow crumpled. 'Yes, you're going to say no? Or yes, you'll marry me?'

Faith laughed, her hair blowing in the breeze, and reached down a hand to pull him to his feet. 'Yes, I'll marry you. Even though you hijacked a bus and proposed to me by flash mob.'

His arms were around her waist in less than a second, before the crowd even started cheering.

'It was the only way I could think of to convince you,' he murmured as he leant in to kiss her.

'Well, it worked,' Faith said, stretching up on tiptoe. 'Remind me not to let you search for wedding speeches on the Internet?'

'Will do.' And then he kissed her and she forgot her sister-in-law-to-be, filming everything from the side, forgot the flash mob, forgot the crowds; she even forgot the pelicans.

She only knew she'd never need to run away again.

* * * * *

THE HEIR OF THE CASTLE

SCARLET WILSON

This book is dedicated to all those little girls who ever dreamed of being Liesl and dancing in the gazebo in a pink floaty dress.

CHAPTER ONE

'THANK YOU FOR coming to the last will and testament reading of Angus McLean.'

The solicitor looked around the room at the various scattering of people, some locals, some not.

Get on with it, thought Callan. He'd only come because the ninety-seven-year-old had been like a father to him. Thoughtful, with a wicked sense of humour, and a real sense of community about him. He'd taught Callan far more than his father had ever taught him.

He wasn't here to inherit anything. He could have bought the castle four times over. He'd offered enough times. But Angus hadn't been interested. He'd had other plans for the estate. And after pretty much living there for part of his life Callan was curious as to what they were.

The solicitor started reading. 'Some of you are here by invitation. Others have still to be contacted. As you may well be aware Angus McLean had a considerable estate.'

He started with some charitable donations, then moved on to the staff that had served Angus over the years—all of them left sizable bequests that would see them into a comfortable age.

Then he cleared his throat and looked nervously

around the room, his eyes deliberately skittering past Callan.

Uh-oh. The castle. What has old crazy done now?

'Most of Angus McLean's friends and relatives knew that Angus was a bachelor. It was always assumed—at least by those of us who knew Angus well—that Angus had no children.' He hesitated. 'But it seems that wasn't the case.'

'What?' Callan couldn't help it. He'd spent most of his life around Angus McLean. Never once in all those years had Angus ever mentioned any children.

Frank, the family solicitor, was clearly not designed for situations like this. His legalese seemed to leave him and he laughed nervously. 'It appears that in his day Angus McLean was a bit of a rogue. He had six children.'

Heads shot around the room, looking back and forth between each other aghast.

But a few heads stayed steady—as if they'd already heard the news.

Callan couldn't believe his ears. 'Six children? Who on earth told you that?' This had to be rubbish. Was a bunch of strangers trying to claim part of the McLean estate?

Frank looked him clearly in the eye. 'Angus told me,' he said quietly.

Callan froze. Every hair on his body standing on end. It couldn't be true. It just couldn't.

Frank cleared his throat nervously. 'As a result of Mr McLean's heirs—and with some further research—we've discovered there are twelve potential inheritors of the estate.'

Callan shook his head. No. Twelve people all wanting a part of Annick Castle. It would be sold without hesitation to the highest bidder. Everyone would want their share of the cash. Angus would have hated that.

'On Mr McLean's instructions, all twelve potential inheritors are to be invited to attend a weekend at Annick Castle.' He bit his lip. 'With true Angus McLean style, they are to be asked to take part in a Murder Mystery Weekend—with the winner becoming the sole heir of Annick Castle. After confirmation of their claim with DNA testing, of course.' His eyes finally met Callan's. 'Mr McLean's last wish was that Annick Castle stayed in the family and was inherited by one person.'

The words chilled Callan to the bone. It was exactly the kind of thing Angus would have said—the only thing they'd ever argued about in this world. But Callan had always assumed there was no real family to inherit, at best, or worst, a few far-flung distant cousins. Nothing like this.

Chaos erupted all around him. Voices shouting and asking questions, people talking amongst themselves, pulling phones from their pockets and dialling numbers frantically.

There was a reporter in amongst the mix who walked out with his phone pressed against his ear. Who inherited Annick Castle was big news—particularly when it was being decided in such an unusual manner. It was one of the few privately owned castles in Scotland.

Callan stood up and walked outside into the rain and biting wind. His eyes landed on the building in front of him. Annick Castle. The place he'd called home for the last twenty-five years.

From the first night Angus had found him cowering in the bushes, hiding from the drunken, abusive bully that was his father, he'd welcomed him into his home. It had become his haven. His safe place. And in later years, when Angus had become frail and needed support, Callan had been the one to provide it.

Annick Castle was the place he'd laughed, cried and learned to be a man.

And it was all, doubtless, about to be destroyed by some stranger.

'Sign here, please.'

Laurie looked up at the electronic screen placed under her nose. She looked around; her secretary had vanished and the courier looked impatient. She lifted the electronic pen and scrawled her signature. 'Thanks.'

She stared at the envelope. It was hardly unusual. A letter from another firm of solicitors. She put it on the pile on her secretary's desk. It would need to be logged in the system.

She rubbed her forehead. Yet another tension headache—and it wasn't even nine a.m. She would be here for at least the next twelve hours. She sighed and picked up the court papers she would need for later and headed back to her office.

Five minutes later Alice appeared at her office door. 'Laurie, did you see who signed for this letter?'

Laurie looked up. It was the heavy cream envelope. 'Yip. It was me.'

Alice looked a little embarrassed. 'Sorry I missed it.' Her hand rested on her slightly protruding stomach. 'I've been at the bathroom three times already this morning.'

Laurie waved her hand. 'No worries.'

Alice smiled. 'I think you should look at this yourself. It's not work-related. It's personal.' She crossed the office and laid the now opened envelope on Laurie's desk. Receiving letters from other solicitors was an everyday thing. But none of them had ever been personal.

Laurie looked up at Alice's retreating back as she closed the door behind her.

Why had she closed the door? Alice had already seen the contents of the letter and unless Laurie was in a meeting with clients her door was always left open. It felt kind of ominous. Was someone suing her? But if they were, surely that would be work-related, not personal?

She picked up the envelope and turned it over in her hands. She didn't recognise the logo on the outside. *Ferguson and Dalglish.*

She pulled the letter from the inside. Heavyweight white bond paper. Exactly like the kind they used for legal documents. Her eyes scanned the page…*'as the daughter of Peter Jenkins you've been identified as a possible heir to the estate of Angus McLean…invited to attend Annick Castle…'* The next page gave contact details and a map of how to get there. The letter dropped from her hands. Her heart was thudding against her chest and she couldn't help but automatically shake her head. This was crazy. This was mad.

As the daughter of Peter Jenkins… Her father had died more than ten years ago. He'd never known who his own father was and had always been curious, but apparently his mother had never told him and refused to discuss the matter. Who on earth was Angus McLean? Was he the father he'd never known?

Because that was what this letter implied. What a way to find out.

She felt her stomach clench a little. Angus McLean could have been her grandfather. Why hadn't he contacted her when he was alive? Why wait until he was dead? It almost seemed pointless. And it was certainly pointless for her father.

Her fingers flew over her keyboard, pulling up a search engine and typing frantically. He wasn't hard to find. Angus McLean, died aged ninety-seven, one month ago. Never married. And apparently no children.

She let out a stream of words into the air. Really?

She scanned the letter again. How many children did this guy have? And had any of the others actually been acknowledged?

The phone rang and she ignored it. Whatever it was it would have to wait. She typed again.

A picture appeared before her and she took a sharp breath, her head moving closer to the screen. Annick Castle. On the west coast of Scotland.

Only, it didn't really look like a castle. More like a beautiful stately home perched on a cliff above the sea with gorgeous surrounding gardens and a swan pond. It was stunning, made of sand-coloured stone, with drum towers at either end and complete with cannons on the walls overlooking the sea.

She looked at the photo credit. The picture was taken twenty years before. Did Annick Castle still look like that?

Her curiosity was definitely piqued. What kind of a man stayed in a place like that? And why would he have family that he never made contact with?

She scanned the letter again. In her haste to read she'd missed the last paragraph.

You are invited to attend Annick Castle to take part in a Murder Mystery Weekend along with eleven other identified family members in accordance with Angus McLean's Last Will and Testa-

ment. The winner of the Murder Mystery Weekend
shall inherit Annick Castle, familial claim shall
be verified by DNA testing.

It didn't say that. It *couldn't* say that.

Lawyers all over the world would be throwing up their hands in horror.

She screwed up her eyes and pinched her nose, then looked from side to side. This was a joke. This was an elaborate hoax. Somewhere, in this room, there must be a hidden camera.

She stood up and walked around. First to the bookshelves on the wall, then to filing cabinets next to the door. She couldn't see anything. But weren't cameras so small now that they could be virtually invisible?

She opened her door and looked outside. Everyone was going about their business. No one was paying her the slightest bit of attention. It was a normal day at Bertram and Bain, one of the busiest solicitors' in London. Twenty partners with another thirty associates, specialising in employment law, partnership law and discrimination law. The phones started ringing around seven in the morning and continued until after nine at night.

Organised chaos.

The tiny hairs on her arms stood on end as if a chilling breeze had just fluttered over her skin. She closed the door and leaned against it.

What if this wasn't a joke? Eleven other family members. Who were they?

She was an only child, and as far as she'd been aware her father had been an only child too. After he'd died, her mum hadn't coped too well and was now living in the sun in Portugal with a little help from Laurie.

She walked back to the desk and ran her finger over the thick paper of the letter.

Family.

She'd felt totally lost since her dad had died. She didn't have a million relatives scattered around the world. There was just her, and her mum.

And now this.

What if she did have relatives she'd never met?

She tried to swallow the lump in her throat as she sagged back down into her chair. Dad would have been so intrigued to receive something like this. He'd always been curious about his father. It made her miss him all the more. She was going to find out the things he'd never known. Who was Angus McLean? Why did he live in a castle? And why on earth hadn't he made contact with his potential family members while he'd still been alive?

She was trying not to be angry. She really was.

She read the letter once more. Property law wasn't her forte, but could this even be legal? There were some differences between English and Scots law, but she wasn't sure if this was one of them.

A Murder Mystery Weekend to decide who inherited the castle?

There was no getting away from it: Angus McLean must have been stark raving mad.

She blinked. A bit like how she'd been feeling lately.

Maybe it was a family trait. The thought didn't really fill her with pleasure—only fear.

She watched as people marched past the glass in her office wall, all with a purpose, all with not a minute to spare.

Exactly as she felt.

How many holidays was she overdue now?

She straightened in her chair, the thick paper between her fingers.

Her father had been a grocer, her mother a shop assistant. No one had been more surprised than Laurie when she'd excelled at school. She liked learning. She liked finding out things. And she'd got swept along with the potential and expectations of her exam results. The careers advisor who'd pushed her towards university. The teachers who'd encouraged her to excel. Her father had cried the day she'd been accepted at Cambridge to study law.

And it had only taken her two months to realise that she hated it.

But, by then it was too late. She couldn't disappoint her dad. Not when he'd spent every waking hour working to help her achieve what he thought was her 'goal'. And especially not when she could hear the pride in his voice every time he told someone his daughter was going to be a lawyer. Turning her back on law would be like trampling on his grave.

She'd been miserable here for months. Always smiling, always agreeing to do more, to work late, to help others out. Never mind the hours she put in at the office, there was never really time off at home. Aches and muscle pains, sleepless nights, tension headaches, all signs that her body needed a break.

And maybe this was a sign.

No matter how ridiculous it sounded.

Her fingers tapped out the email quickly—before she had a chance to think straight and change her mind. She picked up the files on her desk and carried them outside.

Alice was worried. Laurie could tell by the frown on her forehead and the way her pencil was banging on the desk.

Laurie took a deep breath and gave her a smile, lifting a pile of Post-its from her desk. She started slapping them on the files. 'I'm taking some time off. Pink for Frances, green for Paul and yellow for Hugo. After I've been at court this afternoon there's nothing they can't handle. Ask them just to pick up where I left off.'

Alice nodded, her mouth gaping open as Laurie handed her the instructions from the letter. 'Can you book me a train ticket and sort out some accommodation for me?'

Alice put her pencil to good use and started scribbling. 'You're going to go? Really? When do you want to leave?'

'Tomorrow.'

'Tomorrow?' Several heads poked up at the surprise in Alice's voice from the pods around them.

Laurie nodded. 'I'm supposed to be there Friday through to Monday evening.'

Laurie Jenkins taking a holiday. It was unheard of.

Maybe it was time for change.

Callan stared at his watch for the twentieth time. This was his last pickup of the day.

Thank goodness. So far, there had been the loud Canadians, the over-excited Americans, the bad-tempered Irishman with the very sweet Irishwoman, and several others from around Scotland. Once the hoity-toity lawyer arrived from London he was all done.

He must have been mad. Why on earth was he agreeing to be part of this ridiculous debacle?

He sighed. What was the bet that Ms Lawyer was extra tired and extra crabbit? By his estimations she'd have travelled four and a half hours from London to Glasgow, another four hours from Glasgow to Fort William, and the last part of the journey on the steam locomotive.

He leaned back against the stone wall of the old station. He could see the steam in the distance. She could have stayed on the train from Glasgow—it did come on to Mallaig—but like any good tourist she must have preferred to take the *Harry Potter* train and cross the viaduct.

It wasn't really a problem. He couldn't blame her desire to see the stunning Scottish countryside. It just meant she was a later arrival than everyone else.

The train pulled into the station and the tourists piled out. Most of them would be staying overnight in Mallaig—a coach was parked outside the station to transport them to their accommodation.

It took a few moments for the steam and chattering crowds to completely clear.

Wow! That was Mary Jenkins? So, not what he was expecting.

Instead of an iron-faced middle-aged woman the smoke cleared around a long-haired brunette, with slim pink Capri pants, a white loose tunic and a simple holdall in one hand. Far from looking tired, she was fresh-faced and brimming with excitement.

Callan was used to beautiful women—he'd dated enough of them—but this was a shock to the system. Her clothes highlighted her curves, the swell of her breasts beneath the thin tunic and her Capri pants showing a hint of lightly tanned skin.

She walked over quickly. 'Callan McGregor? Thank you so much for meeting me.' She reached over and grasped his hand firmly between both of hers.

Zing. What was that? A wave of tiny electric shocks shot up his arm.

'It's a pleasure to meet you.' She waved her hands around. 'What an absolutely gorgeous setting. I've had an absolute ball on that train.' She pointed to the camera around her neck, nestled next to a gold locket. 'I must have taken around a hundred pictures.'

He was trying to remain calm. He was trying not to let the corners of his mouth turn upwards in surprise. It wasn't just that she was pretty—she was gorgeous. Warm brown eyes, clear skin, curls bouncing around her shoulders and full pink lips. 'Mary Jenkins?' he queried. The name just didn't suit her at all.

She let out a laugh. Nothing quiet and polite, but a deep, hearty laugh that came all the way up from her painted pink toes. 'What? No one has ever called me that! It's Laurie. Laurie Jenkins. My father called me after his elderly aunt Mary, but I've always been known by my middle name Laurie.'

He nodded. The Mary Jenkins he'd pictured in his head had looked nothing like the Laurie Jenkins standing on the platform before him. Around twenty years of nothing.

Was she really old enough to be a lawyer?

She shuffled some papers in the front pocket of her holdall. 'Let me take that for you,' he said as he reached down and swung it up onto his shoulder. It was light. It was surprisingly light. Maybe Laurie Jenkins wasn't planning on staying long? Unlike the Canadians, who appeared to have brought the entire contents of their house with them.

He ushered her along the platform towards his car, trying not to watch the swing of her hips and shape of her curved backside. *Focus.* That zing was still bothering him. Callan McGregor didn't do 'zings'.

He waited for the comment—there weren't many

people with a pristine James Bond DB5 in this world. One of the few over-the-top purchases since he'd made his fortune. But she just happily climbed in the front seat and pulled on her seat belt. 'Do you know much about Angus McLean?'

He was thrown. He was totally thrown.

Not only had every other single person made a passing comment on the car, every other single person's first question had been about the castle—leaving him in no doubt why they were there. They could recognise money at a glance.

He should have walked away. After the reading of the will he should have left the solicitor's office and just kept on walking. Walked away from the madness of all this.

But something deep inside wouldn't let him. Whether it was a burning curiosity of what would happen next. Whether it was some bizarre desire to actually meet some of Angus McLean's relatives. Or whether it was some deep-rooted loyalty to the old guy, and some misplaced desire to try and maintain the integrity of the castle.

He waited until she was settled and then he pulled out of the car park.

'Well?' She was obviously determined to find out a little more. Her fingers were clenched tightly in her lap, her index fingers rotating around each other over and over. It was the first sign she wasn't quite as relaxed as she seemed.

'Angus was a good friend.'

She raised her eyebrows. The sixty-five-year age difference was completely apparent and must be sparking questions in her brain.

'So, you're not one of his relatives?' She hesitated. 'I

mean, you're not one of…my relatives?' Her voice tailed off and she shook her head with a little half-smile. 'I can't get used to the thought of any of this. It was only ever me, my mum and my dad. My dad died ten years ago. I never imagined anything like this would happen. It all seems so unreal—like I'm caught in a dream.'

'Oh, it's real all right,' he muttered under his breath. Then he shook his head and gave a woeful smile. This woman really didn't have a clue how he felt about any of this. 'I guess the *Harry Potter* train will do that to you.'

Her face broke into a wide, dreamy grin. 'It was fantastic. My secretary booked it for me. I haven't had a holiday in a while and she obviously knew I would like it.'

He tried not to let his ears prick straight up. She hadn't had a holiday in a while. What did that mean? Did she work for some hotshot company that made their employees work one hundred hours a week? Or did she just not have anyone to go home to? His eyes went automatically to her hand, but she'd moved it, jamming her left hand under her thigh and out of his sight.

'How did you meet?' Her voice cut through his thoughts. Boy, she was persistent. She still hadn't even mentioned the castle.

A shadow passed across his face and his lips tightened. 'I met Angus when I was a small boy. I spent quite a bit of time at Annick Castle.'

Something flickered across her face—doubtless another question—but something obviously told her to change tack and she let it go.

'So, what's going to happen this weekend? Are you organising things?' Did she think he was an employee? Even though he was offended, it was a reasonable assumption. After all, he had picked her up from the station.

He signalled and turned off the main road, passing some stone columns and an extravagant set of entry gates, and heading down a long, sweeping driveway.

He shook his head and his words were spoken through gritted teeth. 'The Murder Mystery Weekend is nothing to do with me. It's being organised by some outside company.'

She shook her head. 'It's the most bizarre thing I've ever heard. Is it even legal? Inheritance law isn't my field of expertise, but I've never heard of anything like this in my life.'

'Neither have I.' The words almost fell out of his mouth. He wasn't embarrassed to say he'd spent the last week locked in a bitter war of words with Frank. But the solicitor had been unrepentant. He'd tried to talk Angus out of it. He'd talked him through all the legal implications, the challenges that might be brought against the decision. They'd even brought a doctor in to give a statement that Angus was of sound mind as he wrote the will.

But Angus McLean had been as determined as he always was in life. This was the way he wanted to do things, and nothing, and no one, could change his mind.

Callan could see Laurie looking around, taking in the impossibly long sweeping road to the castle, and the huge gardens. The car followed the bend in the road and she let out a little gasp, her hand going to her face.

'Oh. Wow.' Annick Castle was now clearly visible. Rebuilt in the seventeen-hundreds, the impressive building had over sixty rooms and a large drum tower at either side. It was clear the first glimpse of the castle took her breath away.

But instead of feeling secretly happy and proud, Callan could barely disguise his displeasure. Was she thinking that the castle might be hers after the weekend? The last guests from Canada had immediately asked what rooms were the best and whipped out a portfolio with extensive notes on the property. He'd almost ejected them from the car on the spot.

But Laurie wasn't quite so brazen. Or maybe she was just better at hiding it?

She shook her head, her eyes open in wonder. 'I just didn't expect it to be so big.' She pointed over at the sea wall. 'I knew it was supposed to be on a cliff top. I guess I just hadn't really realised how impressive it would be.' She fumbled in her bag and produced a tissue, dabbing at her eyes. 'My dad wouldn't have believed this. He would have thought he was in a dream.'

For the tiniest second Callan almost felt sorry for her. He knew that three of Angus's children had died: Laurie's father, another woman from England and a son who'd lived in Canada. Laurie was an only child, but the son in Canada had three sons and two daughters, and the woman in England had had three children. It took the total number of possible inheritors to twelve. All of whom were now here.

They pulled up outside the main entrance and Laurie jumped out automatically. 'I'll show you to your room and introduce you to the staff,' Callan said gruffly.

'My room?' She looked shocked, and then shook her head. 'Oh, no, I'm not staying here.' She started to fumble in her bag for her paperwork. 'My secretary will have booked me in somewhere.'

Callan was starting to run out of patience. 'She has—here.'

Laurie's chin practically bounced off the driveway.

'But I thought you'd just brought me here to show me where the castle was.'

He shook his head and shrugged his shoulders. 'It's part of the stipulation of the weekend.' Nothing he had any control over.

He waited until she'd extricated the crumpled paperwork from her bag and stared at it a few times as if she was still taking all of this in.

'Like I said, come and I'll introduce you to the staff.'

Her eyes widened. 'There's staff?'

He frowned. 'Of course there's staff. A place like this doesn't look after itself.'

That was the trouble with all these people. None of them knew or understood a thing about Annick Castle. None of them appreciated the people who'd spent their life working here. It didn't matter most of the staff had been left bequests, it was the actual castle that mattered to them—just as it mattered to Callan.

Laurie was still standing in amazement outside. The sun was starting to set over the horizon, leaving her bathed in a warm glow of pink, orange and lilac. With the beautiful sea in the background she could have been starring in a movie. With her dark eyes, long chestnut curls about her shoulders and her curves highlighted in her white tunic, Laurie Jenkins could prove quite a distraction.

She was the youngest relative here by far. And for a second he almost forgot that: the fact she was a relative—a potential inheritor. A complete stranger who would probably sell Annick Castle to the highest bidder as soon as she could.

It made the hackles rise at the back of his neck.

All day he'd picked people up and dropped them off. And there was no getting away from it. Some of them he already hated. They'd asked the value of the property, its potential price on the open market and how soon the inheritance would take to sort out.

So it didn't matter how Laurie looked, or how she acted.

The truth was—she was the same as all the rest.

What was wrong with this guy? Ever since he'd picked her up at the train station he'd acted as if she'd jabbed him with a hot poker.

She had no idea what his role was here. It was a shame, because if he could actually wipe the permanent frown off his face, he would be attractive. And not just a little attractive. The kind of guy you spotted at the other side of a room and made your heart beat faster kind of attractive.

When she'd spotted him at the station she'd almost turned around to look for the film camera. Were they shooting a new film, and he'd been brought in as the resident hunk?

She smiled to herself. His hands had been firm. Was the rest of him? It certainly looked that way—his shirt did nothing to hide the wide planes of his chest.

Mr Silent and Brooding was obviously not planning on telling her much. She was trying to push aside the fact he was impossibly tall, dark and handsome. And she was especially trying to push away the fact he'd fixed on her face with the most incredible pair of green eyes she'd ever seen. Ones that sent a little shiver down her spine.

But nothing he'd said had exactly been an answer, and now she'd finally met someone who knew Angus McLean her brain was just bursting with questions. It was her duty to her dad to find out as much as she possibly could. She followed him inside and tried to stifle the gasp in her throat.

It was the biggest entrance hall she'd ever seen, with a huge curved staircase running up either side around the oval-shaped room. These were the kind of stairs a little girl would dream of in her imaginary castle. Dream that she was walking down to meet her Prince Charming. If only.

Callan dropped his car keys into a wooden dish with a clatter.

Fat chance of that happening here.

She shook hands with a grey-haired woman with a forehead knotted in a permanent frown just like Callan's. Maybe they were related?

'This is Marion. She's the housekeeper. If you need anything you'll generally find her around the kitchen area.'

Laurie couldn't imagine a single occasion she'd want to seek out the fearful Marion but she nodded dutifully and followed him up the stairs.

There was an old full-length portrait at the top of the stairs of a young woman in a long red dress. Something about it seemed a little odd and she stopped mid-step. Callan gave her a few seconds, then finally smiled in amusement. It was the first time today he'd looked even remotely friendly.

'You're the first person that's noticed,' he said quietly.

'But that's just it. I know I've noticed something—' she shook her head '—but I don't know what it is.'

He pointed at the portrait's serious face. 'It's an optical illusion. *She's* an optical illusion.'

'But, what…how?' She was even more confused now.

Callum pointed to the stairs. 'It doesn't matter which

side you walk up. It always seems as if she's looking at you.'

'Impossible!' She couldn't even make sense of the words.

He folded his arms across his chest and nodded to the other flight of stairs. His face had softened slightly. He was much more handsome without the permanent frown. 'Go on, then, I'll wait.'

She hesitated for a second but the temptation was just too great. She could only pray he wasn't playing some kind of joke on her. She raced down one side and halfway up the other.

Her arm rested on the ornate banister, her eyes widening. The serene young woman was staring right at her—just as she'd been on the other staircase. She lifted up her hands in exasperation. 'But that's impossible. How old is that painting? Did optical illusions even exist back then?'

A cheeky grin flashed across his face. 'Did rainbows?'

She felt the colour flood into her cheeks and a flare of annoyance. Of course. Nature's greatest optical illusion. Now she felt like a prize idiot. Something tightened in her stomach.

She hated anyone thinking she was dumb. The only real joy in being a lawyer was the recognition that most people assumed you had to be smart to do the job in the first place.

But Callan didn't seem to notice her embarrassment. He was looking at the painting again. 'Angus liked to have fun. Once he discovered the painting he was determined to own it. It's nearly two hundred years old. He put it there as a talking point.' There was obvious affection in his voice and it irritated her even more.

Who was this guy? He'd already told her he'd spent some time living here. But why?

Why would Angus McLean take in a stranger, but ignore the six children that he had? It didn't make sense.

All of a sudden she was tired and hungry. The long hours of work and travelling had caught up with her and all she wanted to do was lie down—preferably in her bed in London, not in some strange castle in Scotland.

'Nice to know he had a sense of humour,' she muttered under her breath as she brushed past him.

'What's that supposed to mean?' snapped Callan.

She took a deep breath and turned to face him. 'It means I'm tired, Callan. I've been travelling for hours.' She lifted her hands in exasperation. 'And it also means I've just found out about a family that's apparently mine.' She cringed as some of the relatives walked past downstairs, talking at the tops of their voices about the value of the antiques.

She looked Callan square in the eye. If she weren't so tired she might have been unnerved. Up close, Callan's eyes were even more mesmerising than she'd first suspected and she could see the tiny lines around the corners. He was tired too.

She took a deep breath. 'I didn't know Angus McLean, but, just so you know, you might have him up on some sort of pedestal—but I don't. I'm not impressed by a man who lived in this—' she spun around '—and spent his life ignoring his six children.' She folded her arms across her chest. 'Nice to see he got his priorities in order.'

CHAPTER TWO

JUST WHEN, FOR the tiniest second, he thought one of Angus's relatives might not be quite as bad as the rest, she came out with something like that.

Callan felt a chill course over his body as he swept past her and along the corridor. 'You're right. You didn't know Angus. And you have absolutely no right to comment.' His blood was boiling as he flung open the door to her room. 'Here's your room.' He stopped as she stepped through the doorway. Her head was facing his chest, only inches away from his. All it would take was one little step to close the distance between them.

It didn't matter to him how attractive she was. It didn't matter that he'd noticed her curves at the railway station, or the way she kept flicking back her long shiny brown curls. All that mattered to him was the fact she'd said something he didn't like about the old man that he loved.

But Laurie Jenkins was having none of it. She folded her arms across her chest again. 'That's just the thing, Callan. I *do* have a right to comment—because, apparently, I'm family.' She let the words hang in the air as she walked past him into the room.

Callan's blood was about to reach the point of eruption.

The very thing that knotted his stomach. Family. And the fact he wasn't.

He still hadn't got over the fact Angus McLean had six children he'd never once mentioned. The reality was he was still hoping it wasn't true—that someone would give him a nudge and he'd wake up from this nightmare.

Nothing about this seemed right. Angus had been the perennial bachelor, even in old age. Why on earth would he have children and never acknowledge them? It seemed bizarre.

Angus had had the biggest heart he'd ever known.

But then, he'd only known Angus for the last twenty-five years. Maybe in his youth he'd been a completely different person?

It bothered him. It bothered him so much he hadn't slept the last few nights.

And now that he'd met some of the relatives it bothered him a whole lot more.

One of these money-grabbers was going to inherit Annick Castle. A place full of history and rich with antiques. A place full of memories that not a single one of them would care about.

Why hadn't Angus let him buy it? He'd known that Callan loved it every bit as much as he did. It just didn't make sense.

The family stuff. It enraged him more than he could ever have imagined.

Laurie was standing looking out of the window across the sea. Some of these bedrooms had the most spectacular views. He knew—his was just above.

And this complete stranger had just put him perfectly in his place.

She was right—she was family. The one thing he wasn't.

He dumped her bag on the bed. 'Dinner is at seven.'

He didn't even wait for a response. The sooner he got away from Ms Jenkins, the better.

Laurie breathed out slowly, releasing the tight feeling that had spread across her chest.

What on earth was wrong with her? And why had she just offloaded to the one person who could actually tell her something about her grandfather?

Common sense told her it wasn't wise to alienate Callan McGregor. He could probably tell her everything she could ever want to know—and a whole lot more besides.

She sagged down onto the bed. The bedroom was big, with panoramic views over the sea. How many people throughout the ages had stood at her window and looked out at this view? The sun had set rapidly leaving the sea looking dark, haunting and cold. Was it possible that the sea looked angry—just like Callan McGregor?

The history of this place intrigued her. It would be fascinating. If only she could take the time to learn it.

Her hand smoothed the coverings on the bed, taking in the carpet, curtains and other soft furnishings. At one time these must have been brand new and the height of fashion. But that time had clearly passed. How did you update a castle? She didn't have a clue.

It wasn't that anything was shabby. It was just— tired. A little dated maybe. And obviously in need of some TLC.

Angus had been ninety-seven when he'd died. How often had he looked around the castle to see what needed replacing and updating? And how much would all that cost?

She shifted uncomfortably on the bed. She'd heard some of the conversation of the other relatives downstairs. They'd virtually had measuring tapes and calculators out, deciding how much everything was worth and where they could sell it.

It made her blood run cold.

This castle was their heritage. How could people immediately think like that?

She walked over to her bag and shook out her clothes. She was only here for a few days and had travelled light. One dress for evenings, some clean underwear, another pair of Capri pants, some light T-shirts and another shirt. What else could she possibly need?

An envelope on the mantelpiece caught her attention. *Ms Mary Laurie Jenkins* was written in calligraphy. She opened it and slid the thick card invitation out from inside.

It was instructions for the Murder Mystery Weekend: where to report, who would be in charge and a list of rules for participation.

Under normal circumstances something like this would have made her stomach fizz with fun.

But how could she even think like that when there was so much more at stake?

The whole heritage of this castle was dependent on the winner. And the weight of the responsibility was pressing on her shoulders. She fingered the curtains next to her. She knew nothing about Annick Castle. She had no connection to this place. She wouldn't even know where to begin with renovations or upkeep. Or the responsibility of having staff to manage.

Working as a solicitor was a world away from all this. Everything and everyone wasn't entirely dependent on her. There was a whole range of other bodies to share the responsibility. Thank goodness. She couldn't stand it otherwise.

All of a sudden she wanted to pick up her bag and make a run for it. She shouldn't have come here. She shouldn't have agreed to be any part of this.

This whole thing made her uncomfortable. She looked at the invitation again. *Costumes supplied.* What did that mean? There was another little envelope with a character profile included, telling her who she was, and what her actions should be.

1920s. Lucy Clark. Twenty-seven. Heiress to a fortune. Keen interest in pharmacy. In a relationship with Bartholomew Grant, but also seeing Philippe Deveraux on the side.

It was a sad day when the pretend character you had to portray had a more exciting love life than you had.

It could be worse. Her card could have told her she was the killer. But maybe that came later?

Then again what did 'keen interest in pharmacy' mean? Was she going to poison someone?

Under normal circumstances this might be fun.

But these weren't normal circumstances, and now she was here, and had actually seen Annick Castle, the whole thing made her very uncomfortable.

She glanced at the clock. There was still time before dinner to freshen up and get organised.

Maybe once she'd eaten that horrible little gnawing sensation at the pit of her stomach would disappear?

Or maybe that would take swallowing her pride and apologising to Callan.

Maybe, just maybe.

* * *

Callan had finally calmed down. He'd had to. Marion, the housekeeper, had flipped when one of the ovens had packed in and she'd thought dinner wouldn't be ready on time. It had taken him five minutes to sort out the fuse and replace it.

Dinner would be served on time.

Served to the twelve strangers who were roaming all over the castle.

Which was why he was currently standing in his favourite haunt—the bottom left-hand corner of the maze in the front garden.

Callan could find his way through this maze with his eyes shut—and he had done since he was a boy. It was one part of the garden that was kept in pristine condition with the hedges neatly trimmed.

Other things had kind of fallen by the wayside recently. Bert, the old gardener, couldn't manage the upkeep of the gardens any more. The truth was he probably needed another four staff to do everything that was required. Twenty years ago there had been a staff of around six to look after the grounds alone, but gradually they'd all retired or left. And the recession had hit. And Bert had become very set in his ways—not wanting others to interfere with 'his' garden. In the meantime the maze, the front garden and the rose garden were almost in pristine condition. As for the rest…

He was thankful for the peace and quiet. All of a sudden his safe haven seemed like a noisy hotel. Everyone seemed to talk at the tops of their voices, constantly asking questions. He'd tried to hide out in the library for a while, but even there he'd been disturbed by some of the relatives wondering if there were any valuable first editions.

If he'd had his way he would have locked some of the rooms to stop their prying eyes, not to mention their prying fingers. He'd caught one relative in his room earlier and had nearly blown a gasket.

A flash of red caught his eye, along with the sound of laughter and heels clipping on the concrete path. He took a few steps forward, crashing straight into Laurie as she rounded the corner of the maze.

'Oh, sorry.' She was out of breath and her eyes wide. 'Isn't this just fabulous?'

As much as he hated to admit it her enthusiasm was clearly genuine.

'How long has the maze been here? I had no idea something like this existed. It's amazing.'

He narrowed his gaze. He could barely focus on the question because his eyes and brain were immediately struck by the sight in front of him. The 1920s-style flapper dress skimmed her figure, hiding it beneath shimmering red glass beads. A feather was slightly askew on her head and he automatically reached up to straighten it. 'What on earth are you wearing?' Damn. There it was again—as soon as his hand touched the soft hair—the mysterious spark from earlier.

'This?' Her eyes widened again and she gave a little spin, sending a cascade of sparkling red lights scattering around them. She wrinkled her nose as she came to a halt. 'Well, I hardly brought it with me, did I? I got it from the costume room. Haven't you got into character yet?' She held out her black-satin-gloved hand to shake his hand. 'I'm Lucy Clark. Apparently an heiress and up to all things naughty with two different men.'

If he'd been anywhere else, at any other time, he would have acted on the current of electricity that was sizzling between them. He thought he might have imagined it, but his palm was tingling. He rubbed it fiercely against his thigh.

The Murder Mystery Weekend. The last thing on his mind right now. He hadn't even opened the envelope that had been sitting above the fireplace in his room. And he had no idea what room in the castle had been deemed the 'costume' room. His fingers burrowed into his jacket pocket and he pulled out the crumpled envelope. 'Oops.' He shrugged.

She shook her head. 'Come on, Callan, get into the spirit of things.' She reached out to grab his envelope, then pulled her hand back. 'I better not.' She leaned forward and whispered, 'I don't want to find out you're secretly a mass murderer.'

He shook his head and pulled the card from the envelope. He must have been out of his crazy mind to have agreed to be part of this.

Then again, he hadn't really agreed. Frank, the solicitor, had informed him that Angus had expected Callan to make his guests feel welcome and help oversee the weekend's activities. He'd had half a mind to walk away.

But his loyalty to Angus ran deep. Too deep.

If he walked away then he'd never find out who inherited the castle, or their plans for it. A tiny seed started to sprout in his brain.

Maybe being here wasn't so crazy after all. Sure, inheriting a castle sounded good on paper, but once Angus's relatives realised the implications, the upkeep, the financial commitments, he was pretty sure they would all run screaming for the hills. Maybe he could make them an offer? He'd always been prepared to pay a fair price, and if Angus wouldn't accept it, maybe one of his children would?

His eyes fixed on Laurie. She was young. She was a

lawyer in London. She wouldn't want to be landed with a castle in the Highlands.

For the first time this weekend he actually paused to think. Maybe he should play nice?

He squinted at the name on his card. He hadn't paid attention to any of the instructions about the Murder Mystery Weekend. 'It appears I'm Bartholomew Grant, thirty-three, a stock-market trader.'

A cheeky smile appeared on her face along with the tiniest flush of red. 'Hmm…Bartholomew Grant. Well, whaddya know? I believe you're one of my two adoring men.' She gave a little wave of her hand. 'Here's hoping you can play the part, Callan.'

The feather was bobbing in the wind. The shimmering red glass beads picking up the soft lights from the open doors of the drawing room. She hadn't donned a short bob wig in keeping with the time; instead she'd left her long brown curls snaking around her shoulders.

She was watching him through her dark lashes with her big brown eyes. His eyes dropped automatically to her left hand. He couldn't see anything through the satin gloves. No telltale lumps with giant diamonds. Surely a successful woman like Laurie must be attached?

She leaned forward again, this time the round neck of her dress gaping and giving a little glimpse of cleavage.

He blinked. What was he doing? Why was his brain even going there? He had far too much to think about this weekend. The last thing he needed was to get distracted by someone he'd never see again.

'Do you think you can play the part, Callan? Or is it all just too much for you?' Her voice was low and husky. She tilted her head to one side. 'Do you even know how to play nice?'

The words made him start. In another world Laurie Jenkins could be quite mesmerising. But he wasn't the kind of guy to fall for a coy smile and the flutter of some eyelashes.

'Maybe I just like to pick my play friends carefully,' he shot back.

She folded her arms across her chest. 'Well, that's a shame. You're the only person around here who looked as if they might be capable of holding a normal conversation. I couldn't get a word in edgeways with the Americans, the Canadians were too busy Googling antiques, and—' she flung her hands up '—the two people that I think are my aunt and uncle from other parts of England have spent the last hour dozing on one of the sofas in the drawing room.'

He couldn't help but smile. He'd already figured out she wanted to meet her family, but it seemed nothing was going to plan. He reached out his hand and grabbed hers, leading her over to a bench near the entrance to the maze and pulling her down next to him.

'What did you think was going to happen this weekend, Laurie?'

He could see her take a deep breath as she glanced around them. The splendour of the castle was behind them and even though the grounds weren't officially lit, the smooth front lawn, maze and rose garden were impressive to say the least. And she had no idea that just beyond that copse of trees lay a swan pond with slightly untrimmed foliage. She really had no idea about this place at all. She shrugged her shoulders, 'I thought this would be a chance to meet some family. There's only me and my mum now, and she lives in Portugal.' She gave a little shake of her head. 'She really couldn't cope when my dad died.' Her eyes had lowered and he resisted the temptation to reach over and squeeze her hand. But her fingers had already moved, automatically going to her throat and catching the gold locket around her neck.

He might not know her, but the pain on her face was real. She'd clearly adored her father.

She lifted her head, turned and stared up at the castle. 'I have no idea what my dad would have made of all this.' Her eyes were shimmering now with unshed tears. 'He so wanted to know about his father. His mum just wouldn't tell him anything.' She lifted her hand and held it out. 'This would have fascinated him, and the thought that he had other brothers and sisters scattered around the world...' She let out a sigh and shook her head. 'That would have blown his mind.'

Callan shifted uncomfortably on the seat. All of a sudden his reaction earlier seemed a bit snappy.

Now he understood a little of what she'd said. It seemed odd to him that Angus had never acknowledged the fact he had children. How must it seem to the newly acquired relatives? To know that Angus had provided for them in his will, but never acknowledged their existence?

He'd been so wound up with how he was feeling he hadn't given much thought to anyone else.

'I had no idea that Angus had children. He never mentioned it. Never mentioned it at all.' He pressed his lips together. 'It just doesn't seem like him at all. The Angus McLean I knew had the biggest heart in the world.'

'How did you know Angus? You seem a bit young to have been friends.' Her brow was furrowed, as if she was trying to sort out in her head where Callan fitted into all this.

He chose his words carefully. Her question wasn't

unexpected. 'Angus helped me out when I was younger. And friends—that's exactly what we were. He was one of the best friends I had.'

'And you stay here—in the castle?' He could almost see the questions spinning around in her head.

'Not exactly. I live in Edinburgh most of the time. I have a house there. But I've always had a room here with Angus. He needed a bit more help in the last few years.'

There was so much more she clearly wanted to ask. He could almost sense her biting her tongue. Instead her eyes fixed on the maze and gardens in front of them.

'Do you know much about the estate?'

The words sent his hackles up. He tried not to let it show, but every question he'd more or less been asked by the relatives in the last twelve hours had revolved around money. He found it impossible not to grit his teeth. 'I know every field, every tree, every fence and every stream. I've been in and around Annick Castle since I was a young boy.'

But Laurie hadn't noticed his tension; she was lost in a world of her own. 'Lucky you.' There was a wistful tone in her voice as she leaned back on the bench and looked up at the elegant façade of the castle. She sighed. 'This would have been my dream when I was a little girl, living in a place like this.' She held out her hand. 'I can only imagine what it must be like to play in a maze like this every day or to run up and down those fairy-princess stairs.' She gave him a mischievous smile. 'Go on, tell me. Did you ever slide down those banisters?'

He could feel his natural protective instincts kick in. Did he really want to tell her that he and Angus had regularly had competitions to see who was the fastest sliding down either side?

All of a sudden this was personal. These were his personal memories of his time here with Angus McLean. And he didn't want to share them.

He didn't want any of these people staying here. He really just wanted them all to leave. The piece of paper in his hand crumpled under his grip.

She was puzzling him. She wasn't talking about money. She was talking about people and family. But maybe she was just cleverer than the rest? And what was more she was persistent. 'Or did Angus forbid you from doing things like that?'

The words jolted him. Jolted him from a whole host of memories that flooded his brain. Diving in the swan pond, trying to build a raft to sail across it, swinging from the rope swings that he'd made amongst the trees. Angus wasn't the kind to forbid him anything. He lifted his heavy eyelids and caught her staring at him with those big brown eyes. 'Only if he caught me,' he said quietly.

The moment passed just as quickly as it appeared. 'Shouldn't we be going?' He stood up. 'You've got a Murder Mystery to solve.'

'Oh, that.' She stood up, her dress catching the light again. 'I'd almost forgotten about that.'

How could she forget about that? It was the key to owning this castle. Surely it should be the first thing on her mind.

He led her towards the open doors to the drawing room. 'Let's get this over with.' She sighed, then turned around. Her hand reached up and rested on his chest. 'Callan, tomorrow, will you show me around the

grounds of Annick Castle? I'm only here for the weekend and I'd like to see as much as I can.'

His immediate response caught in his throat, because
his immediate response was to say no.

The last thing he wanted was to be the genial host,
showing everyone around the castle he considered a
home.

But Laurie seemed a little more measured than the
rest. A little more interested in the history of the castle
as a whole.

Her hand was still resting on his chest, almost burning a hole through the thin cotton of his shirt. She bit her
lip. 'I was also wondering if I could see some pictures
of Angus. See what he looked like.' Her eyes drifted
off... 'I kind of wonder if my dad looked like him at
all...' then came back to meet his '...or if I do.'

The hairs were standing up at the back of his neck—
and it wasn't the cool evening breeze. It was her. And
the effect she was having on him.

Had anyone else asked to see pictures of Angus?
He couldn't remember, but they must have—surely? If
someone told him he'd a long-lost relative the first thing
he'd want to do would be see what they looked like.

He gave a little nod. 'I know where some of the family pictures are kept. Leave it with me. I'll let you see
them tomorrow.'

She gave a nervous kind of smile. 'Thank you, Callan. That will be nice. And the tour?'

Her big brown eyes were fixed right on him. She obviously wasn't going to let this go.

He wanted to say no. He really did. But how could
he?

He could almost hear Angus's voice in his ear. *Show*

them around, make them fall in love with the place as much as we did.

'Fine. I'll meet you just after breakfast.'

She gave a little nod of her head. 'Thanks.'

He gestured towards the dining room. 'You better go on. I'll be a few minutes getting changed.' He turned and walked off along the corridor.

Dinner with the twelve potential inheritors of Annick Castle.

He really couldn't think of anything he wanted to do less.

CHAPTER THREE

By the time Laurie reached the dining room most of the other guests were already seated. It seemed there was no opportunity to pick your own seat. The calligraphy from the character envelopes had been carried on to the name cards on the table.

She gave a little sigh as she sat down. Her character was between both men she was apparently seeing, which meant that Callan would be next to her again.

A man around twenty years older than her sat down on her right at the *Philippe Deveraux* card. She tried not to smile. In real life he wasn't exactly her taste, but she held out her hand politely. 'Pleased to meet you.' She nodded at her card. 'I'm Lucy Clark, but I'm really Laurie from London. My father was one of Angus McLean's children.'

Her companion smiled. 'Then that makes you my niece. I'm Craig Fulton. From what I can gather, I think I am the youngest of Angus McLean's children.' He leaned forward conspiratorially. 'And I'm not sure that I'm comfortable with dating my niece.'

Laurie felt a wave of relief rush over her. Thank goodness. This could have been awkward.

'What do you do in London, Laurie?'

'I'm a lawyer.'

His eyebrows rose. 'Well, that will come in handy with all these shenanigans. Is this even legal?'

She shook her head. 'Scottish law and English law can differ. I'm just as in the dark as you are.'

The chair next to her was pulled out and Callan sat down beside her. He'd changed into a hunting-style jacket, obviously in keeping with the style of the evening.

But Craig persisted. 'But you must know something?'

He was making her uncomfortable. 'Actually, I don't. This isn't my area of expertise. I practise employment, partnership and discrimination law.'

Craig threw up his hands. 'What use is that to anyone?'

Now he'd really annoyed her. And it was clear that Callan was about to intervene, but she lifted her hand and laid it on his jacket sleeve to stop him. She smiled sweetly at Craig and spoke quietly. 'Why don't you ask my last client? I won him an award of half a million pounds.'

Craig choked on the wine he was currently necking down at a rate of knots. Leaving his neighbour on the other side sharply hitting his back for him.

Callan shot her a smile. 'Touché,' he whispered.

She smiled. 'I'm nobody's shrinking violet…' she leaned forward to whisper in his ear '…and I hate anyone implying otherwise.'

Callan lifted his glass. 'I'll remember that.'

The food appeared moments later, all served by a harassed-looking Marion and a young girl who looked too terrified to speak.

Everything was beautiful. From the chicken liver

pâté, to the chicken breast stuffed with haggis. All accompanied by copious amounts of free-flowing wine.

After such a long journey Laurie could feel the wine go straight to her head and stopped after the second glass.

The doors to the garden had been left wide open, and, instead of feeling cold, Laurie found herself appreciating the clean sea air that circulated around them. It was the first time in for ever she could remember having a clear head. Sure, if she'd drunk much more wine it could have made her wobbly, but for the first time in months she didn't feel at her muggiest, with a persistent headache thumping in the background.

She tried to remember when the headache had actually left her. It had been there so frequently she couldn't recall. She really should get out of the city more. Was it on the steam railway that she'd finally felt her head clear? Maybe there was a lot to be said about highland views and sea breezes.

It didn't matter that the air in the room was fraught with tension. It didn't matter that she was lost amongst a sea of relatives, some of whom she wasn't sure she even liked. It didn't even matter to her that Callan was constantly prickly around her.

This was the first time, in a long time, she finally felt relaxed. Her body almost didn't recognise the signs. What she really wanted to do right now was climb the curved staircase, open her bedroom window to the sea air and slip under the covers of that comfortable-looking double bed.

She almost didn't care about the inheritance aspect of the journey.

Almost.

Because from the moment she'd set foot in this place she'd loved it.

It made her toes tingle. It made her breath catch in her throat. It made the tiny little hairs on her arms stand on end.

She couldn't even begin to imagine the fabulous history of a place like this. And all she wanted to do was drink it in.

And if that meant having to play nice with Mr Callan McGregor, then she would. Because he seemed to be the only person who could tell her what she wanted to know.

The dinner passed by in a flash, then Frank the solicitor appeared again and ushered them all into the drawing room.

Laurie almost let out a sigh. It was after nine o'clock at night and after a long day's travel she really just wanted to go to sleep.

She'd tried to speak to Frank earlier but it had been very apparent he didn't want to be seen in discussion with her. Maybe he was worried he would get accused of showing her favour because she was a fellow professional? All she'd wanted to ask him was a little about Angus McLean. But it wasn't to be.

Frank read out a list of rules about the Murder Mystery Weekend, about them staying in character and when they would be expected to meet. He also introduced some people from the company running the weekend's activities: Ashley, a blonde woman in a pale pink 1920s dress, Robin, a dark-haired man dressed in hunting regalia and John, who was dressed as a butler.

Tea and coffee were provided on a table at the side and Laurie made her way over to grab a cup. The rest of the guests were told to mingle and familiarise themselves with each other. As she poured the coffee into one of the pale blue china cups another one was slid alongside.

'Pour me one too, would you? I'm going to fall asleep in here. Playing nice doesn't agree with me.'

Laurie smiled at Callan's voice. 'You and me both. I had no idea I'd be so tired after the journey. All I want to do right now is go to bed.'

Should she have said that out loud? There was kind of an amused glint in Callan's eyes. For a second she felt a flare of panic. What did he think she meant? For a horrible moment she thought he might have taken it as an invitation. The colour started to flood into her cheeks, and she did what she always did when she was embarrassed—she babbled.

'It's such a long journey up by train. The steam locomotive was fabulous, I wouldn't have missed the gorgeous scenery for anything, but when it gets to this time at night, and especially after that beautiful dinner, I just want to go and lie down. Alone—I mean,' she added hastily.

But Callan was laughing and shaking his head. It was obvious he'd picked up on her anxiety.

She said the first thing that came into her head. 'What about you, Callan? Is there a Mrs McGregor to go home to?'

Had she actually just said that out loud? Please let the ground open up and swallow her whole. Wine and tiredness obviously weren't a good mix for her.

Callan shook his head, and was it her imagination or did he just glance at her left hand?

'No. There's no Mrs McGregor. I've been a bit of a workaholic these last few years.'

'And any mini McGregors?' In for a penny, in for

a pound. It seemed prudent to ask, particularly after what had been learned about Angus McLean in the last few weeks.

There was no hesitation. He shook his head. 'I can assure you, if I had any kids they would be permanently attached to my hip.'

There was no mistaking that answer. Callan McGregor would never do what Angus McLean had—whatever his reasons might have been.

'What about you, Laurie? Are you like your character—do you have more than one attachment?' There was a cheeky glint in his eyes as he asked the question.

Laurie rolled her eyes. 'I should be so lucky. I don't have enough hours in the day for myself let alone anyone else. Do you know, I think this is the first time I haven't had a headache in months.'

He leaned forward. 'It's all this good Scots air. It does wonders for your health.' For a second, her breath was caught in her throat as the aroma of his woody aftershave invaded her senses. It was delicious.

She gathered herself and smiled. 'Yeah, but it's making me exceedingly tired.'

'You mean you don't want to go and play nice with the relatives?'

Laurie took a deep breath. She knew the correct answer to this question, but it just couldn't form on her lips. She gave a little shrug. 'Yes, yes, I do. But right now I'm just too tired to care.' She looked over to the middle of the room where they were all currently holding court, talking—no, shouting—at the tops of their voices.

She gestured over to the other side of the room. 'The person I'd really like to sit down with at some point is Mary from Ireland. She'll have been my father's half-sister. And she looks really like him. I'd like to get a chance to talk properly to her.'

The lights flickered out and the room was plunged into darkness, followed by a theatrical scream. And even though she should have half expected it, it really did make her jump.

Callan's arm slid around her waist. Even though she couldn't see a thing, she could sense him leaning closer to her. And it was her natural instinct to move a little closer to him. 'You okay, Laurie?' His warm breath tickled her cheek. More of the aftershave. It was scrambling her senses and rapidly turning into her new favourite smell.

She clutched the cup in her hands. Her hands had started to tremble. The last thing she wanted to do was shatter some priceless china on the parquet flooring. 'Yes, thanks,' she whispered.

'I'm sure this will all be over in a second...' his voice was low, the curls around her ear vibrating with his tone '...and hopefully then we can all get off to bed.'

The words sent a shiver down her spine. Something she hadn't felt in a long time. Something she hadn't had *time* to feel in a long time.

The realisation was startling.

She'd only been here one evening and everything about this place was surprising her.

She'd yet to feel a connection to any of her relatives—the one thing she would actually have liked.

But she couldn't get over the connection and tingle she'd felt to this place from the moment she'd stepped inside. She was under no illusion that Annick Castle would actually ever be hers. But she hadn't expected the place to take her breath away. She hadn't expected

to get the tiniest sensation of belonging from just looking out of a window across an ocean.

None of that made any sense.

But what made even less sense was the man standing
next to her, and the fact her skin was on fire beneath his
fingertips. She didn't even know him. She wasn't sure
if she even *liked* him. He was grumpy. He was prickly.

But something made her feel as if Callan McGregor
was the one true person about here she could trust.

Then there was the fact she knew he was single. It
seemed to have made her stomach do dangerous som-
ersaults.

And he seemed fiercely loyal to a man she knew
nothing about.

The lights flickered back on around them. It only
took her eyes a few seconds to adjust. The blonde
woman Ashley from earlier was now lying on the floor,
with a blood stain on her dress. Thank goodness she
could still see the woman's slight chest rising and falling, otherwise she might have been totally convinced.

Robin—the man in hunting clothes—immediately
launched into his act. 'Call the police, there's been a
murder! Everyone stay where you are—you'll all be
questioned.'

Callan took a deep breath. 'Oh, joy. Let the mayhem
begin.' He was shaking his head again and he moved his
arm from her waist. She was surprised by how much
she could feel the imprint of his hand on her side. She
was even more surprised by how much she still wanted
it to be there.

He took a few steps over to the door, looking back
across the room. There was something in his eyes, and

she couldn't tell what. Was it a memory? Happiness or sadness? No, it was something else, a wistfulness.

'Angus would have loved this,' he said under his breath as he headed out of the door.

CHAPTER FOUR

LAURIE PUSHED OPEN the door to the kitchen. It was ridiculously early but there seemed to be a whole army of pigeons nestling outside her castle window. And the truth was she'd had the best night's sleep in a long time. Whether it was the good Scottish clean air, or the immensely comfortably mattress, something had made her feel as if she were sleeping in a luxury hotel.

Marion the housekeeper was *not* in a sunny mood. She glanced at her watch. 'It's only six. Do you want breakfast already?' Her face was red, her brow wrinkled and her shoulders hunched as if an elephant were sitting on top of them. And there was a tiny little red vein throbbing at the side of her eye. The woman looked as if she were about to spontaneously combust.

Laurie crossed the huge kitchen and laid her hand on Marion's arm. 'No, of course not, Marion. I'm more than capable of fixing my own breakfast.'

Totally the wrong thing to say.

'That's what I'm here for, that's what I get paid for! You shouldn't be in here at all.' Her feet were crossing the kitchen in shuffling steps like a tiny little wind-up toy. 'I've got sixteen people to fix breakfast for and four staff. Then there's the morning coffee and cakes and all the veg to prepare for lunch. The butcher meat hasn't arrived yet and someone pushed *this* under the kitchen door.' She brandished a crumpled piece of paper in her hands. 'I mean, how many allergies can one person have? What on earth am I supposed to do? And did they have these allergies last night? Because no one said a word then—and all the plates came back clean. How am I supposed to deal with that?'

Laurie nodded her head and took the piece of paper from Marion's hand. She blinked at the list. It was the kind of thing that got printed in national newspapers when movie stars handed them to their chefs. She glanced at the name and stifled her smile.

She put the piece of paper on the table and tried to smooth it with her hand. 'Why don't you let me deal with this, Marion?' She met the woman's angry eyes. 'Let's face it, if they were this allergic to food they probably died in their bed last night after the amount they put away at dinner.'

There it was. The tiniest glimmer of a smile. The slightest sag of her shoulders showing a bit of relief. 'Do you think?'

Laurie nodded. 'Leave it with me. If there's anything that is a true allergy and not just a preference or a request, I'll let you know.'

She looked around the kitchen, trying to choose her words carefully. 'Is there anyone else to give you a hand? You're not expecting to do all this yourself?'

Marion bristled and Laurie winced, bracing herself for another onslaught. But it didn't come. It was almost as if it hovered in the air for a few seconds before Marion took a deep breath and calmed herself down.

'One of the girls from the village nearby is coming to help out. She should be here at seven. She's good with breakfasts—just not so good with baking.'

Laurie ran her hand along one of the dark wood worktops leading to the Belfast sinks. There was a huge Aga stove taking up one end of the kitchen and a gas hob with sixteen burners in the island in the middle. There was a huge range of copper-bottomed pans hanging along one wall and shining silver utensils hanging along another. At some point this kitchen had been renovated, keeping the best of the old with the most practical of the new. It was the kind of kitchen used in TV shows, or period dramas.

She loved it. She absolutely loved it.

There was a navy and white striped apron hanging on a hook at the side and she picked it up and put it over her head. 'Okay, if you have help with the breakfasts that should be fine. I'm happy to help with the baking. What kind of thing would you like?' She bent down and started opening cupboards looking for cake tins and mixing bowls. 'I can do carrot cake, fruit loafs, lemon drizzle, cupcakes, tray bakes or sponges.'

She straightened up. Marion was looking at her in horror. 'You can't possibly help with the baking. You're a guest.' She looked as if she was about to keel over and faint.

Laurie smiled and shook her head. 'And you're a member of staff that has had their workload increase tenfold overnight.' She sighed. 'Let me help you, Marion. Baking is about the only skill I have to offer.' She shrugged. 'To be honest I'm not that enamoured by some of my potential relatives and I'd prefer to stay out of the way in the meantime.' She glanced out of the kitchen window and across to the beautiful rose gardens. 'I'd much prefer to be in here.'

Marion frowned. The wrinkles in her forehead like deeply dug troughs. It seemed to be the natural position her face returned to after every interaction. 'You really want to help?'

Laurie nodded. 'I really want to help.' Just being in the kitchen helped. She could already feel some of the tension starting to leave her body, particularly around her neck and shoulders. The thought of staying in the kitchen and not having to participate in small talk with the crazy relatives was like a weight off her back.

The thought of not being under the watchful glare of Callan McGregor was also playing around the back of her mind. Why did he bother her? Why was he floating around in her thoughts? And more importantly, why had he hovered around the edges of her dreams last night?

Marion thudded a stained and battered recipe book onto the worktop. 'Can you follow a recipe?'

Laurie smiled. 'Of course I can.'

And that was it.

Acceptance. Acceptance into the murky depths of the castle kitchens.

Marion bustled around her. 'You'll find all your ingredients in here…' she opened the door to a huge walk-in pantry '…all your fresh goods in here…' another door to a chilled walk-in larder '…and all the equipment you'll need here.' She flung open a door to every baker's dream—a full array of scales, mixing bowls and every baking implement known to man.

Marion folded her arms. 'We've just had a delivery of strawberries. How do you feel about making a fresh cream and strawberry sponge?'

'Sounds good.' Her mouth was watering already.

'And an iced gingerbread and some flapjacks too?' The frown was on its way back.

Laurie nodded. 'No problem, Marion. Leave it with me.'

Marion gave her a little nod and bustled off to the other side of the kitchen where the girl from the village had arrived and was hanging up her coat.

Laurie started to gather all the things she would need. Peace perfect peace. Just what she wanted.

Callan pushed open the door to the kitchen and immediately started to choke, the thick white smoke clawing and catching at the back of his throat.

But it wasn't smoke, and the immediate burst of pure adrenaline started to fade. In amongst the white cloud around him, all he could hear was raucous laughter.

And what was more he recognised that laughter. He just hadn't heard it in a while.

Marion's laugh seemed to come from the very bottom of her feet and reach all the way up her tiny frame to the top of her head. It was a deep, hearty laugh that should come from someone double her size. And he loved it.

Callan waved his hands in front of his face, trying to clear the white, smoky haze.

'Marion? Are you all right in there?'

There was another sound, another laugh. This one verging on hysteria. And he recognised it too. He'd heard it at the train station yesterday.

The white haze gradually cleared, settling around his shoulders and every surface in the kitchen in a fine white powder.

Marion was holding onto the side of one of the worktops to keep herself from falling over. Laurie was sitting in the middle of the floor, a huge sack of white flour burst all around her, covering her hair, face, shoulders and legs and making her look like a snowman in the middle of summer.

He shook his head, taking in the scene around him. 'What on earth happened?'

Laurie opened her mouth to speak, then burst into a fit of laughter again.

Marion shook her head. 'Miss High-and-Mighty on the floor didn't realise quite how heavy the flour sacks were. She thought she could just pick it up and throw it over her shoulder.' Her shoulders started to shake again. Even though she was dusted in white powder her cheeks were flushed with colour. She rolled her eyes. 'Seems like the sack taught her a lesson.' She started laughing again.

Callan held out his hand. 'Laurie? Are you okay?'

Her slim hand fitted easily inside his and he gave her a firm tug to pull her up from the floor.

'Whoop!'

Maybe the tug was a little more than he realised, as she catapulted straight towards him, her flour-coated hands landing squarely in the middle of his navy jumper. 'Oops, sorry, Callan.'

She even had flour smudged on her nose. And he resisted the temptation to wipe it clean.

'What are you doing in the kitchen, Laurie?'

She tried to shake off some of the flour. 'I'm helping. I got up early and offered to help Marion with the baking for later.'

'You did?' He was astounded. It was the last thing he was expecting.

Laurie was a potential inheritor of the castle and estate. Why on earth would she want to be helping in the kitchen? She was a lawyer, for goodness' sake. His suspicions were immediately aroused.

She reached over and started trying to brush the flour from the front of his jumper. Long sweeps with the palm of her hand across the breadth of his chest, sweeping lower and lower... His body gave a jolt at his immediate reaction. He stepped back. Seemed as if it wasn't only his suspicions that could be aroused around Laurie Jenkins.

He lifted his hands and brushed the cloud of flour off for himself. 'Leave it,' he said a little more brusquely than he meant to.

Laurie stepped back and rested her hand on Marion's shoulder. 'I'm so sorry, Marion.' She looked around the powdered kitchen. 'I'll clean up, honest, I will.'

But Marion shook her head firmly. 'Forget it. You've done enough this morning.' She gave her an unexpected wink. 'Anyway, you'll not clean to my standards. June and I will manage.'

Callan shook his head. 'Marion, if you needed help in the kitchen, why didn't you let me know? I could have tried to get you some extra help for the weekend.'

He was cursing himself inside. He should have planned ahead. But the truth was, he'd been so angry about the whole scenario—the whole some-stranger-will-inherit-Annick-Castle—that he hadn't properly considered the staff there.

He knew they'd been catered for in Angus's will. But that wasn't the same. That wasn't the same as considering the pressure they would be under this weekend, or the way they would feel about having to deal with a whole host of strangers—one of whom could become their new potential boss. It wasn't just the twelve potential inheritors—some of them had brought husbands or wives with them, then there was the Murder Mystery Weekend staff too.

It wasn't like him to be so blinkered. He hated that he hadn't considered the people he'd been amongst for years.

But Marion didn't seem so bothered. It was odd. For as long as he'd known her she'd been prickly and difficult. As if a little invisible force field stopped those around her from getting too close.

The laughing he'd heard a few moments ago had been the first he'd heard her laugh like that in years. She had a twinkle in her eye. Laurie Jenkins was currently digging her way under that force field. And he'd no idea how she'd managed it.

Marion tilted her chin, a stern look in her eye. The kitchen was her domain. 'Let me manage things in here, Callan.' Her hand swept towards the table at the far end of the kitchen. 'Laurie seems to be managing fine. She's done a good job.'

He tried not to flinch. Praise indeed from Marion and he followed her gaze to three cakes covered with glass domes and protected from the flour attack, sitting on the far-away table.

He walked over. 'You made these?' It didn't matter that he tried to hide his surprise, the rise in inclination of his voice was a dead giveaway.

He felt Laurie appear at his side, their arms almost touching. She was smiling. She looked happy—no, she looked relaxed. The first time she'd appeared that way since she'd got here. 'Strawberry sponge, orange-iced gingerbread and flapjacks for Mr Allergy.'

He raised his eyebrows. 'Mr Allergy?'

She waved her hand. 'Don't ask. I think a pop music diva has a shorter list of demands than he has.'

He wrinkled his nose. 'So, if you've made all these, what's with the flour?'

She smiled. 'I was going to make a chocolate cake for dessert tonight.'

'Aren't you supposed to be taking part in the Murder Mystery Weekend?'

His head was spinning. Surely, the whole point of coming here was to see if she could be the potential inheritor of Annick Castle. Everything had been clearly spelled out in the letter. Why on earth was she wasting her time in the kitchen?

'Yeah, well, I suppose so.' Her eyes fixed on the gardens outside, drifting away to her own little world. What was the story about Laurie Jenkins?

There it was. That little flicker on her face. Did she even know that happened? That little glimmer that looked a lot like hope. Right now it was fixated on the rainbow explosion that was the rose flower beds outside. Usually the castle gardens had regimented colours, red in one, pink in another, yellow and white in others. But this year he suspected Bert the gardener had fallen foul of his own poor eyesight.

Nothing had been mentioned. Nothing had been said. And the effect was actually startling. An explosion of colour right outside the kitchen windows.

Laurie turned to face him. 'To be honest I was hoping to take a walk around the gardens today.' She hesitated. 'You've already shown me the maze—how about the rest of the gardens? Isn't there a swan pond?'

Callan nodded automatically. 'Aren't you supposed to take part in all the designated activities?'

She shrugged. 'I'll make an excuse. As long as I hand in my card at the end saying who I think the murderer is, I don't suppose it will matter. Anyway, I'll be there for dinner tonight.'

She really didn't care. She really didn't want to take part.

He was astonished. Did she know what she was giving up?

But Laurie was peering out of the window again, across the gardens to the wall next to the sea that was lined with cannons. 'Can we get down on the beach from here?'

He nodded. 'It's not the easiest path.'

'I think I'll manage.' She'd lifted one eyebrow at him, as if daring him to imply anything otherwise.

He wasn't sure whether to be angry or intrigued.

The whole purpose of the weekend was to find out who would inherit the castle. Laurie was a lawyer. Maybe she'd found a loophole in all this and knew she could mount a legal challenge. The thought sent a prickle across his skin.

He'd been assured that no matter how crazy this whole scheme appeared, legally it was watertight—whether he liked it or not.

But that would be an explanation as to why she didn't really want to engage with the Murder Mystery Weekend. Why she wanted to spend her time exploring the estate. Maybe she was already drawing up plans in her head about what she wanted to do with the place, or how to sell it off for the highest profit.

'Callan?' Her voice was quiet and her hand rested gently on his.

His mind was running away with him again. Every time he thought about this place or the people in it, his mind naturally went for the worst-case scenario.

He looked down, trying to ignore the warmth spreading up his arm. She was looking up at him with her smudged nose and hair and her big brown eyes. Questioning the fact that for a few minutes he'd been lost in a world of his own.

There was still a light dusting of flour across the pink shoulders of her shirt. Her dark brown hair was swept up in a clasp, with stray strands escaping. The flour was like the first fall of snow at the start of winter.

She blinked, her cheeks flushing a little as he continued to stare. Her head tilted to the side. 'What time can we meet?' she prompted.

He started. Meet. Yes. That was what he was supposed to be doing.

'Half an hour.' His words came out automatically. 'I'll meet you in the entrance hall.'

She gave a little nod of her head and disappeared through the kitchen door.

Callan stared at his hand. The skin that she'd touched felt on fire. He couldn't understand. It just didn't figure.

Laurie just didn't figure.

A movement caught his eye. Marion was staring at him with her arms folded across her chest.

'What?' The words snapped out, louder than intended.

She gave him a little knowing smile, then turned her back and started busying herself around the kitchen.

For the first time, in a long time, Callan felt unnerved. And he couldn't quite work out why.

CHAPTER FIVE

LAURIE WASN'T QUITE sure why her stomach was churning, but it was. She frowned at her reflection in the floor-length mirror. Red Capri pants probably weren't the most appropriate for a cliff-side clamber but that was the trouble with travelling light. Thank goodness Marion had found her a pair of wellington boots, and they even matched her trousers.

She took a deep breath, grabbed her jacket and headed along the corridor towards the stairs. The phone in her pocket beeped and she pulled it out. Work.

Her stomach sank like a stone. Funny how a simple text could have that effect on her. A missing file. On a Saturday. She glanced at her watch. If she'd been in London right now she'd probably have been in work too. How sad was that? She couldn't help but glance at the mysterious woman in the portrait at the top of the stairs. Was it possible that her glare was even more disapproving than normal, and even more focused on Laurie?

She wondered if this castle had any ghosts. She'd need to ask Callan about that later. She tapped out a quick reply with a number of locations for the missing file.

As she reached the bottom of the curved staircase Robin, the Murder Mystery Weekend co-ordinator, rushed over, clipboard in hand. 'Ms Jenkins, I didn't see you at breakfast this morning. Was something wrong?'

Yet another person with a disapproving glare. She shrugged. 'Sorry, I was busy.'

He frowned. 'You do realise that in order to get a good idea of who the murderer is, you have to take part in all the activities.'

She bit her tongue to stop the words rolling off that she really wanted to say. It wasn't his fault Angus McLean had made this a stipulation of his will. This was just a guy doing a job.

She gave him her sweetest smile. 'Some of the activities just aren't for me.'

He looked horrified. 'But you have to take part. You have to speak to as many of the other characters in order to build up an idea of who the murderer is.' He eyed her haughtily. 'And they need the opportunity to speak to you too.'

She sighed. 'Listen, you and I know that I'm not the murderer, so it doesn't really matter whether the other "characters"—' she lifted her fingers in the air '—speak to me or not. As long as I tell you at the end who I think is the guilty party, everything will work out fine.'

'Ms Jenkins, you're really not entering into the spirit of things. It spoils things for all the other participants too.'

She was starting to get annoyed now, and feel a little guilty, which made her even madder. She straightened herself up to her full five feet five inches. 'Well, I guess since the other participants are my new-found family, it's up to me whether I want to spend time with them or not.'

She turned and strode away as best she could in the ill-fitting red wellies. Callan was leaning against the wall next to the door with his arms folded across his chest and an amused look on his face. He pulled the main door open and picked up a jacket. 'Ready?'

There was a little spark of something in his eyes and if he said something smart right now she would take one of these wellies off and hit him over the head with it.

'Ready.' She barely turned her head as she walked straight out of the door and onto the gravel courtyard.

This place was driving her crazy.

She spun around, hands on her hips, and Callan nearly walked straight into her.

'What kind of person was Angus McLean?'

He started. 'What?'

'What kind of person was Angus McLean? Was he some kind of sick sadist that would try and pitch his unknown relatives against each other for some kind of pleasure? Did he actually think anyone would agree to this?' Now the words were coming out she couldn't stop them. 'Was he sane? Did a doctor check him over after he wrote that mad will?'

Callan hesitated for the tiniest second, then obviously thought better of getting into an unwinnable fight with an angry woman. He put his arm around her shoulders and steered her in the direction of the stairs, leading down to the impeccable gardens, fountain and maze. Her feet moved without her even really realising it, the weight of his arm behind her just making her flow along with his body. Before she knew it she was guided along to the bench in front of the trickling fountain.

Callan nudged her to sit down and she did. With a thump.

It was as if all her frustration was coming out at once.

Callan waited for a few minutes, letting them sit in silence and listen to the peaceful trickle of the fountain.

It was a beautiful setting. The bronze fairy was spouting the water from her mouth, through her hands. The water flowed down into the round pond with a mosaic bottom of blue and green tiles. The sun was high in the cloudless sky and the temperature was warm in the shelter of the lowered set of gardens.

Eventually Callan spoke, his voice deep and calm. He was leaning forward, his arms resting on his knees. 'Angus McLean was completely sane. Frank Dalglish, the solicitor, was worried there might be a legal challenge to the will and made sure that Angus was examined by a doctor.'

'Oh.' Laurie's brain was spinning, questions firing everywhere, but Callan's voice had a real weight to it. He was completely sincere. And she realised he probably wasn't amused at her outburst. She could smell his aftershave again, the one that seemed to play with her self-control and turn her brain to mush. Or maybe that was just the sight of his muscled arms?

'He was no sadist. And he certainly wasn't sick. Angus McLean was one of the best guys I've ever met.' He leaned back against the bench and ran his fingers through his hair, mussing it up. She liked it better that way. He shook his head. 'Truth is, Laurie, I don't understand any of this any more than you do. I spent twenty-five years around Angus McLean. I never suspected for a second that he had children. I could never understand why he wouldn't sell me the place. He kept telling me he wanted to keep it in the family—but as far as I knew, there wasn't any.'

He was upset. He was hurting. No matter what her thoughts were on Angus McLean she had to try and remember that this was someone who had been dear to Callan. His experience was totally different from hers.

Something registered in her brain. She looked up at the castle.

It was hard to believe but as a potential inheritor of Annick Castle she hadn't even given a moment's thought to how much it could actually be worth.

She gulped. The figures dancing around her brain made her mind boggle. She turned to face him. 'How on earth could you afford to buy a place like this?' She held up her hands. 'I have no idea how much Annick Castle would cost, but what kind of job do you have?'

She couldn't even begin to understand how someone could make enough money to buy Annick Castle. Her question probably seemed cheeky, but she was the kind of girl who usually said what came to mind. And she wasn't going to stop just because she was here.

'If I tell you will you be able to reply in one hundred and fifty characters or less?'

It took a few seconds for the penny to drop. She couldn't help it; her mouth fell open.

'You? You own Blether?' She couldn't believe it. The Scottish equivalent of Twitter, with a slightly longer letter count, had started as a rival company six or seven years before. It had taken the advertising market by storm. Those ten little letters made all the difference, but still allowed short, sharp messages.

He gave a rueful smile and nodded. 'Guilty as charged. I owned an Internet search engine before that. Blether came about almost by accident.'

She was stunned. Everyone knew exactly how successful the company was, but she'd never really heard anything about the owner. 'How so?'

'I was annoyed one night and came home and spouted off to Angus about it. He told me to stop bellyaching and do something about it. He challenged me to make something bigger and better.'

She shook her head. 'And the name?'

He shrugged. 'How could it have been anything else? Blether—the Scots word for people who talk incessantly.' He raised his eyebrows at her. 'You should be able to relate.'

Her reaction was automatic; she elbowed him in the ribs. 'Cheeky.'

They sat quietly for a few more seconds as she tried to take in everything he'd just told her. He must be worth millions—no, probably billions—and here he was, sitting at Annick Castle for a crazy Murder Mystery Weekend. It just didn't make sense.

'So, your background is in computers, then?'

He shook his head. 'It should be, but it isn't. I did pure mathematics at university.'

'You did?'

He smiled and looked up at the castle. She could see the fondness in his eyes, see the memories flit across his face. 'I wasn't doing too well at school before I met Angus. My father didn't believe in homework. And as a child I had other skills that were my priority.'

Something about the way he said the words sent a chill down her spine. He hadn't emphasised them, or been too explicit, but it was almost as if the skills he was hinting at were survival skills.

'Once I started spending time with Angus he used to sit me down at the kitchen table at night and go over my homework with me. He was methodical—and strict. He discovered I had a natural aptitude for maths and he bought me textbooks and journals that challenged me.'

'So you did your homework here?' It seemed the safest question to ask, without prying too much.

'Pretty much. Angus helped me with my exams. He even helped me fill in my application for university.'

'Where did you go?'

'I got into Cambridge—and Oxford, but in the end I went to Edinburgh. I didn't want to leave Scotland.'

'You didn't?' She didn't mean to sound so surprised; it just came out that way. It hadn't even occurred to her for a second to turn down her university place at Cambridge. Did people actually do that? And how distracted would she have been if she'd met Callan at university?

He stood up and arched his back, obviously trying to relieve some tension. 'Look around you, Laurie. What's not to love?'

It was the way he said the words. So simple. Without a second thought.

And she did look around her.

At the magnificent sand-coloured castle looking out over the Scottish coastline.

At the immaculate maze.

At the colourful, impeccably kept gardens.

At the forest and vegetation around them, set against the start of a mountain range.

It was almost as if something sucked the air out of her lungs.

She lived her life in London. She spent her day jumping on and off the tube, breathing in other people's air. She was surrounded by high-rise buildings and streets that often never saw any sunlight. Continual fights over parking spaces, and eternally rising rents.

She didn't have a single friend in London that had a garden. Her own flat had a window box that she rarely filled with flowering shrubs—on the few occasions that she had she often forgot to water them.

She couldn't remember the last time she'd walked

on grass. How long had it been since she'd gone to Hyde Park?

'You want me to tell you a little of the history of the place?'

She nodded. She knew absolutely nothing about Annick Castle.

Callan sat back on the bench, resting his arm along the back as she settled next to him. His arm was brushing the top of her shoulders. It was as if a whole host of butterflies were flapping their wings against her skin. 'The castle was built originally in the fifteen-hundreds.' There was a gleam in his eyes. 'There's even a rumour that Mary Queen of Scots once stayed here. It was enlarged, rebuilt and the gardens planted in the seventeen-hundreds. The Earl of Annick's family owned the estate for years. They were connected to the Kennedy family in Scotland who can trace their ancestry back to Robert the Bruce. In later years they had connections with some of the most powerful families in America.'

'I had no idea. So how did the castle end up in the hands of Angus McLean?'

'There were a number of properties like this all over Scotland. Some of them were poorly maintained because of the costs involved, others just weren't lived in all year round. In 1945 a lot of them were handed over to the National Trust in Scotland. But this one had caught the eye of Angus's father—he owned a pharmaceutical company and was about the only person who hadn't gone bankrupt after the Second World War. He bought the place for a song.'

Laurie let a hiss of air out through her lips. Maybe not this castle, but something had been here for five hundred years. It was amazing. All that history in one place.

She could be sitting in the same place that Mary Queen of Scots had once stood.

Callan had reached out his hand towards her and she took it without question, letting him pull her up from the bench. Warmth encapsulated her hand. There was a chilly breeze coming off the sea and part of her wished he would wrap her in his arms.

'Come on,' he said. 'You wanted to see the grounds. Let's go down to the swan pond.'

She followed him along the gravel path, winding past the fountain and flower beds. Small things started to prick her mind. Some of the plants here were a little wilder, a little less trimmed. The bushes weren't quite as shaped as the ones underneath the castle windows.

'Who looks after the grounds, Callan?'

He turned, his hand gesturing towards another set of steps. 'Bert mostly. He has a few of the local boys who come and help him, but he generally scares them all off within a few months.' He pointed back at the perfect green lawn. 'Last year Angus persuaded him to let another company come in and cut the lawns and do the edging.' He rolled his eyes. 'You've no idea the fight that caused.' There was a real affection in his voice.

She walked down the steps that were sheltered by some thick foliage. When she reached the bottom she let out a little gasp. She turned to face Callan. 'When you said swan pond I was thinking of something much smaller.'

He gave a nod and a smile. 'Some people don't even know it exists. The castle grounds are sheltered and on an incline. It means that you have to walk down steps at each level.' They walked closer to the edge of the pond. It was the size of around four football pitches and Laurie could see a few white swans bobbing in the middle.

'What's that over there?' There was an elegant glass and white metal gazebo on the other side of the pond. 'It looks as if you lifted it straight out of *The Sound of Music* and put it there.'

Callan nodded. 'What if I told you it had a bench that ran all the way around the inside?'

'Really?' Her stomach gave a little flutter. Her mind instantly had her inside the gazebo with Callan twirling her around in his arms. The chemistry between them seemed to increase the more time she spent with him; it was getting hard not to acknowledge it. Did Callan think so too?

She wasn't sure. He nodded and gave her a half-smile. 'Really. It's just coincidence. It's more than a hundred years old. Angus's parents had it built. The swan pond was his mother's favourite spot, but she didn't like sitting in the sun.'

'It's gorgeous. Can we go around?'

He glanced at his watch. 'Maybe later. We've still got a lot of ground to cover.'

Laurie glanced down at her footwear. If she was going to visit the castle's own *Sound of Music* gazebo she didn't really want to do it in red wellies. It kind of spoiled the mood. 'Okay, then, where to next?'

Callan led her up another set of steps that took them around the other side of the castle. They passed outbuildings that looked a little worse for wear. A set of unused stables and a round stone building that was almost falling down.

The stonework on this side of the castle wasn't as clean as the front and there were a number of slates on the ground. Were they from the roof?

The round building was fascinating and she couldn't

help but go and peer through the doorway. 'What was this?'

'It was one of the old icehouses on the estate. They used to cut ice from the swan pond and store it here for use in the house. The old icehouses were the forerunners of refrigeration. And watch out—you probably need a hard hat to go in there.'

'Wow. What other buildings are there?'

'As well as the gazebo at the swan pond, there is an orangery. It was built in 1818. It was used later as a camellia house and had one-inch-thick glass, a dome top and a furnace at the back of the building to supply under-floor heating. They used to think that delicate flowers needed to be grown in hothouses. There also used to be a pagoda overlooking the swan pond, but it fell into ruins—only the foundations are left now.'

This place was truly amazing—she didn't even know the half of it. No wonder Callan loved it so much. 'What was that for?'

'The lower level was the swan house and aviary with the gazebo or teahouse above. During its time the aviary housed specimens of gold and silver pheasants, pigeons of fancy varieties, kites and hunting hawk. It's also thought that one time a monkey was housed here, giving the pagoda its local nickname of the "monkey house".'

She shook her head. 'I had no idea the estate was so big.' She was also astounded at Callan's knowledge and the way everything just tripped off his tongue. 'Did you ever see it?'

He wrinkled his brow. 'It was partially standing when I was a boy. There was still some glass and stone remaining. And there's more. There are old gatehouses, a water house and a gas house all around the grounds of the estate. There's an old dairy, a stonemason's and another set of stables.'

Laurie had no idea about any of this. When she'd done the Internet search for Annick Castle, she'd only really looked at the pictures of the actual castle. She hadn't read up on how big the estate was or what it contained.

They'd reached the wall again that looked out over the sea. She placed her hands on her hips and looked around her. 'This place is just amazing.' She sighed.

'Yeah. It is.' Callan had that look again, the one where he just drifted off and she couldn't help but wonder what was going on in his head.

She cleared her throat. 'I hope you don't mind me saying, but parts of it look a little…run-down.'

He didn't hesitate. 'I know. You're right. I tried to speak to Angus about it for the last few years. But I've got no control over what happens on the estate, and I had no right to order repairs—even though I was willing to pay for some of them myself.'

'He didn't want to maintain the castle?' It sounded odd. And she couldn't imagine why.

Callan leaned back against the wall. 'He just grew old—and stubborn. And he wouldn't let me help him with his finances.' He shrugged his shoulders. 'I was worried he didn't actually have any money left. He still had his faculties but his decision-making processes, well—they just seemed to disintegrate.'

'And yet he still managed to make the strangest will in the world?'

'There's no cure for old age, Laurie.' He gave a nod towards the next set of steps. 'Come on. Let's put those wellies to good use.'

He removed a thin piece of rope closing off the

steps and started down them. Laurie made to follow and stopped dead. It wasn't a traditional set of steps. They were precarious, cut into the cliff side with only a thread rope as a handhold. At places they looked almost vertical.

Callan moved down them easily, sure-footed without a second's hesitation. He made it look easy.

Except it was far from easy.

'Come on,' he shouted over his shoulder. 'If you fall you'll only land on me.'

Part of his confidence annoyed her—which was silly. He'd lived here for a good part of his life. He could probably go down these steps with his eyes shut.

Venturing down them in a pair of somebody else's ill-fitting wellies was an entirely different story. In some ways she might have taken great pleasure in landing squarely between his shoulders. In another, despite his bravado, it was likely they would both tumble down the cliff face and land in the rocks below. Quite frankly, she wasn't that brave.

She took her time as she edged down the steps, shouting down to Callan in an attempt to appear casual, 'You never told me, how did you end up going from pure mathematics to computers?'

He was so far beneath her now. The noise from the crashing waves below almost drowned out his reply. 'Boredom, or luck, I guess.'

She took the next few steps a little quicker. She was becoming more sure-footed, the thin rope slipping easily through her fingers. She knew her brow was wrinkled as she took the last few steps towards him. 'I don't get it. Boredom? Whoops—'

The last few steps were slicked with moss and lichens, the thick soles of the wellies having hardly any grip at all. His hands planted firmly on her hip bones, stopping her from losing her balance completely.

She was one step above him, meaning they were almost face-to-face.

If the breath hadn't exited her lungs so quickly she might have smiled. The view was good here.

Any woman would tell you that from first glance Callan McGregor was a fine figure of a man. But this close she could see everything—his slightly tanned, slightly weathered skin. The smattering of tiny freckles across his nose. Her hands had lifted to stop her falling and were now naturally placed on the breadth of his chest. After a few seconds she could feel the heat from his skin seeping through his cotton shirt onto the palms of her hands.

She should move them. She really should. But right now they felt superglued to his chest.

She caught her breath. 'Boredom?' she asked softly.

They were so close now the crashing waves were merely background noise. He hadn't moved his hands; they were still firmly on her hips, steering her closer to him.

He blinked. If he'd been any closer those long eyelashes of his might have brushed her cheek. She shouldn't feel so comfortable. Under normal circumstances she would have jumped back, hating her personal space being invaded without her say-so.

But nothing about this weekend had been normal. Why change anything now?

From this position she had a real clear view of his green eyes. Bright green eyes. Unlike any she'd seen before. There was nothing pale or wishy-washy about them. She'd seen an emerald this green once before on the jewellery shopping channel. Was it from Colombia?

It had been three carats, with a single carat diamond on either side. Probably the most gorgeous ring she'd ever seen and well out of her price range. Funny how the billionaire's eyes reminded her of that.

He tilted his head to one side. 'Just because I had a natural talent for maths didn't mean I had to spend my life doing it.'

He said it as if it made perfect sense.

A gust of wind swept past her, pushing her even closer to him. Every hair on her arms stood on end. But it wasn't the wind. It was him. His touch. And his words. Doing a whole host of strange things to her.

It was more than unsettling. She tried to pull her tongue down from its current position of sticking to the roof of her mouth. It wasn't often in this life that Laurie found it difficult to talk.

'But what did Angus say? Didn't he tell you to find a career related to your degree?' She'd already realised there was no point asking what his father thought. He hadn't even mentioned his mother at all. And she couldn't ask the question that was throbbing in her head right now: *What would my father have thought if I'd walked away from law?* Because neither Callan nor she would know the answer.

Callan smiled. A smile that reached right up into those green eyes. Little wrinkles appeared around them. Good wrinkles. He looked so much better when he smiled rather than the permanent frown that had been on his face since she'd met him.

'Angus would never have told me to do something that made me unhappy. I'd completed my degree. It was up to me to find my place in life.'

He said the words so easily. As if it was the way it

should be for everyone and she felt her stomach twist in tight knots.

Why couldn't she have said something like that to her father? Only hers hadn't been an ordinary kind of degree. What else could you do with a law degree if you didn't practise law? Sure, there were some students in her class who hadn't gone on to complete their professional qualifications after sitting their exams. They'd moved into other professions.

But she wasn't exactly sure what. Truth was, she'd been too scared to pay too much attention to any other options. It had almost been easier to work on the assumption that there was none. She would never have disappointed her father. She just couldn't have.

Horrible things were jumping around in her mind. What would have happened if she'd told her father that she didn't like her degree? What would have happened if he'd still been alive and she'd told him she hated her job? She could feel tears prickling in the backs of her eyes. All of a sudden she felt cold. Really cold. Did this make her a coward?

'Laurie?' Callan's voice was quiet; she could feel his warm breath on her cheek, see his eyes full of concern.

'But what if you can't find your place in life?' she whispered. *Or, you're too scared to.*

She was going to cry, any second now she was going to burst into tears, on the edge of the Scottish coastline with a virtual stranger.

Callan didn't say a word. He slipped his arm around her shoulders, holding her close to his side, and guided her down the last few steps onto the thin line of shingle beach. Judging from the moss and lichen on the shingles, this part of the coastline must regularly be underwater.

The warmth from his body was comforting. The feel of the arm around her shoulder was reassuring—protective almost. He hadn't asked her any questions. It was almost as if he knew she was upset and he sensed not to push her.

They walked a few hundred yards along the coastline and he stopped at the rock face. 'Look,' he said, his mouth brushing against her ear.

She lifted her head. Carved into the rocks in front of her were three arches—as if someone had tried to create a house out of one of the natural caves. The arches were on three levels, almost as if it had been someone's home.

'What on earth is this?' It was a perfect distraction. So unusual, and so mysterious that she couldn't help but ask the question and push the other heavy thoughts from her mind.

'Welcome to the history of Annick Castle. This part of the coast was a notorious centre for smuggling and the fortified caves beneath the castle were ideal for hiding contraband from the Revenue Officers. For centuries the Annick Kennedys and others on the estate were either directly involved in smuggling, or turned a blind eye to it, in exchange for a share of the profits.'

'No.' Laurie felt her eyes grow wide. 'Really?' This was fascinating to her. A whole part of her family history she knew nothing about. 'So, you're telling me my relatives were involved in smuggling?'

Callan smiled as they entered the cave. 'It seems that way. This was all long before Angus's time, but it is amazing, isn't it? And it's part of the heritage of Annick Castle.'

He sounded a little wistful as he said those words. They stood for a moment in the cave. It wasn't quite as dark as she'd thought, the carved windows letting in lots of light. It was damp and slimy, with the water lapping around her wellies. There was a ledge high above her at the second window.

Laurie pointed. 'I take it the contraband had to be moved up there at high tide?'

Callan shrugged. 'I would assume so.' He walked over and touched one of the walls. 'Just imagine if these walls could talk. What do you think they would tell us?'

She walked over and laid her hand on the damp, cold wall next to his. 'How many of those smugglers died on the rocks out there? This doesn't look like the easiest bit of coast to navigate—not that I know anything about sailing.'

Callan nodded. 'That's a good point. This is a pretty treacherous part of the coast. Even today, sailing around here isn't really encouraged. I can remember a few wrecks over the years.' He gave a little smile. 'When I was a young boy I spent most of my time down here fighting imaginary pirates.'

She could almost imagine him dressed up with a pretend sword, swooping in and out of the atmospheric cave. 'Was it safe to play down here?'

He laughed. 'I take it these days it would need a whole health and safety check before anyone set foot on those steps. But when I was young Angus could always tell me the tide tables. As long as it wasn't high tide, I was allowed to come and play.' He gave her a measured look. 'Do you think you would have come and joined me?'

The question took her by surprise. A million thoughts and possibilities had floated around her head. What if Angus McLean had made contact with her dad years ago? What if she'd had a chance to spend summers here—to spend summers playing in *The Sound of Music* gazebo, pretending to be Liesl? What if she'd had a chance to grow up around Callan McGregor?

She pushed the thought from her mind and met his smile. 'I was a girl's girl. Pirates and damp caves would have horrified me. I guess, as every little girl would, I would have dreamed of being a fairy princess in the castle. To be honest, I would probably have spent most of my time sweeping up and down that fabulous stair-case. Hours of fun presenting myself at the ball.' She gave an imaginary curtsey. He went to speak but she raised her finger. 'But as a teenager, I would have put a no-fly zone around the gazebo and spent every eve-ning re-enacting the dancing scene, singing "Sixteen Going on Seventeen" with the gentleman of my choice.'

Callan raised his eyebrows. 'And who might that have been?'

He moved a little closer. Or did she just imagine it?

Nope. His fingers had definitely edged nearer hers on the wall. 'That all depends.'

'Depends on what?'

His voice had grown quieter, huskier. It was send-ing shivers down her spine and her body was reacting in the most natural manner—moving even closer to hear his words.

'Depends on who the hero of the moment was.' It was the perfect time to tease him. And she had to tease him. Because otherwise she might end up wishing for something else entirely. 'When I was sixteen I went through a real retro phase—I loved Marty McFly from *Back to the Future*. I wanted him to magically appear in his DeLorean and take me off. By seventeen I'd moved on completely and thought I would marry a member of Take That.'

Callan cringed. 'Save me from boy bands!'

She shook her head. 'It was downhill all the way from there. I still had a tiny bit of retro films going on. Indiana Jones was definitely my overall favourite.'

He raised his eyes. 'So, no pirates?' His eyes were darker in here. He was standing with his back to the incoming light, making his pupils even bigger.

It was easy to imagine what film he was talking about now. She smiled. 'No, funnily enough, pirates never did it for me.'

He blinked. Thick, dark lashes over bright green eyes nearly obliterated by the huge pupils. 'Pity.'

He said the word so quietly it was almost a whisper. But it was the hidden implication. The expression on his face. Laurie was frozen. She couldn't move. No, she didn't want to move.

She knew exactly what he was thinking. Because her mind was in the same place.

She was in the same position as earlier. Inches away from Callan McGregor. Except this time she wasn't standing on a set of exposed steps; this time she was standing in a darkened cave.

Any second now he might move closer. She couldn't help it. Her lips felt instantly dry and she ran her tongue along them.

He lifted his hand and her breath caught in her throat. Was he going to kiss her? But no. He reached up and touched a long brown curl, pushing it back over her shoulder. 'You're a strange one, Laurie Jenkins.'

She tilted her head to the side. 'What do you mean?'

He sighed. 'I mean, I haven't found you stealing the family silver. You don't seem that interested in the Murder Mystery Weekend, but you *do* seem really interested in the castle.'

'That's because I am.' It was the simplest answer because it was true. It was cold in here. If she just inched forward a little…

'But why? Because of how much it will be worth if you inherit it?'

His words sounded harsh. And they offended her. She pulled back.

'Is that what you think?'

Callan hadn't moved his eyes from hers. 'That's just it, Laurie—I'm not sure what I think.'

She moved a little backwards. His gaze was starting to unnerve her. But she was determined to speak her mind.

'I want the opportunity to meet other members of my so-called family. I'm still not sure how I feel about all this. Most of the time it makes me angry. You talk about Angus McLean with great affection, Callan, but for me—he's just some unknown guy that ignored his children. I can't get my head round that at all.' She lifted her hands up. 'And this, a castle, spectacular grounds, caves and a history just waiting to be learned. It's more than I could ever have imagined. I'm trying to decide how much I want to be part of all this—if at all.'

His expression changed quickly. He looked almost scornful. 'You mean you don't want to inherit the castle?'

She shook her head. He really didn't understand her at all. And she wasn't even sure she could put it into words. She could barely understand it herself. 'I mean, I don't know what I would do with it, Callan. Look at me.' She put her hand on her chest. 'I'm a London girl from a small family. I'm a lawyer. What do I know about castles? I've never seen anything like this before. How on earth would I fit in? You've had the benefit of being here since you were young. You grew up here. You know everything there is to know—'

'Or not.' His words were quick. She'd forgotten Angus hadn't told him about his children either. This must be even harder for him than it was for her.

He'd cut off her frustration mid-sentence. And she just couldn't find the words to continue. She needed some time. She needed some time to get her head around all this.

She took a deep breath in the vain hope it would fill her lungs and straighten out her head.

Work. Getting away from work had been the first step for her.

The letter and invite to Annick Castle had been the starting point in the process, but now she was away and out of her usual environment she was scared of how she was feeling. She was scared by how much she was embracing things, relishing the change and enjoying little things she would never usually experience.

She was scared of the horrible feeling in the pit of her stomach when she realised she would have to board a train in a few days to head back down to London.

Back to the long hours, aching muscles and tension headaches. Back to a life that revolved completely around work. She'd long since abandoned her gym membership after she'd only found the time to go twice. Was that what she really wanted?

The waves started to lap in around her feet. Callan looked down. 'Time to go. The tide comes in quite slowly at this time of day. We've got around twenty minutes to get up the steps.'

He strode out of the cave into the bright sunlight while Laurie stood for a few seconds longer.

She took a deep breath. What was she doing? She

had no idea who Callan McGregor was. Every time she was around him she was unsettled.

She couldn't help but feel a tiny bit envious of the fact he'd grown up here.

She couldn't help but feel even more envious that Angus never had any expectation of him beyond going to university.

She squeezed her eyes tightly shut. This was disloyal. She wasn't even going to allow herself to think like that.

It was time to get a hold of herself. Time to stop with the crazy thoughts and focus on the reason she was here—to try and get to know her family members.

She lifted her head and walked back outside into the sunlight.

CHAPTER SIX

'Knock, knock.'

Callan cringed. He'd recognise that high-pitched voice anywhere. It was Robin, the Murder Mystery Weekend organiser. It didn't matter where in the castle he tried to hide, the guy seemed to have an inbuilt antenna and could find him anyway.

Robin stuck his head around the door. 'Dinner will be served in ten minutes. We were hoping you would have made it to the pre-dinner drinks. You did agree to participate.' There it was. That tiny disapproving edge to his voice that he seemed to have in every conversation with Callan. It was almost as if he were an eighty-year-old grumpy headmaster trapped inside a gangly twenty-five-year-old's body.

Callan tried not to say what he was really thinking. He stared at the crumpled piece of card he'd been given earlier with his instructions. They included *Flirt with Lucy Clark, get into an argument with Philippe Deveraux*. No problem. If the man was drunk again and put his hands on Laurie he'd do more than argue with him.

Where had that come from? The thought surprised him. He'd only known the woman two days and already she was getting under his skin.

Who was he kidding?

She'd probably got under his skin from the second the smoke had cleared at the railway station and he'd caught sight of the curvy brunette. But when they'd been standing on the steps earlier and he could see her brown eyes filled with tears he couldn't help but feel protective towards her. Something was going on with Laurie Jenkins—and it was nothing to do with inheriting a castle. The question was, did he really want to find out?

Did he want to get to know any of Angus's relatives who were milling around the place he thought of as his home? Once one of them inherited it, he would have to clear out his things and start staying in his Edinburgh town house. And even though he owned a beautiful home he couldn't bear the thought of that.

The place he called home was here.

'Callan, can I count on you?'

Robin. He'd forgotten he was even there. He gave the organiser a quick nod and watched him scuttle off.

Callan closed his computer. He was doing exactly what he'd been dreading. Examining the castle accounts. In the interim period between Angus dying and the castle being handed over he'd been appointed as caretaker. The upkeep of the castle was huge. Heating, lighting and maintenance costs were astronomical. The roof needed some repairs. They needed to employ more staff to help Bert with the grounds. Whoever inherited Annick Castle was going to get a nasty shock.

A horrible little coil of guilt was snaking around him. He should have stepped in earlier. He should have spoken to Angus about how run-down parts of the estate were becoming.

But the truth was he had too much respect for Angus to ever have done that.

But maybe there was a little hope. Maybe if he made more of an effort to talk to the relatives he could plant the seeds about how costly the castle would be. With any luck he could put in a generous offer and buy the castle, just as he'd always wanted to.

It seemed mercenary. It seemed calculating. But none of these people felt the way he did about the castle. The only one who'd shown any real interest in anything other than its retail value was Laurie, and even she'd admitted that she'd be out of her depth.

He picked up the jacket that was sitting on the Louis XV armchair. It was the same one he'd worn the night before. He'd no idea whose idea it had been that all the guests should dress in 1920s clothes but this was as far as he'd go.

He could hear the noise in the main drawing room as he descended the stairs, some laughter louder than others.

He saw Laurie as soon as he entered the room. She was sitting next to another woman on one of the red velvet chaises longues. It was Mary, from Ireland, the one aunt that she'd really wanted to talk to.

She was wearing an emerald-green dress with beading around the scooped neckline. It skirted the top of her knees and she had a matching pair of shoes. Her hair was swept back on one side with an elaborate clasp made of jewels and blue and green feathers. Was that a peacock? He couldn't help but smile.

The dress could have been made specifically for her. It skimmed her curves, hinting at them without giving too much away. The dress colour accentuated the light tan of her skin and the glossy chestnut of her hair that hung in curls around one shoulder. She'd applied some heavier make-up, her eyes outlined in kohl and her lips red and glossy. It was all he could do to stop himself staring at them.

But what he noticed most about her was how animated she seemed. She was clutching a photograph in one hand that she'd obviously been showing to her aunt and the two of them were talking at once. Her eyes were sparkling, her other hand gesturing frequently, and her aunt Mary seemed equally engaged.

Laurie was the only person in the room he was interested in talking to, but he couldn't disturb them. He walked over to the sideboard where a vast array of drinks was laid out. He didn't for a second imagine that any of the bottles had been half empty when they'd been put out, but most of them were well on their way to being finished.

He poured himself some soda water and gritted his teeth. He did drink alcohol himself—in moderation. But he hated being around people that were drunk. Having an alcoholic as a father did that to you. When his father had succumbed to alcoholic liver disease a few years ago Callan had actually felt a sigh of relief. It was as if he could finally shake off that part of his life.

He looked around the room again. He was still finding it hard to get his head around the fact that he was surrounded by Angus's relatives—Angus's *family*. Twelve people who'd never had a single conversation with Angus McLean in their lives, one of whom could inherit the thing he'd held most dear. No matter which way he looked at it, it still didn't make sense.

But as much as he didn't want to admit it, he was noticing a few similarities in some of the guests. Two of the sons definitely looked like Angus—one so much so that Marion had commented it was like being around a younger version of him.

One of his daughters had identical blue twinkling eyes and a dimple in her right cheek. He couldn't see any physical similarities in any of the other relatives.

Family. Why hadn't Angus surrounded himself with these people?

He'd never really understood the whole 'Annick Castle should be kept in the family' ethos and had questioned Angus about it on more than one occasion.

But Angus had made comments about family on other continents. Callan's problem was he'd imagined that was some distant far-flung second cousin who'd eventually inherit the castle. He'd always had the thought at the back of his mind the said cousin wouldn't want to move continent and change their life, so would be happy with a financial offer instead.

But he hadn't imagined this. He hadn't imagined children.

It made it all so much more personal.

He watched as Laurie threw back her head and laughed, revealing the paler skin of her throat. It was the same hearty laugh he'd heard in the kitchen earlier. He liked it, but from the way Laurie had acted earlier today he guessed she didn't get to do it often enough.

It was as if the rest of the room just faded into oblivion whenever she was around. At least that was what happened in his head. This woman was invading every part of his senses. Even when he wasn't with her he was thinking about her, and when he *was* with her it was all he could do to keep his hands to himself.

What had she meant—*What if you can't find your place in life*? She was a lawyer living in London. She'd gone to Cambridge to do her degree. Surely she'd already found her place in life?

He knew she was successful—he'd Googled her.

There didn't seem to be any bad reports about her work and the case she'd quoted the other night—about winning a client half a million pounds—had been entirely true.

And why was Laurie Jenkins intriguing him so much? Why, when she'd looked as if she was about to burst into tears on the coastal steps, had he just wanted to put his arms around her?

Everything about her drew him in like a magnet. Her sparkiness, her ability to cut through the crap, but still have a hint of vulnerability about her. She spoke with love about her father, disappointment that he hadn't got to meet Angus McLean and she didn't try to hide her disdain that Angus hadn't met his children.

He couldn't blame her. And as much as that hurt him, part of him was pleased that she didn't tiptoe around him.

So what was it that was making Laurie Jenkins unhappy? Because he could see it. See it in her eyes when she had those fleeting moments off in a little world of her own. He could sense it in the little gaps in conversation as she tried to take in the beauty of Annick Castle and its surroundings.

All he knew was he liked it better when Laurie had a smile on her face and that twinkle in her brown eyes. He liked it better when he could hear the laughter that seemed to come from the very bottom of her soul. Just as she was now.

Her eyes met his across the room and she paused for a second, then lifted the glass of rosé she had in her hand towards him and gave him a little smile of acknowledgement.

'Dinner is served, everyone.' Robin's voice jolted him.

Callan caught Robin's steely glare clearly directed at

him. Darn it. He'd forgotten about flirting with Laurie and causing an argument. To be frank it was the last thing on his mind. Flirting with Laurie he could do in a heartbeat, but the argument? He really couldn't be bothered. He'd just need to remedy that at dinner.

Laurie walked straight over to him as they entered the dining room and reached the table, her green dress swishing around her with the sway of her hips as she moved. 'I met my aunt Mary,' she said. 'And she's fabulous. It's so strange how some of her mannerisms are the same as my dad's. Even though they never met. I can't believe it.'

She glanced at the table with the name settings and promptly reached over and swapped hers with someone else's so she could sit next to Callan. He raised his eyebrows at her but she shook her head and said quietly, 'Don't want to be stuck between those two—they've spent the whole evening arguing.'

He smiled and whispered in her ear. 'Don't you think you might be spoiling the activities of the night by doing that?'

She gave him a wink. 'I'm quite capable of sorting out my own activities for the night.'

He liked it. Her cheeky side that he'd only glimpsed on a few occasions. Most of the time Laurie Jenkins was obviously on her guard around him. And who could blame her? She'd walked into a weekend full of strangers. Some of whom were friendlier than others.

'I'll bet you are,' he replied. If he thought about that too long his imagination would run riot.

'Did you speak to any of your other relatives?'

She rolled her eyes. 'Yes, and no. Mary was great. Joe from Canada was great too.' She wiggled her hand

and pointed at the name cards she'd moved. 'I'm not so sure about Arnold and Audrey.'

Callan raised his eyebrows. 'Were they taking pictures while they spoke to you?'

Laurie nodded and moved to the side as her dinner plate was put in front of her, the feathers in her hairclip brushing against his face. 'Yes! And what's that little black book they continually scribble notes in? What on earth are they up to?'

She straightened up, leaving her perfume wafting around him. Something spicy, more sensual than the floral scent she'd been wearing today. It wound its way around him, prickling his senses.

He waited until all the other guests had been served, then picked up his knife and fork, trying to clear his head. Marion had got some help this evening and things certainly appeared to be going more smoothly. Like all the food that came out of her kitchen the chicken Caesar salad looked delicious. If only he could concentrate on it.

He gave her a smile. 'I hate to think what they're up to. You know I caught one of them in my rooms yesterday?'

'You're joking? Really?' Her mouth was hanging open. 'What on earth were they doing?'

He shrugged. 'I didn't wait to find out. I just shouted at them, told them my rooms were private and showed them out.'

Laurie shook her head. 'That's just ridiculous.'

'I think we should change seats.' The interruption was brisk. Callan heard the male voice in his ear and felt the hand pressing heavily on his shoulder. He resisted his first reaction. Although Craig had obviously had a bit too much to drink again this evening, Callan's

instruction card for this evening had told him to flirt
with Laurie's character and get into an argument with
Craig, or his alter ego Philippe Deveraux. He'd paid little enough attention to the Murder Mystery Weekend
without trying to wreck the one small part he'd been
asked to be involved in. He would give him the benefit
of the doubt. For five minutes only.

He stood up. 'I think you'll find Ms Clark has decided she wants my attention this evening.' He looked
down at the dinner table. 'I think you'll also find that
the entrées have already been served. Take a seat, Mr
Deveraux.'

From the corner of the room he could almost see
the Murder Mystery Weekend organiser clapping his
hands with glee.

Craig looked momentarily confused, then obviously
realised he was supposed to be in character. 'You've
monopolised Laurie—I mean, Ms Clark's attention all
day. It's time to let her mix with some other company.'

Callan wondered exactly how far he was supposed
to go with this. As Laurie lifted a glass of wine to her
rose-red lips he had an instant spark of inspiration. Or
maybe it was her scent that was still permeating his
skin? Whatever it was, he reached down and pulled
her to her feet.

After all, he had agreed to play along.

'I think you'll find Ms Clark is already spoken for,
Mr Deveraux. I suggest you take your seat.' And at
that, he bent down and brushed his lips next to Laurie's.

He felt her instantly stiffen in shock. He hadn't given
her any warning. He hadn't given it much thought himself. He was just playing along and it seemed like the
natural thing to do.

Bartholomew Grant would surely want to stake his claim on his girlfriend?

His hand was around her waist, supporting her as she leaned back a little. Across the table Auntie Mary burst into a round of applause.

Her lips were soft and pliable, but, oh, so inviting. He meant just to brush the slightest touch, but his lips caught the taste of wine from her and his gentle brush became instantly more intense. He felt her hands place on his chest. For an instant he wondered if she was going to push him away, but she didn't. Instead her hands rested lightly—just as they had done earlier that day on the steps.

Her scent wound its way around him, rich, sultry and exotic. It was truly intoxicating. If he didn't stop now, he never would.

Only the briefest few seconds had passed but he was conscious of the audience around them, and conscious of the fact if she did object, she might not want to do so in front of others.

He pulled back but felt her lips still connected with his. It was as if she didn't want the kiss to end. Had she felt the same connection he had? As their noses brushed against each other he opened his eyes. Her dark brown eyes were already open, staring straight at him.

She looked a little stunned. As if she didn't quite believe the kiss had happened. Her hand came up automatically to her lips, which seemed even redder, even fuller than before.

Her eyes still hadn't left his. All he could see was how chocolate-coloured they looked in this light and a definite dilation of her black pupils. His body reacted instantly—a natural response. Her hips were still pressed against his and her eyes widened, but the smile that appeared on her face was one of pure mischief.

As if on cue, one of the other guests stood up and started shouting—obviously all part of the activities. Callan stepped back, releasing his hand from around her back, and reluctantly sank back down into his seat. 'Sorry, if I took you by surprise,' he murmured.

She lifted her glass and took another sip of wine. There was a cheeky glint in her eyes. Laurie Jenkins wasn't upset or offended. Quite the opposite, in fact. It made the blood race through his body. 'Seems like it was surprises all round,' she said softly.

Up close the green dress was perfect for her skin tone and chestnut-coloured hair. Her cheeks glowed and the red gloss on her lips shined. The beads around the neckline caught the candlelight in the room and dazzled. She looked as if she belonged on a magazine cover, or an old-fashioned portrait. But here she was sitting at his side.

He wanted to sweep the rest of the guests away. He wanted to erase the Murder Mystery Weekend completely. He wanted the chance to get to know Angus McLean's granddaughter on his own, with no distractions.

But the long evening stretched ahead of them. He spoke solicitously to the other guests around him. He ate the steak placed in front of him. But all the while his eyes were watching her every move. Every sip of her wine. Every mouthful of delicious food.

Laurie knew it. And she was enjoying it. Seemed like teasing Callan was the order of the night.

The play-acting continued around them. Callan hadn't paid attention to a single part of it. He leaned over and whispered in her ear. 'Do you have any idea who the murderer is?'

She looked up through her darkened lashes. 'Of course I do, Callan. I've known from day one. But it wouldn't be fair if I told you. You have to guess for yourself.'

'But I don't need to guess. I don't have anything to inherit.' As soon as he said the words he could feel them wash over his body like an icy wave.

It kept coming back to this. One of the people at the table would inherit the place he called home.

Part of him wanted to behave like a child. Part of him wanted to scream and shout that even though DNA might say they were related to Angus, none of them had been his family.

He was Angus's family.

He'd been the one to make adjustments to Angus's rooms so it was easier for him to get about. He'd been the one who'd eventually had to help him in and out of the bath and shower. He'd been the one who'd tried to persuade him to eat and drink as he'd started to fade away. He was the one that had sat by his bedside while his chest rattled night after night.

He was the one that held his hand while he died.

He was the one that shed a mountain of tears.

Not one person in this room knew a single thing about Angus. They weren't family. No matter what the DNA said.

And it made him angry.

It made him angry to see relatives examining the antiques and trying to find their value on the Internet. It made him angry to hear them discussing market values. Had they no respect?

'Callan? Are you okay?'

Laurie was looking at him with those big brown eyes again.

It was so easy to get distracted by her. It was so easy to forget that she might actually be the person to inherit Annick Castle.

Why couldn't he have met her in a bar? Why couldn't he have just met her in the street?

Anywhere but here. And any set of circumstances but these.

Callan was usually good with people. He could usually tell the charlatans at fifty paces.

And there was definitely more to Laurie than met the eye.

But could it all just be a game?

He had to remember she could inherit this place. He had to push aside the way his pulse quickened when she entered a room, and raced when she shot him one of her winning smiles.

She was a lawyer. She was on the ball. And despite how uninterested she acted, she'd probably checked out all the legal implications before she got here. Was there a chance she was playing him?

A horrible sensation crept over his skin. Who better to tell her everything she'd need to know about Annick Castle than him? There was no one. No one else.

He'd noticed her talking to Frank Dalglish yesterday when she'd arrived, but Frank wasn't giving anything away. He was much too cautious for that.

And she'd just told him she already knew who the murderer was. At the end of the day that was all that was needed to inherit Annick Castle. He had no idea what would happen if more than one person got it right. Doubtless, Frank would have instructions for that scenario too.

He'd thought Laurie was genuinely interested in the place and the people. But maybe she was just killing time? Come Monday and the announcement of who would inherit, a totally new Laurie Jenkins might appear.

'Callan?' Laurie was tugging his arm now, concern written all over her face. 'What's wrong?' she hissed.

Robin was finishing a long diatribe at the end of the table. It seemed everyone had been listening but him. Some people were even taking notes. Had he given away a clue as to who the murderer was—or wasn't?

Truth was he didn't have a clue. About anything.

'Tomorrow night, more will be revealed as Annick Castle hosts its very own ball.' Robin's normally high-pitched voice was practically squeaking with excitement. 'Formal dress will be required—all available from our costume room, of course. I look forward to seeing you all there.'

Laurie gasped and put her hand up to her mouth. He could almost see all her childhood fantasies dancing about in her head.

Callan pushed his chair out and stood up. 'Sorry, Laurie, something's come up. We'll talk later.' He couldn't stand it. He couldn't stand the thought of all this merriment in Annick Castle.

Not when Angus McLean wasn't here to see it.

None of this seemed right. None of it at all.

CHAPTER SEVEN

THIS WAS, WITHOUT doubt, Laurie's favourite room in the whole castle.

She leaned back in the well-worn leather chair and turned the pages of the book in front of her. It was one of the classics—*Anne of Green Gables*—and she'd never had the chance to read it before.

Her feet were tucked under her and the sun was streaming through the multi-paned windows. She took a deep breath. She loved that. The inhalation of the smell of books and wood.

The library was one of the grandest rooms in the castle. Set in the base of one of the large drum towers, the circular bookshelves ran along the inside of the room on three different levels. There was even a sliding set of stairs that allowed you to reach the books on the top level. But the real pièce de résistance was the views all around the tower. Sitting in the middle of the room Laurie could see the sea on one side and the beautiful gardens on the other. The room was every book lover's dream.

The knock at the door startled her. She'd closed the door and turned the key in the lock in order to try and have a little privacy. Just her, the views, the books and a steaming-hot cup of lemon tea.

She shrank down into the chair. It was silly. No one could see through the door. No one could really know she was in here. Maybe if she just kept quiet they would go away?

But no. The knock was more insistent this time, sharper and louder. She cringed.

'Laurie? Laurie, I know you're in there. Can you open the door, please?'

She straightened in her chair. Callan.

After his abrupt departure last night she hadn't seen him again.

She had no idea what she'd said or done to upset him. One minute they'd been almost flirting, the next second he'd disappeared. She'd made excuses as soon as she could and tiptoed up the stairs to bed. She hadn't really been in the mood for socialising after that, her excitement about the ball all but crushed.

The knock came again. 'Laurie? Will you let me in, please?'

She sighed. Callan. This was his home. She couldn't really keep him locked out. He probably had a master key somewhere anyway.

She walked over and opened the door, not even waiting to speak to him but crossing back to her chair, sitting down and picking her book back up.

He was carrying a tray in his hands that he set down on one of the tables before turning and locking the door again.

The fresh smell of his aftershave drifted across the room. She was trying to make a point by ignoring him.

But ignoring a six-foot-four man who'd just locked them both in a room was kind of hard.

That and the smell of bacon rolls that was floating across the room towards her.

Her stomach betrayed her and rumbled loudly. A plate landed on her lap. 'Can I interest you in some breakfast?'

She looked up. 'Is this an apology?'

He hesitated. 'It's a peace offering.'

'Did you bring ketchup?'

He lifted the bottle and shook it.

She held out her hand. 'Let me think about it while I'm eating.'

He sat down in the chair next to her with his own bacon roll and a cup of tea.

He smiled. 'I see you went for the old lock-the-door-and-keep-them-out trick.'

She was mid-chew. 'Sometimes it feels as if there are just too many people about. I mean, I know it's a big place—it's a castle, for goodness' sake. And I can always lock myself away in my room. But it's weird—sometimes I feel I just need a little space. A little time out.'

He nodded. 'I get it. I do. And I get agitated every time I see a measuring tape.'

She burst out laughing. 'I know. They were doing it again last night as I was going to bed. What is the obsession with that and taking pictures with their phone?'

He shook his head. 'I'm trying hard not to think about it. I'm sure if I go online I'll probably see half the furniture and antiques in this castle listed for sale.'

She was horrified. 'Callan? Do you really think that?'

He shrugged his shoulders. 'What other reason is there? I take it they're sending the pictures to someone to get things valued first.'

She shook her head. 'That's horrible.'

'That's life.'

He said the words so simply. As if he was finally trying to accept the fact that in the next few days Annick Castle would have a new owner. She couldn't imagine how he must be feeling. If people came into her home and started doing things like that—well, she couldn't be held responsible for her actions.

Their eyes met and there it was again. That connection she felt every time she was around him. Her breath hitched in her throat. She didn't want to drag her eyes away from his. What she really wanted was to get to the bottom of what was happening here.

They hadn't discussed it. They hadn't acknowledged it. Surely this wasn't just in her head?

Callan looked away and she took a steadying breath, bringing herself back to reality. She had to think about normal things. Things that weren't Callan McGregor.

Focus. She took a sip of her tea and looked around the room. That bacon roll had really hit the mark. 'I still don't get it. How did Angus McLean manage to have so many children that no one knew about?' She stood up and started walking around the room.

There were a few pictures of Angus in here. One with him in his army uniform in World War II. Another with him looking a little older and standing in front of the sign for Ellis Island in New York.

Callan walked over next to her. 'I've been trying to figure it out—believe me.' He pointed to the picture of Angus in his uniform. 'I've worked out that Angus was stationed in a few places throughout World War II. He was down in England for a time, then over in Canada just after the war. I think that accounts for two—or maybe even three of his children.'

'What about this one—the New York picture?'

He nodded. 'He was apparently sent there after the

war to negotiate deals for the pharmaceutical company.'
He raised his eyebrows. 'That would be another child.'

'Wow. The guy certainly got about.' She wrinkled
her nose. 'What about my Irish relatives, then? Did he
go to Ireland?'

Callan shook his head. 'I don't think so. But Mary
said her mother was originally from Scotland and
moved over to Ireland as a young woman.'

'A young woman with a baby on board?'

Callan shrugged. 'It's just as much a mystery to me
as it is to you, Laurie.'

She couldn't help it. Talking about Angus McLean
just made her frustrated. 'But how? How could he have
six children and not bother with them?'

Callan slumped down into the chaise longue and put
his head in his hands. She was staring out at the gardens thinking what a beautiful environment this would
have been to be raised as a child. 'I've got some boxes of
paperwork—old things, to go through. Maybe I'll find
something there that will shed some light on all of this.'

'Should you be doing that?' Her lawyer head was
instantly slotting into place. Callan wasn't related to
Angus.

He looked up at her. His brow was wrinkled again
and the green of his eyes seemed to make her want to
step closer. He ran his fingers through his dark hair.
'That's just it, Laurie. I might not be family, but I was
named as Angus's next of kin. So, until all this is sorted,
I'm pretty sure I'm allowed to sort things out. At least
that's what Frank tells me.'

'Wow.' She sat down next to him and automatically
put her hand on his leg. It was meant to be friendly. It
was meant to be reassuring—or supportive. But it was
none of those things.

It was her fine fingers feeling his thick, muscular thighs. How did a guy with a desk job get thighs like that? And what did they look like when he wasn't fully dressed?

The wayward thoughts made her blush and her instant reaction was to pull her hand away. But Callan stopped that. He put his hand over hers and gave it a squeeze.

She could swear that right now a thousand butterflies were fluttering over the skin on her hand. She couldn't stop staring at him. Even though she wanted to.

She must look like some star-struck teenager, hardly appealing.

'Didn't you know he'd named you as his next of kin?' Great. Her voice had turned into an unintelligible squeak.

He shook his head. 'Maybe I should have guessed. As far as I knew, Angus didn't really have anyone else to name as next of kin. But we'd never talked about it. I found out as he became really unwell. Frank told me.'

'But he didn't tell you the rest?'

Callan raised his eyebrows. 'That he had six mystery children? Oh, no. Frank didn't mention that.'

'Have you asked him about it?'

'That's just it. I'm not entirely sure how much Frank knows. He said he's checked back and Angus's family have dealt with Ferguson and Dalglish solicitors for years. As far as he can see, Angus was contacted at various points in his life and made payments.'

'What kind of payments?'

'I guess it must have been some sort of child support. All of this happened before I was even born.'

Laurie shook her head. 'Isn't there anyone else you can ask?'

He lifted one hand and held it up. 'Like who? Angus was ninety-seven. All his friends and acquaintances are long since gone.'

It made sense. Whether she liked it or not.

But here was the thing. She wasn't really concentrating on why Angus McLean had only acknowledged his children financially. She was far too interested in the fact that their fingers were still intertwined on his thigh. Her ability to concentrate on anything else was fading fast.

Laurie pointed at one of the photos. Anything to try and keep herself distracted. 'I have to say, I can't really see any family resemblance between Angus and my dad. I can definitely see a resemblance with some of the other relatives. I notice lots of subtle similarities between Mary from Ireland and my dad. They're half-siblings. It's only natural. But it just feels really strange. It's almost like having a little part of him back.'

Her eyes instantly filled with tears. She hadn't meant to say that out loud. She didn't want to get emotional in front of Callan.

But Callan didn't hesitate. He stood up in front of her and pulled her up, enveloping her in his arms.

She'd never been the kind of girl to act like a shrinking violet. She'd never been the kind of girl that needed rescuing by some dashing guy.

But just that act of kindness—that feeling of someone putting their arms around her—made her breath hitch in her throat. How long had it been since this had happened?

It was so nice to feel the warmth of someone's body next to hers. It was so nice to be comforted—to not feel alone any more—that for a few seconds she went with her natural responses and just buried her head against his chest. She could hear his heart thudding in her ear through the thin cotton of his shirt. She could feel the rise and fall of his chest next to her skin.

It was warm. It was comforting. It was something else entirely.

What would it be like if this could be the sound she woke up to every morning?

Her brain was doing crazy things to her today. If he'd hovered around the edges of her dream the night before, then there was no denying that he'd had the starring role last night. It was funny the things an unexpected kiss could cause to pop up in a dream.

He pulled back a little. 'Are you okay?' Before she had a chance to speak, his hand came down and tilted her chin up towards him. 'I'm sorry, Laurie. I don't mean to be a bear. I've been so caught up in the fact that Annick Castle will soon be gone that I've not really thought about how all this might be affecting others—affecting you.'

There was real sincerity in his words, real concern in his eyes. She should feel comforted. She should feel reassured. But all she could feel was the blood currently buzzing around her body.

'Angus's funeral was only a month ago. And all this has come as a bolt out of the blue. I still wake up in the morning and it takes me a few seconds to remember that he's not here any more. It takes me a few seconds to realise I'm in the middle of all this. I feel as if I haven't really had a chance to say goodbye to him yet.'

His words stopped her blood buzzing. Stopped it dead.

She could relate. She could totally relate. Grieving was a completely individual process, but Callan's sounded similar to how she'd felt.

This time she reached out to him. And it was the most natural thing in the world for her. Her hand reached up and cradled the side of his cheek.

'I hated that. That few perfect seconds where everything was all right—just as you woke up. Then, that horrible sicky feeling you got as soon as you remembered. It was like that when my dad died. It took months for it to go away, Callan—and even now, ten years later, tiny little things—a headline in a paper, a picture of something, or someone saying something totally random to me—can bring it all flooding back. It doesn't go away. It never goes away.'

He hadn't moved. He was just watching her with his steady green eyes. He probably didn't realise it, but she could see the myriad emotions flitting behind his eyes.

She was starting to see a clearer picture now. She'd been making assumptions. But it was clear to her now that, in Callan's head, Angus had been his father figure. The person he'd relied on, the person he'd looked up to. How would she feel if she were in his shoes?

His arms were still around her waist. Her hand was still on his cheek. She almost felt frozen in time. She could stay like this for ever.

For the first time, in a long time, she felt as if she was home. Home in Callan McGregor's arms. The realisation was startling. It didn't matter how she felt about Angus McLean. She had to respect the fact that, for Callan, he'd been family.

'What happened to your own mum and dad, Callan?'

It was an intrusive question and she felt him bristle under her touch. But it was just the two of them, with no interruptions. If she wanted to understand Callan McGregor better, she had to ask.

His eyes fixed on hers and she could almost see his

mind jumble around trying to decide what to say. 'My mother was never really around. I'm not entirely sure what happened in their marriage. It was only me and my dad since I was a young boy. My dad would never talk about her.'

'Do you remember anything about her?'

'I remember the police coming to the door of our house when I was fifteen to tell my dad she was dead. I was more or less staying with Angus all the time by then, but I went home on occasion.'

'What happened to her?'

He shook his head. 'I didn't actually find out until years later. She had a mental health condition—schizophrenia. She'd taken an accidental overdose.'

'That's awful. Do you think she left because of her mental health problem?'

'No. I think she left because of my dad.'

His answer was instant. The next question was poised on her lips, but something told her not to ask it. Not to pry. Callan took several deep breaths. Even sharing that little part of himself had been hard for him.

He pulled back and she was surprised by how hurt she felt as he walked across the room, picking up the plates and cups and putting them on the tray.

She didn't want him to leave. She wanted him to stay here, with her. And that made her insides curl up in confusion.

'I'll take these back to the kitchen. Are you baking today?'

The conversation was clearly over. At least that part of it was.

She took a deep breath and smiled. 'I think Marion has me lined up to make a raspberry cheesecake and some more gingerbread.'

'You could leave the staff to it, you know.'

'No. I couldn't. I like being in the kitchen. Next to this room—' she held out her arms '—it's the place I feel most at home.'

She hadn't meant to say it like that. She hadn't meant to imply that she was thinking of this place as home. Because she wasn't. Really she wasn't. Her mind was getting jumbled with the huge range of emotions Annick Castle was conjuring up for her. And something flickered across his face. A look of discomfort, that was quickly replaced by a quick nod of the head.

'I'm going to go for another walk later—back around the grounds. Or, do you want me to help you with Angus's boxes?' It was a measured question. It was her trying to offer a hand of friendship.

Was she really comfortable making that offer? Who was she to go through Angus's things? Grandfather or not, she hadn't known him and never would. Not the way Callan had.

But she'd seen the look in Callan's eyes earlier. She'd seen how hurt he was, how he was struggling with his bereavement. And while she didn't have any loyalty to Angus, she did have a burning desire to support Callan.

She'd been there. She knew how hard this was. Her mother had fallen to pieces and if it hadn't been for her university friends, she would have too. Having people around to support you made all the difference.

Callan shook his head. 'I'll be fine. I probably won't get much done today. I have to make some calls and answer some emails for the day job.'

She smiled. 'You mean you need to Blether?'

He laughed. 'Absolutely. I need to Blether.'

She took a deep breath. This was difficult. She was struggling with this. She didn't really know who Callan

McGregor was. But he'd shared a little of himself with her today. He'd held her at the bottom of the cliff steps. He'd kissed her last night. He'd hugged her today. This was the closest she'd got to a man in months. And he set every nerve in her body on fire. There was something between them. For her, there were blurred lines all over the place. She just wasn't sure what this was.

'Well, you know where I'll be if you're looking for me.' Her eyes fixed on his.

And he held her gaze. For longer than ever before. She could practically hear the air in the room sizzle between them. Was something else going to happen?

He tore his gaze away and fixed a smile on his face. 'Yes, I do. Thanks, Laurie.' Then he picked up the tray and disappeared down the corridor.

She didn't know whether to laugh or cry.

At first glance the kitchen seemed empty and Laurie walked across the room and started washing her hands at one of the Belfast sinks. It only took her a few minutes to collect all the ingredients from the larder, including the fresh raspberries that had been picked from the castle gardens this morning. She breathed in deeply; they smelled gorgeous.

She lifted the large glass mixing bowl and whisk out from the cupboard at her feet and started adding her ingredients for the cheesecake. Marion appeared at her elbow. 'Hi, Laurie, are you sure you're still happy to help?'

She jumped about a foot in the air. 'Where on earth did you come from, Marion? I was sure there was no one else in here.'

Marion laughed and tapped the side of her nose. 'I'm

like the genie in the lamp. I know all the hiding places around this kitchen.'

Laurie stared at her for a few seconds, trying to work out if she was joking or not.

Marion smiled. 'I was in the pantry. You were so deep in concentration that you didn't notice me when I came out. What are you fretting about? Is it about the castle?'

Laurie set down the wooden spoon she held in her hand. 'No. It's not about the castle. Not at all.' She looked around her. 'But that's probably what I should be worrying about, isn't it?'

'Aha.'

'Aha? What does that mean?' Marion was giving her a strange kind of smile as she started to collect her own set of ingredients.

'It means I always know what's going on in this place.'

'Well, I don't. Why don't you share it with me?'

Marion was practically chuckling. 'I bet it was Callan that was on your mind.'

Her cheeks flushed instantly. The woman was a mind reader. 'Why do you think that?' Had people noticed they'd been spending time together?

'Because I've been here a long time. I notice things. I particularly notice things when it comes to Callan.' Her voice had a little protective edge to it. 'I heard about the kiss,' she added.

'How long have you been here, Marion?' Curiosity was piquing her interest, particularly now Callan had revealed a little part of himself to her.

'More than forty years.' She said the figure with pride.

'And you haven't thought about retiring?' She knew

instantly it had been the wrong thing to say as Marion bristled.

'I have no intention of retiring,' she said stiffly. 'As long as I can still do my job I'll be here.'

'Of course. I didn't mean anything by it, Marion. Forty years is a long time.' She started mixing the ingredients in her bowl. 'You must have been here when Callan first appeared,' she added carefully.

Marion's keen eyes locked with hers. 'What did he tell you?'

'He told me Angus found him as a young boy. He told me about his mother. And about the fact Angus named him as next of kin.'

Marion raised her eyebrows. 'He told you quite a lot, didn't he?' Her eyes swept up and down the length of Laurie. 'He doesn't usually share much about himself.' She stopped, then added, 'But then he doesn't usually kiss girls in front of a room full of strangers.'

Laurie gave a little smile. 'I get that.'

She mixed slowly. Had she been misleading about how much Callan had told her? She was itching to know more, but she didn't want to come right out and ask.

After a few guarded seconds Marion started to speak, her eyes fixed on the wall. She'd obviously drifted off into some past memory. 'I'll never forget that night for as long as I live. When Angus came in here with Callan bundled up in his arms, freezing and soaking wet after hiding from his brute of a father.' She shook her head. 'We made a pact.'

Laurie felt her heart start to race. Did she really want to know this? Should she be upfront and tell her Callan hadn't told her this part? But the truth was she did want to know this. She wanted to understand why Callan was so fiercely loyal to Angus. She wanted to try and understand the connection between the two men.

'All of us. Me, Angus and Bert. We were the only three here that late at night. But we promised there would always be a place here for Callan. There would always be somewhere safe he could come where people would be concerned about him.' Her voice drifted off a little, and Laurie could see the tears forming in her eyes. 'Where people could show him that they cared what happened to him.'

She looked out of the window. 'Social services weren't the same as they are nowadays. Children were left in conditions they shouldn't be. Everyone knew that.' She turned to face Laurie. 'Do you know after his drunken rage his father didn't even know that Callan had gone? It was two days before he turned up here looking for him.' Laurie could hear the disgust in her voice. 'We all knew that his mother was gone. But no one really knew why. We didn't know about the schizophrenia then.' She waved her hand. 'That all came much later.' She shook her head. 'We guess that his father got worse after his mother left. But we don't know that for sure. Maybe his father's drinking contributed towards his mother's mental health condition? All I know is, that must have been a terrible environment for a wee boy to be in.'

Laurie was shocked. No wonder Callan only shared little pieces of himself. What had he been subjected to at home?

Marion hadn't said the words but the implication about his father being a drunk was clear. She couldn't help the automatic shiver that ran down her spine. No child should be subjected to a life like that.

Her eyes fixed on the contents of the bowl as she

stirred. She could feel the tears prickling in her eyes. Her natural thoughts were to compare Callan's upbringing with her own.

She'd had a mum and dad who had loved her dearly and doted on her. Callan's life had been nothing like that. And no matter what her thoughts about Angus McLean, thank goodness he'd recognised a child in need and had reached out to him.

She felt a hand resting on her back. Marion's. 'I know,' came the quiet words of understanding. Marion could obviously see the whole host of emotions flitting across her face.

She waited a few minutes, lost in her thoughts. 'Marion, if you've been here that long, tell me about my grandfather. Tell me why he didn't acknowledge his children.'

She couldn't stop this. It played on her mind constantly. She already knew Callan's thoughts on all of this. Maybe Marion could offer better insight?

Marion shrugged her shoulders. 'I'm not sure, Laurie. It seems odd. But Angus McLean's life wasn't entirely easy. He was much more involved in the pharmaceutical business than his colleagues thought. He would spend hours in the laboratories. He was involved in all the developmental work. Lots of people just thought Angus dealt only with contracts and sales—but that wasn't true at all.'

There was something strange about her words. Something Laurie couldn't quite put her finger on.

'But lots of people have difficult jobs, Marion. That doesn't stop them keeping in contact with their kids.'

Marion's lips pressed firmly together. 'Things aren't always what they seem, Laurie. And remember, times have changed rapidly over the last few years. Angus did what he thought was right for his children.'

Money. Marion was talking about money. So, she wasn't wrong about this vibe. There was definitely something that Marion wasn't telling her.

'All the money in the world doesn't make up for not having your dad when you need him, Marion. I can't imagine not having my dad there. I'm a grown adult now, and I still struggle with the fact I can't pick up the phone and speak to him every day.'

'I understand that, Laurie, really I do. But everyone's life circumstances are different. That's all I'm saying.' She picked up the mixture she'd been preparing and started dividing it into tins. It was clear that from her perspective the conversation was over.

Laurie followed suit. It only took a few minutes to finish whisking the cheesecake and put it in the fridge to set. The gingerbreads were ready for the oven and now all she had to do was wait.

'Have you finished up?'

She nodded. 'Is there something else you need a hand with?'

Marion shook her head. 'We're all ready for the ball tonight. The turkey and the beef joints are in the oven. The veg are all prepared. And I've got a few girls coming in from the village to help serve again.'

'What else is happening tonight?'

Marion rolled her eyes. 'I have no idea. I do know that there's a string quartet coming. They are expected to arrive in the next few hours. As for the rest of Robin's plans? Your guess is as good as mine.' She brushed her hands together and glanced over at the ovens. 'If you're finished up I'll be happy to take everything out of the oven for you.'

Laurie smiled. 'Has Callan been nagging you about me being in the kitchen?'

Marion laughed. 'Don't you worry about Callan nagging me. I've been dealing with that for years.'

Laurie took off her apron and hung it back up. 'I'd quite like to go for a walk around the grounds before tonight—you know, to clear my head.'

Marion nodded and looked at her carefully. 'We all need to do that sometimes. Even Callan.'

Her feet had already carried her to the door but she turned as Marion spoke again. 'Laurie—just so you know. That's the first time I've ever known Callan to be so...' she was obviously searching for the right word '...affectionate in public.'

Laurie's heart gave a little leap. She gave Marion a little smile and fled out of the door. Annick Castle was going to land her in a whole heap of trouble.

CHAPTER EIGHT

CALLAN CHECKED THE records one more time. Annick
Castle was in trouble. Lots of trouble. It was losing
money like a leaky sieve. In a few weeks' time he and
Frank would have to hand over all this information to
the new owner. What would they think? Because right
now, all paths seemed to lead to the fact that Angus
McLean hadn't been managing at all.

He could see what the problems were. The biggest,
and most obvious, was that Annick Castle had no income. The gas and electricity bills had quadrupled in
the last ten years, but, then again, so had every family's in the country.

Annick Castle wasn't environmentally friendly. It
was a draughty old girl, in rapid need of some maintenance. But even then his hands were tied. There were
no modern windows to keep the freezing winter tem-
peratures out, no proper insulation, no modern heating
or modern appliances. The whole place really needed to
be rewired. But rewiring was more than a little expensive, and the damage that would be incurred rewiring a
building like this would be astronomical. The heritage
people would have a fit. As for the roof…

He hadn't even had a chance to glance at Angus's
boxes yet. All his time had been taken up with trying

to sort out the accounts. It wasn't just the castle. The family fortune had been damaged by the stock-market crash, some unlucky investments and poor interest rates. He was going to have to try and find some solutions—fast.

He closed the computer program and grabbed his jacket. The walls were starting to close in around him. He needed some fresh air and that was one thing Annick Castle had in abundance. It was time to find Laurie. She was the only person around here he wanted to spend any time with.

Part of him felt a little guilty that he didn't want to spend more time around Angus's children or grandchildren. Truth was, some of them he didn't even like.

And a tiny part of him said why should he spend time with people that Angus hadn't? And until he got to the bottom of that he wouldn't be able to understand it.

But Laurie was different. She wasn't constantly assessing the value of the castle. She wasn't aligning herself with estate agents as he'd heard one of Angus's sons doing yesterday.

Laurie was the only one of Angus's relatives he felt a connection to. He couldn't understand it. He couldn't understand it at all, but after several hours surrounded by computers, paperwork and figures he found himself craving her company again.

It would be so much easier if he could put Laurie Jenkins in a box where she wasn't a possible inheritor of the castle, and she wasn't Angus McLean's granddaughter. Then maybe he would be free to try and figure out what it was about her that drew him like a moth to a flame.

The scent of gingerbread had drawn him to the kitchen. But the evidence of her baking was sitting on two wire cooling trays with no sign of Laurie at all.

He walked out into the grounds. His first guess had been the gazebo next to the swan pond. He'd noticed the gleam in her eyes when she'd first seen it and the whole host of other thoughts that was obviously flitting around her mind. But even from the top of the steps leading to the lowered gardens it was clear she was nowhere in sight.

His steps carried him onwards, quickening as his brain went into overdrive. *Please don't let her have headed to the caves.* It was odd. He hadn't given a second thought to any of the other relatives injuring themselves on the cliff-side stairs—even though they would probably sue Annick Castle—his only thought was for Laurie. The thought of her on those stairs sent a shudder down his spine. He really needed to see about something more substantial than a piece of rope to block them off.

He rounded the drum tower and stopped dead.

There she was. A yellow hard hat perched precariously on her head as she skirted around the edges of the round icehouse. She hesitated at the entrance, glancing at the roof, then in the blink of an eye she disappeared inside.

He resisted the temptation to shout at her, striding over and grabbing one of the other hard hats outside and jamming it on his head. He'd warned her about this place. It wasn't safe. Part of the roof had already fallen in, and other parts looked distinctly dangerous.

He stuck his head inside. It was much darker in here. The only window was boarded up and there was no lighting, no electricity. The place hadn't been used in over one hundred years.

'Laurie? What are you doing?'

She was standing in the middle of the icehouse, looking up at the part of the ceiling that had fallen in. Could she be any more dangerous?

'I just wanted to get a feel for the place, Callan. You talked about the history of the caves, but what about the history of this place?'

He folded his arms across his chest. 'It was an ice-house. It stored ice that was brought up from the lake. It took the ice to the kitchen. End of.'

She walked over towards him. Even in this dim light he could see the sparkle in her eyes. Her voice changed timbre. 'Callan McGregor, are you using your stern voice on me?'

'Do I need to?' His response was instant because Laurie Jenkins had gone from the middle of the room to directly under his nose. Didn't she realise what those big brown eyes did to the men around her? Had this woman no idea of the electricity she could spark with those few words? She was flirting with him. She was definitely flirting.

'Hmm…' She was looking up at him through half-closed lids. In another life he'd have called them come-to-bed eyes. But Laurie didn't seem the type.

But type or not, her very presence was having instant effects on his body.

She gave a shiver and he frowned. 'Are you cold, Laurie?'

Why hadn't he even considered that? He'd picked her up from the railway station; he knew she'd travelled light. He was wearing a big thick parka, the one he always used for tramping around the grounds of Annick Castle. But Laurie only had on a light summer jacket. It might be nearing the end of summer, but she obviously hadn't banked on the Scottish coastal winds.

'Isn't it weird? How even though this place hasn't

been used in years, it's just still so…cold.' She gave a shudder and wrapped her arms around herself.

Callan moved closer, opening his jacket and putting one arm around her shoulders. He couldn't quite fit her inside, but she slid her arm behind his waist and pressed her body up next to his.

He tried to focus. 'What are you doing in here anyway?'

She smiled. 'It's this place. I like it. I love the shape—the circular building is gorgeous. And it's bigger than you'd expect. Why didn't Angus do something with this? Turn it into something else?'

Callan shook his head. 'Like what? He's already got two unused sets of stables, a gazebo, an orangery, an old water house, an old gas house, and—' he gestured out beyond the doors '—a whole set of mystery caves.'

But Laurie was deep in thought, her mind obviously taking her off into her own world. 'This could be a gorgeous coffee shop,' she murmured, 'right next to the castle, with views over the sea and over the gardens if this place had windows in it. It could make a fortune.'

The words sent prickles over his skin. Did Laurie know more about Annick Castle than she was letting on?

But she was obviously wrapped up in her own ideas. 'Can't you see it, Callan?' She held her arms out. 'Just think, wooden tables and chairs with red and white checked tablecloths. A whole variety of teas.' She pointed to the other side of the round house. 'There could be a whole circular serving area over here and one of those gorgeous coffee machines.' Her eyes were lit up. 'I can practically smell the different kinds of scones, gingerbread, sponges and chocolate buns. You could serve local produce from the neighbouring farms, maybe even from the castle gardens?' She was walking around, obviously seeing the whole thing in her head. 'It could be great. Two kinds of homemade soup every day and a different variety of scone.' She came back over and slid her arm around his waist again.

He could feel himself bristle. 'What's the point? The castle isn't open to the public. Who would come to a coffee shop?'

'But maybe it should be.' Her eyes looked up and met his.

He drew in a sharp breath. Her words put him instantly on the defensive.

And Laurie seemed to sense that, but she waved her hand. 'Oh, don't get all crabbit with me, Callan. I'll be the first person to admit I know nothing about Annick Castle. But I'm not blind. I can see buildings lying in ruins. I can see the tiles and slates off the roof. That can't be safe. That can't be good for the castle. Don't you want to see things restored? Wouldn't you like it if that gorgeous pagoda that used to house birds down at the swan pond could be rebuilt? You already told me the upper floor used to be a teahouse. It seems like somebody, somewhere, at one time thought it was a good idea.'

He tried not to be defensive. He tried not to take it as a criticism. But the thought of a whole bunch of strangers tramping around Annick Castle didn't fill him with joy.

He had to be rational about this. He had to put his business head on and think with his head and not his heart. 'Do you think people would want to come and see around Annick Castle?' There were a hundred little thoughts currently sparking around his brain. He'd only ever thought of Annick Castle as a home. He'd never even considered anything else. And deep down he knew Angus wouldn't approve of having strangers on his property. But the sad fact was that times had changed, the comfortable nest egg the family used to have was gone, and so was Angus. It was certainly something that the new owner could look into.

'Why ever not? There's another castle about a hundred miles down the coast that's open to the public. They have a kids' playground, a teahouse, an old bookshop and stables too. Why couldn't Annick Castle be like that?'

He could feel the hackles go up on the back of his neck, instantly suspicious of her wider knowledge. 'How do you know that?' His voice was low. It was practically a growl. But Callan McGregor couldn't hide how he felt about things. Had she been planning this all along? He hated feeling as if he'd been duped.

Her arm slid out from around his waist. She folded her arms and stood in front of him. All of a sudden the dim light in the icehouse didn't seem tranquil or romantic, it felt oppressive.

'I know because I looked it up on the Internet, Callan. What did you think? That I'd planned all this before I got here?'

The words stuck in his throat. He was being ridiculous. He *knew* he was being ridiculous. He just couldn't help it. As soon as anyone started making suggestions about Annick Castle he could virtually feel his own portcullis slide down in front of him.

The protection of Annick Castle lay at the very essence of his heart and soul. He couldn't see past it. He couldn't see around it.

And being around Laurie just seemed to heighten every emotion that he felt. Magnify it ten times over.

He seemed to seesaw between high as a kite and lower than the belly of a snake all in the blink of an eye.

Laurie was annoyed. It was practically emanating from her pores. And boy was she beautiful when she was angry. Her dark eyes flashed, 'Get over yourself, Callan. I *get* that you love this place. I *get* that it means everything to you. But if you find yourself unable to have a rational, reasonable conversation about the place then I've got to ask the question if you're the right person to be custodian of this place in the first place. I'm making one tiny suggestion.' She held up her finger and thumb with the minimum of space between them. 'That's all. The very least you can do is listen.'

'It's not one tiny suggestion, Laurie.' He held up his finger and thumb too, but then he held his arms open wide. 'This is the kind of suggestion you're making. Annick Castle hasn't been open to the public since its first building was put up in the fifteen-hundreds. That's more than five hundred years of history.'

She stepped closer, gritting her teeth. 'Exactly. Five hundred years of history that should be shared with others.'

Their faces were inches apart. Even in this dim light he could see the normally hidden tiny freckles that were scattered across her nose. He didn't even want to start thinking about those brown eyes again. In years gone by Laurie Jenkins would probably have been labelled an enchantress with eyes like those.

And she was obviously determined to get her point across. 'Don't you think visitors would love to know about the links with Mary Queen of Scots? Don't you think there must be dozens of little boys who'd want to explore the smuggler's caves and think about pirates? Don't you think there must be a hundred crazy women like me who'd love a chance to sit in the gazebo that matches the one in *The Sound of Music* and dream their afternoon away?'

He could see the passion in her eyes. Passion in them for Annick Castle and what it represented and he couldn't help but smile.

'You've really got it bad for that gazebo, haven't you?'

His words broke the tension in the air between them in an instant.

Her face broke into a smile too and she rolled her eyes. 'You have *no* idea how much I love that gazebo.'

'Every little girl's dream?'

'Oh, *way* more than that.'

'Better than the castle double staircase?'

She grinned. 'Yip. Even better than the castle staircase.' She moved back towards him. 'Why is it that we always head towards a fight? What is it I do that upsets you so much?'

'I keep asking myself the same question.' His voice had deepened; it was quieter—a virtual whisper. The words seemed to echo around the circular building.

She edged a little closer and he found himself doing the same thing. Any second now he could reach out and touch her. Touch the soft skin of her face, run his fingers through her loose curls. Or just grab her with both hands and pull her body next to his.

Her sultry perfume was winding its way around him again—like the Pied Piper's music had lured the children of Hamelin. He couldn't control it.

He couldn't help the grin spreading across his face.

She blinked, her long dark eyelashes brushing against his lowered head. It was torture. 'And have you found the answer yet, Callan?'

Even the way she said his name sent shivers down his spine. His hands reached up and cradled her hips. 'It's as much a mystery to me as it is to you. Maybe we're just two people with a lot at stake.'

She squeezed her eyes shut. 'Not the answer I was looking for.'

It wasn't the answer he'd wanted to say either. But he couldn't articulate what he really wanted to say. He couldn't sort it out in his head. And until he did that, how could he say anything?

He couldn't tell her that she was driving him crazy. He couldn't tell her that he hadn't been able to sleep since he'd kissed her. He *definitely* couldn't tell her what she'd been doing in the five minutes' worth of dreams he'd had last night.

And no matter how much his body was reacting around Laurie, no matter how much he felt drawn to her. No matter how much he was attracted to her both physically and emotionally, he still had the tiniest doubts in his head. Doubts placed there by his love of Annick Castle. And until that was resolved he couldn't feel free to make any kind of other decision.

'It's the best I can do right now.'

She stepped backwards and gave him a gentle smile. 'I know, Callan, I'm finding this just as hard as you are. You aren't the only person with something at stake.'

She gave him a wink, but it wasn't the playful kind of wink he'd experienced from Laurie before. This was different. It was more resigned. Almost sad.

She looked out of the doors, her eyes drifting over towards the crashing waves. 'There's something about this place, Callan. I can't tell you what it is. I can't put my finger on it. But Annick Castle, it just draws you in and holds you here.'

He understood. He understood completely. He always had, right from the first time he'd stayed here. Was it the dream of living in a castle, or was it just the austerity of the building, the magic of the surroundings?

And this was it. This was the tiny thing that kept creeping up on him. It was the long tendrils of jealousy that flickered around him when someone else said those words. When Annick Castle had that effect on *them*.

Her words tailed off. 'But is it the castle…' then her dark eyes fixed on his again and a jolt shot through him '…or is it you?'

She disappeared out of the door before he could reply.

His skin prickled. It didn't matter what his selfish thoughts were. Laurie Jenkins had just laid it on the line.

Big time.

She'd only lain down on the bed for a few minutes. But it seemed as if the comfortable mattress and high thread-count sheets had lulled her off into a deep sleep. As her eyes flickered open the sun was lowering in the sky outside her window. It wouldn't be sunset for a few hours yet but she'd slept much later than she'd expected.

A wave of panic swept over her as she glanced at her watch. She jumped from the bed and ran to the door. The ball was tonight and she had nothing to wear. She hadn't even given it a thought; she'd been too busy baking in the kitchen and spending time with Callan. The costume room was on the floor underneath and her feet thudded heavily down the stairs. She'd always managed to find something suitable before; she would just have to grab the first thing that fitted.

Robin was flapping around the room. Flapping. It was the most accurate expression for him. 'There you are! Where have you been? You're the only person who hasn't chosen a costume.'

'Sorry, Robin, I fell asleep. I'll just take whatever you think is appropriate.'

He pointed to the wall. 'I'd already picked out a few possibilities for you.'

There were four dresses hanging from part of the coving on the wall. Should he really be doing that? Wouldn't that damage the paintwork? She shuddered to think.

The costume room was packed full of colourful clothes, all hanging in rails by gender and size. Some women would absolutely adore this, but Laurie had never been the kind to spend hours mooning over clothes. She appreciated beautiful things, but didn't want to spend the time having to find them. The last two dresses she'd had from this room Robin had recommended to her.

She walked over to the four dresses. All beautiful. All full-length. She wasn't quite as elegant as others might think. There was a high possibility of her catching her feet in these dresses and tumbling down the curved staircase. That would make for an interesting ball.

She reached out and touched one. There was a variety of colours. Gem colours. Ruby red, emerald green, sapphire blue and silver. All sparkling. All gorgeous.

She wrapped her arms around herself and turned to face Robin.

'What's wrong?' he demanded. 'Don't you like them?'

She screwed up her face; she really didn't want to hurt his feelings. She hesitated before speaking. 'I think they're all beautiful. But I'm worried about wearing something full-length. It just isn't me. There's a strong likelihood I'll fall over and ruin them.'

He scowled and touched the red one. 'It's a ball, Laurie. You're supposed to wear something full-length—you know, a *ball* gown. I thought you might go for this one. It's almost identical to the dress the girl is wearing in the picture at the top of the stairs.'

He was getting tetchy. She looked again. It was. It was perfect. A little more old-fashioned than the others but almost a perfect replica. Why couldn't she imagine herself wearing it? It was so thoughtful that Robin had tried to take in the surroundings. But she just couldn't picture herself walking down the stairs in that dress. If there were ghosts in this castle they'd probably push her down in disgust at her attempts to look regal.

She shook her head. 'I'm sorry, Robin. I just don't think they're right for me.'

He let out a loud sigh and threw up his hands. 'Okay then, Laurie. What is it? What is the dress you see in your dreams?'

She laughed. 'It depends entirely what I'm dreaming about.'

'Pfft.' He waved his hand in disgust and touched his finger to the side of her forehead. 'What is it, Laurie? What's the one that you keep in here?' Then his finger came down and pressed on her chest bone. 'Or more importantly, what's the one you keep in here?'

She flinched. 'It's the dress Liesl wore in *The Sound of Music*.' The words came straight out without a second thought.

'No!' He was excited, and obviously a little surprised. He didn't even have to ask what dress she was referring to as he clearly already knew. He flung his arms around her. 'Oh, Laurie, you are going to love me!'

He disappeared in a flurry, snaking amongst the rails of clothing.

She caught her breath; he couldn't have what she was looking for—could he? She stood on her tiptoes. Robin had disappeared from sight. She'd no idea where he'd disappeared to, then she heard an exclamation of pure pleasure. 'I've got it!'

He snaked his way back through to her, a pale pink dress held in a plastic cover in his hands. Her heart started to beat a little faster and she was sure her eyes must have been as wide as saucers. 'No. You can't have.'

'I can.' He swept the dress past her in pleasure, holding it up under the light. 'A genuine, replica Liesl dress.' She'd never seen him look so pleased with himself.

Laurie could hardly contain her excitement. She reached out her hands to touch the dress, then snatched them back again.

Robin lifted his eyebrows; it was almost as if he understood. He slipped the dress out of its protective cover and held the hanger in one hand and let the dress rest on his forearm.

It was the palest pink chiffon, as light as a whisper. Elbow-length chiffon sleeves, a tiny bow in the middle of the gathered bodice, and a knee-length swishy skirt. It was exactly the same as the dress in the film.

There were no sequins. No floor-length glamour. No jewels. But beauty was in the eye of the beholder and it was the most perfect dress she'd ever seen.

The colour was so pale. On so many other women the colour would completely wash them out. But Laurie had slightly sallow skin, and with her dark eyes and long brunette curls there was no doubt it would suit her to perfection.

'Will it fit me?' She was almost too scared to ask.

She had curves. She certainly wasn't the tiny frame of the actress who'd played Liesl in the film.

Robin nodded with pride. 'I promise, it will be a perfect fit.'

She held out her hands. She had to touch it and she couldn't wait to try it on.

Her feet flew up the stairs even quicker than she'd come down. She slammed the door behind her and stripped off her clothes in an instant, sliding her arms through the delicate material.

It fell over her head as light as a feather. Her eyes were closed and she spun around to where the full-length mirror was, praying inside her head that it would look okay.

She opened her eyes. It looked more than okay. It was more perfect than she could have imagined. It was almost as if it had been made especially for her.

She glanced at her watch. She'd only half an hour to get ready. She pulled the dress over her head again and switched on the shower. It only took her a few minutes to put her long hair in sticky rollers. There was a knock at the door.

She panicked and grabbed a towel to hold in front of herself in her undressed state. She opened the door just a crack. It was Robin, holding two pairs of shoes in his hands.

He rolled his eyes at her. 'You dashed off so quickly I didn't have time to give you some shoes. Take your pick.' He held up the first pair. 'Nude shoes—' then held up the other '—or gold sparkly sandals. Not strictly Liesl,' he whispered, 'but aren't they gorgeous?'

He set them on the floor just outside her door. 'I'll leave them here.' He sashayed back down the corridor as she clutched at her towel and grabbed the shoes.

She could hear the strains of music downstairs. The string quartet had obviously arrived and was setting up. Robin had also left her a card with her instructions for her character this evening. She hadn't even glanced at it and it made her feel guilty. He'd obviously just pushed the boat out to give her what she wanted. The least she could do was try and fulfil her duties for this evening.

But the shower was calling and time was ticking onwards. She didn't want to be late.

She got ready in double-quick time, pulling out her rollers at the last possible second and letting her curls tumble around her shoulders. At the last minute she fastened her gold locket around her neck, giving it a little kiss. 'You've no idea what's going on, Dad,' she whispered. 'I just hope you'd approve.'

She slipped one foot into one of the nude shoes and pulled the straps of one of the gold sandals over the other. A quick glimpse in the full-length mirror told her everything she wanted to know.

The nude shoes were abandoned and the straps on the sandals quickly fastened into place. A little brush of eye shadow and mascara and some rose-coloured lipstick and she was ready.

She read over the instructions on the card once more. She really didn't have much to do this evening. A simple conversation with one of the other guests, which would obviously lead them to think her a suspect. Robin was planting red herrings all over the place.

She didn't really care. It wasn't important. Not to her.

She wanted to enjoy herself. She wanted to enjoy spending the evening in Annick Castle when it would look at its finest. Where she could imagine bygone eras and what the nights had been like for the people who used to be residents here.

Where she could spend some more time with Callan McGregor.

Where she could try and figure out what was going on in her head whenever she was around him.

Tiny pieces were fitting into place. Callan had opened up a little, but after Marion's telling comments she finally felt as if she could start to appreciate the loyalty he felt towards Angus McLean.

It was exactly the same as the loyalty she felt towards her father. She had one final glance out of the window towards the sea and then walked across the room, pulling the door closed behind her.

She walked along the corridor. How would she feel about going back to her flat in London? Being surrounded by the compressed air of the city again instead of the fresh coastal winds of the Scottish Highlands?

Her feet carried her along the corridor. One foot in front of the other.

One foot in front of the other. Much as her life had been for the last eight years. But was that enough? Didn't she want more out of life?

Her eyes had been opened in the last few days to a whole host of possibilities—both personal and professional.

How would it feel to get up every morning feeling excited about going to work? How would it feel to be doing something else entirely?

She reached the top of the curved stairways and looked down to the magnificent hallway. Which set of stairs, one or the other? And how did you choose?

She glanced at the red-dressed woman in the portrait at the top of the stairs. Her haughty expression hadn't changed. But there was more. Something else when you looked a little closer. Something in her eyes. Something pleading. Was it desperation?

There was a shift in her peripheral vision.

Callan. He was waiting at the bottom of the stairs for her. It didn't matter which set of stairs she walked down. The outcome would be the same.

It was almost as if someone had turned on a glistening chandelier in her head.

The last few days had been the oddest of her life.

Relief. That was what she'd felt as soon as she'd set foot in Annick Castle.

No tension headaches. No aching joints or sleepless nights. Her stomach coiled at the realisation that was coming over her.

She couldn't go back. She couldn't go back to Bertram and Bain. No matter what happened here.

Just the recognition in her brain felt like a huge weight off her shoulders. The logistics of how she might do that were too complicated for her to figure out herself. She had ongoing cases—responsibilities to clients. It was only fair that she work a period of notice.

The fear of stepping outside her ordered life was terrifying. She really needed to speak to someone about it. But who? Most of her friends were in the profession, and they would be horrified and try to talk her out of it.

Callan. He was the only person she could talk to about it.

He was the only person she wanted to talk to about this.

And there he was—waiting for her. Everything about this just seemed right.

She took the first step.

CHAPTER NINE

CALLAN WAS AGITATED. He'd spent the last five minutes walking about the drawing room, dining room and kitchen. Searching everywhere for Laurie, but she wasn't here yet.

Everyone else seemed to be accounted for. Most were sipping drinks and listening to the string quartet—who were surprisingly good. Marion was a blur in the kitchen; service would begin shortly. So where was Laurie?

For a horrible fleeting second he wondered if she'd decided to leave. To get away from Annick Castle and to get away from him.

She'd left that question hanging in the air between them. She'd been disappointed he couldn't acknowledge what was happening between them. And he'd been disappointed too.

If he got her on her own again he wouldn't make the same mistake.

The momentary thought of her leaving vanished as quickly as it had come. He'd seen the look in her eyes. He'd seen the way she felt about her surroundings. Laurie wasn't ready to leave yet. No matter how many difficult conversations they had.

Then he froze. There she was. Standing at the top of the curved staircase.

Looking as if she belonged. Looking as if she was meant to be here.

She was a vision. No ball gown. Nothing ostentatious.

It took him a few seconds for the vaguely familiar-looking dress to click into place in his head. Of course. He should have known.

He watched her carefully. She was deep in thought, her hand resting on the carved banister. She was taking long slow breaths, then her eyes met his and she gave him a smile as her feet started to descend the stairway.

She was breathtakingly beautiful. Her shiny dark curls danced around her shoulders. The simple pink chiffon dress floated around her, emphasising the curves of her breasts and hips.

But it wasn't just her beauty that was captivating. It was something else. It was the feeling that she looked totally at home—that walking down this staircase was what she was supposed to be doing.

He met her at the bottom of the stairs. 'Should I break into song?' he said quietly.

He couldn't wipe the smile from her face. Her eyes sparkled and her cheeks were flushed. 'I need to talk to you. I need to tell you something.'

He frowned. 'Is something wrong?'

She shook her head, making her curls bounce around. 'No. I think for the first time in a long time, something is right.'

He had no idea what she was talking about. All he could see was how happy she looked, how relaxed. It was almost as if the weight of the world had been lifted off her shoulders. What on earth had happened?

He crooked his elbow towards her. 'Shall we go into dinner?'

She nodded and slipped her arm through his. 'I can't wait for this to be over,' she whispered in his ear.

'Me either. Do you have anything to do this evening?'

She shrugged. 'I've to have a conversation with someone and say a few things that will make them suspicious of me.'

'I've to do something similar.' They'd reached the dining room by this point and he pulled out her chair for her, ignoring the seating plan at the table. As she sat down he moved the cards around.

She arched her eyebrow at him. 'I've taught you well.'

He sat beside her. 'You have. I feel kind of guilty—I haven't really paid much attention to what's been happening this weekend.' He didn't mean for the words quite to come out like that. He'd been paying far too much attention to what was happening between them, just not the events of the Murder Mystery Weekend.

He could see her pause momentarily before she took a sip of her rosé wine. 'I haven't either,' she said, her eyes fixing on his.

For a moment he felt relief. She hadn't misunderstood. She was staring at him with those big brown eyes. He couldn't blink. He didn't want to do anything to break this moment. She knew he was invested heavily in Annick Castle. She knew how important it was to him. She knew he loved it with every breath that he took.

So, to allow himself to be distracted away from the events of the weekend spoke volumes. He was only just beginning to realise how much.

Laurie Jenkins was occupying every waking minute

of his thoughts. She was burrowing under his skin with her questions, her logic and her passion for everything around her. Maybe he should be worried. Maybe, given the set of circumstances he was in, he should be acting with more caution. But Laurie was the first woman he'd ever really felt a true connection with.

Of course, he'd had girlfriends. He'd even lived with one woman for a couple of years. But he'd never felt this. He'd never felt drawn to someone so much.

And it wasn't for any of the reasons most people would suspect. It wasn't her connection to Angus—if anything, that was more of a hindrance than a help. And it wasn't the possibility she could inherit Annick Castle.

No. This was simple. This was all about her, Laurie Jenkins, and him, Callan McGregor.

He would have felt this way no matter where he'd met her. Whether it had been some noisy bar in London or Edinburgh, or some workplace environment. The fact that he'd met her here—in one of the most beautiful settings in the world—was just an added bonus.

One he fully intended to take advantage of.

He gave her a smile. There was a whole host of other thoughts going on in his head that he almost hoped she could see. 'I guess it's only good manners for us to stay as long as it takes to fulfil our duties.'

She nodded solemnly, with a wicked smile dancing across her lips. 'I guess you're right.' She leaned forward and whispered in his ear, 'How long *exactly* do you think that will take?'

Their eyes met again and stayed that way until Robin clapped his hands together to draw their attention. 'Good evening, people. This is the last night of our Murder Mystery Weekend. There have been more than enough clues left for you all to have some idea of who the murderer could be. I'd ask you *all*—' he emphasised the word and looked pointedly in the direction of Laurie and Callan '—to pay special attention to the actions you've been asked to take this evening that will help all parties have an equal chance of winning the castle.'

Callan felt a cold wave wash over his skin. Robin made it sound as if they were winning the lottery— not an ancient piece of history. He tried to push his thoughts aside. He had to come to terms with this. He had to move past this and accept Angus's decision. The boxes upstairs flickered into his mind again. He had to spend some time looking through them. Not that it would make any difference to the eventual outcome.

A slim hand slipped under the table and gave his hand a squeeze. Even now Laurie was taking his thoughts into consideration. The touch of her silky skin sent a shot of electricity up his arm, setting his senses on fire. And in a world of uncertainty there was one thing that he knew for sure. Nothing would douse these flames.

He kept his voice low. 'How quickly can you eat dinner, Laurie?'

She smiled as a bowl of soup was placed in front of her. 'Quicker than you can imagine.' She looked around her. 'This is my last night in Annick Castle. Let's blow this place as quickly as we can.'

She was laughing. She wanted to escape the confines of the dining room and their other companions and he felt exactly the same.

Dinner had never seemed such a protracted affair. The food was as delicious as always. But every single mouthful seemed to take for ever. People were too busy talking to eat their food. In between courses Callan walked around to the other side of the table and had the conversation that his card had instructed him to. It was over in the blink of an eye. He made sure of it.

And Laurie had done the same. But she didn't seem to walk—she floated. Something was different with her tonight. And he couldn't wait to find out what.

The clock ticked slowly. By the time dessert arrived Callan wanted to refuse it and leave. But it was Marion's speciality, rhubarb compote with crème anglaise and he could never offend her by not eating her food.

Laurie was more relaxed. She happily sipped her wine and ate her food, chatting to all those around her. By the time Robin announced time for coffee in the drawing room Callan was almost ready to explode.

He didn't hesitate. He grabbed her hand and pulled her towards the open glass doors leading out to the gardens. 'Ready to leave?'

She flashed him a smile. 'Around two hours ago.'

'Really? You seemed so comfortable.'

'I'm just a better actor than you.' She squeezed his hand. 'Where are we going?'

They'd walked out to the stone patio that overlooked the maze. There was smoke around them, a haze. A natural mist that was lifting from the sea as the warm summer air met the cool sea breezes. If he didn't know any better he'd suspect some film director was pumping it around them to set the scene.

But Callan didn't need anyone else to set the scene for him. He'd arranged that for himself.

He looked down at her. 'In that dress? There's only one place we can go.'

They didn't even wait to walk along the paths but just cut across the lawn towards the stairs that led to the lowered gardens. His hand was grasping hers tightly and she could scarcely keep up with his long strides, the damp grass wetting her feet through the open gold sandals. As the grass was wet the ground underneath it was soft, her spindly heels sinking rapidly into the pliable earth. She stumbled as her heel caught and her foot slipped out of the shoe.

Callan's strong arms closed around her, catching her before she collided with the damp grass. 'Careful!'

He reached back and extracted her shoe from the ground, kneeling down to slip it back over her foot. His gentle touch around her foot was sending a whole host of delicious tingles down her spine as he refastened the straps. 'Isn't this what Cinderella did? Lose her shoe as she ran away from the ball?'

She smiled at him. Her one leg that was on the ground was feeling distinctly wobbly. 'I guess that makes you my Prince Charming, then?'

His hand slid along her lower leg. The tingles were getting *so* much worse. 'I guess it does.' He stood up, stopping in front of her for a few seconds. She caught her breath.

This was so real now.

Tonight was their last night together. And expectations were causing the air between them to sizzle.

He reached out and took her hand again, this time walking with a little more care, a little more measure.

As they reached the top of the stairway she let out a little gasp. Something she totally hadn't expected. Lights around the gazebo.

'I didn't realise,' she began. 'Is there an electricity supply down there?'

The rest of the swan pond was in complete darkness. Even the steps they were standing on now had no lighting.

'No. Just be thankful for modern technology.'

She took a few tentative steps down the first few stairs and screwed up her nose. 'What is it then?'

'Solar lights. Small white ones lighting around the base of the gazebo, and some coloured butterfly lights strung along the outside.'

'They're beautiful, Callan. Just beautiful.' She tilted her head as she looked at him. 'Have they always been there? I didn't notice them the other day.'

He shook his head. 'I put them there today.'

There was a little soar of pleasure in her chest. It was almost as if, with every step, a notch on the dial between them turned up. She felt curious. 'Did you know? Did you know about the dress?'

'No. But I knew about your daydream. You told me. You told me what you wanted to do.'

Her heart squeezed in her chest. She hadn't told him everything she wanted to do. Some thoughts were entirely private. But here, and now, someone had valued her enough to make her little girl dreams come true. Someone she'd only known for a few days, but felt a whole-hearted connection to.

'Thank you,' she whispered.

He kept her hand in his as she walked gingerly down the steps and they walked along the white stone path around the edge of the swan pond. She could hear the swans rustling in the bushes at the side of the pond. Some of them were floating near to the edges, obviously asleep. It was such a peaceful setting at night.

The gazebo with its soft lights was glowing like a beacon in the middle of the pitch-black night. Twinkling like a Christmas tree in the middle of summer. The air around them was still with hardly a breath of air. Apart from the occasional animal noise all she could hear was their steps on the path, the stones crunching beneath their feet. It was magical.

They reached the entrance to the gazebo and Callan pushed the door open. It creaked loudly. Almost in protest at being disturbed. She liked the idea that none of the other guests had been here. She liked the thought that this was her and Callan's private space.

It probably wasn't too surprising. Most of the other guests were older than her and Callan. The steps to the lower garden were steep, not the most conducive to those who weren't as steady on their feet.

She held her breath as she stepped inside. Wow. The glass panels inside reflected the string of tiny butterfly lights outside. And as they bobbed around outside, the multicoloured lights reflected across the floor inside like a rainbow.

It was better than a movie effect. This was real.

She felt his hands on her waist and spun around to face him, her hands reaching up and resting on the planes of his chest.

He smiled down at her. 'So, Laurie. What is it you wanted to talk to me about?' He was standing over her. Only inches away.

She was trying to concentrate. She was trying not to focus on the rise and fall of his chest beneath the palms of her hands. She was trying not to dare recognise the fact she could feel the gentle echo of his beating heart beneath her fingertips.

It was time. It was time to tell someone else her plans. Her hopes for the future. It didn't matter that she didn't know where those plans would take her. She only knew they wouldn't keep her in London any more.

Callan's green eyes were focused on her. And they

soothed her. And they ignited a fire within her belly. A surge she hadn't felt in a long time.

'You know I work as a lawyer in London.'

He nodded.

'When you told me that you worked in computers instead of mathematics I was surprised.'

'Why?' His voice was quiet. 'Lots of people do degrees in one field and take jobs in another.'

She hesitated. This was hard. She was trying so hard not to say anything she would regret. 'It's a bit more difficult when you've studied law. It's not such a generic field. Once you've done a law degree there's really only one way you can go.'

'I get it. Like why would you study medicine if you don't want to be a doctor? But why would you do a law degree if you didn't want to be a lawyer?'

It made so much more sense when he said it out loud. It also made her feel foolish. Foolish for taking so long to put this into words.

She lowered her head, blinking back the tears that had automatically formed in her eyes. There was a lump in her throat. She felt his warm hand sweep back the hair that had covered her face, pulling it back to the nape of her neck where his gentle figures rested. 'Laurie?'

The tears started to flow. 'I knew right from the minute I got there that I didn't want to do a law degree. I'd done well at school. My guidance teacher persuaded me to apply for the best possible degrees for my results. It seemed natural. It seemed the sensible thing to do.'

'You were thinking with your head instead of your heart?'

He whispered the words as if he understood.

She nodded desperately. 'My dad—he was just so

happy, so proud when he knew I'd been accepted to Cambridge. He'd never imagined his daughter would do so well. And neither did I. It all seemed like a dream at first.' She shook her head, fixating on the flickering lights outside. 'Then my dad just worked so hard, such long hours to make the dream a reality and all of a sudden I felt as if I couldn't get out. I couldn't say anything. How could I disappoint him when he was working so hard? What kind of a daughter would that make me? It was like being on a train ride I couldn't get off.'

His hand cradled the side of her cheek and his fingers brushed away one of her tears. 'You felt like you couldn't tell him?'

She nodded again as the tears just seemed to flow from her eyes like a tumbling river's stream. 'I didn't want to do anything to disappoint him. I didn't want to do anything to make him sad.' She could hear the desperation in her own voice. 'But when you said that Angus had no expectation of you beyond finishing your own degree...' Her voice tailed off. 'It just seemed unfair. You make it sound so easy.'

Her hands were resting on his shoulders now and one of his hands drifted along the length of her arm, settling back to her waist where he pulled her closer.

The temperature had dropped around them. Or maybe it was just the atmosphere that was making her breath send little clouds in the air around them. The hairs on her arms were standing on end. Or maybe it was being here with Callan, the man who had no expectations of her and only a steady admiration in his eyes.

'I know you lost your dad a few years ago, Laurie. So what now? You're an adult. There's no one to disappoint. You can decide what happens next. You can decide what steps you take. Where do you want to go, Laurie? Where do you want to end up?'

The words were measured. His other hand had reached her waist and both were pulling her even closer to him. She could almost hear music in the air between them. And it was as if they weren't talking about her career choice any more. It was so much more than that.

Where do you want to end up? The million-dollar question. It was everything that sparked in the air between them. Every impulse that fired in her skin whenever he touched her. Every dream that featured him in high-definition detail.

A smile came across his face. The air in the room was closing in on them. Pressing around every inch. His grip on her waist tightened and he lifted her in the air, as if it were something he did every day, making her breath catch in her throat as he took a few steps and stood her on the thin bench that ran around the inside of the gazebo.

'Maybe it's time to forget, Laurie. Let's pretend you don't need to think about any of these things.' He waited, then reached and wiped another tear from her cheek before adding, 'And neither do I. You told me earlier what you wanted to do. Why don't you just let me give you your dreams tonight?' She heard his voice break and it squeezed at her heart.

Tomorrow everything changed for both of them.

Tomorrow the person who would inherit Annick Castle would be announced. She doubted it would be her. And in a way, she didn't want it to be. She had no idea what to do with a place like Annick Castle, even though it had wound its way into her heart.

Right now, she was more concerned about what it might do to Callan. What it might do to the small boy who had found a haven—a safe place in Annick Castle. It didn't matter what she thought of Angus. It didn't matter to her at all.

All that mattered to her was what Callan thought of him. How Callan McGregor would feel. Because Callan McGregor was a keeper. She knew that in her heart.

She would never do anything to hurt him. Never do anything to keep him from his dream.

The realisation was startling. Two, in one night.

And even though she couldn't think about it right now they were probably interconnected. The decision about walking away from her job felt freeing. Like spreading her wings and flying high in the air.

She didn't feel guilty about it. She didn't feel irresponsible. It was time to start living her life for herself. Not for anyone else.

Her legs were trembling. She looked around her. It was beautiful. It was the perfect setting. And Callan was the perfect man to share it with.

'Are you going to be my prince tonight, Callan?' She held out her shaking hand towards him.

He gave a little smile. 'Aren't I supposed to be your Rolfe?'

She wrinkled her nose. 'He turned out to be a traitor. I'd rather go with the prince theme.'

He took her hand in his. 'Does this mean I have to dance and sing? Because, I warn you. This might not work out the way you imagined it.'

Her voice was low and husky. 'You've no idea what I've imagined, Callan.' His eyes widened as his smile spread across his face. He gave a mock bow.

'Ms Jenkins, can I have this dance?'

She gave a little curtsey as he took her hand and her steps quickened around the circular bench. Callan laughed, keeping pace with her as she started to run, letting the rainbow-coloured reflections of light dance across the pale chiffon of her dress. Her gold shoes sparkled in the dim lights but the one thing that stood out for her was the green of Callan's eyes. They didn't leave her. Not for a second.

'You're planning on making me dizzy, aren't you?' he quipped as she started around the circle for the fourth time.

'I might never get to do this again,' came her instant response.

He stopped dead. As if the realisation had just hit him.

Her breath caught in her throat, her heart beating rapidly against her chest. Did she really want this to be the last time for her and Callan?

She could see his quick breaths, see the glimmer of uncertainty across his eyes followed by a look of firm decision.

His hands swept around her waist, lifting her up and spinning her around as if she were as light as a feather. Her arms caught around his neck and she laughed as he continued to spin her round, her dress billowing out around them. He stopped slowly, holding her in place for a few seconds before gradually beginning to lower her down. Her face was just inches above his. She didn't want him to stop touching her; she didn't want him to stop holding her.

'Are you going to kiss me again, Callan?' she whispered. 'Do I get a little warning this time?'

'How much warning do you need?'

'About this much.'

She started to kiss him before he'd completely lowered her to the floor. This time she was ready. This time she initiated it. This time there were no spectators.

There was just her and Callan. A perfect combination.

It wasn't a light kiss. She wasn't gentle. She knew exactly what she was doing. This was happening because she wanted it to happen. This wasn't about her job. This wasn't about Angus McLean. This wasn't about Annick Castle.

This was just about her and Callan.

And it felt so right.

Their kiss was intensifying; the stubble on his chin scraped her skin. His hands ran through her curls, locking into place at the back of her head as he tried to pull her even closer.

The chiffon material on her dress was so thin, all she could feel was the compressed heat from his body against hers.

Her hands ran across the expanse of his back; she could feel his muscles rippling under his shirt. One of these days she'd ask him how he got those.

Or maybe he could show her...

He pulled his head back from hers, still holding her head in place. With slow sensuous movement he slid his hands down her back, around her hips, and stroked upwards with his palms towards her breasts.

She wasn't in a fairy tale any more. She was in a positively adult dream. One where she only dared imagine the outcome.

'Laurie,' he murmured as he rested his forehead against hers.

'Yes.' She could hardly breathe. She would scream if he stopped touching her. This was meant to happen. They were meant to be together.

She'd never felt a connection like this. Her one-track mind knew exactly where this would go. And she couldn't think of a single reason to stop it happening.

She didn't want to have regrets in life. She had too many of those already. And Callan could never be regret. Not when he made her feel like this.

She stood on her tiptoes and kissed his nose. She ran her fingers through his dark hair as she looked into his eyes. He didn't need to ask the question out loud.

She already knew her answer. Her hands cupped either side of his face. 'Yes, Callan,' she breathed.

And he took her hand in his and led her back to the castle.

CHAPTER TEN

HE DIDN'T WANT to wake up. He didn't want this day to begin.

This was the day where two things he loved could slip through his fingertips.

All of a sudden he was instantly awake, his eyes fixating on the rain battering on the windowpane. Love. Where had that come from?

With the exception of Angus, Callan couldn't remember the last time he'd ever had a thought like this. Callan 'cared' about people. He didn't love them.

He'd 'cared' about some women in the past. He'd worried about them. He hadn't wanted to hurt their feelings. He'd wanted to take care of them.

None of these things applied to Laurie. He'd have to multiply everything by a thousand to get even close.

From the first second he'd glanced her through the steam on the train platform she'd started to burrow her way under his skin and into his heart.

Her reactions had been totally different from everyone else who could inherit the castle. She'd walked the estate, she'd asked questions, she'd shown an interest that was above and beyond the monetary value. She'd seemed invested in the place.

Her connection with Marion had taken him by surprise. He suspected it had taken Marion by surprise too. She wasn't known for sharing her domain. But apparently Laurie had sneaked under her radar too. She'd done nothing but sing Laurie's praises to him—all with a twinkle in her eyes.

What sat heaviest on his chest was his loyalty to Angus. He knew instantly that if Angus had met Laurie he would have loved her. He would have loved her spark, her inquisitiveness, her cheek and her ability to run rings around Callan.

He just couldn't understand why Angus hadn't met his children. Hadn't loved his children the way he'd loved him. Nothing about it seemed right. And until he could sort that out in his head he would never be able to move forward.

And today was a day for moving forward.

He turned on his side. Laurie currently had her back to him, the cotton sheet had slipped from her shoulders and his eyes carried along the curves of her skin. She was sleeping peacefully and his hands were itching to touch her again.

He wanted to ask her to stay. He wanted to ask her to stay here with him. To stay anywhere with him.

But what could he offer her?

Her words had almost broken his heart last night when she'd told him how she hated her job. It would be so easy for him to tell her just to pack it all in, forget about everything and move up to Edinburgh with him. Money wasn't an object for Callan.

But he knew in his heart that Laurie wasn't that kind of girl.

And the outcome of Annick Castle was still hanging over his head like a black thunder cloud. Until that was resolved his stomach would constantly churn.

He slid his feet to the floor as something flickered into his brain. Laurie had told him she knew who the murderer was. How on earth could she know? He was embarrassed to say that he hadn't been paying enough attention to even hazard a guess.

Was there even a tiny chance that Laurie could inherit the castle?

A shiver crept down his spine. How would that make him feel? He didn't even want to consider that for a second. What was developing between him and Laurie could be destroyed by something like that.

He took a deep breath as he watched her sleeping form. She had a one in twelve chance of inheriting the castle. He watched her gentle breathing, in and out, in and out, her hair framing her face and her tongue running along her rose-pink lips.

He didn't want anything to mess this up. Nothing at all.

He stood up. The boxes. He still hadn't had a chance to go through Angus's boxes. He had to do it now. Time was running out. He might have access to these things now, but in a matter of days he would have to walk away from Annick Castle and leave everything behind. He had to use the opportunity to find out what he could now.

He pulled a shirt over his head and some trousers on. He would do it now while Laurie slept. There was no point disturbing his sleeping Cinderella.

Her eyes flickered open and for a second she was startled. For the last few days she'd woken in a room with a peaceful yellow colour scheme. The pale themes of blue unsettled her. Her reactions were instantaneous.

She pulled the sheet over her naked body and flipped over onto her back.

Nothing. No one.

Callan wasn't there.

She was instantly caught by the pain in her chest. The expanse of the bed seemed huge. The dip where he should be lying seemed like a giant chasm. Where was he? Was he embarrassed? Was he ashamed of what had happened last night? Why wasn't he still lying here next to her?

Her beautiful pale pink chiffon dress was lying in a crumpled heap on the floor. Robin would have a fit. Her gold glitter sandals were strewn across the floor, obviously left exactly where they'd fallen. She cringed as she looked around the rest of the room. Even though this was obviously Callan's room, there was no visible sign of him.

It made her stomach churn. She pulled the sheet around her like a toga as she stood up and her eyes swept the room. There was nothing else for her to wear except the clothes she'd discarded last night. And who knew where her underwear was?

She rummaged around the floor eventually finding her bra and pants and pulling them on. Her Liesl dress was a crumpled wreck. It seemed to echo exactly how she felt. Talk about doing the next-day walk of shame.

Thankfully the corridor was empty. She fled down the staircase as quickly as possible and slammed her door closed behind her.

Her half-empty rucksack lay on the floor. Going home. After the announcement today she would be going home.

Her eyes filled with tears. Everything last night with

Callan had been perfect. But deep down both of them had known they were saying goodbye.

How could there be a happy ever after for them? What on earth did she expect to happen?

She pulled out some clothes. A pair of Capri pants and a slightly wrinkled shirt that she'd already worn. If she'd thought about it a bit more she could have asked Marion where she could launder her clothes. But there was no point now. No point because she wasn't staying.

There was something pushed under the doorway. She'd completely missed it. She tore the envelope open. Was it from Callan?

Of course it wasn't. He'd left her sleeping alone in his room; why would he push a note under her door? It was from Robin. Asking her to write the name of the person she suspected as the murderer and return it to him before eleven that morning.

That was easy. She grabbed a pen and scribbled the name. She didn't even have to think about it.

Part of her wanted to hide away in her room. *Her* room. It wasn't her room. It was part of the castle. After today she would probably never see this place again and it was about time she accepted that.

She'd probably never see Callan again. But that thought made her legs buckle and left her sitting on the window seat looking out at the crashing sea.

The rain was battering down outside. It was the first day of bad weather she'd experienced here and all of a sudden she felt very sorry for the bygone smugglers. It must be terrifying down at the caves in weather like this. She could feel the wind whistle through the panes of glass. The temperature was distinctly lower. Or maybe it was just her mood.

It was time to step away from Annick Castle and Callan McGregor. It was time to go back to London and sort her life out.

One thing hadn't changed. She didn't want to be a lawyer any more and she needed to take steps to make a change. She could do that. She could do that now.

Annick Castle had changed her. It had given her some perspective on life. Meeting some of her unknown relatives had been enlightening.

She would have preferred it if some of them had remained unknown. But there was a few she had felt some kind of affinity towards. She would love to go and visit her auntie Mary in Ireland some time. She would love to show her some more pictures of her father so she could see the family resemblance between the two of them.

As for Angus McLean? She'd grown tired of wondering why he'd abandoned his children. She'd grown tired of wondering why he'd been able to show love to some unknown child, then split his heart in two with the contents of his will.

She'd grown tired of it all.

There was a thin layer of dust over the boxes. No one had touched them in years.

He'd found them in the back of a cupboard in Angus's room, hidden amongst shoes and old smoking jackets. He'd been curious at first, wondering if they would reveal something about Angus's unacknowledged children.

But they were something else entirely.

Medical files. And lots of them.

It took Callan a few minutes to work out what he was looking at. At first they seemed totally random. Patients allocated numbers instead of names. They were ancient—some more than seventy years old. And the initial sense of unease he'd felt at looking at someone's medical files rapidly diminished.

The files all seemed to have one thing in common. A big red stamp with deceased across the front.

But there was more than that. All of these people seemed to have died within a very short period of time. A window of six months back in the 1940s just after the Second World War had ended.

It took him a little longer to work out entirely what they were telling him.

Angus's father had owned a pharmaceutical company. These were all records of drug trials. Nowadays clinical drug trials were scrutinised, monitored and regulated beyond all recognition. Seventy-five years ago—not so much.

And whatever drug these people had been trialling seemed to have had an extreme adverse effect. All the patients taking it had died within six months.

All except one. Patient X115. Otherwise known as Angus McLean.

It was a horrible moment of realisation. Scribbled notes were all over the file that was obviously Angus's.

Scribbled notes that revealed that as one drug trial patient after another died, Angus McLean had fully expected to die himself within a few months.

He'd had no idea what was wrong with the medication, but all the other patients—twenty of them—had died within a short space of time.

Callan leaned back against the desk. He'd been sitting on the floor, the files scattered all around him. People had been paid a fee all those years ago to take part in drug trials. Things weren't so carefully monitored.

And although the medical files were full of things he didn't understand, there were a few things that he did understand.

According to the post-mortem results most of the patients had died of some kind of accelerated blood disorder. Angus McLean had thought he was living on borrowed time. He'd fully expected to die along with the rest of the group.

Except he hadn't. He'd outlived them all by almost seventy years.

Was this the reason? The reason why he hadn't had contact with his children, but had instead made some kind of financial recompense?

From the dates he could see, at least three of his children had been born during wartime. Communications were limited. It wasn't like today where a ping of an email signified the arrival of a message from half-way round the globe. He'd moved around a lot during, and directly after, the war. It was entirely possible that Angus hadn't found out about some of his children until after the war—right around the time he'd just taken part in the disastrous drug trial.

Callan's head was spinning. He couldn't really draw any conclusions from this. He was guessing.

But Angus had been a gentle-natured man. Callan didn't really want to believe he'd deliberately left his children without a father. But how would Angus have coped, forming a relationship with these children, whilst he was living in fear he would die at any moment? Leave them to suffer the bereavement of losing their dad? Maybe, if Angus had died quickly, it would have been better not to meet them. And although he didn't agree with it, he could maybe understand it a little better.

* * *

But Angus would never have left his children unsupported. That did seem like something he would do. Provide for them. And if this was the only explanation Callan could find, then he'd take it.

Maybe he'd thought leaving them Annick Castle would make up for the fact they hadn't had a father figure in their lives. How had he felt as one year after another had passed? Had he realised he'd managed to run the gauntlet that the others in the drug trial had failed?

Callan leaned forward. There was a collection of black-and-white photos at the bottom of the box. Some of women. Some of children. One, a picture of Angus with his arm around a woman.

This was it. This was the only sign that Angus McLean actually had family. No letters. No gushy cards. No sentimental keepsakes.

Callan felt a rush of unease at the similarities between himself and Angus.

If someone searched his personal belongings what would they find? No pictures or memorabilia about his father. No trace of the man at all. One slightly crumpled picture of his mother, along with an album of family snaps of him as a baby or a young boy accompanied by an unknown arm holding him, or a set of unidentified legs.

He opened the lid of the other box, fully expecting to find similar contents. But this was different. This held a leather-bound photo album.

He opened the first page. It was some old pictures of Angus as a young boy with his mother and father. Family snaps had obviously been few and far between then.

He flipped the pages. Angus as he was growing up.

In school uniform. In hunting gear. In his army uniform. In a dinner suit.

And then there was Callan. As a small child sitting at the kitchen table that still existed, laughing heartily with Angus laughing next to him. Callan had no recollection of the picture ever being taken, but that tiny snapshot in time struck him like a bullet through his heart.

He flicked again. Him and Angus on every page. Fishing. Horse-riding. Sitting in the grounds. Digging the gardens with Bert. Standing on the cannons in the castle grounds. Sailing across the swan pond in the most rickety paddle boat that ever existed. It had subsequently sunk to the bottom of the pond never to be seen again.

Callan standing at the castle doors holding some kind of certificate in his hands. He had a vague recollection of it being his exam results that gained him his place at university. All little moments in time.

He'd been feeling annoyed. He'd been feeling spurned by the fact Angus wouldn't sell him Annick Castle. Deep down he'd been hurt that Angus hadn't considered him in his will.

But here it was. Captured for posterity. Exactly what Angus had left him.

A life.

A safe haven.

Love.

The things he'd needed to shape him and become his own man.

A tear dripped down his face.

Now he understood.

He'd always known how much he'd owed Angus. But here was something to cherish and keep. To help him remember that memories were more precious than material things. None of Angus's children had shared any of these moments with him.

The gift that Angus had left him was the most precious of all.

CHAPTER ELEVEN

THE GONG SOUNDED dead on eleven. Laurie had never heard the gong used before. She'd noticed it standing in the entrance hall and wondered what it had ever been used for. It was almost like the start of one of those movies, except Robin wasn't dressed in a loincloth.

Everyone was gathering in the drawing room. It seemed to be the room where Angus's relatives had spent most of their time.

The rain was battering the windows with a ferocity she'd never seen. It seemed fitting on a day like this. It was almost as if the weather could read how she was feeling.

She filed in and took a seat. Frank, the family lawyer, was standing in the corner of the room. He looked as if he wanted to be sick. Robin stood next to him along with the guy John who had been playing the butler, and the girl who'd been murdered on Friday night.

There was the sound of hurried footsteps outside. Callan appeared with Marion and Bert by his side. It was only fitting. They should all hear who would own Annick Castle together.

Her eyes fixed on the floor. After Callan had abandoned her in the bedroom she didn't even want to look him in the eye. She certainly didn't want to have a conversation with him in front of anyone else. Whatever she had to say to Callan she could say in private before she left.

But Callan seemed to have entirely different thoughts.

He crossed the room in a matter of seconds, sitting on the chaise longue next to her. 'Laurie, I'm sorry. I had to go and look through Angus's papers this morning. You won't believe what I've found.'

What? Her head whipped up. She couldn't help but frown. 'But you left this morning.' She shook her head. 'I woke up and you were gone.' She couldn't hide the confusion in her voice. And she didn't care what he'd found.

He smiled, obviously unaware of the turmoil she'd felt. 'You looked so peaceful. I didn't want to wake you. I meant to come back and bring you breakfast in bed, but once I started going through Angus's boxes I just lost all track of time.'

There was no time to reply. No time to try and think clearly. Frank cleared his throat loudly. 'Thank you for gathering here this morning. In accordance with Angus McLean's will, today we will reveal who has inherited Annick Castle. Once the announcement is made, we will make suitable arrangements for a DNA test to be carried out to confirm the family connection. Once this has been confirmed, the process of passing on Annick Castle will take a few weeks.'

Frank looked around the room. He was clutching cards in his hands—the cards where everyone had written who they thought had carried out the murder.

He was obviously feeling the strain. The colour in his face was rising, probably in line with his blood pressure. He gave a nervous smile. 'It turns out that only one person correctly identified the murderer. There was provision in the will if more than one person had guessed correctly, but that won't be necessary now.'

Heads were glancing around the room. Everyone wondering who had been right. 'So, who was the murderer?' Craig snapped, the tension obviously getting too much for him.

Frank nodded. 'The murderer was John. The butler did it,' he said simply.

There were gasps around the room, along with several expletives.

'That's not fair!'

'I hardly spoke to him.'

'He was only ever in the background.'

'I never even had a conversation with him!'

Robin was instantly on the defensive. 'We conducted everything with absolute precision. The clues were all there if you looked for them.'

Laurie was frozen. Her throat dried in an instant. She couldn't hear anything. She couldn't hear because the thudding in her ears was getting louder and louder. Sweat. She'd never experienced sweat like it. Appearing instantly all over her body, running down the length of her back and collecting between the cups of her bra. She was freezing. She felt as if someone had just plucked up her body and dropped her in the raging sea outside.

People were still ranting. Callan was just frozen in the chair beside her, holding his breath while he waited for the announcement.

The announcement that would mean any chance they had of having any kind of relationship would disappear in an instant.

Frank's grey eyes locked on hers. 'Congratulations, Laurie. Pending a DNA test, Annick Castle is yours.'

The room erupted.

'It's a fix!'

'She's obviously in league with Frank—you lawyers stick together.'

'She's hardly even been here!'

'She's in cahoots with that man—Callan. The rest of us never really stood a chance!'

She felt numb. There was good reason she didn't like some of her relatives. Her vibes about most of them hadn't been wrong. Any tiny flicker of doubts she'd had about the personality traits of some her relatives were now being revealed in 3D multicolour. She felt as if she couldn't breathe. The air was coming in, but she couldn't get it back out.

From the corner of her eye she saw her auntie Mary give her a little smile and blow her a kiss. She was sitting on the other side of the room and her elderly bones couldn't possibly navigate the melee between them.

It was the first sign of hope. The first glimmer of a good-luck wish.

She was scared to look sideways. She was scared to look at Callan. Part of her wished he'd jumped up to defend her once the rabble had started. But he hadn't—he'd been silent.

Frank was trying to push his way through the crowd. At this point it looked as if he might be trampled by the objectors.

She stood up and turned to face Callan.

He hadn't moved. He looked shell-shocked. The smile on his face earlier had vanished. His green eyes lifted and met hers.

She could read everything on his face and in his eyes. He'd been taking steps forward. He'd been try-ing to move past the fact that Annick Castle would be inherited by someone else. And he'd been getting there. In tiny baby steps.

But this was entirely different. This changed everything. The pain and confusion was etched in his eyes. Both of them knew this wasn't her fault. This was something that neither of them had control over. Or did they?

Could she have done something to prevent this happening? Could she have done something to allow them to cling onto the hope of developing a relationship together?

She was so confused right now.

Panic started to grip her. She'd written that name on the card without a second thought. Her reactions had been automatic. She should have guessed wrongly. But it hadn't even occurred to her at the time.

Pain started to spread across her chest. She was starting to feel woozy. The room was closing in around her. She couldn't bear the look on Callan's face. The look that said everything had just changed. His pain was too much for her to bear. And the ramifications made her feel as if everything was out of her control.

Her feet started to move. She started to push her way through the bodies. She had to get outside. She had to get some air.

Marion reached out to her on the way past but she didn't even slow her steps. She couldn't.

She pulled the main door open. The wind and rain howled around her but she didn't even care. She just walked. And kept on walking.

Her shirt was soaked in seconds, her hair whipping around her face. But all she could think about was the air. It was what she needed.

Her legs carried her around to the front of the castle—

the most exposed edge facing the sea. She leaned against the wall and tried to take some deep breaths.

The wind was working against her—almost sucking the air from her lungs as she tried to pull it in. She bent over, arms around her waist and counted to ten. One, two, three…

She lifted her head again. This time she felt the cold coursing through her. This time she looked at the castle she could inherit.

Tears started to pour down her cheeks. This was hers. This *could* be hers.

It was almost unbelievable. To go from a girl with only one known living relative, to a girl with a huge array of aunts, uncles and cousins, and the inheritor of a castle all in the space of a few weeks.

The castle loomed in front of her. Dominant. Intimidating. A whole world of problems.

But she didn't feel like that about it. She looked at the sandy-coloured storm-battered building with its intricate-paned glass windows and drum towers.

She loved it.

She loved it with her whole heart.

But she loved something or someone else a whole lot more.

Genetically she might have a right to Annick Castle. But there were some things so much more important than genes.

'Laurie!' The shout came from her side.

Callan was running towards her, followed by Frank bundled up in a rainproof mac. Frank's umbrella caught in the high winds, turning instantly inside out and making him spin around blindly.

Callan reached her, soaked and windswept by the battering rain. He put his hands on either side of her shoulders. 'Laurie, are you okay? What happened? You ran out before we had a chance to talk.'

She shook her head. Would he notice her tears in amongst the torrent of rain?

Callan was shaking his head in wonder. An amazed smile appeared on his face. 'How did you know? How did you know it was the butler? We've hardly been there this weekend.' He was shouting now. She could hardly hear him above the roar of the waves below.

She lifted her hands. 'Who else could it be? There were twelve of us. It couldn't be any of us, Callan. That would have been unfair. It had to be you, Robin or John. And when the murder took place, you had your arm around me the whole time.'

The recognition dawned on his face. He'd obviously never given the whole weekend much thought. He'd been too wrapped up in the outcome. Too wrapped up in the fate of Annick Castle.

He grabbed her hand. Frank had reached him now and was starting to babble. She couldn't hear a single word he was saying in the braying winds. 'Come on,' shouted Callan. 'Let's get inside.'

He pulled her towards a back door. It must have been a servants' entrance and it took them along a back corridor until they reached somewhere she was much more familiar with. Much more comfortable with—the library.

Callan waited until Frank had joined them and locked the door behind them. Rain was dripping from every part of her. Callan lifted a throw from the back of one of the chairs and stood in front of her, gently rubbing her sodden hair and face.

Callan was so wrapped up in what he wanted to tell her he couldn't contain himself. 'I found medical files,

Laurie. Files that were part of a drug trial seventy years ago. Angus was a participant. Everyone else died within six months. He must have thought he was going to die too, Laurie. That's why he didn't meet his kids—just provided for them financially.'

She hadn't spoken. She hadn't responded. And his voice tailed off to be replaced with a concerned expression on his face. There was a second of recognition. Recognition that she was long past the point of caring about Angus McLean.

'Laurie? Isn't this what you wanted? You're the only relative here who has shown any real interest in Annick Castle.' He hesitated. 'I'll need to go over the castle accounts with you, but some of the things you suggested might be part of the way forward for Annick Castle.'

Frank stepped forward. 'I have to warn you I think there might be some legal challenges from some of the unhappy parties. There's nothing we can do to prevent that. But no matter what their challenges, Angus's will is rock solid. He made sure of that. It might just tie us up in court proceedings for some time.' He rustled some papers. 'Now, can we make some arrangements for your DNA test? It's just a simple cheek swab, and I'd expect the results back relatively quickly.'

'Stop.' She lifted her hand. 'Stop it. Both of you.'

Callan froze. He'd been mid-rub of her hair, which was still stubbornly dripping on the floor below. She shivered. The impact of the rain and wind was starting to affect her body's reactions. Frank's mouth was still open—poised mid-sentence.

'I can't do this.'

'What?' Both voices, in perfect unison.

Callan's brow instantly wrinkled. 'What do you

mean you can't do this? You are the perfect person to do this, Laurie.'

'No. No, I'm not.' She shook her head fiercely. 'If I'd thought about this more carefully I would have put the wrong name on the card.' Frank looked horrified, but she continued before he could say anything else. 'I'm not the right person to look after Annick Castle. It doesn't matter that I'm a relative of Angus McLean. It doesn't matter at all.'

She walked over and picked up one of the photographs of Angus in his army uniform. 'I didn't know this man. I didn't know this man at all.' She pointed to herself. 'And he didn't know me. I didn't matter to him. My father didn't matter to him. I don't care what his reasons were.'

Her brain felt as if it were scrambled. She didn't feel rational. She didn't feel in control.

'Laurie, hold on. Let me show you what I found—'

'No. Don't, Callan. I don't want to hear it. The fact is, I'm a lawyer. And I'm not even going to be that for much longer. But it doesn't matter. What do I know about a place like this? I wouldn't even know where to begin. It's already starting to fall apart.' She held out her hands. 'This is a piece of history. This is something that should be protected and preserved. This is something that other people should enjoy.'

'But you can do that, Laurie. You've already considered what could happen with Annick Castle. Let me tell you what I found.'

She felt herself start to sway. Her legs were turning to jelly underneath her and she slumped down into one of the nearby chairs.

She took a few seconds, then lifted her head. 'Frank,

if you need to do a DNA test on me, then that's fine. Do it. But I need you to do something else for me.'

'What?' Frank looked bewildered, as if the whole event were taking place in a parallel universe.

She loved Callan. She absolutely loved him. If she kept Annick Castle they would never have a chance. This would always be Callan's home. And she would always be the person that had taken that away from him. And she loved him too much for that.

She'd seen the flash in his eyes back in the drawing room. She didn't need him to spell it all out to her.

She wanted to believe that he really hadn't meant to leave her this morning. But deep down she couldn't entirely be *sure*.

And she needed to be sure. She needed to know that Callan McGregor was with her because he wanted to be, not because she was a route to something else that he loved.

She needed him to love her, just as much as she loved him. The only way to find out if that was true was to take Annick Castle out of the equation.

To put right something that was wrong.

She looked over at Callan's face. She loved him. She loved him with her whole heart. There was only one action she could take right now and it was something she was proud to say that her dad had taught her. *Do the right thing*.

'I want to give Annick Castle to Callan. I want the castle to be looked after by the person who deserves it most.'

CHAPTER TWELVE

'WHAT?'

Callan couldn't believe his ears. This day was getting madder by the second.

'You can't do that.'

'Yes, I think you'll find I can. Can't I, Frank?'

Frank nodded numbly.

Callan knelt down in front of Laurie. She looked exhausted and she was still soaking wet. They were all soaking wet. 'Laurie, you've had a shock. You're not thinking clearly.'

Her words were crisp. 'I'm thinking perfectly clearly, Callan. If Annick Castle is mine, then I can do what I want with it.'

He shook his head. 'But Angus wanted it to go to family. *You're* his family, Laurie, not me.'

She leaned forward, her face inches away from his. 'And I can see exactly how much that hurts you, Callan. What is a family anyway? Is it the person that created you genetically? Or is it the person that's loved you, protected you and sheltered you from the world? Isn't family the people who've taken care of you, helped you do your homework, played with you and looked out for you when you were a kid? Shaped you into the adult you've become? What does the word family mean to you, Callan?' She reached out her finger and touched his chest. 'What does it mean to you in here?'

He couldn't speak. He felt totally blindsided by her. It was as if she could see inside his head. See every bad thought that had entered his brain. Every time he'd bitten his tongue this weekend to stop him saying something he shouldn't.

He knew exactly what she meant. He'd heard her talk about her father. She'd loved him unconditionally—much like the way he'd loved Angus. Whenever she was thinking deeply about something she fingered the gold locket around her neck, the one her father had given her. The love she felt for her father had lasted long after her father's death. And he felt the same; he'd never forget Angus.

'Angus was my family,' he whispered. His throat felt dry and scratchy. Saying the words still hurt. Facing up to the fact that Angus hadn't thought of him as family still hurt. But now he'd discovered so much more.

He reached over and took her hand. 'Let me show you something—something I just found.'

He didn't wait for her response; he just pulled her along behind him. Down the corridor and up the carved staircase towards the room that held Angus's things.

Laurie hadn't stopped crying yet. Slow tears were still trickling down her cheeks. She reached over and put her hand on his cheek. 'What is it, Callan? Because I can't deal with this right now. I can't deal with you.' She pressed her hand to her chest.

He dropped down onto the carpet and pulled the photo album from the top of the box. 'I don't want you to give me the castle, Laurie. It's not right. It's not the way it's supposed to be.'

She lifted her head up. He could see the determined

look across her face. The kind of look that dared anyone to argue with her. 'I don't agree with what Angus
has done. And I don't need to. But I can put right what
I think is wrong.'

Callan shook his head. Every other relative had
looked as if they wanted to sell the castle. Laurie was
the only person who hadn't considered that. Did she
have any idea what the castle was really worth?

'Laurie, I have to tell you. I'd planned to speak to
whoever inherited the castle to see if they would accept my offer. I'd always planned to try and buy Annick
Castle. I certainly don't want you to give it to me.' He
placed the album in her hands. 'But this is what Angus
McLean left me. Something so much more important
than a castle.'

He was starting to panic. This didn't feel right. Callan McGregor was always entirely above board. He
didn't want Laurie to give him the castle. No way.

How would that look?

Particularly now—when he wanted her to stay.

This confused everything. He'd wanted to ask her to
stay this morning. Before any of this happened. And he
should have asked her. He should have asked her then.

He wanted her to understand everything. He wanted
her to look through the album and realise he believed
she was right. The gift that Angus had given him was
security. A place where a little boy could thrive and be
loved by a family. The people who stayed here were
his family. Blood didn't matter. Genetics didn't matter.

But Laurie's face was blank. Was she listening to
him at all? She still hadn't opened the album. The album
that told the story of his life. He had to try something
else.

'I'll buy it from you. We'll get an independent sur-

vey, an independent evaluation.' He was starting to babble, but he just couldn't help it. He felt as if everything
was slipping through his fingers. Which was strange,
because up until a few days ago his priority had been
Annick Castle. A few days ago, this would have been
exactly what he wanted.

And part of him still wanted it. Just not without her.

He shook his head. 'I've looked at the accounts.
Things aren't good. Annick Castle is in trouble. The
nest egg that Angus used to have just isn't there any
more. You've seen for yourself that there are areas that
need attention. And with a place like this there are no
simple fixes. Even things that seem simple need a master craftsman. Traditional materials, specialist trades,
everything has to meet the standards for listed building
consent. Things need to change around here.'

Laurie stood up. 'What are you talking about, Callan? I've told you. I want to give you Annick Castle. I
don't want your money. I don't want you to buy it from
me. It doesn't even feel as if it should really be mine.'
She flung her hands in the air, letting the album fall to
the floor. 'It's ridiculous. I inherit this place on the basis
of the name I wrote on a card?' She turned to face Frank
too. 'Tell me this isn't fundamentally wrong—because
we all know it is. This place, never mind its monetary
value, what about its heritage value, its history? These
are the things that are important. These are the things
that make Annick Castle special.' She turned back to
Callan. 'Angus was wrong. Annick Castle should always have been yours. You're the one with the connection with this place. You're the one who loves it. It
should be yours.' There was real passion in her voice.
As if she knew, as if she understood.

And he could recognise it. Because he understood completely.

He placed his hand on her arm. 'But that's just it, Laurie. I'm not the only one with a connection to this place, am I?'

He watched her eyes widen. She started to stutter, 'B-but...'

'Tell me.' He stepped forward and placed his hand on her chest. 'Tell me how Annick Castle makes you feel in here, Laurie.'

She didn't answer. She couldn't answer.

'I could see it, Laurie. I could see it in your eyes, in everything you did this weekend. From the moment you saw this place, from the moment you set foot in this place, Annick Castle started to get under your skin. You asked questions, you took an interest in everything that happens around here. You looked at this place with a fresh set of eyes.' His voice lowered. 'You introduced me to ideas that I would never have considered myself.' He shook his head as he grew more determined—as he started to see in his head exactly what he wanted to happen.

It was like standing at the railway station again, watching the smoke clear around Laurie's curves. He just knew.

'I can't do this without you, Laurie. I don't want to do this without you. This morning, when I woke up I watched you sleeping. I wanted to ask you then. I should have asked you then.'

'Asked me what?'

'To stay. To stay with me.' The words that had been skirting around the edges of his brain for the last few hours. It was so much easier to say them out loud than he could possibly have imagined.

He sat her down on the chaise longue next to the window and put the album in her lap, flicking past the first few pages of Angus's photographs and onto the pages that showed him as a young boy.

He could see her sharp intake of breath. 'Laurie, I don't care what you do with Annick Castle. If I ever want to move on, I have to let it go. I have to get past this. But I can't get past you.'

Her eyes widened as he turned the pages, letting her see every year of his life recorded by Angus. Letting her see the love between them, letting her see the warmth and security that he'd been provided with. Letting her see his family.

'What is this?' she murmured.

'This is me. This is the legacy that Angus left me.' He put his hand over hers and squeezed tightly. 'It means so much more than bricks and mortar. Angus, and the people here, helped me grow into the man I am today.' He traced a finger down her cheek. 'One that knows if you love someone, you should always put them first.'

Her voice trembled. 'What do you mean you can't get past me, Callan? What are you saying?'

'I'm saying whatever your decision—about Annick Castle, or about your job—I want to be in your life. I want to be part of your life.' He put both of his hands on her cheeks. 'I want to be your family.'

Tears glistened in her eyes.

'You have to know that I've never connected with anyone the way I've connected with you. I don't want to let you go. I don't want this weekend to end.' He held up his arms. 'I wanted to ask you to stay with me this morning, Laurie, but I didn't know where I'd be. I didn't know what I'd have to offer you.'

Her voice cracked. 'Why would you need to offer me anything, Callan? I don't expect anything from you.'

'But that's just it, Laurie. I want you to. I want to be part of your life. I want to be here for you. Wherever you want to be, just tell me. I can find a way to make this work.'

He could see her breath catching in her throat.

Her head was spinning. He was asking her to stay. He was telling her he wanted to be with her. But he hadn't said the words. The three little words she needed to hear.

She took his hands from her cheeks and intertwined her fingers with his. It had finally stopped raining and the sun was peeking out from behind some clouds. Beneath them the gardens lay out in all their coloured glory. Who wouldn't want to look out at that every single day?

She took a deep breath. 'I've been so confused, Callan. You're right. From the moment I set foot in Annick Castle I feel as if it's got a hold on me. I love this place. I love every single part of it.'

She hesitated. Should she say the next part?

'You've made some of my dreams come true, Callan. I never expected it. I never imagined it.'

His hand clasped over hers. 'Every girl should have their own *Sound of Music* gazebo. Every girl should have their own princess staircase.'

'But I don't want every girl to have you.' Did she just say that out loud? In another life she might have cringed, but not here, and not now. This was the moment she found out if her life was going to change for ever.

His voice was low and sincere. 'Every girl can't have me. There's only one girl I want. There's only one girl I want in my life, now and always.' His hand reached up and stroked her cheek. 'Know that I will go anywhere with you, any time.' He shrugged his shoulders. 'I can Blether all over the world, but there's no one else I want to blether with. It's you or nobody. I love you, Laurie Jenkins. Please say you'll stay with me. Please say we have a future together.'

She reached up and caught his finger in her hand. 'I love you too. I can't imagine spending a single day without you.'

She was going to cry again. The tears were building in her eyes.

'Can I interest you in an Edinburgh town house, Laurie Jenkins?'

'Can I interest you in a slightly dishevelled castle, Callan McGregor?'

He smiled, his eyes crinkling as pulled her towards him in a kiss. 'Let's begin negotiations. I think I'm going to need a good lawyer.'

She laughed. 'I know just the person.'

EPILOGUE

As SOON AS he walked through the doors all he could smell was the wonderful array of baking. Gingerbread, chocolate cake, freshly baked scones and the bubbling smell of lentil soup. His stomach growled in instant response but there was a bus tour due in an hour. He had to keep his mind on the job. 'Laurie, where are you?'

The former icehouse was exactly as she'd planned. Windows all the way around showing views of the gardens and views of the sea. Red and white checked tablecloths, comfortable chairs at the tables, a separate play area for kids and a *very* expensive coffee machine that Callan had already burned himself on. Still, it was red and matched perfectly. *And* it had put a huge smile on Laurie's face.

She appeared from behind the counter, looking a little flushed, wiping her hands on a towel. 'It can't be that time already?'

He raised his eyebrows. 'It is.'

'But I haven't got changed, or fixed my hair, and my make-up must be halfway down my face.'

He shook his head and put his hands on her waist. 'You look perfect.'

'But I've still to—'

He bent down and kissed her to stop her talking. It

was amazing how often he had to do that. But it worked like a charm every time. She wound her hands around his neck. 'You're distracting me,' she murmured.

'It's my job.'

He pulled back and smiled. 'I have two special customers that we can't keep waiting.'

Fourteen months of blood, sweat, tears and lots and lots of special memories. Annick Castle was theirs. Together. And it was now open to the public. The repairs had been put in order. They'd been exhausting and daunting. There had been hours of planning and negotiations with local authorities. They'd even had to redo the steps down the cliff side and install a proper handrail.

But the important thing was that they'd done them together.

And the truth was he'd never seen her look happier. She gave a nervous laugh. 'Customers. Now I'm really scared.'

'Oh, don't worry. I think they'll like this place,' he said with confidence as she flicked the sign on the door from Closed to Open.

Marion and Bert didn't waste any time. Bert went straight to the strawberry and cream sponge sitting under a glass dome. 'I'll have a bit of that and a mug of tea.' He wagged his finger at Laurie. 'Don't be giving me any of those fancy china cups.'

Marion was the extreme opposite. 'I'll have a toasted scone with butter and jam, and a pot of tea.' She nodded at Laurie. 'And I do want a china cup.'

Laurie scurried off, obviously overjoyed by her first customers. Callan sat down at one of the round tables, staring out at the crashing ocean. It was August. The doors to Annick Castle opened today. His stomach was churning a little at the thought of it.

Part of it was genuine nerves about what people might think of the place he loved. Part of it was fear that things wouldn't work out. Laurie would be devastated. He was beginning to suspect she loved this place even more than he did. Could that even be possible?

He heard the clink of china being set on a table, appreciative voices, then he felt a hand on his back and Laurie slid into the chair next to him, putting a large piece of his favourite chocolate cake on the table in front of him.

'How does it feel?'

She smiled and glanced out of the window, looking the other way towards the gardens. 'It feels right,' she said quietly as she reached over and squeezed his hands.

'No regrets about leaving London?'

She shook her head fiercely. 'Not a single one. I haven't had a tension headache since I moved here.'

'Even with all the hassles with the castle?'

'They weren't hassles. They were teething problems.' She leaned over and kissed him. 'Besides I had someone I could moan to every night in bed with me.'

He gave her a wink as he put a piece of chocolate cake in his mouth. 'I hope that wasn't the only reason you were moaning.' He didn't wait for her reaction before he let out a yelp. 'Ouch! What's that?'

Laurie jumped up. 'What's wrong? Is there something wrong with the cake?'

'There's something very wrong. I just got a lump of something in it.' He couldn't stop the gleam in his eyes as he pretended to fish something out of his mouth.

She still hadn't clicked. 'What is it?' she demanded as she made a grab for his palm. 'Oh!'

The emerald and diamond ring lay in the palm of his hand. He'd wanted to propose to her from the moment she'd moved here. But there was never a more perfect time than now—the first day of their new life together.

'Is that all you can say—oh?'

She smiled. 'Oh, no, you don't, Callan McGregor. I want the whole shebang.'

He slid down onto the floor, kneeling in front of her. 'I should have taken you to the gazebo, shouldn't I?'

She leaned forward and whispered in his ear. 'Don't worry, our last trip to the gazebo seems to have left us with more than memories.'

'Really?' He jumped straight back up and pulled her into his arms, swinging her around. 'Really?' He couldn't believe it. Nothing could be more perfect.

'Really.' She smiled as he lowered her to the floor.

For the first time in years Callan felt flustered. He grabbed the ring and knelt down again in front of her. 'Then I better make this quick, before people start getting out calendars and looking at the date.' He took both her hands in his. 'Laurie Jenkins, I love you more than life itself. Will you do me the honour of walking down our gorgeous staircase in a wedding dress and becoming my wife?' He slid the ring onto her finger.

'I think you're supposed to wait for my answer.' She smiled.

He leaned forward and kissed her, laying his hand gently on her stomach. 'It seems to me that you've already realised I've got no patience. How about we get ready for a castle full of them?'

'I can't wait,' she replied as she kissed him again and again.

* * * * *

THE HEIRESS'S
SECRET ROMANCE

MARTHA KENNERSON

I'd like to dedicate this story to all my faithful readers. If not for you I would have all these stories and characters stuck in my head with nowhere to go. Thank you for your continued support.

I would like to acknowledge all the survivors of Hurricane Harvey. Houston showed the world just how resilient we are.

Chapter 1

Kathleen Winston walked into her office, still in shock at how badly her meeting with her boss had gone. Twenty-nine-year-old Kathleen was an heiress to the multibillion-dollar Winston Construction fortune, but still worked as a special agent for the Occupational Safety and Health Administration. She released a string of profanity under her breath, dropping down into her chair. Kathleen turned away from the desk and looked over at the framed picture of her parents sitting on the credenza. Memories of the day her parents had sat their children down to explain their mother's illness were very vivid. It was also the day that changed the trajectory of her life.

Hearing her mother say the words *I have cancer* had been a knife piercing Kathleen's heart. She still felt as if the conversation had just taken place versus seven years earlier. Initially, Kathleen thought her parents were playing a very bad joke. At least she hoped they were. After all, their mother showed no signs of being sick. She was still strong, energetic and very beautiful.

But Kathleen quickly realized how serious things were by the pained look in her father's eyes.

Don't worry, Mom. I'll get them, just like I have all the others.

"What's wrong?" a voice from behind asked.

"Everything," she replied, immediately recognizing the speaker. "Simpson just killed my investigation into Kingsley Oil and Gas."

"And you're surprised? Girl, you know you can't trust no Simpson," Gilbert replied, laughing as he approached her desk.

Gilbert Ray was Kathleen's assistant and best friend since they were kids. He was one of two people at her office, the only one besides her boss, who knew her background and wealth.

"What did he do now?"

Kathleen turned and faced Gilbert. She smiled at the baby-blue suit and white dress shirt he'd paired with a blue-and-white bowtie and blue-and-white loafers. Kathleen loved the fearlessness of her friend. He always knew who he was and he never cared about what others thought about him.

"My...my, don't you look fabulous."

"Don't I?" He glanced down at himself. "I love that green Michael Kors camouflage dress you're rocking too."

"Thanks."

"Dish—what happened at the meeting?"

"Just what I said—Simpson pulled the investigation into the Kingsleys and their company," she explained.

Gilbert gave a nonchalant wave before he took a seat in one of the round chairs that sat in front of her desk. "Girl, I don't know why you are tripping. You know how you beautiful, rich, bougie people do stuff like that. If you want something to go away—" he used his hands to imitate making a phone call "—like on that game show, you use a lifeline and call a friend."

Kathleen sighed. She knew Gilbert was still upset about the way his wealthy boyfriend of nearly a year had recently ended their relationship. Kathleen sat up in her chair. "First, I know you're still salty about what Vince did, and I hate that he made me tell you what an ass he'd been, but I couldn't have you thinking something happened to him when he stopped returning your phone calls."

Gilbert smacked his lips. "I know, and I love you for it."

"Good. And I love you too. Second, I told you to stop calling me that and don't lump me in with all bougie rich people."

"But you are…both. Rich and high-class and you know it too." He frowned.

"I'm a melting pot of things, and I embrace them all," she stated matter-of-factly.

"Okay, Miss Thing. You beautiful, long haired, high-cheekbone-having, sophisticated, successful, thick-lipped melting pot you," he teased. "You're certainly rich, though."

"Excuse me, Miss Winston. Mr. Ray, the postman just dropped off the mail."

Gilbert looked over his shoulder. "You see that tray on my desk with the sign that reads Mail Here? Why don't you drop it right there?" he asked sarcastically.

"Oh… Okay." The young lady turned and hurried off.

"Thank you," Kathleen yelled after her. Her eyes bored into Gilbert. "Really?"

"What?"

"Why are you so rude to that young lady?"

Gilbert shrugged. "She's an intern."

"And you're acting like a mean girl. Stop it. It's not a good look."

"Fine." Gilbert rose from his seat. "I'll go buy the child a cookie or something. Speaking of buying things, when are you going to give me one of those black cards of yours and let me buy you some better chairs? Something nicer than these fake leather things you're forcing your guests to endure. Better still, a whole new office set for us both."

"This is a government office. We have to accept the furniture they already provided us. So deal with it."

"At least you get to fix your office up with a few antique knickknacks and those beautiful and costly contemporary artworks that grace these ugly walls while I'm stuck out there in a world full of gray."

"Oh please, talk about knickknacks. Your colorful accessorized cubicle brightens up the whole floor," Kathleen complimented him, smiling.

"True. I do love all the colors in my rainbow flag."

Kathleen laughed. "That you do."

"What were we talking about?" He tapped his index finger against his temple. "Oh yeah, the fact that you're rich and still hiding it."

"No, we were talking about what Simpson did, and my father's rich," she corrected.

"So what do you call that mega trust fund you got when you turned twenty-five or what you'll get at thirty?"

"My father's legacy…not mine," Kathleen stated expressionlessly. Her cell phone rang, and she looked at the screen. "Speaking of which…"

"You talk to him. I'm going to make a coffee run. Will you be having your usual?"

"Yes, thanks." Kathleen answered her phone. "Hi, Dad."

"Hello, Kathleen. How's my beautiful daughter?" he asked in his native French.

"I'm fine, Dad. How are you?" she replied in English. The phone fell silent, but she could hear background noises, so she knew what had happened. Kathleen repeated her statement and question, only this time in French.

Kathleen's Creole father was from the North American island of Sint Maarten. Along with her mother, the product of a Caucasian and Afro Caribbean relationship, he raised their children to speak both French and English. However, her father preferred that they converse using his native language.

"I just want to confirm that I'll be picking you up tonight at your sister's place."

"We talked about this, Dad. I have a lot going on at work and I really can't afford to—"

"What? Take a little time out to celebrate your mother's legacy and help raise money and awareness for her foundation's mission?"

"That's not fair, Dad. Of course the work of our foundation is important. But so is my job. I'm helping to ensure others don't have to go through what we did."

"And I'm proud of you for it too. Yet you have a responsibility to your family as well," he reminded.

Kathleen sighed. "Well, it looks like my workload has just lightened a bit, so yes, Dad, I'll be there."

"Good. Make sure your sister is on time. You know how she can be and I hate being late," he stated, his voice firm.

"Yes, Dad. We know. We'll both be ready when you get there." Kathleen heard her boss's voice before he appeared at her door. "Dad, I have to go. Love you, and I'll see you later."

Simpson stood in the door with his hands in his pockets. "The French language is beautiful."

"Yes, it is," she agreed.

"You didn't have to end your call on my account," he stated as he entered the office.

"Are you all right, Mr. Simpson?" Kathleen frowned. His gray suit was a bit wrinkled; he could use a haircut and he looked like he needed a nap.

"I haven't been getting much sleep, and I'm not feeling well."

"Maybe you should go see a doctor," Kathleen suggested.

"I'm on my way now, but I wanted to tell you that I think you're right."

"About the Kingsleys?" Her eyebrows snapped to attention.

"Even though all the allegations of wrongdoing by the Kingsleys and their company have been proven false, and Evan Perez, the man behind the false narratives, is behind bars, this most recent accusation didn't appear to come from anyone Perez hired. I still can't believe he thought he could get away with trying to ruin the Kingsleys, who were basically defending themselves from his many attacks. He was the one who started their war in the first place," Simpson offered, shaking his head and taking a seat.

"No, it did not. Mr. Silva seems credible and is not a part of some big conspiracy," Kathleen stated with conviction. "His only concern is about the safety of his fellow employees and ensuring their company has competent leadership."

"Yet how can we know that for sure?" Simpson challenged.

"Because he's still around. He didn't pull his complaint, and he's very specific with his concerns too."

Simpson nodded. "That's true. Yet his motives aren't completely unselfish."

"Fine, he has stock options he wants to protect against bad management. There's nothing wrong with that either. He claims the Kingsleys are putting their employees in danger because they changed leadership to someone inexperienced and inappropriate who altered policies, and their safety practices now don't follow OSHA standards. He states these changes are putting people at risk. That's reason enough to do an investigation. The man didn't even ask for confidentiality."

Kathleen remembered the detailed and painful explanation of how her mother's former employer had exposed her to dangerous chemicals, causing her to contract such rare cancers. It had been hard to take. Hearing Mr. Silva's concerns made Kathleen wonder what might have happened if someone from her mother's company had spoken out against the poor conditions in which they worked. The desire to make someone pay for what happened to her mother fueled Kathleen's desire to act. Her need for revenge became a lifeline, a reason for her to keep breathing every day. Kathleen was determined to make sure no other family would go through what they had. The Winstons lost their matriarch within a year of that conversation.

"How long has he worked for the Kingsleys?"

Kathleen reached for the file that sat on her desk. "Let's see." She flipped through the pages. "Ten years."

"It's only one complaint, but all things considered it would be prudent to do a cursory and very discreet investigation at least. With everything this family has gone through we have got to be careful."

"I can do that," she promised, clapping her hands. "Be discreet and careful, I mean."

"I'm serious, Kathleen. You have to go in under the radar and if—and that's a big *if*—you find anything, then we will bring in the cavalry. I know you're a professional, but you have to make sure your personal feelings and family history of dealing with bad chemical companies don't interfere with you getting the job done…the *right* job."

"I won't," she promised.

"Now, how do you propose to do that?"

"I can go in as one of our policy trainers. Offer them our free services. That always works and will give me access to one of the areas he's complaining about too, not to mention free rein with their staff."

Simpson shook his head. "They train their people themselves. Hell, we even sent some of our trainers to their sessions."

Kathleen tapped her fingers on the desk. "They don't have the new regulatory updates yet. I could offer to go in specifically to talk about them and help update their training materials."

"That might work, but I still need to sweeten the tea." Simpson reached into his pocket, pulled out a Kleenex and wiped his forehead.

"'Sweeten the tea'?" Kathleen held back her laughter. She always found Simpson's use of colloquialisms amusing. "Why?"

"The Kingsleys have been through hell this last year,

and if we're wrong we both could be out of jobs," he informed her, concern written all over his face.

"I'm not wrong, and if I am, I deserve to lose my job."

"Easy for you to say, Kathleen. You've been here seven years, and you come from money. I put in over fifteen years at this agency, and I can't afford to lose my job," Simpson stressed.

Kathleen came from around her desk and leaned against its edge in front of him. She reached for his hand and gave it a quick squeeze. "You won't. I promise. Mr. Silva has no connection to Mr. Perez. There have been a couple of recent changes in their senior management team and policies that have been altered that raised a few eyebrows in the industry. All these changes could be legitimate, but we won't know that for sure unless we check into it. Now how do we sweeten the tea?"

"I'm going to offer our services as a form of an apology for all the false accusations they've had to endure from government agencies as a whole. Show it as a positive PR move on both our parts."

"Do you think that will work?" Kathleen asked, feeling hopeful.

"I guess we'll see." Simpson stood. "I'll let you know after I give their company's chairman of the board and family matriarch, Victoria Kingsley, a call on my way to the doctor's."

"Great. I hope you feel better."

"Talk soon," Simpson said, walking out the office.

The moment the door closed, Kathleen stood in the middle of her office and did a happy dance. "I'm coming for you, Kingsley."

Chapter 2

Morgan Kingsley, the twenty-nine-year-old VP of field operations for Kingsley Oil and Gas, walked into the plant's cafeteria, rubbing his hands together with one thing on his mind: food. It was a room designed to make the Kingsley employees feel at ease and have a sense of home. With all the hours they all spent there away from their families, the Kingsleys felt the least they could do was make sure their employees were comfortable doing their downtime.

He walked into the brightly lit tan-and-white room, which offered various types of wood-and-steel tables paired with large cream leather folding chairs, to find his plant manager, Adrian Jones, standing in the buffet line.

"What are you doing here so early on a Friday, boss?" Adrian asked.

Morgan picked up a tray and plate and surveyed his choices. "I'm about to have breakfast."

"I can see that," Adrian replied, accepting a plate with an omelet from one of the craft service members.

"Lately you've only been around for lunch or dinner."

Skipping the special-order omelet line, Morgan filled his plate with eggs, bacon and pancakes. "Yeah, well, now that all those bogus investigations are over and that bastard Perez is behind bars, I can stay at my own place here and come right to the plant every day and enjoy some of the best breakfast in town."

After spending a few moments at the juice-and-coffee bar, both men made their way to a vacant table. "Cool," Adrian replied, pouring syrup over his stack of pancakes. "You're wearing overalls and work boots. Where are you working today?"

"Maintenance is shorthanded, and I don't want my welders falling behind." Morgan reached for his glass of juice.

"I can pull a couple of people from the south bins to help out."

"That's not necessary. Ernest and I can handle it." Morgan popped a piece of bacon in his mouth.

"Someone call my name?" Ernest Walker, the plant's maintenance director, asked, approaching the table, holding a tray of dirty dishes.

Adrian and Ernest shook hands. "I hear you got the boss doing some heavy lifting today."

"He can handle it," Ernest insisted.

"Damn right," Morgan agreed, diving into his food.

"There you are," a small, gray-haired woman called out as she approached the table, wiping her hands with her apron.

Morgan and Adrian rose from their seats. "Good morning, Ms. Monica," all three men greeted. Ms. Monica, as everyone called her, was the sixty-year-old craft service manager and head chef who had worked for the Kingsleys for nearly thirty years. She was like a grandmother to all the Kingsley boys and pretty much everyone else too.

Ms. Monica was just one of the many reasons Morgan was so happy to have the Perez fiasco behind his family and their business. The plant, located just outside of Port Arthur, Texas, and their oil rigs were his safe haven. The death of his father and uncle were beyond difficult, but his extended family at their plant made growing up without them a bit more bearable.

Often, their mother's love could be suffocating, so when she finally allowed them to spend time at the plant with a few people she trusted who weren't bodyguards, Morgan relished those moments. The plant became his second home and he was fiercely protective of it too.

"We need to talk about the menu that nutritionist lady sent over the other day."

"What's wrong with the menu, Ms. Monica?" Morgan pulled out a chair for her.

Ms. Monica took the seat. "Nothing's wrong with it. Your mother was right. Healthier, balanced diets are something we should all strive for. None of us are getting any younger, you know. In fact, nearly half the folks working have been here since the doors opened. It's just going to be too much money buying so many organic vegetables from that company they recommended. I know where we can get everything we need for much less money. I know y'all rich and all, but it never hurts nobody to save a little money."

Morgan laughed. "You are so right, Ms. Monica, and I appreciate how you look after us—"

"But…" She crossed her arms.

"We have some pretty solid agreements with a number of vendors. Agreements that my mother negotiated personally."

Ms. Monica laughed. "Well, in that case, I'm sure Victoria got you a rock-bottom price."

"Yes, ma'am, I'm sure she did."

"Well, I better get back to my kitchen. It'll be time to serve lunch before I know it. Speaking of lunch, my friend's beautiful daughter—"

"Ms. Monica, we've talked about this already." Morgan helped her out of her chair. *Here we go again. I really wish everyone would stop trying to fix me up. Can't a brother just get back to work and enjoy the fact that no one is coming after us for one thing or another?* "I appreciate your concern, but I don't need help getting dates."

"I'm not trying to help you get hooked up with some hussy," Ms. Monica said and playfully swatted at his hand. Morgan pressed his lips together, preventing his laugh from escaping. "I'm trying to help you find a nice girl you can marry."

"Ms. Monica—"

"And not like that gold digger Bonnie Ford," she continued talking, shaking her head as if he hadn't said a word. "I still can't believe she tried to use your relationship to advance her family's business interest. Ridiculous! Compared to your family's other refineries, that small oil refinery of theirs would look like one of those ugly hateful stepsisters standing next to the beautiful princess. Not to mention all the times he's filed for bankruptcy."

"It was a long time ago," he replied, still feeling a mixture of anger and embarrassment. Morgan had no idea that his three-year, loving relationship with Bonnie—at least he'd thought it was loving—had meant so little to her. He certainly didn't know her and her parents' only agenda for them was to forge a business empire between their families.

"That's my point. It's time for you to stop playing with all these silly little girls and find a woman with some substance. It's time you found yourself a wife."

Morgan checked his watch. "Look at the time. I should get over to the shop."

"Fine, go, but we are not done with this discussion, young man," she insisted, walking toward the kitchen.

Yes, we are. The last thing I need is a wife.

Ms. Monica was like family and Morgan knew she meant well, but he was happy with his life just the way it was. Sexually satisfying liaisons with temporary companions and keeping his heart protected from another bad break suited him just fine. Morgan threw his trash away and set his dishes in the collection pans. He walked toward the exit when his cell phone rang. "Hey, what's up, A?" Morgan answered, stopping shy of the exit.

"China's in labor," Alexander, Morgan's elder brother and CEO of Kingsley Oil and Gas, replied.

"Oh. Snap. Is China all right?"

"She's…emotional but strong," Alexander replied.

"That she is," Morgan agreed.

"And beautiful…so damn beautiful," Alexander murmured.

Morgan heard something in his brother's voice, something unfamiliar. Fear maybe. "Are you okay, A?"

"Yeah, but I could use some backup," he admitted.

"I'm on the way."

"You sure, Morgan?"

"I'm sure. Where am I coming?"

"Woman's Hospital. Thanks, man."

Morgan could hear the relief in his brother's voice. "I'll take the chopper and see you in about an hour."

Morgan put his phone away, pivoted and walked toward another exit, one that would get him to his car the fastest. He still couldn't believe another Kingsley would be arriving soon. Now Morgan had two brothers with children, something he never thought he'd see— so soon, anyway—and briefly wondered if that was a journey he'd ever take.

"I can't believe I let you talk me into this," Kathleen grumbled that night, trying to sit still in the makeup artist's chair. She was anxious to find out if the Kingsley investigation would move forward and kept thinking about all the things that needed to be done before she could get started.

"Like you could go to the Irene Winston Cancer Foundation gala with Dad and me looking like—"

"Like what, Hannah, myself?"

"No, not you. Not the real you, anyway. Maybe a more sedated you," her younger sister conceded.

"I work in the real world where all this excess is not necessary and frowned upon. Just because I don't walk around looking like a glam goddess like you, little sister, Miss TV Chef, doesn't mean I don't look good."

"I didn't say you didn't. What I am saying is that you need to showcase all of our mother's wonderful gifts. The high cheekbones, seductive eyes and—" she ran her hands through her own hair "—all this thick beautiful black hair."

"Hannah, you sound like a beauty commercial," Kathleen said, laughing. "Why aren't Wesley and Kennedy going to this thing tonight?"

"You know our big brother and sister are workaholics just like you. They're out of town on business. Plus they're always at these things. Our foundation's charity events usually have us traveling all over the country. Since this one was local, right in your backyard, we figured you could step up for once," Hannah explained.

"For once?"

"Yes, Kathleen. You rarely make an appearance to any of our social events, be they personal or charitable."

Kathleen bit her lip. "I like my privacy. Besides, my job—"

"Has nothing to do with your family. Stop hiding behind it."

"I'm not," she murmured, knowing her sister was right. Kathleen had enjoyed attending their charitable functions just as much as her sister until their mother got sick. Her mother's illness and trying to find ways to deal with her anger became her focus.

"Whatever. Which dress do you want to wear? They're both Versace." Hannah held up a black, low-backed lace gown in one hand and a red, strapless, flowing gown with a high split in the other. "If I were you—"

"I'll take the black one, please."

"Red, it is," Hannah replied. "You need to show off your banging body and gorgeous face if you want to catch a worthy man."

"I'm not looking for a worthy man, Hannah."

"You should be. You're twenty-nine and haven't had a man since college."

"I've been focusing on my career. Making a difference in people's lives is important to me. I don't need any unnecessary distractions."

"You can still fight your crusade and have a man too. You'd be amazed what great sex can do for a working woman's disposition."

Kathleen rolled her eyes. "My temperament is just fine, thank you very much. Anyway, I don't think there are many men out there like Dad. It would take someone pretty substantial to get me to deviate from my course."

"You won't know until you try and find one," she said challengingly.

"I don't see you running to the altar with Peter."

"And you won't. We've outlived our usefulness for each other," Hannah explained, picking up a comb, running it through her hair and admiring her own beautiful makeup job.

"What? When did that happen?"

"That's a story for another time. You look fabulous." Hannah turned and hugged her makeup artist. "Lisa, you are amazing."

"Thank you, but you both offer a beautiful canvas for my work. I'll see you on the set in the morning. Have a good night, ladies," Lisa said before walking out the door.

"The set?" Kathleen frowned. "I didn't know you were working."

"They booked a couple of promos for me while I'm in town. Houston's one of my biggest markets," she declared proudly.

Kathleen's phone beeped. She reached for it and read the message. A huge smile crawled across her face. Kathleen had just received the go-ahead to go after the Kingsleys. She felt giddy. Like she'd just found out that her favorite book was being turned into a movie. Her boss might believe the Kingsleys were innocent but her gut wouldn't let her join that bandwagon just yet and Kathleen always followed her gut.

"Good news?" Hannah asked.

Curiosity was written all over her sister's face. "The best. I just got my new assignment."

"Oh. Here." Hannah handed Kathleen the red dress, brushing off her news. "Put this one on with the sexy red-and-gold Versace heels I pulled out."

"What are you wearing?"

"Versace, of course, only my dress is a deeper red." Hannah gave her sister a Cheshire cat smile.

"If I didn't know that your IQ was as high as mine or that you were a beast when it came to cooking, I'd swear you were a spoiled, rich woman enamored by the trappings of your lifestyle," Kathleen stated.

Hannah shrugged. "There's nothing wrong with me enjoying the fruits of Dad's and my own labor. Anyway, most of my wardrobe comes to me free."

"Yes, I keep forgetting. People *actually* want to see you in their clothes."

Kathleen walked into her sister's oversize dressing room, dropped her robe and stepped into the gown her sister had selected. It fit her perfectly, accentuating all of her physical assets. Kathleen stared in the full-length mirror and smiled. Her light eyes sparkled, the makeup highlighted her golden-bronze skin beautifully, her black hair full of curls. Kathleen was thankful her hair was pulled up and out of her face.

She hadn't seen the woman staring back at her in quite some time. Not only did she look like a younger, slightly darker version of her mother, which made her both happy and sad, she rarely wore makeup or such fancy clothes anymore. Kathleen only cared about stopping companies from hurting their employees and making the bad guy pay, and she didn't care how she looked doing it. Her heartbeat increased, and she had to fight back her tears. She knew her sister would kill her if she messed up her makeup.

"Ready or not, I'm coming in," Hannah called out before walking into the room. "Oh wow, sis. You look divine…and just like Mom."

Kathleen swallowed hard. The fact that her job didn't require her to dress up was only one reason she didn't like to do it. The other was because it reminded her of just how much she missed her mother. Hannah was right. Irene Winston had blessed her daughters with her beauty.

"So do you," Kathleen replied, smiling at Hannah through the mirror. She turned to face her sister. "I'd say we could pass for twins, except your dress leaves little to the imagination with such a low cut in the front."

Hannah turned around. "And the back," she added, smiling.

Both women laughed. "You are a mess, Hannah."

"I know. Here you go." Hannah handed her sister a black velvet box.

"What's this?" Kathleen's eyebrows snapped together.

"Just a few accessories," she explained.

Kathleen opened the box and her breath caught in her throat. "Oh no, I'm not wearing these." She quickly closed the box and tried to hand it back to her sister. It was like the box held a deadly secret or something. It was one more thing bringing up emotions she was trying to keep buried. The loss of her mother might have fueled her career, but personally it was something she'd never completely dealt with.

"Will you stop being silly? We don't have time to go by your house and get yours so you'll just have to borrow my set tonight."

"That would be a waste of trip since my set isn't at my house," she murmured.

Kathleen heaved a sigh and slowly opened the box as if she'd expected the million-dollar diamond-and-ruby choker and matching stud earrings had disappeared. They had each gotten a set when they'd turned twenty-one. Their father had showered them with jewelry their whole lives. He told them it brought him joy especially since their mother was no longer around to buy things for and spoil.

That was another example as to why Kathleen didn't waste her time dating. There were too many ideals a man would have to live up to, and spoiling her had nothing to do with it. It was the unconditional love that made them want to do such nice and extravagant things for one another. Kathleen just knew that type of love would be hard to find.

"Don't tell me something happened to yours." Fear crossed Hannah's face. "Dad's going to be heartbroken."

Kathleen frowned at Hannah as she reached for the earrings. "Don't be silly. Most of my jewelry is in my safety deposit box. I only keep a few pieces in my home safe." She removed the necklace from the box and placed it around her neck.

"Why not keep all your stuff in your home safe?"

"Because it's not like I wear so much jewelry every day."

"Good point." Hannah adjusted her diamond neck-lace. "How's work going anyway? I know you can't tell me who you're going after but whoever it is had better watch out."

Kathleen smiled. She had gone up against some powerful people in her career and while ambition had never been a motivating factor for Kathleen, she knew bringing down the Kingsleys would be a big feather in her career cap. "Let's just say it's a really big fish that I can't wait to catch and fry."

"You go, girl. Ready? I just got a text. Dad's here, and you know how he feels about being late." Kathleen heard her phone beep. She knew she'd just received the same message. "You ready to spend your Friday night with Dad?"

"I might as well be." Kathleen gave herself one final look in the mirror and smiled. She knew how much her mother had loved to dress up and that she'd be really happy right now. "Let's go celebrate Mom and raise a lot of money for cancer research." *Tomorrow I'll start the process of bringing down another company that won't make the safety of their employees a priority.*

Chapter 3

After an eventful weekend, Morgan walked into the plant's operations director's office, drinking from his travel mug, to find his mother standing in the middle of the room looking out the window. She was wearing a blue pantsuit that showed off how physically fit she was, emphasizing the fact that age was nothing but a number. Her bag sat on the desk next to her personalized hard hat.

"Mother, what are you doing here?" Morgan asked, checking his watch. His mother wasn't exactly a morning person these days, so he was trying not to let her unexpected visit concern him, but the last couple of times she'd surprised him it had been to share bad news.

Morgan was actually looking forward to getting back to work and focusing on expanding into new territories—all the things he'd been working on before Perez entered into their lives. Still reeling from the excitement of the weekend, the birth of another Kingsley and seeing how happy his brothers were, Morgan was actually considering taking Ms. Monica up on her offer to introduce him to her friend's daughter. Although he knew that particular thought would soon pass.

Victoria turned and faced Morgan. "Good morning, son. I realize we've had an exciting weekend and that you might be a little out of sorts on this bright Monday morning, but I'm sure you haven't forgotten the appropriate way to greet your mother."

Morgan sighed and placed his cup on the desk next to his mother's hat. He leaned in and kissed her on the cheek. "My apologies. Good morning, and to what do I owe the pleasure of this visit? Is everything good with Baby A?" His heart skipped several beats at the thought that something could be wrong with his new nephew. Morgan never imagined that something so small could knock him off balance and make him feel so much.

Victoria's face lit up with pride. "Alexander the third is wonderful," she reassured, smiling, taking a seat in front of the desk. "I'm here because with all the excitement around little Alexander's birth this weekend I failed to mention that you'll be receiving a visitor today."

"A visitor?" He reached for his coffee.

"Yes. I got a call Friday afternoon from another one of my well-placed sources in our state government offering me a few olive branches so to speak for all the trouble we've…our company had to endure this last year."

"Oh, really, what type of olive branch?" Morgan questioned, narrowing his eyes while the hairs on the back of his neck rose. At this point Morgan didn't trust anyone from any government agency.

"The only one you need to worry about is the one from OSHA. They're sending one of their trainers to update our material and orientate our employees on some new regulatory updates."

"They're what?" Morgan frowned. *Why in the hell would I need or want to use any of their trainers?*

"You heard me, son."

Morgan went around the desk and dropped down in the chair. He knew better than to argue with his mother about the decisions she made for the company, especially those that might have political ramifications. He had to pick his words carefully.

"Do you really want someone from any government agency in our business after everything we've been through? I certainly don't. I can send a couple of our trainers for a train-the-trainer session and they can come back and train everyone else here. You realize they send their trainers to our training center for a number of different programs we conduct?" he reminded his mother, trying to keep his annoyance under control.

"I do, son, and while that sounds like a great idea, unfortunately I've already agreed and given my word."

Morgan gave his head a quick shake. "When will they get here?"

Victoria gave a nonchalant shrug. "I have no idea. All I know is that they arrive today."

Morgan grabbed his cup and took a sip. "I'll listen to what they have to offer, but if it's not up to our standards, the ones you set, I'll send them packing."

Victoria rose from her seat and smiled. "I wouldn't expect anything less. Now, let's go." She reached for her hard hat.

Morgan stood. "Where are we going?"

"To talk to some of the line staff. It's been a while since I've been out here. I'd like to see a few people.

Just deliver me to Adrian, and you can wait for our guest in his office."

"Yes, ma'am." Morgan offered her his arm, and they walked out of the office.

Kathleen arrived at the Kingsley plant close to ten, much later than she would have liked thanks to an unexpected traffic jam on the freeway. She was impressed by the level of security just to gain entrance to the property and the plant itself, although part of her wondered if that was a sign that the Kingsleys were trying to hide something. Kathleen exited her vehicle, pulled out her roller bag and purse and made her way to the guard's stand.

"Good morning, ma'am. May I help you?" one of the three guards greeted.

"Yes." Kathleen pulled out her ID and flashed it to the guard. "I'm Kathleen Winston from OSHA, and I'm here to conduct some training sessions."

"One moment." The officer reached for his phone at the same time Kathleen's rang. She checked the screen and saw that it was her father calling. Instead of answering she sent him to voice mail.

The guard handed Kathleen a visitor's badge. "You'll need to keep this on you at all times. Please follow me. May I help you with your bag?"

"No, thanks. I have it."

Kathleen followed her escort over to a small truck. He handed her a hard hat. "You need to put this on." He gave her the once over, and the corners of his mouth turned down as he nodded.

"Is everything okay?"

"Yes, ma'am. It's just most of our female visitors don't think to wear sensible shoes like the ones you're wearing."

Kathleen looked down, past the conservative black suit and white blouse she wore to the black leather loafers on her feet, and laughed. "This isn't my first time working in a plant." She got in the truck and watched the guard load her things while she put on the hat. Kathleen was glad she'd remembered to put her hair in a low, tight bun when she got dressed.

"My name is Van, ma'am," the guard stated as he got in the truck behind the wheel.

"Pleased to meet you," she replied, smiling.

Van gave Kathleen a map of the plant in the form of a brochure before giving her the layout as he drove around the outskirts. He highlighted the major points of interest. Van explained that she'd have to have an escort to each location.

"Will you be that escort?"

"No, ma'am. That will either be the plant manager, Adrian Jones, or someone he assigns."

Kathleen had done her research and she knew all the names of the key staff and the positions they held at the plant; however, several of their photos hadn't been available. She especially found it surprising how little she was able to find out about the Kingsleys. Yes, there was a great deal of detail about their recent troubles, their financial fortune and of course their family's matriarchs, but minimal information beyond tabloid gossip was available about the personal lives of the heirs.

They drove toward a large one-story white building with the Kingsley name on it. "Is that where I'm going?"

"At some point I'm sure. That's the administrative building where you'll find the training center. However, I was told to bring you to the plant manager's office."

They rode in silence through the middle of the plant on what was a main street, and Kathleen was surprised to see a five-story glass office building surrounded by several other equally impressive buildings of varying sizes positioned in the center of the plant. *Wow. You can't judge a book by its cover but this place is pretty great.* "This plant is like a small town."

"You haven't seen anything yet. The Kingsleys take good care of their people." They pulled into an assigned parking space and exited the truck.

I'll keep that in mind.

Kathleen collected her things and followed Van into the building where another security guard met them. Before the guard could offer a greeting, a tall Hispanic man wearing jeans and a white button-down shirt with Kingsley Oil and Gas monogrammed above his left shirt pocket said, "Good morning, Ms. Winston. I'm Paz Villarreal, operations manager." He offered her his hand.

"Pleased to meet you," she replied, accepting his callus-riddled hand, and smiled.

"Thanks, I got it," he told the officer from his building as he patted him on the back. "Thanks, Van, I got it from here. You can get back to your post."

He nodded. "Thank you, Van," Kathleen said.

"No problem, ma'am."

"May I help you with your bag?" Paz offered.

"No, thank you. I'm fine. We passed your training center coming in. Will I not be working there?"

"Eventually." They walked over to the elevator and took the short ride up to the fifth floor. He led her past a small waiting area and down a long hall with offices on each side. They came to the end of the hall and stood in front of a door with a sign that read Operations Administration. Paz opened the door and stood aside as Kathleen entered. It wasn't at all what she'd expected. The waiting area had two low-back leather sofas sitting against the left and right walls with framed blueprints of the plant hanging above them. An expensive Persian rug covered the slate floors, and a long fish tank filled the back wall.

"Very nice."

Paz laughed. "You haven't seen anything yet. Follow me." He led her toward a door in the corner.

Kathleen's forehead creased. "No receptionist?"

"It's not necessary. You can't get up here without an escort unless you're an employee or a Kingsley." He led her through the door.

Time to get to work. "I was wondering, are they here often...the Kingsleys?" She gave him a half smile.

"Sure."

"How involved are they with the staff? I mean, do they spend much time with the employees? What do they do while they're here?" Kathleen tried not to sound like she was going down a checklist but she knew she was failing in that effort. She prayed her face didn't show how unsettled she was. It was not as if this was the first time she had to come into a facility incognito to find out what was going on, but something felt different about this one. Her boss was right—the Kingsleys were a big deal—and she couldn't mess this up. Kathleen knew the outcome of her investigation could have far-reaching ramifications.

Paz looked at Kathleen as if she was speaking a foreign language and he didn't understand a word she was saying. "They work just like the rest of us," he replied, frowning.

They walked down another corridor, passing several more offices until they made it to the large double doors at the end of the hall. "You can wait in here, and Mr. Jones will be right with you." Paz opened the door, and Kathleen walked in, stopping before she could get more than a foot into the room.

"Back again, Adrian?" a baritone voice said, sending an unfamiliar chill down Kathleen's spine. The sound came from a olive-skinned man with a short haircut and a fine beard. His long jean-clad legs were propped up on the desk, and he was reading through what appeared to be a report. When he raised his head, and Kathleen caught his gaze, his hazel eyes rendered her mute. Kathleen's throat was suddenly dry, and she blinked rapidly. The short-sleeved white shirt he wore with the company's logo on the pocket accentuated his wide chest and big arms.

"Oh my," she whispered to herself. Kathleen had seen handsome men before, but this man was unlike any of those. The ruggedly handsome gentleman sitting before her looked like someone from one of the old black-and-white Westerns she and her mother used to enjoy watching together. Her mother would tell Kathleen, "That's what a man's man is, darling," when one appeared on the screen. Today was the first time she'd seen one in person, and the thought made Kathleen smile.

Morgan slowly lowered his papers to the desk, brought his feet to the floor and stood. He felt like his whole body was moving in slow motion. Morgan had seen beautiful women before, but the exquisite creature standing in front of him was different. Her heart-shaped face and flawless skin was mostly makeup free. She appeared to be a foot or so shorter than Morgan; her smile was faint but stunning, and while she tried to cover her perfectly shaped body in conservative clothes, Morgan could see that she had curves in all the right places that called out to him, and his body was responding. It was something that never happened by the sight of a woman.

Damn!

Paz stepped forward. "This is Kathleen Winston. Kathleen, this is—"

He raised his left hand and waved him off. Morgan hadn't heard anything beyond her name. What he didn't recognize were the emotions she had provoked in him. He felt warm, he couldn't seem to focus and he had a sudden desire to touch her. He'd heard about this happening before, only he was usually watching from the sideline of his brothers' lives.

Morgan quickly righted himself. "You must be the trainer from OSHA," Morgan forced out, extending his hand. "I'm—"

"Yes," Kathleen interrupted, offering her hand.

Morgan felt a spark as he gave her small, delicate hand a shake. *Get it together.* "Excuse the calluses."

Kathleen smiled, sending another spark through his body, the sweet scent she was wearing attacking his senses. "No problem." She freed her hand.

"May I?" She gestured toward one of the two large leather wingback chairs that sat in front of the mahogany wood desk.

"Please."

Morgan returned to his seat and watched as Kathleen quickly removed four medium-sized binders from her bag and placed them on the desk. He told himself he would listen to what she had to say, but he would send her away as soon as she read her last page. There was no way in hell this beautiful woman could teach anything to his men. They wouldn't be able to concentrate. He sure as hell couldn't right then.

Kathleen removed her electronic tablet from her bag and turned it on. She handed Morgan a binder and said, "I've taken the liberty of highlighting a few deficiencies in your training program."

"Deficiencies?" Morgan sat forward and opened the binder, feeling annoyed by her assumption in spite of being so turned on by her presence.

"The first tab has my résumé and all my credentials and certifications. If you look behind the second tab, you'll find my recommendations for improvement," Kathleen explained.

"That was mighty presumptuous of you, considering the state uses our material as part of its training program." He hardened his expression as he glanced down at the pages.

"Not really. It's my job to ensure all safety protocols are adhered to regardless of whose name is on the building.

"I—"

"Look, I'm sure you're loyal to the Kingsley family." She shook her head as if that was the most ridiculous thing she'd ever heard.

"You have no idea," Morgan replied.

"However there are some things where loyalty isn't a part of the equation."

That was when Morgan realized she had no idea who she was talking to. He remembered that she'd launched into her presentation before he had a chance to introduce himself. *She's arrogant and another know-it-all when it comes to my family.* "In my mind and my family's, loyalty is everything."

"This isn't about you or your family. Making improvements to your systems is about protecting you and your coworkers. Shall I continue?" Kathleen's eyebrows stood at attention.

The girl's got spunk. The way her eyes bored into him was wreaking havoc on his system. Morgan folded his arms across his chest. "Please."

Chapter 4

Morgan sat back and watched Kathleen make her presentation as he flipped through the pages of her binder ahead of her. He tried to focus on her words, but her green-gold eyes and luscious lips scrambled his brain. Only a few phases broke through the fog of annoyance and attraction, one of which he had to address.

"Wait, did you say we need to switch from our computer-based training program to a more group-based, interactive one?" *That's not going to happen.* "The industry, the world for that matter, is moving more toward digital and you want us to pull back."

"Yes, statistics show people respond better in a working group setting like the one I'm recommending. They learn from their peers, and it strengthens relationships between coworkers."

Morgan dropped his hands. "My team already works well together. They don't need a feel-good session to make them better at their job." He closed the binder. "Stick to the regulatory updates, and I'll make sure our systems are brought current based on those changes."

Kathleen raised her chin and held his gaze. "While I appreciate your opinion, it doesn't count, Mr. Jones."

"What do we have here?" Victoria asked as she entered the office with Adrian on her heels. She placed her hat back on the desk.

Morgan and Kathleen got to their feet. "Victoria Kingsley, meet Kathleen Winston, the trainer OSHA sent."

Victoria extended her hand. "Pleased to meet you, and welcome to Kingsley Oil and Gas. I take it things are going well."

"Not exactly," Morgan stated.

Unfortunately, thanks to Mr. Tall, Handsome and Too-Damn-Sexy-for-His-Own-Good.

"Miss Winston seems to think we should abandon our tried-and-true computer-based training in favor of her more interactive-type program," Morgan explained. His jaw tightened.

Kathleen glared at Morgan before turning her attention to Victoria. "It's not my program, and I didn't suggest you abandon your computer-based training altogether—just adjust it a bit."

"A bit." Morgan pointed to the binders that sat on his desk. "According to the data in your unnecessarily long, although well-put-together, presentation, you recommend we cut our program by fifty percent."

"And replace it with a more productive method of training," she countered.

"Says you." Morgan crossed his arms.

"Says several experts. How did you even see that? We haven't even gotten to that section yet." Kathleen made her annoyance clear. She thought he was acting like a petulant child.

I bet you stomp your feet and hold your breath, too, if a woman doesn't drop to her knees on command. Oh, my goodness. Where the hell did that come from, Kathleen?

"I'm good at multitasking, and I pay attention to details."

Another warm sensation ran through her body. "I bet you do," she murmured.

Victoria laughed as she reached for her buzzing phone. "Well, I see you have everything under control, son." She started reading her incoming text.

"'Son'?" Kathleen's forehead creased; she was clearly shocked by the revelation. "I thought you were the plant manager."

"No, that would be me," another man replied, raising his right hand.

Victoria placed her hands on her hips. "Morgan Kingsley, did you not properly introduce yourself to this young woman?"

"I tried, but she launched right into her presentation. I think she was a bit awestruck." Morgan smirked.

Kathleen's left eyebrow rose. "As were you," she snapped back before she could stop herself.

"Touché," Morgan acknowledged.

"Enough." Victoria picked up her bag and hard hat. "I have to get back to Houston."

Morgan dropped his hands. "I'll see you out, Mother."

"No, Adrian will. You and Miss Winston are going to get to work." Victoria turned and faced Kathleen. "While I appreciate your input and we will take your recommendations under advisement, we will continue to do what we feel is best for our company. If you can't accept that, I have to rescind my offer to allow your presence at my plant."

That can't happen. "Yes, of course. I understand," she replied nervously.

"Good, now pass me one of those binders, and I'll read through it on the ride home."

Nice going, Kathleen—you almost get yourself kicked out of here before you can even get started. Kathleen handed Victoria a binder and watched as she kissed her son goodbye and left. She had heard and read a great deal about Victoria Kingsley but nothing compared to meeting her in person. While she was very firm and definitive in regard to her business, watching her maternal interactions with her son was something clearly not many got to witness. She felt honored.

"Well, I guess that's that." Kathleen started packing up her bag. "I'll focus on the regulatory changes as you requested, Mr. Kingsley."

Kathleen watched the handsome Kingsley drop his shoulders and lean against his desk. The closer he got to Kathleen, the more out of control she felt. Kathleen knew she had to bring her wayward mind and body under control. He was part of her investigation, after all.

"It's Morgan, and if you prefer you can conduct your sessions using your interactive method. If the team is receptive to the idea, I'll consider incorporating your way into *some* of our program."

Kathleen offered up a small smile. "Was that too hard?"

"Not at all. I can be a reasonable man when I want to be, Miss Winston."

"I guess we'll find out just how reasonable you are when you attend my class, and please call me Kathleen."

"All right, Kathleen, but I have no intention of attending your class," he said matter-of-factly.

Kathleen felt a slow smile spread across her face. "Why? Are you afraid you just might learn something and realize my method is better than the program you so covet?"

"Not at all." His face went blank, and he held her gaze.

Kathleen dropped her eyes and reached for her rolling bag. "Shall I get started?"

"Absolutely."

Morgan came from around the desk and reached for Kathleen's bag. "I got it," she said.

"I insist," he replied as he placed his large hand over hers.

Kathleen felt a spark that wasn't electrical and quickly pulled her hand back. *You have got to get it together.* "Fine."

"And if I may suggest…you are open to suggestions, right?"

Annoyed by the sarcasm, Kathleen rolled her eyes. "Yes, of course."

"You should lose whatever that perfume is you're wearing. The men might find it distracting if you want them to focus on your class. Don't worry—they'd never be inappropriate."

"I'm not, and I know the drill. Besides, I'm not wearing perfume," Kathleen explained, walking toward the door.

Morgan stepped in her path, preventing Kathleen from moving forward. He stared into her eyes and said, "If you're not wearing perfume, then it's you. All you," he concluded, his voice low and husky.

Kathleen felt light-headed. She thought for a moment

that somehow all the oxygen had been sucked out of the room. *Focus, Kathleen.*

"I want my men to concentrate on the training and not the trainer," he continued.

Kathleen pushed her shoulders back and raised her chin defiantly. "Maybe it's you with the concentration problem. Every consider leading by example?" She stepped around him and walked out the door.

Kathleen's first day wasn't as difficult as she'd imagined. It was just the opposite. Everyone was extremely nice but not in a sucking-up type of way, either. The assistance offered to Kathleen no matter where she went or what she requested was unlike anything she'd ever experienced. Everyone seemed genuinely happy to help. Even her initial class, in which she'd expected to receive pushback, especially from the more seasoned staff, went well. Everyone appeared open to the training, and some were even excited about the opportunity to explore her new methods. Other than that initial hiccup in the office that morning, she had a good day. Kathleen still couldn't get over the effect Morgan Kingsley had on her mind and body. Her attraction to him was an unexpected hurdle she had to get over. The jury was still out on Morgan and his company.

While Kathleen had limited access to the Kingsley systems, she was given the ability to review all the training material including their archived programs. A big part of Mr. Silva's charge had been that the new COO had implemented policy changes that put the staff in danger. Kathleen was in the perfect position to prove or disprove that allegation. The first thing she did was check the company's policy change log against what they had filed with the state. She found no irregulari-

ties. In fact, she was impressed with just how well orga-
nized they were. However, Kathleen knew just because
the paperwork was in order didn't mean everything
was aboveboard. Yet for some reason she felt relieved
that the paperwork confirmed what she'd seen so far.
It was like she was rooting for them, which was something that she never did this early in the investigation.

Employers often put one thing in writing but expected their employees to cut corners to get the job
done faster and cheaper, regardless of the potential
risk to themselves and their families. Most employees went along with such antics because they felt they
had no choice. Kathleen was determined to make sure
the Kingsley employees knew they had a choice. Over
the next couple of weeks, Kathleen conducted what
she called "featherlight interviews" with her trainees. She would weave investigative questions into her
training sessions and found nothing out of the ordinary.
While Kathleen appreciated his hands-off approach to
her work, she found herself looking forward to their
check-in moments, as Morgan called them, at the end
of each day.

But Kathleen combed through old and new training records and found a smoking gun. Unfortunately,
it wasn't what she'd expected. The most damaging evidence she found was against a senior-level welder by
the name of Mundos Silva. While Kathleen couldn't review the Kingsley employees' personal records, she did
have access to their training files. It seems Mr. Mundos
Silva had experienced a great deal of difficulty passing
most of his required training. It had taken him longer
than others and multiple times to pass. There were notes
in his files indicating that his supervisors had offered
him assistance and additional training in areas where

he was having difficulty. Unfortunately, Mr. Silva refused the help. Kathleen found that the outside training specialist recommended that Mr. Silva be demoted to a position more appropriate for his current level of ability. The recommendation and change took effect long before there was a change in leadership.

"Damn," Kathleen replied, after reading the last note in his file. She called her boss.

"Kathleen, what's up?" Simpson answered.

"I found something."

"What?" She could hear the anxiousness in his voice.

"It's not against the Kingsleys, but Mr. Silva."

"Tell me."

After going over everything she'd found out so far, she read the final note in the file. "'Mr. Silva is a valued employee who we should do everything we can to try to help according to the Kingsley Family Stay Whole policy.'"

"What the hell is the Kingsley Family Stay Whole policy?" he asked.

"Apparently anyone who's been here for more than five years is eligible to receive any form of help they may need in the event of a crisis, to stay whole."

"What?"

"I just heard about it. The Kingsleys believe in taking care of their employees. There's even something for those who've been here for fewer than five years," she added.

"Maybe we can get a job there after we're both fired. It's time to come home, Kathleen."

"Not yet. You need to bring Mr. Silva in for a follow-up conversation."

Kathleen was experiencing a whirlwind of emotions. Confusion and anger that she might have let herself get played and pleasure that it appeared the Kingsleys were actually what she was finding them to be: good people with a great company.

"I'm already ahead of you, but there's nothing to find," Simpson insisted.

"You may be right, but I have to be sure. Besides, I have to finish the training and system updates. That way I can leave, and no one will ever know the real reason for my visit."

"Fine, but make it fast," he said before hanging up on her.

Kathleen had a feeling that Simpson was right, but for reasons she didn't want to explore she just knew she had to stay a little longer…for Morgan.

Chapter 5

The pledge that Morgan made to keep his distance proved to be harder than he thought. He spent the next two weeks doing everything he could to avoid spending any time alone with Kathleen. Whenever she came near him with questions, concerns or comments his brain seem to shut down, allowing his hormones to take control. After turning down several recent offers for female companionship, putting himself through grueling workouts in his home gym and riding his horses until he started to smell like one himself, Morgan spent the entire weekend wondering what Kathleen was doing. She never wore rings, so he figured she wasn't married, but it seemed impossible for a woman like that to be single. The question and idea had made him nuts all weekend.

Morgan had a history of dating beautiful and compliant women, but none of them affected him like Kathleen. Her beauty aside, it was her passion for her work, the compassion he'd seen her show his team, but most of all, the way she challenged him when she believed she was right about something that attracted him.

It was another Monday afternoon when Morgan sat

at a table in the cafeteria across from where Kathleen was sitting talking to several of his employees. However, this time she seemed to be focusing her attention on Troy, one of his senior welders. The way she threw her head back when she laughed at whatever he was saying to her grated at him and he had no idea why.

"I'm surprised Kathleen hasn't filed charges against you," Adrian said before biting into his chicken.

"What?" Morgan frowned and he looked over at his friend.

Adrian wiped his mouth with his napkin and said, "The way you're attacking her with those glares."

Morgan turned his head and pushed his plate forward. "I don't know what you're talking about."

"Sure you do. Just ask Kathleen out already," Adrian suggested.

"Don't be ridiculous. First, Kathleen works here. Second, she may be married or at least have a man. And third, I'm not—"

"Don't say you're not interested because I know better."

"Do you now?"

"We've been friends for over ten years, and I know when someone's piqued your interest. Considering all the hard labor you've put in these last couple weeks, I'd say Kathleen has more than done that."

What she's doing is driving me crazy. "Like I said, she works here—"

"She's working here. She doesn't *work* here, and as far as her being married or having a man, she isn't, and she doesn't."

Morgan could feel his anger on the rise, and he didn't understand why. Had Adrian asked Kathleen out? Did she turn him down? Had he already gone out with her?

Those questions were racing through his mind and driving him crazy. "How the hell do you know that?"

Adrian must have sensed the change in Morgan's demeanor. "Chill, man, I heard one of the welding guys asked her out."

"Who?" Morgan hadn't realized that he'd fisted his hands on the table.

Adrian shrugged and took another bite of his food. "I'm not sure, but I think it might be one of the guys she's sitting next to. I don't know if she said yes."

I'm going to fire his ass. Wait, where the hell did that come from? He used the palm of his right hand to rub against his temple.

Adrian turned toward his friend. "Look, man, just ask the woman out. You know you want to. Didn't you say she seemed interested when you first met?"

"Yeah, when she thought she was talking to you. Ever since she found out who I was, Kathleen's been tense and standoffish."

"Probably because you've been quiet and brooding." Adrian wiped his face and took a drink of his soda.

"Quiet and brooding?"

"Yeah, that's what the women around here call you," Adrian explained with a half smile.

"Do they now?"

"Yes. You haven't even attended one of Kathleen's classes," Adrian noted.

"I don't need to," he defended.

"She might appreciate the gesture, and you'd be surprised how cool it is."

Morgan's eyebrows rose. "Would I?"

"Hell, perhaps Kathleen would like a man who can make her laugh like that." Adrian directed Morgan's attention to the area were Kathleen now stood talking to Troy and two additional women. They were all laughing and standing near the exit, and Kathleen had her hand resting on Troy's arm.

"Perhaps we should both get back to work. Those containers aren't going to clean themselves."

Morgan stood, threw his trash out and headed for the exit away from where Kathleen stood. Morgan knew Adrian was right, he couldn't stop thinking about her, but he also knew he had to get his foreign and inconvenient feelings for Kathleen under control before he did anything. It was time to talk to one of his brothers, and he knew the perfect one too.

Kathleen had been keeping an eye on Morgan from the moment he walked into the cafeteria. Their encounters over the last couple of weeks were very professional, although she found herself having more inappropriate thoughts and dreams about the man she was investigating, a probe that had only yielded positive responses from his employees.

As part of her investigation, she got to see how well prepared his administrative team as well as his frontline staff were. Kathleen needed to make sure she wasn't allowing her personal whatever she was feeling for Morgan to interfere with her ability to do her job. It had never been a problem before, and she was going to make sure it didn't become one now. It was time to deal with Morgan Kingsley.

Kathleen figured if she could interview him about the complaint one of two things would happen. She'd either be able to clear the charges once and for all or find a reason to move forward with a full investigation. Now all she had to do was find a way to interview Morgan without him catching on. Kathleen knew just the person to ask for help too.

Morgan stood in the immaculately decorated living room of his younger brother Brice's home and smiled. He remembered how not very long ago when he'd visited his brother, Brice would direct him downstairs to his man cave and away from the living room. The painful memories of his then soon-to-be ex-wife were too much to handle. Morgan was happy his brother and sister-in-law had since reconciled, even though at first he hadn't seen it happening. Watching Brice handle his conflicting feelings for Brooke while being forced to work with her told Morgan that Brice would be the perfect person to ask about his foreign feelings for Kathleen and how best to handle them.

"Here you go." Brice handed Morgan a bottle of beer.

"Thanks, man. You sure this is cool? I haven't interrupted anything, have I?" he asked, noticing his brother's wet hair, pajama bottoms and T-shirt.

"Not now," he replied, smiling.

"Good, I'd hate to disturb Brooke. How's she doing with everything?"

"She's fine. She hasn't had an MS flare-up in a while."

"That's great. I still can't get over how well you two are handing Brooke's multiple sclerosis diagnosis. I'm proud of you, bro."

"I appreciate that. We've made a decision."

"About what?"

Brice's face lit up. "We selected a surrogate, and we're starting the process next week."

"For real?"

"Yep." Brice nodded.

Morgan hugged his brother. "Congratulations, man. I know how much you want kids, but I also know how much you need to keep Brooke safe." He took a long pull from his bottle as he watched Brice's expression morph from happiness to fear back to happiness again in the matter of seconds.

"Let's sit down."

Morgan took a seat in one of the two large wingback chairs across from his brother, who was now sitting on a sofa. "Have you shared it with the rest of the family?"

"No. You're the first. Mother won't be surprised, since she's the one who made the recommendation and found us the perfect agency."

"Why am I not surprised?" Morgan took another drink from his bottle.

"Because she's Victoria Kingsley. Now, what brings you out here? You were all cryptic when you called," he asked, finally getting around to taking a drink from his beer bottle.

Morgan placed his now empty bottle on the coffee table. He leaned forward, resting his forearms on his thighs, clasping his hands. "There's this woman—"

"Oh wow…wait." Brice held up his left hand and put his beer bottle down on the floor. "You came to see me about a woman?"

"Yeah, so…"

Brice clapped his hands and started laughing. Morgan knew he deserved his brothers' ribbing after all the hard times he'd given all of them about their problems with women while he incessantly played the field after Bonnie broke his heart, but now really wasn't the time. He needed his help. Morgan sat back in the chair. "You done?"

"Sorry, man. I'm done. What's going on and who is this woman who has finally got Morgan Kingsley, the king of the bachelors, Mister No-Woman's-Worth-the-Drama all twisted up in his feelings?"

"Her name is Kathleen Winston—"

"The trainer from OSHA?" Brice frowned.

Morgan rose from his seat. "That's the one."

"Damn, man, she just got there, and you've already—"

"No, I haven't." Morgan started a slow pace around the room. "I haven't done anything, and that's the problem."

"I don't understand."

Morgan released an audible sigh. "Neither do I, which is why I'm here. So, what do I do?"

Brice frowned. "About what?"

"Men…" a small, soft voice called out as Brooke descended the stairs and entered the living room, barefoot and wearing a robe.

Morgan stopped midstride, and Brice stood. He reached for his wife's hand and pulled her into his arms, kissing her on the cheek. "Sorry if we disturbed you, sweetheart," Brice stated.

A warm feeling came over Morgan watching the sweet exchange, and while normally such a sight never affected him, he was finding himself thinking about how nice it would be to have such a moment, maybe with a beautiful stranger who he couldn't even have a real conversation with.

"Yeah, sorry about that, sister-in-law."

"Don't be silly—you didn't disturb me. I was ear hustling from the top of the stairs, and I couldn't take it anymore."

Brice laughed. "You were eavesdropping?"

"Well, yeah. It's rare that Morgan comes to anyone for help about anything and I knew it couldn't be about business this late. I figured it had to be good." Brook cupped Brice's face with her right hand. "I love you, sweetheart, but you suck at translating stories."

"True," Brice agreed.

"I knew if I wanted to find out what was going on I'd better find out for myself," Brooke confessed.

While the exchange between his brother and sister-in-law was cute, it wasn't helping him at the moment. "I should probably go," Morgan stated, moving toward the door.

"You will do no such thing. Sit…both of you," Brooke ordered, taking the twin chair next to Morgan. She angled her body toward him. "Let me see if I got this right. You've developed feelings for the OSHA trainer. You're not sure if you should act on them nor are you sure that you can't either. Is that the gist of the situation?"

Morgan smirked. "That about covers it. Except I can't seem to stop thinking about her or putting my foot in my mouth whenever I'm around her."

"Damn…you got it bad," Brice teased.

"Stop it," Brooke chastised her husband. "You've never had trouble talking to women. I'm sure she's beautiful," Brooke suggested.

"Breathtakingly so," Morgan confirmed.

"And that's never been a problem either. What makes this one so different?" Brooke's eyebrows came together.

Brooke's apparent confusion merely matched his own. Morgan leaned forward again and briefly lowered his eyes to the floor before returning his attention to his sister-in-law. "She's so much more. It's not just her looks. I've seen her be strong and she won't take crap from me or any of those roughnecks around the plant. Talk about smart. Kathleen has an impeccable résumé and she knows the ins and outs of the oil and gas business. Talking business with her is like talking to one of you, which is why everyone seems to respect her so much." He felt two sets of eyes bore into his face.

"Wow. I wasn't sure I'd live to see the day," Brice said in a hushed tone.

"I was," Brooke acknowledged, smiling.

"What are you two talking about?" Morgan's frustration with himself and his family was rising. He needed answers.

"You're falling in love," Brice stated.

"I'd say he's already fallen," Brooke corrected.

"No… I'm not. Hell, I can't even talk to her," Morgan declared.

"We know," the two replied in unison.

"Look, Morgan, just ask her out. I bet you'll be surprised to find that she's into you too."

"At first I thought she might be until she found out who I was," Morgan informed, feeling annoyed with himself and remembering the moment.

Brooke's forehead creased. "What does that mean?"

After explaining his first encounter with Kathleen, Morgan added, "Ever since that day, things have been just professional."

Brooke rose from her chair, and Morgan and Brice mimicked her move. "You're a smart guy with a good heart. Show that side of yourself to her. Find a way to push past your fear and think of a clever way to ask her out. Life is too short to miss out on or run away from…" Brooke's eyes cut to her husband briefly before landing back on Morgan "…any opportunity that could change your life and bring you untold happiness."

Morgan hugged Brooke. "Thank you. My brother is one lucky man."

"We're both lucky." Brooke kissed Brice before she headed back upstairs.

"She's right, you know," Brice added.

Morgan shoved his hands in his pockets. He still couldn't believe how twisted his insides were behind a woman he'd spent nearly no time with at all. "I know she is, but I still don't know what to do about it."

"You can start by taking a nonjudgmental interest in what her training program has to offer."

Morgan glared at Brice. "You think I should sit through her touchy-feely training to do what? Get her to like me…to go out with me?"

"If that's what you want. *Is* that what you want?"

Morgan stared at his brother but held his tongue while his body stirred, making its opinion known. "Thanks, man. I'm going to head out."

"Anytime."

Morgan walked out Brice's door, contemplating the answer to his brother's question. He knew what he wanted and what he had to do to get it.

Kathleen sat with her back against the headboard of the king-size bed in her Port Arthur hotel room. The entire room was half the size of her bedroom at home, but Kathleen didn't mind. She never reveled in her wealth and privilege, unlike her siblings. Kathleen spent most of her time focusing on righting perceived injustices in the world within her reach. Although she did have one vice: collecting art, antiques specifically.

Having just showered and changed into a long nightshirt, Kathleen settled in for the night. When her phone rang, she stared down at the screen and froze. Morgan Kingsley was calling her. Kathleen wasn't sure if she should answer it or send him to voice mail but before she could decide the ringing stopped. A feeling of disappointment came over Kathleen until her phone beeped, alerting her to a newly received message. Her disappointment quickly was replaced by a mixture of excitement and fear. Kathleen pushed out a quick breath and played back the message.

"Good evening, Miss Winston. This is Morgan Kingsley. Forgive the intrusion, but I want you to know that I'll be joining your training session in the morning. See you tomorrow."

Morgan's smooth, baritone voice sent a warm feeling throughout her body. Kathleen replayed the message several times, not because it wasn't clear, but because she was enjoying what his voice was doing to her body, specifically to the lower half of her sexually deprived body. All of her fantasies about Morgan were closing in on her.

Kathleen closed her eyes and ran her right hand across her breasts and down her stomach to her sex. Morgan's handsome face and the sound of his voice filled Kathleen's mind. Her hand slipped under her panties and slid through the fine hairs to her core. She lay flat on her back, spread her legs and inserted one, then two fingers inside as she thought about Morgan and all the sexy things they could do together. Before long she'd found temporary relief to desires he'd managed to tap into.

"You've got to stop this, Kathleen," she murmured between breaths. "You can't keep using this man to get off. He could be a criminal, for goodness' sake." It was a statement she knew probably wasn't true and one that hurt to consider seriously. Kathleen's heart and body ached for a man she couldn't be one hundred percent certain was innocent.

Kathleen took another shower, only this one was as cold as she could stand it. She was hoping to drown out the smoldering desires she was still experiencing for Morgan. After several minutes, Kathleen dried herself off, wrapped her body and hair in thick towels and sat on her bed. Kathleen knew she had to get her feelings under control and she needed advice on the best way to handle her situation with Morgan. She reached for her phone and called her sister. For the first time in her career, Kathleen was afraid that she was about to break a cardinal rule in investigation. A rule she'd always believed in and followed. It was the first thing her boss told her when she started: never get emotionally or physically involved with a target. Deep down inside, Kathleen knew she was about to do both.

Chapter 6

Kathleen set her phone on the nightstand while she changed back into her nightclothes. She was using her towel to squeeze the excess water from her hair when her video call connected. "Kathleen, why am I looking at one ugly-ass lamp?" Hannah asked.

"Oh sorry. Hold on a second." Kathleen pulled her hair up into a high ponytail and reached for the phone. She smiled at Hannah, a near mirror image of herself. "I was getting ready for bed."

"Bed?" Hannah checked her watch. "It's only nine."

"Yes, in California. I'm in Texas, remember, and it's eleven here."

"Oh yeah. I forgot."

"Where you going all dressed up? Not like you need much of a reason." Kathleen laughed.

"True, but tonight I have one. I'm going to the opening of a friend of mine's new restaurant."

"Oh...well I guess we can talk later," Kathleen replied, trying but failing to hide the disappointment in her voice.

"Oh no, you don't. I know that look. What's going on?"

"I don't want to keep you from your friends."

"Stop that." Hannah leered at her sister and sat down. "You know the rules. Family comes first. I got lots of friends but only two sisters. What's up?"

"Thanks, Hannah, and I'll be quick."

"Don't worry about it. What's going on?"

"I need your advice about something, but for you to help me, I have to share some things with you about my work."

"Okay." Hannah's eyes widened with surprise just as Kathleen expected.

Kathleen knew she had to keep the specifics of her investigations secret. However, Hannah had to know that she had developed feelings for someone and the situation around that person but not his identity, to know just how complicated things had gotten.

"I met this man…" Kathleen watched the small smile spread across Hannah's face as she searched for the right words. "He's the target of my investigation."

Hannah's smile disappeared. "What? Kathleen, you've been without a man for a long time, and the first one you fall for is a criminal?"

"Don't call him that. He's not a criminal." That was a conviction that had started taking root in her mind and heart the more time she spent with Morgan. The revelations about Mr. Silva didn't hurt, either.

"He can't be a Boy Scout, either, if you're investigating him. You've never been wrong about the targets you've gone after before. Don't let hormones screw up your professional success. Trust me when I say mixing business with pleasure doesn't work."

"This isn't about you, sister dear. Now can I finish?"

Hannah crossed her arms and pursed her lips. "This should be good."

Kathleen was having second thoughts about sharing the dilemma with her sister until she remembered Hannah's response was coming from a place of love and real concern. "Ever since I met this man I can't seem to stop thinking about him…dreaming about him."

"That's your hormones talking. Maybe it's just a bad boy phase you're going through. You'll get over it," Hannah concluded.

"It's not a bad boy phase, and I told you he's not a criminal. Morgan's strong…a man's man. He's extremely smart and family oriented. He reminds me of Dad."

"Then why are you investigating him?" She raised her left eyebrow.

Kathleen knew her sister's question was rhetorical, but she couldn't leave it out there in the universe like that, so she said, "All I can say is that a claim was brought against his company and not him personally."

"Remember what Dad always says?"

"We are our company," the two women chorused.

"Yes, Hannah but that's *our* company. I think this family is much like ours in that regard. There is no way his mother would do anything to hurt her company or their reputation."

Hannah frowned. "His mother?"

"Never mind that, what do I do?"

"About what?"

"These feelings…"

Hannah dropped her arms. "Do you think he's into you too?"

"I think so…maybe." Kathleen released an audible sigh. "I don't know."

"Well, if you're really into him, ask the man out."

"I thought about that, but I don't want to taint my investigation."

Hannah reached for her ringing phone. "Isn't it already tainted?" She sent the caller to voice mail. "You are having what I assume are sexy dreams about the man."

Yes, they are. "The dreams just started, and I pretty much have my answers regarding the investigation."

"Putting your hormones aside for minute. Can you honestly say with one-hundred-percent certainty that he is innocent of whatever it is you're investigating?"

"I'm ninety percent there."

"Then I recommend that you find that other ten percent before you do anything," Hannah stated.

"Looks like I'm about to get that chance tomorrow." She nodded in agreement.

"If you do, then bring him to Vista."

"Vista?"

"Yeah, that's the restaurant my friend is opening in Houston this weekend. It's their soft launch, so it won't be too crowded, no press and I'm his guest chef. That way I'll be able to check out the man who finally reminded my beautiful sister that she's a woman." Both women laughed. "But promise me one thing."

Kathleen was afraid to ask but replied, "What's that?"

"You won't do anything until you know for a fact that this man and his company are innocent of whatever it is that they are being accused of, okay? I know you, Kathleen. If you're wrong about him, you'll hate yourself."

Kathleen knew her sister was right and she couldn't put the lives of others in jeopardy because she was suddenly all hot and bothered for Morgan Kingsley. "I promise. I won't make a move until I'm one-hundred-percent sure."

"Good."

"But…"

"But what?" Hannah's phone rang again.

Kathleen rolled her eyes. "Please answer your hot-line."

"Hold up." Hannah put the caller on Speaker. "Yes?"

"Hannah, where are you? Everyone's waiting," the frantic-sounding person on the line asked.

"I'll be there soon. Chill." Hannah ended the call.

"You should go, sis."

Hannah gave a nonchalant wave. "But what?"

Kathleen ran her right hand through her damp hair. "What if he says no or isn't interested in me?" she asked, her voice barely above a whisper. "You know I haven't dated in a while, so maybe I'm misreading the signals."

"I'm sure you're not. If he's not interested, then he's weak," Hannah stated matter-of-factly.

Kathleen burst out laughing, and before she knew it, she said, "Morgan Kingsley is most certainly not weak."

Hannah's eyes widened, and her whole face lit up like a kid discovering a favorite toy under the Christmas tree. "Morgan Kingsley? You want to do the nasty with Morgan Kingsley?"

Both hands flew to Kathleen's mouth. "Dammit!"

"Girl, you should've started with that. Morgan Kingsley is fine as hell, and you're right. I don't care what anyone says…they couldn't have done anything they're being accused of doing. The Kingsleys are good people."

"Wait, you know the Kingsleys?" A horrifying

thought popped into her mind. Had her sister and Morgan dated?

"Of course I know the Kingsleys. We all run in the same social circle. A circle you rarely visit."

Kathleen didn't want to ask, but she couldn't stop herself. "Have you and him ever…"

Hannah smiled. "You *really* do like him. No, we've never even met, not formally anyway. I wish you could have seen your face. If I'd said yes, you would have come after me through the phone," she replied, laughing.

Kathleen threw up her hands and shook her head. "Not funny, Hannah. Talking to you is like talking to a toddler sometimes." Hannah stuck out her tongue. "What does 'not formally' mean?"

"He's escorted his mother and her sister Elizabeth Kingsley to a few charity events that I've attended with Dad. You know, the ones you usually refuse to go to."

"Not this again. I don't refuse. It's just most of the events I'm asked about happen when I'm extremely busy with work, or they're halfway across the country."

"Which is why we have our very own planes, Kathleen."

"Cut me a break. I just went to one, remember?"

"Yes and only because it was about Mom," Hannah reminded her sister, her voice turning somber.

A sense of sadness seemed to hit them both at the same time. "Yeah, well, I was there," Kathleen murmured.

"We have some obligations that we as a family should address. We just need you to do better when it comes to your responsibilities to the foundation and all of us. Now I'm done. Okay?"

"Okay."

"Be careful with Morgan Kingsley."

"Why do you say that?" Kathleen frowned. She was nervous about what her sister was about to say.

"I hear he's not much for long-term commitments."

"Neither am I," Kathleen offered, knowing that was a lie. She'd never really been one to date. Her life had been centered on her work; she had no idea how she felt about commitments.

Hannah burst out laughing. "Seriously, Kathleen? You're no virgin, but you're not a serial dater either. All I'm saying is Morgan Kingsley is the type of man you play with…not marry."

"Why do you keep trying to marry me off? I told you, I'm not looking for a husband."

"Then what are you looking for…a one-off, a hit-and-run? Are you looking for Mr. Goodbar?"

Kathleen felt her whole face contort. "What?"

"A one-night stand…just sex."

Kathleen looked away from her sister for a moment before returning to glaring at Hannah. "Maybe. Maybe I want to sow a few wild oats myself."

Hannah gave her head a slow shake and picked up her purse. "You couldn't find an oat if you stood in the middle of an oat field."

Kathleen gave her sister the evil eye. "Go to your opening and thanks for the advice."

"Anytime. Be careful, and I love you."

"Love you more." Kathleen blew a kiss at the screen and disconnected the call.

Kathleen turned off the light and lay down on her bed. She thought about everything her sister said and realized she had no idea what she wanted from Morgan. The only thing Kathleen knew for sure was that everything about the man intrigued her and she was attracted to him in a way she'd never been with anyone else.

Kathleen had to find out why and what it meant. Was it just physical or might it go deeper than that? But first, Kathleen needed to see if the picture everyone painted about the Kingsleys was accurate, and she had to figure out how. As Kathleen closed her eyes, an idea started to take shape.

Chapter 7

The next morning Kathleen dressed in her favorite gray Vera Wang pantsuit. It showcased her curves and gave her an added level of confidence whenever she was a little nervous about the day's outcome. She paired it with a scoop-neck white blouse, offering only a hint of cleavage, and low-heeled gray shoes. Kathleen told herself that she was just changing up her wardrobe and dressing up had nothing to do with the fact that she was expecting Morgan to attend her eight o'clock class that day.

From the moment Kathleen arrived at the plant, she found herself staring at all the time-tracking devices in her wake. If it wasn't the watch she wore on her wrist to help track her steps, it was the large clock on the wall and every computer screen she passed in the Kingsley training center. They all read the same, sending her a clear message. It was ten forty-five in the morning, and Morgan was nowhere to be found.

Kathleen was using the small training room, which usually held fifty individuals; today there were only thirty people in attendance. Normally she'd have a packed house, but she was competing with another required policy training session down the hall. Kathleen had considered that Morgan might have forgotten he needed to be there instead of her safety training class, so she checked. After finding out that he wasn't there either but on the grounds, she deduced that he'd changed his mind and blown her off. Kathleen couldn't figure out what angered her the most, the fact that Morgan hadn't shown or that her disappointment was overpowering and purely personal.

"Five minutes, everyone. You should be wrapping up your test now," she announced to the class.

"I'm done. Easiest test ever," one of the trainees stated, his voice loud and full of pride.

Kathleen smiled. "We'll see in four minutes, won't we?"

Everyone laughed, then suddenly the room fell silent, and everyone's attention returned to their computers. Kathleen, standing with her back to the door, could feel the presence of someone behind her as the mood in the room shifted. She turned to find Morgan standing in the doorway wearing a pair of blue coveralls and work boots. While most of the men who worked in the plant wore the same uniform, it was something about the way he wore his. It fit his tall, fit body like a well-cut suit. Morgan took three steps into the room, and like a magnet, Kathleen was drawn toward him, matching his movement.

Kathleen's eyes roamed his body, and her mouth suddenly became dry as a desert, her mind going blank. Only one word snapped in her head and unfortunately escaped her lips before she could stop it. "Yummy." *Dammit.* Kathleen was thankful that the trainees couldn't hear her. Too bad Morgan did.

The corners of Morgan's mouth rose as he stared down at Kathleen. "What was that?"

Kathleen gave her head a quick shake, pushed her shoulders back and stared up at him. "May I help you, Mr. Kingsley?"

Morgan took another small step forward, ignoring a few of his onlooking staff. "You just might be able to, only now isn't the time or the place," he replied in a hushed tone.

Kathleen cleared her throat and bit the inside of her lip. "Is that so?"

Morgan nodded slowly. His eyes scanned his team, sending them an unspoken message to mind their own business. Kathleen folded her arms across her chest. "You're late. You promised you'd come." Kathleen knew she was sounding more like a disappointed girlfriend than a professional trainer, not to mention a top investigator for one of the government's most trusted and respected agencies, but for reasons she couldn't explain she just didn't care.

Morgan reached for Kathleen's hand, sending very familiar shockwaves throughout her body. He led her out into the hall, closing the door behind him. Morgan didn't release Kathleen's hand, and she didn't bother pulling herself free. "I apologize for not showing up. I should've sent someone to explain where I was. We had a situation in one of our tanks that needed my attention this morning and you can't make calls from inside the tanks. Whenever one of my people could be in danger, I need to be on-site."

"Oh… I understand." Kathleen had heard that Morgan would never ask anyone to do anything he was not willing to do himself and if something dangerous was happening, he was always lending a helping hand.

Morgan pulled Kathleen closer and intertwined their hands. "I didn't make you a promise. I made a statement that I hoped to be able to keep. For me a promise is personal, and I keep my promises, which is why I rarely make some."

Kathleen lowered her head, and a sense of disappointment was suddenly upon her, fighting the desire she had for the man who was openly holding her hands. Morgan freed his right hand, captured her chin with his thumb and index finger and raised her head. He gazed into her eyes and said, "The promises I make to you, Miss Winston, I plan to keep."

They stood staring into each other's eyes as Morgan ran his thumb slowly across her lips. It was like he was lighting a match. Kathleen knew the fire he'd ignited inside her could consume them both if she weren't careful. Needing to break the connection, Kathleen closed her eyes, pushed out a slow breath and took a small step backward.

Morgan was afraid he might have gone too far too fast. He knew he had to act. Now that he'd decided to pursue Kathleen there was no way he was giving up now. "Is it too late?"

"Too late for what?" she whispered.

"To join your training. Would you prefer to try again tomorrow morning?"

"No. It's not too late. In fact, you're right on time."

Morgan opened the door and gestured for Kathleen to enter. "After you."

"Thank you." Kathleen walked back into the room. "Excuse me, everyone. Now that you've finished with the sectional quiz, I assume you're all done and passed." She scanned the room for signs that anyone hadn't. Having found none, she continued. "Now I would like to move on to our next test."

Everyone moaned, and Morgan raised his hand. "Excuse me. There's a test? Do I need time to prepare?"

The room broke out into laughter. "It's not that type of test," Kathleen said, smiling up at Morgan, sending his heart and mind racing. Kathleen turned her attention to the rest of the class. "The new regulations require that you be able to put your protective gear on in less than two minutes during a level-three emergency."

"And we can," Morgan declared proudly. "Some of us can do it in under a minute."

"Really?"

"You doubt me?"

"As a matter of fact I do," she replied, winking at the class. "I think you'll need to prove it."

"Excuse me, Kathleen," one of the male trainees called out from the front row.

Morgan was irritated by the casual nature of how he addressed Kathleen. It seemed a little too personal. Morgan's eyes lasered in on the trainee. He walked over to the young man and read his badge. "Bloom, is it?"

"Yes, sir," he replied, sitting up in his chair.

"We haven't met yet. I'm Morgan Kingsley, and I'd prefer it if you were less casual when you address our guest."

"It's fine—"

"No, it's not. It's either Miss Winston or Miss Kathleen. It's more appropriate in this setting," he instructed.

"Yes, sir," the young man replied.

Morgan could feel Kathleen's eyes boring into his skin. He knew she didn't agree, but he didn't care. He didn't like the idea of anyone getting too personal with

Kathleen. Morgan turned toward her. "Shall we continue, Miss Winston?"

"We most certainly can. I need everyone to join me at my exhibit area." Kathleen walked over to a long cafeteria-style table positioned on the side of the room and covered by a red tablecloth. "As I was saying, you need to be able to change into all of this gear in two minutes or less."

"And like I said, with the exception of a few new people in the room, most of my men can."

Kathleen folded her arms at her breast. It was a move he loved and hated. "When was the last time you had a level-three crisis at this plant, Mr. Kingsley? You know, severe weather, explosions and fires."

"Yes, I know. Never, but we have monthly drills, so if it happens our brain will kick in, and thanks to the repetitiveness of our actions, we'll know just what to do," he stated confidently.

"Yes, the brain stores repetitive actions. However, that area of the brain is like any other muscle. If you don't use it on a regular basis, it can go limp when you need it the most." Kathleen heard gasps and snickers spread throughout the group and she instantly regretted her choice of words. She was hoping she wasn't turning as red as her tablecloth.

"Trust me—that would never happen," Morgan stated in a lowered tone.

Kathleen needed to bring the room back under control. She picked up a pair of glasses and headphones. "To ensure that it doesn't, you need to do your monthly drills under similar circumstances as a level-three emergency."

"And how do you suppose we make that happen?" Morgan asked.

"By using these." Kathleen held up the glasses and headphones for everyone to see. "The eyeglasses offer a blurred view, and the headphones will play the noises you'd expect to hear during such emergencies. While wearing these, you'll have to put all your emergency gear on in less than two minutes."

"Is that so?"

"Yes, it is. Does everybody understand?" Everyone nodded, except Morgan. "So who's first?"

The room went still, and all eyes landed on Morgan. "Looks like I'm it."

The room broke out in loud cheers and claps. "In under a minute," Kathleen reminded Morgan.

Morgan smiled. He turned his back to his staff and lowered his voice. "Once I get all that gear on, even with the distraction, in less than a minute, you'll allow me to take you to dinner." Morgan held her gaze as he waited for Kathleen's response.

Kathleen couldn't think rationally whenever he set his gorgeous eyes on her. "Fine. And if you don't, I'll take you out, and I get to pick the place," she replied, deciding to take her sister's advice.

Morgan offered Kathleen a brittle smile. He took the glasses and headphones out of her hand and went over to the table. "When do we start?" he asked, looking down at everything before him.

"Once you put the glasses and headphones on, I'll tap your shoulder, and you can begin." Kathleen held up a timer that was also on the desk. "We'll track your time with this. Ready whenever you are, Mr. Kingsley."

Morgan put the glasses on first. "Wow, I can't see a thing with these on. Everything's all fuzzy."

"Yes, I know. The glasses are designed to distort your vision the way smoke or excess water coming down on you might."

"Water?" one of the female trainees asked, touching her hair.

"Yes, from the heavy-duty sprinkler system the plant must have in place. Trust me, in such an emergency the last thing you'll be worried about is how your hair looks." Kathleen replied.

"Unless it's on fire," she rebutted.

"Which is why you'll be grateful to have those sprinklers functioning properly and ready to go… They are ready to go, right?" she asked, scanning the room for any tempered responses. Kathleen felt ridiculous for even asking the question, but she couldn't seem to turn off the investigator in her.

A number of different positive responses came flying at her. "Would you like to see the schematics?" Morgan asked.

"That won't be necessary."

"Let's get this show started," Morgan said, placing the headphones over his ears.

Kathleen tapped Morgan's shoulders and hit the start button on the timer. She stood back and watched as Morgan selected each piece of clothing and safety apparatus, slipping them onto his body as if he could see where each piece lay. It took him fifty-eight seconds to become fully dressed, having put each safety piece on in its appropriate order. The order in which things should be put on was a little tidbit she usually held back so she could see how much each person knew and understood. Once he finished, the room broke out in a loud cheer, and Morgan removed his glasses and headphones.

"Congratulations, Mr. Kingsley. That was quite impressive," she stated, surprised he was able to complete the task so quickly.

"Thank you," he said as he placed the glasses and headphones back on the table.

"I'll go next," Bloom offered, making his way to the table.

"Sure. Why doesn't everyone partner up? There are four sets of gear. One can dress while the other keeps time." Morgan had removed all his gear and was now standing close to the door.

"Going somewhere?" Kathleen asked, secretly hoping that he wasn't.

"Of course not. I'm here for the duration of the class. If you don't mind?"

"'Course not." Kathleen suddenly felt very warm and extremely happy.

"So how's Friday?"

Kathleen tried to hold back her broad smile but couldn't. "Friday's fine."

"And to show how good of a sport I am you can pick the restaurant. As long as there's meat."

Kathleen covered her mouth and laughed. "You're a carnivore. Why am I not surprised?"

Morgan smirked.

Chapter 8

Morgan sat back and watched as his team tried to complete the task in less than two minutes. Most were successful and for the few exceptions who struggled, Kathleen walked them through the process in such a way they got it on their second try. He was impressed with her approach and her extensive knowledge of not only the equipment but the proper order and manner in which it should be used. He was rethinking his position on her interactive approach, at least for this portion of their safety training.

He struggled to stay focused because no matter how hard Kathleen tried to downplay it, her gorgeousness was a distraction, to him anyway. Wearing little to no makeup only enhanced her natural beauty, and now he knew how soft her skin was too. The simple outfit she wore showed off how physically fit she was, and Morgan found himself wondering what she wore underneath it. Morgan had been with many women, but none of them affected him in such a way, especially at work. He knew he had to keep things professional while at the plant but staying away from Kathleen was no longer an option.

"Great job, everyone," Kathleen announced. "It's nearly lunchtime, so let's stop here. Thank you for the terrific work this morning. For those of you coming back this afternoon, I'll see you at one thirty sharp. Those who aren't—" her eyes jumped to Morgan "—thanks for your participation."

Morgan watched as his team filed out of the room one by one. "Wonderful job."

"Thank you." Kathleen packed up her things.

"Let me help with that." Morgan reached for the box on the floor at the same time as Kathleen, and his hand covered hers.

Kathleen released an audible gasp. Morgan dropped the box, took Kathleen's hand and pulled her into him. "You're the most beautiful woman I've ever seen."

"I doubt that, but thank you," she replied, her voice barely above a whisper.

Morgan ran his right hand slowly down the side of her face and stared into her eyes. "To me, beauty goes beyond how a person looks. It was a thing of beauty how you handled my team, especially the ones having difficulty meeting the task. It's beautiful to see how much you know and understand, not to mention how passionate you are about our business. Yes, I understand that as a trainer, it's your job, but your level of understanding comes from somewhere else, and I can't wait to find out where. Your physical beauty is gravy to the meat and potatoes of who you are."

Kathleen lowered her eyes. "That's very kind of you to say, considering…" She freed her hand, picked up the box and continued packing up her supplies.

"Considering the hard time I gave you when you first arrived."

"Yes. Not to mention the distance you kept."

Morgan helped her pack. "I had my reasons."

"Care to share?" The question was out of Kathleen's mouth before she could do anything about it.

Morgan's phone rang. He pulled it out, read the name and sent the caller to voice mail. "Not really but I will say this. I'm done avoiding you." He placed his hands in his pockets.

"So it wasn't my imagination?"

"No." Morgan's phone rang again.

Kathleen saw it was a woman's name that appeared. "Care to take that?" Kathleen had never been the jealous or possessive type, and Morgan didn't belong to her, so she didn't understand why all of a sudden she felt like taking his phone and throwing it against the wall.

"It can wait."

"You mean *she* can wait," she replied, giving him the side-eye as she placed the last of her supplies in the box. "Look, if you're seeing someone—"

"If I was seeing someone, I wouldn't have asked you out. I most certainly wouldn't be standing here, forcing myself to keep my hands in my pockets, so I won't keep touching you."

Thank goodness, and the feeling is mutual. But I have to know.

Kathleen turned and faced Morgan, placing her right hand on her hip. "We both know you have a bit of a reputation when it comes to women."

"We do?"

"Are you denying that you're a serial dater?" Kathleen asked, using her sister's words.

"A serial dater. That's an interesting analogy."

"Yes, but is it an accurate one?"

Morgan removed his hands from his pockets and crossed his arms at his chest. He leaned against the table. "If your definition of 'serial dater' is a single person who dates a number of women over a certain period of time, then I guess that would be accurate. But I only date one woman at a time."

"I appreciate your honesty."

"What about you?" he asked.

"What about me?" She scrunched up her face.

"Are you a serial dater too?"

Kathleen shook her head. "Hardly. *Serial* usually implies three or more. My two relationships wouldn't make the cut."

"I find that hard to believe. So you're more the relationship type," Morgan worked out.

"You make that sound like a bad thing."

"Not at all. I watched my brothers' lives change for the better, thanks to their wives."

"But that's not something you want for yourself."

"I just haven't been so lucky when it comes to relationships," he said, his face expressionless.

"I'm sure there's a story behind your lack of luck."

"What about your two relationships? Were they serious?"

Kathleen's phone rang. "One second."

"Saved by the bell."

Kathleen laughed as she moved over to the desk and picked up her cell phone. She saw that it was her father calling. "Excuse me for one moment."

"I'll step out," Morgan offered.

"No!" Their eyes collided, and Kathleen only hoped

she didn't look as desperate as she sounded. "I mean, you don't have to leave."

Morgan stood, poker-faced, and nodded.

Kathleen turned her back to Morgan and answered the call in French. "Hello, Dad, is everything okay?"

"Yes, can't a father just call and check on his children?"

"Of course you can, but I'm working, and you know that, so if everything's okay, you must have a reason for calling me in the middle of the afternoon."

"Well, I was hoping you'd come home for the weekend. I'll send your plane for you. It's just sitting in the hangar."

Kathleen would have loved to spend the weekend in New Orleans but she had a date with Morgan, and she wanted that just a little more. "I'd love to, Dad, but I have plans in Houston this weekend. I'll come home soon—I promise." Kathleen ended the call and turned to face Morgan. She was expecting to get hit with some questions regarding her bilingual status, only to her surprise he smiled and said, "So where's home?"

Kathleen blinked. "You speak French?"

"Only a few words here and there. I understand it more."

"Did you take a class in high school or college?" she questioned, smiling.

"Not exactly," he replied, offering her a knowing look and scratching his chin with his right thumb.

"Oh, an old girlfriend taught you."

"Something like that," he admitted, clenching his jaw.

Kathleen shifted her weight from one leg to the other. "I sense there's a story there."

"One for another time. So where's home? I gathered your dad wants to see you," he asked.

"New Orleans."

"So—"

The door opened. "Oh, sorry if I'm interrupting," Adrian announced as he entered the room.

Kathleen checked her watch. "Oh goodness, I lost track of time. You're not... I mean—"

"I'll get out of your way," Morgan said.

"No, I can come back?" Adrian offered.

"It's cool," he replied before turning his attention back to Kathleen. "We'll finish this conversation later."

"I look forward to it." As Kathleen stood and watched Morgan walk out the door, for some reason she felt like all the air left the room with him.

"Are you all right?" Adrian asked with a concerned look on his face. "You look like you're going to be sick."

Kathleen walked over to her desk, picked up an unopened bottle of water and cracked the seal. She took several unladylike gulps, trying to extinguish the thirst brought on by Morgan's mere presence.

"I'm fine. Let's get started. What did you need help with again?" Kathleen was embarrassed about her lack of professionalism. She'd forgotten about her meeting with Adrian, and now she didn't recall why he was there.

"You wanted to see me, remember?" He frowned, looking at her like he was about ready to call for help. "Are you sure you're all right?"

Kathleen's mind had been filled with thoughts of Morgan, and she completely forgot her plan: she'd decided she needed to find out once and for all if her initial instincts about Morgan and the Kingsleys were wrong, or had her judgment been clouded by desire? What better way than to try to gain additional insight about the family than from someone who knew them well? Someone who might feel comfortable enough to tell her the truth, no matter what that truth might be, since he'd come to see her as just another fellow employee.

"Yes, of course. Forgive me, my mind was elsewhere. Please have a seat." Kathleen directed Adrian to a chair in front of her desk.

"What's up?"

"You've worked for the Kingsleys for a while now, correct?" Kathleen sat in the chair next to him.

"That's right."

"From what I've heard and seen, this seems to be a pretty great place to work."

"It is," he said and offered a laid-back smile.

"I was just wondering why, after all the bad publicity and bogus charges brought against them were dropped, they would make such major management changes now?"

Adrian shrugged. "I guess Ms. Victoria decided the time had come to step aside and let Alexander take over. She'd been training him for the role for years."

"Morgan's cousin...what's her name?"

"Kristen Kingsley."

"Yes, she stepped into Alexander's former role. I know she was VP of Operations but we're talking about a high profile COO position. No offense but she's a bit of a party girl according to social media. I would have thought others with less of a media presence would be more qualified for the role although Morgan would have been the next and best logical choice in my opinion." Kathleen only hoped Adrian thought she was advocating for Morgan versus investigating the choice.

The lazy smile he gifted her with told Kathleen he

was going down the path she led him to. "You don't need to worry about Morgan. He loves the role he plays. As for Kristen, yeah, she likes to party, but she too was trained for her role. Like her aunt Victoria, Kristen is smart and tough as nails. That's one bad bitch. Excuse my French. I mean that in a good way."

I hate that saying. That's not French. "It's fine."

"One thing about the Kingsleys—birthright only gets you the option of being first. You have to earn roles just like everyone else."

"Really? Most wealthy families with businesses expect their kids to be part of said business." *Mine most certainly did and Dad and my siblings remind me of that fact all the time.*

"True, and the Kingsleys are no different. However no one's forced to join the company and Victoria would never let nepotism ruin her bottom line," he said, laughing.

"I believe that." Kathleen was coming to realize she'd been wrong about the Kingsleys.

"Are you thinking about trying to come to work here full-time? I know we could use a smart trainer like you on staff. I can put in a good word for you with Morgan, if you like," he offered, seeming excited by the idea.

"Thanks, but that won't be necessary."

Adrian rose from his chair. "I'd better get back to work, unless you need something else."

"No, I'm good. Thanks for the information."

"Anytime. You really should think about my offer," Adrian reminded before walking out the door.

Kathleen touched her cheek where Morgan had caressed her skin. "I'm thinking about a lot of things."

Chapter 9

The next few days came and went with little interaction between Morgan and Kathleen. While Morgan was no longer avoiding her, he'd make sure when they did spend time together others were around. Morgan had never wanted a woman the way he found himself wanting Kathleen. Not even the woman he'd once planned to marry. There was just something about Kathleen that both enticed him and scared the hell out of him too.

It was Friday, and Morgan found himself watching the clock. He was excited about the fact that he'd soon have Kathleen alone and all to himself. The hours seemed to be moving slower than normal. Morgan was sitting at a table in the back of the cafeteria, watching his team members interact with each other when Kathleen approached him holding a tray with one of Ms. Monica's famous chef's salads and a bottle of water on it.

"May I join you?" Kathleen asked, smiling down at him.

Morgan stood, and his heart sped up. "Please."

Kathleen took a seat. "Thank you. You're not eating?"

Morgan sat down. "I had something earlier. How's your day going?" His cell phone rang and he sent the caller to his voice mail.

"Good. In fact, I'm done with my last class, so I thought I'd cut out early, if that's okay with you. My older sister has a few things she needs my help with this weekend."

Morgan puckered his brow. "Sure... No problem." *There goes our date.* They hadn't talked about it since Monday, so Morgan assumed Kathleen had either forgotten about it or changed her mind. Either way, he felt like a fool and had a sense of disappointment unlike anything he'd ever known.

Suddenly, he was drowning in it and had to get away from Kathleen before he said or did something that would embarrass them both. Morgan picked up his ringing phone. "Excuse me. I should take this. Have a good weekend, Kathleen." Morgan stood and made his way to the nearest exit. He had to use every bit of pride he had not to turn around and demand an explanation and try to change Kathleen's mind.

Kathleen watched Morgan disappear through the door before she could find out what the hell had just happened. She thought they'd reached a turning point. He was no longer avoiding her, and he'd sat in on several of her classes. He told her he was just auditing her work, but she knew there was more to it than that, and she loved it. She even caught him staring at her from across the room a few times. Now this... He just blew off their date. Kathleen was no longer hungry, but before she could dispose of her tray, she saw Ms. Monica and her assistant heading right for her table. They'd never officially met, but she certainly knew who she was.

"How's the salad, baby girl?" Ms. Monica asked.

"It's great," Kathleen replied, forcing a smile.

"Really? How would you know since you haven't touched it?"

"I mean, I'm sure it's great. It's just my stomach is a little upset all of a sudden," Kathleen explained, hoping it would appease the woman. It didn't.

"Roughage is what you need, then. It'll get things moving. Excuse my manners. I'm Monica, and this is my sous chef, Lori."

"Pleased to meet you," Lori replied, offering her hand, which Kathleen shook.

"I've been cutting onions so I won't shake your hand, but I will bump your elbow," said Monica. "You can call us Ms. Monica and Ms. Lori. Yes, I went to culinary school, but I never liked being called chef."

"Me either," Lori agreed.

"The titles go along with these fancy new uniforms." Ms. Monica looked down at the black pants and double-breasted black coat and pointed out the personalized embroidery. "They even got our names and titles on them. Rich people, I swear."

Lori laughed. "You should try putting something in your stomach. It might make you feel better."

Kathleen appreciated the concern and suggestion but she knew only one thing could make her feel better and he'd just left. "Thanks, but I'll be fine."

Ms. Monica placed her right hand on her hip. "A little stomachache isn't all that's wrong with you."

Kathleen could feel her emotions rising. Soon her face would flush, and she'd be fighting back tears. She had to bring herself back under control, and she needed a distraction. She picked up her fork and took several bites of her food. "This is good," she complimented through bites.

"I'm glad you like it, but I know something's up." Ms. Monica and Lori took seats across from Kathleen. "Care to talk about it?"

At times like these, even after seven years, she missed her mother very much. Irene Winston had been very easy to talk to, and Kathleen knew she'd know just how to make her feel better. Although Irene would never tell her what to do, she always informed Kathleen and her siblings that people were the sum of their decisions and while others might offer advice, ultimately, it was up to the individual to make the right choices for himself or herself.

"I'm fine… Really."

"Mm-hmm. Lori, you believe this child?"

Lori folded her arms across her ample breast. "Not at all."

"I bet Morgan said something he shouldn't have," Ms. Monica guessed.

Kathleen could feel her expression close up. "Not at all. Everything's—"

"Fine?" Ms. Monica supplied. "Child, I've known that boy most of his life, and I know the effect he can have on women."

"I've seen you too," Lori added, shaking her head.

"I've watched him watching you these last few days. There is an intense interest there, which means only two things."

Kathleen couldn't help but ask, "What's that?"

Ms. Monica held up her index finger. "One, he's feeling you. Isn't that what the kids call it?"

Kathleen laughed. "Yes, ma'am."

"And two—" another finger went up "—he's feeling you."

Kathleen presented a shy smile. "I—"

"Let me finish. Morgan's not like his brothers or his mother. He's a man of few words. With Morgan, actions speak louder. He doesn't like drama. Morgan tends to avoid things, leave things unsaid, which can cause problems."

"He has issues with communicating unless it's about work," Lori added.

"He's dated other women," Kathleen murmured, speaking without thinking. Fearing she'd said too much she quickly added, "Not that we're—"

"Child, please." Ms. Monica gave Kathleen a knowing look. "A blind man can see something is going on between you two. If he's gone all quiet on you or shut down, you'll have to make him tell you what's going on."

"That is, if you want him. If not, there's plenty in this town and elsewhere that do. Hell, if I was twenty years younger and a few pounds smaller..." Lori smiled and winked.

"You'd still be too old," Ms. Monica said, giving Lori the evil eye. She reached for Kathleen's hand. "Morgan's a good man. He just protects that heart of his. It has been broken once, and he's afraid to take a chance on letting it happen again."

"Really, when? Who was she? What happened?" Kathleen was spitting out questions like rapid fire. This new information took her completely by surprise, and she didn't know how she felt about knowing that Morgan once loved someone so much that he became afraid to let anyone else get close. Loving someone else like that again was something she didn't think he would be willing to do. Kathleen had never experienced that type of love before, and she was jealous of whoever this mystery woman was, the one who'd managed to steal Morgan's heart.

"That's not my story to tell. You should ask Morgan about it yourself unless, like you said, you two aren't dating." Ms. Monica rose from her seat, as did Lori. She reached for Kathleen's plate. "I'll go wrap this up. You can take it to go. I'll be right back."

"Thank you." Kathleen's eyes jumped between the two older women.

Kathleen sat back and waited for the wise women to return. She let Ms. Monica's words take hold as Kathleen recalled her sister's advice to make sure she was positive about Morgan before she did anything. *He doesn't want to get close to anyone.* Maybe he felt things were getting too close already. She certainly did.

That's why he blew off our date. Kathleen's heart dropped like she was riding on a roller coaster. She hated the idea that some mystery woman from Morgan's past was preventing them from finding out if what they were experiencing was real. She understood how ghosts from the past could stop her from pursuing things and people that might be good for her. She knew she'd been doing that most of her adult life, focusing solely on her career, driven in part by a need to avenge her mother's death, something she knew wasn't rational, but until now there hadn't been anything she'd wanted enough to make her think twice about her choices.

But her attraction to Morgan was proof that she needed more in her life than just work. He needed to improve his communication skills a bit. She was still very annoyed about the way he'd handled the situation.

Plus, his heartbreak had been a while ago. Maybe he had some other reason for not keeping their date.

Regardless, Kathleen had to tell him the real reason behind her visit before she left town. Now that she could officially clear them he deserved the truth, especially since her boss could confirm that Mr. Silva's concerns were misguided but there was no malicious intent.

Kathleen stood when she saw Ms. Monica approaching. "Here you go, my dear." She handed Kathleen a to-go box.

"Thank you…for everything."

Ms. Monica gave a nonchalant wave. "No problem. If you want to talk to Morgan, he's in Adrian's office right now."

"How do you know that?"

"Because I called to find out," Ms. Monica said, frowning like Kathleen's question was a waste of oxygen. "You two should talk. You might be surprised by the outcome."

Kathleen hugged Ms. Monica and walked out the door. It was time to end her stay at Kingsley. She'd done what she'd come to do. The charges were unsubstantiated, so it was time to go. Kathleen could send someone else to complete the rest of the training, as well as help with incorporating new regulations into their policy. Kathleen fought back tears. She couldn't comprehend continuing to work side-by-side with Morgan, knowing how much she wanted him…cared for him.

It was time to get her mind off Morgan and find some real bad guys to chase. The case of Kingsley Oil and Gas versus OSHA was now closed, and so, it seemed, was the budding love affair between her and Morgan Kingsley, and it was breaking her heart.

* * *

"So does everyone agree with the final sale price?" Alexander asked. A ripple of yeses came through the phone, but Morgan's mind was on the woman who'd just blown him off and not a piece of property their mother wanted.

"Morgan... Morgan, you still there?" Alexander asked. Morgan, who had been standing and staring out the window, turned and sat down behind the desk. "I'm here, and I'm fine with it too."

"Good—"

"Wait, you did say that included the mineral rights, correct?" Morgan asked.

"Yes, of course," Alexander replied.

"Are you okay?" Kristen Kingsley, the company's newly appointed COO, questioned, her concern coming through loud and clear.

"Yes, I'm fine. Just a bit distracted," Morgan replied.

"Anything you want to share?" Alexander asked.

Not in the least bit. The last thing he needed was for his family to know that the one woman he wanted didn't want him back. "No, I'm good."

The office door opened and an angry Kathleen walked in and slammed the door behind her. She was holding what looked like a to-go container. "The next time you want to blow off a woman for a date, you should at least have the decency to tell her."

Chapter 10

Morgan slowly rose from his seat. "Excuse me." He came from around his desk.

Kathleen placed her food container on the corner of his desk and stood defiantly in front of him. "At first I was going to let it go…exit gracefully. But you asked me out, then what…you changed your mind or did you just get a better offer?"

Morgan was confused, but by the scowl on Kathleen's face he knew she believed what she was saying. "I have—"

"And another thing, mister." She used her right index finger and poked him in the chest. "You don't say all those beautiful things to a woman and just kick her to the curb without an explanation. What, are we back in high school?"

Morgan grabbed her finger and held it at his heart. "I didn't kick you to the curb, and I certainly didn't blow you off. You said you were leaving early and doing something with your sister this weekend. I'd say *you* blew me off."

"No, I didn't." Kathleen stepped forward, closing the gap between them. "I wouldn't."

Morgan watched as Kathleen's expression morphed from angry to confused to desirous. He could see how sincere she was and he was overwhelmed with emotions. Morgan lowered his head, scanning Kathleen's face for any sign of rejection. Seeing none, he gently kissed her on the lips. Kathleen slid her hands up and around his neck, pressed her body against him and moaned his name in his mouth. Morgan deepened the kiss. Soon he heard, "Hello... Morgan."

Morgan broke off the kiss and looked over at the phone. "Dammit!"

"What's wrong?" Kathleen asked before she heard the laughing. "What was that?" Kathleen looked around the room.

"I was on a conference call when you came in."

Kathleen buried her face in his chest. "Oh no. I'm sorry," she replied.

"I'm not. It's okay. Chill, you guys," he ordered, his voice taking on a husky tone.

"I'll go," she whispered.

"Oh no, you don't. I'm not dealing with that crew by myself," Morgan said, snaking his arms around her waist.

"Who?"

"My family. Alexander, Brice and Kristen, I'd like to introduce you all to Kathleen Winston. Kathleen, the laughter coming through the phone is from two of my brothers and my cousin."

"Hi, everyone," Kathleen reluctantly replied, and everyone responded with an array of hellos.

Morgan bid farewell and ended the call. "Sorry about that. So…"

"So… What?" Kathleen asked, gifting him with a sexy smile.

Morgan captured a loose strand of hair and placed it behind her ear. "Can I have the pleasure of your company for dinner tonight?"

Kathleen smiled. "Yes."

"Where are we going?"

"I don't know yet. I haven't heard from that sister."

Morgan tilted his head. "That sister? How many sisters do you have?"

"Two, and one brother."

Morgan tightened his hold on Kathleen. "I don't care where we go. I just want to be with you."

Kathleen rose up on her toes and collapsed her hands around his neck. "I want to be with you too," she replied before kissing him passionately on the lips.

After finally coming up for air, Morgan asked, "Where do I pick you up?"

Kathleen stepped out of Morgan's hold, and he missed her instantly. She reached for his cell phone that sat in its dock on the desk and handed it to him. "Pull up my contact information, and I'll add my address."

Morgan did as she asked and handed his phone to her. After inputting her address, she said, "I live in Houston. I'll text you the time and location once I know the information."

Morgan looked down at his phone. "This zip code looks familiar. Do you live near Hermann Park?"

"Yes, my house isn't far from the park at all. I live in the North MacGregor Way area."

"Nice. That area has a lot of newly renovated homes."

"Yes, they do. I should go." Kathleen picked up her lunch container and walked toward the door. She looked over her shoulder and said, "I'll see you later."

Morgan gave a quick nod but kept his feet planted. He knew if he didn't he'd reach for Kathleen again and wouldn't be able to let her go. Morgan had never felt like this before, and while the power this woman suddenly had over him scared the hell out of him, he couldn't wait to explore where it would lead. Morgan turned his back to the door and picked up a stack of documents he had to review, knowing how difficult a feat that would be. He was having a hard time concentrating on anything except Kathleen, but had to give it a shot.

When Morgan heard his door open again, his heart started beating so hard, he just knew she would hear it. He grinned. "Forget something, Kathleen?"

"No, but apparently you did," Adrian stated as he entered the office.

Morgan checked his watch. "Oh man. You're right. I forgot all about the meeting."

"No worries, I stalled. Van is taking them on a quick tour of the plant. We have a few minutes." Morgan was sitting in his chair so Adrian took a seat in one of the chairs in front of the desk. "I assume this lack of memory has something to do with Kathleen."

The corners of Morgan's mouth turned up. *It has everything to do with her.* Morgan knew he couldn't admit that to Adrian because he would never hear the end of it. "Where are we meeting the Ultra Tech executives?"

"Ignoring the question only means that I'm right. That's cool. They're in the executive conference room back at the administration building," Adrian informed him, leering at his friend.

Morgan's smile widened. He knew there was a chance he'd get another glimpse at Kathleen before she left for the day. "Oh man, you got it bad," Adrian concluded as he stood and walked toward the door. "I know my office is pretty cool but you do know that you have an office somewhere down the hall."

"Technically the whole plant is my office," Morgan countered.

"In that case why don't you set up an office next to the training room," he said, laughing as he walked out the door.

"That's not a bad idea," Morgan murmured to himself.

After spending a few hours with her eldest sister, Kennedy, Kathleen had finally made it home. Hannah had given her the information for the restaurant, and she texted it to Morgan. His reply, See you soon, baby, had her feeling all warm and fuzzy inside, something she'd never felt before.

Between her work and hobby of collecting unique antiques, Kathleen never seemed to have the time, energy or desire to date. She stood in her exceptionally large walk-in closet—which was a dressing room much like her sister's—trying to determine what to wear when her doorbell rang. "Who could that be?" She made her way down the stairs. Kathleen knew Morgan wouldn't dare show up three hours early, especially after she told him to be there at eight thirty. After checking her security screen, she heaved a sigh, but, deep down she was happy to see her guest.

Kathleen opened the door. "Hello, Lisa. Hannah sent you," she stated.

"Yes. Hannah thought you might need a little help getting ready for your date."

Kathleen waved Lisa inside. "Sadly, she's correct. Wait, please tell me you were already in town."

"I was," she said, laughing.

"Good, follow me."

The two women climbed the stairs and returned to Kathleen's closet. "See the problem?" Kathleen pointed to her wardrobe.

The luxurious dressing room with a designer closet system would make anyone swoon.

Kathleen nodded and walked over to each compartment where her clothes were held and opened the doors.

"May I?" Lisa asked.

"Please."

Lisa walked up to each compartment and flipped through all the garments. Nearly everything had a designer label, but it was all conservative professional business attire. Only one compartment had what could be perceived as business casual clothes.

"Is that it?" Lisa frowned.

Kathleen shrugged and nodded. "Except my jeans, leggings and casual tops, that's it."

"I see why Hannah did what she did."

Kathleen exhaled noisily. "What did Hannah do?"

The doorbell rang, and Lisa smiled. "Right on time."

"Shall I get that?" Lisa asked with a gummy smile.

Kathleen dropped down on one of the two gray-and-white chaise longues in the closet. "Might as well." Kathleen knew her sister must've made arrangements for her to have something more appropriate to wear tonight. While she wanted to strangle her, Kathleen also wanted to thank Hannah. She only hoped there would be something she could wear that didn't scream *jump my bones*, in spite of the fact that was exactly what her wayward body wanted.

"Here we are," Lisa announced, returning to the closet. She held up two large stuffed garment bags that she hung on a freestanding rack. Lisa unzipped one, removed the clothes and hung them on the rack. She removed a small gift bag that she set on the dresser. Kathleen walked over to the rack, flipped through everything her sister sent and was pleasantly surprised. Everything suited her perfectly. All the outfits selected were sexy but not over-the-top, like those Hannah usually preferred, especially when she was going out.

"Wow, these are great. I can't believe she picked these out," Kathleen replied.

"She didn't," Lisa said, unpacking her makeup bag. "She sent me shopping for you. I've gotten a sense of what you like based on the few times I've had the pleasure of working with you."

"You most certainly did. Thank you. Now, how many do I get to pick and when do they go back?"

"You aren't some frumpy stepsister and we're certainly not your fairy godmothers. They don't go back."

"What?"

"Hannah bought them all. She figured this would be the first of many dates you'll be going on."

"There's, what, twenty outfits here?" Kathleen couldn't hold back her surprise.

"There're twenty-four actually," Lisa corrected.

Kathleen fought back tears. She knew Hannah always had her back and doing something like this was right up her alley, but it still touched her heart knowing that her sister always seemed to know when she needed her the most.

Lisa looked over Kathleen, who had her hair in a messy ponytail; she was wearing leggings and a long white T-shirt. She shook her head and said, "We better get started. We only have two and a half hours before Prince Charming arrives."

Kathleen giggled like a little girl. "He most certainly is that."

"But first." Lisa picked up the small gift bag she'd placed on the dresser and handed it to Kathleen. "This is from both of us."

Kathleen's brows drew together. "What's this?"

"Something we both hope you'll need, if not tonight, then very soon."

Kathleen pulled out the decorative tissue paper and looked inside the bag. Her mouth fell open and her heart raced at the idea of using their gift. She bit her bottom lip and smiled. "Thank you," she whispered.

Chapter 11

Morgan admired all the different style homes he passed as he made his way to Kathleen's house. North MacGregor Way community was well-known for its historic and eclectic homes near downtown Houston. Morgan pulled his silver Aston Martin—a passion for expensive cars was the one indulgence all the Kingsleys shared—into Kathleen's circular driveway, which sat on a corner lot in a tree-lined area. Morgan grabbed the bottle of Domaine Ramonet Montrachet Grand wine on the front seat and exited the car.

He stood back and admired the single-family home and its large wooden door with a stained-glass center. Morgan rang the bell and nervously waited for Kathleen to answer. When the door opened, Morgan stood speechless as his eyes took their fill of the ravishing creature before him.

For three weeks Morgan had had the pleasure of getting to know the brilliant and charming woman who tried to downplay her beauty. Kathleen never even wore jewelry at work. However, the radiant woman standing before him, wearing a formfitting black wrap dress, high heels and had her hair held up with a black crystal clip, was a sight to behold. Teardrop diamond earrings were the perfect elegant accessories to the outfit.

"Good evening, Morgan," Kathleen greeted him with a broad smile.

Note to self: she likes diamond earrings. Get it together, man. "Good evening. This is for you," he said, offering her the bottle of wine.

"Thank you. Please come in." Kathleen stepped aside and allowed Morgan to enter. Kathleen read the bottle's label. "Very nice, and it happens to be one of my favorites."

"Really?"

"Yes, my sister Hannah is a chef and insists on nothing but the best and she introduces me to a lot of really cool things."

"Good. My cousin Kristen recommended it," he confessed.

"You're not much of a wine person," she guessed, laughing.

"Not really. I mean, a glass or two at dinner is fine, but it's not my go-to choice when I want to sit back and chill."

"Let me guess. You're more of a beer-and-whiskey guy," she said, leading him out of her foyer.

"That I am," he confirmed. They walked into the open living area, and Morgan was taken aback by how nicely she'd infused a contemporary style that didn't diminish the historical feel of the house.

"You have a beautiful home."

"Thank you. Let's take this into the kitchen. This way."

Morgan's heart nearly stopped when Kathleen turned and offered him a view of her perfectly round behind.

He commanded his body, which was starting to stir, to behave. "When was it built?"

"In 1940. It came up on auction, and I bought it. Renovated it myself," Kathleen announced proudly.

"You renovated it?" He raised his eyebrows.

Kathleen stopped in her tracks and turned to face him. "I most certainly did. Yes, I had help, but I designed it, picked the materials and you see these wood floors?" She pointed down. "I refurbished them myself. In fact, I did all the flooring throughout the house myself, including the tiling."

"Seriously?"

"Just me with these." She placed the wine bottle under her arm and presented him her hands. "My own two hands."

"Wow. I'm impressed."

Kathleen smirked. "Don't be. It's kind of in my genes."

"What does that mean?"

"My family's into construction, and I picked up a thing or two. Along with my love of antiquing, renovating turned into a hobby," she explained.

"That's some hobby."

"I guess…" Kathleen led him through an open set of French doors that took them into the dining area and to a gray-and-white, gourmet-style kitchen. The large marble island with seating for six offered in-kitchen dining. There was plenty of storage and modern appliances, except for the old-fashioned six-burner yellow stove and oven.

"Damn, Kathleen, this kitchen is something else. Where did you find that stove?"

"I didn't. My sister Hannah is a chef, remember."

"Okay?" He frowned, not sure what that meant.

"Well, she found it for me." Morgan nodded while he gave the stove a closer look. "She cooks for me from time to time, so she insisted that I have a stylish and quality stove for her to use."

Morgan laughed. "She sounds like my mother and cousin Kristen. They're all about quality and style."

Kathleen had all but closed the case against Kingsley Oil and Gas, yet she was still curious about the reason behind the recent change in leadership. She figured now was the best time to ask about Kristen and Alexander's promotions, get it straight from the horse's mouth, so to speak. "We have a few minutes before we have to go. Can I get you anything?"

"No, I'm good."

Kathleen placed the bottle in the refrigerator. "Do you mind if I ask you about something?"

"Of course not."

"You mentioned your cousin Kristen…" Kathleen bit the inside of her lip.

"Yeah, what about her?"

"I know she has just been promoted to COO for your company, and please don't take offense to this, but she doesn't seem like the obvious choice." She presented a small smile.

"Obvious to whom? Those idiots out there who think she got the job just because she's a Kingsley?" His jaw clenched. "Or maybe those assholes in our social circle who think just because she's had a few episodes in her personal life splattered all over social media that she's not serious enough to get the job done. Or could it be our competitors, who are trying to taint her reputation? They are the same ones who've gone up against us and know she's a brilliant businesswoman who's been trained by the best and is the perfect person to help my brother run our company and take us to the next level."

Morgan's mood had changed, and Kathleen wanted to kick herself for even bringing it up. His passion for his family and their company rivaled that of her own family, something she lacked and was coming to realize had been a disservice to herself. "I didn't mean to upset you."

"*You* didn't. Some people think that, because we're a privately held company and can manage things the way we wish, we'd overlook quality people for roles in favor of a family member. Victoria Kingsley would never do such a thing. Now, have we all been groomed to join our family's business? We most certainly have, and we've been trained from the ground up in fact. But if we weren't up to the task we wouldn't be given the opportunity to destroy something our parents spent their lives building just because we're family. My mother's not built that way. In fact, my brother Brice nearly got fired for letting his personal life interfere with business. Plus, not all the Kingsleys are in the business."

"Yes, your mother's one intense woman," she said, leading him back into the living room.

"You have no idea."

She did. Victoria Kingsley had a well-earned reputation for being a hard-ass when it came to her business, dealing with the regulatory branches of the government and being very protective when it came to her family. Facts she knew from her investigative role at OSHA that she wasn't ready to share with Morgan just yet.

Kathleen reached for her clutch purse that sat on the antique table behind the sofa. "Did you not want the job?"

"Hell, no. I hate wearing suits, let alone dealing with them all the time."

Kathleen admired the expensive, well-tailored black Giovanni suit and black collarless shirt he was wearing. "You certainly look great in them," she complimented.

"Thank you, and I believe I failed to mention how breathtakingly beautiful you look tonight."

Morgan's words and the way he was looking at her sent warm tingles to the lower half of her body. Kathleen knew her face was probably as red as the bottoms of her expensive shoes. "Thank you. Shall we go?"

"After you." Morgan gestured with his hand for her to lead the way.

Kathleen set her house alarm and walked out the door. She felt Morgan's eyes on her before the warmth of his hand was placed on the small of her back. Kathleen inhaled quickly. Morgan opened the car door and helped her inside. "Thank you," she said, her voice barely above a whisper. Kathleen cleared her throat as she watched him walk around the car. His model good looks, alpha male demeanor and sweet nature made Kathleen want him even more.

Morgan got into the driver's side. "So where are we headed?"

"There's a place in the Museum District called Vista." She opened her purse and pulled out a small piece of paper with an address written on it and handed it to him." *Hannah better be on her best behavior.*

"I know where this is. There used to be a bar in that spot," he informed, pulling out of the driveway.

"I wouldn't know. I don't go out much."

"Why is that?" he asked, making his way out of her neighborhood and onto the highway. "You can't expect me to believe men aren't lining up to take you out. I'm sure a few of mine are asking you out, in fact.

Kathleen saw Morgan's hands grip the steering wheel and the muscle in his jaw twitched. His eyes glanced over at her before returning to the road. Kathleen liked the idea that the thought of her going out with someone else annoyed him. She wished she'd worn her hair down so she'd at least have some cover when her cheeks started to warm from the embarrassment.

"Well…"

"Yes, I get asked out—"

"By my men," he finished.

"A couple, but I haven't dated anyone since college." There was a slight tremor in her voice that she couldn't hide.

Morgan tightened his grip on the steering wheel as she fell silent. He pulled into a vacant lot and Kathleen could see they were just down the street from the restaurant. Morgan turned off the engine and angled his body toward her. "Did something happen to you in college?" he asked, his tone hard.

Kathleen watched the emotions on Morgan's face morph from shock to anger, and his eyes narrowed. For several seconds Kathleen wasn't sure what he might be thinking. Then it finally dawned on her. Women on college campuses were being sexually assaulted every day. Kathleen reached for his forearm and squeezed it.

"Oh no, nothing bad happened to me. I promise." Kathleen could almost see the anxiety leaving his body. Morgan had no idea who she really was. If he did, he would have known about the security team that attended school, including their Ivy League colleges, with all the Winston girls. Their security's presence and antics on campus had made several media outlets' coverage.

"After my mom died all I wanted to do was focus on my career. I had a new purpose in life and relationships never fit into my plans," she explained.

Morgan tilted his head. "And now?"

"Now—" Kathleen captured his hand and intertwined their fingers "—I guess we'll see."

He brought her hand to his lips and kissed the back of it. "Yes, we will."

When he thought Kathleen might have experienced sexual harassment in college, Morgan's mind flashed back to what that bastard Perez had tried to do to both his aunt and sister-in-law. Morgan figured she might not have been able to fight off some bully trying to take advantage of her had she not had the financial means to exact vengeance the way his mother had when Perez attacked her sister.

"When my father and uncle died over twenty years ago, our lives changed significantly," he said.

"I can imagine and relate." Kathleen rubbed the top of her hand over his.

"We all handled our grief differently, but my aunt Elizabeth took it exceptionally hard, as you'd imagine. She went away for a while."

"What do you mean, she went away?"

His mouth set in a hard line. "Aunt Elizabeth had a bit of a breakdown. When she started getting back to her old self again, she would go out and see people. You know, in social settings."

Kathleen nodded her understanding but remained quiet.

"Well, one of those people was Perez—"

"The man who tried to ruin your company."

"Yes. Perez attacked my aunt...tried to..." Morgan

focused on the warmth of Kathleen's touch to help him stay in control.

Kathleen squeezed his hand. "Tried, so he didn't hurt her, right?"

"No."

"Thank God."

Morgan nodded. "By the sad look that transformed your beautiful face, the change in your voice and the way you avoided looking at me, I assumed the worst. I thought someone—"

"No one did anything—I'm fine." Kathleen brought Morgan's hand to her mouth and kissed his palm. "Let's go have dinner."

Morgan started the car and pulled onto the street, steering with one hand while keeping a strong grip on Kathleen's with the other. The idea that anyone would try to hurt any innocent person, especially a woman, made Morgan crazy. His heart was racing as he drove. Morgan ran his thumb across hers, and Kathleen squeezed his hand. His heart began to slow its rapid pace. It was as if she was sending him a message that she was fine. Morgan could feel her eyes on him, and when he glanced over at her, she gifted him with a relaxed smile. In that moment, he swore to himself that no one would ever hurt his woman…including him.

Chapter 12

Kathleen was surprised by the lack of fanfare typical of Hannah's events. Morgan pulled into the front of the restaurant and waved off the approaching valet. Exiting the car, he came around and opened Kathleen's door, then he helped her out and held her hand. Morgan gave the key to the valet along with two one-hundred-dollar bills and said, "Keep it close." That shouldn't have been an issue since he noticed all the up-close spots for valet cars were empty.

"Yes, sir," the young man replied, his eyes roaming between the money in his hands and the expensive car he was about to drive.

There were two big floodlights outside lighting the way, a red carpet had been rolled out and several valets were waiting at the ready, yet no one was around. "Are you sure this is the right spot?" Morgan asked Kathleen.

Kathleen, who looked just as confused as he felt, said, "I'm sure. This is the address my sister sent me."

"Well, for a grand opening, they're not getting much business. The owners should fire their PR agency," Morgan joked.

They both laughed. "Yes, they should."

Morgan led Kathleen inside, and a pretty blonde woman greeted them with a big smile on her face. She was obviously the hostess. The woman was wearing a short black dress and high strappy heels, a look obviously meant to grab the attention of the male customers. While she certainly would meet her goal with other men, Kathleen noticed that Morgan didn't seem fazed by the woman.

"Welcome to Vista," she announced, directing her attention to Morgan.

"Thank you," Kathleen replied as Morgan gave a quick nod. "I'm Kathleen Winston, and we have a reservation."

"Yes, ma'am. We've been expecting you. Please follow me."

"We've," Morgan whispered in Kathleen's ear.

Kathleen shrugged and did as she was asked. The young woman led them into a room that was dimly lit in spite of the many chandeliers that hung from the wooden ceiling. Slate tiles covered the floors and a ceiling-to-floor glass bar ran along one wall. The focal point of the beautiful space was the Japanese Fruticosa tree placed in the middle of the room. A single and inviting table for two sat underneath the artificial tree's wide spray.

"Here you go," she said, smiling.

"Thank you," Kathleen replied as Morgan pulled out her chair. "Excuse me, miss, but if this is a grand opening, where is everyone?"

"It's a soft launch, actually," a voice said, coming from a woman who could have been Kathleen's twin. "Welcome to Vista, big sis."

Wow, Kathleen's sister is very pretty and they look a lot alike. But my baby is stunning.

Kathleen smiled as she watched her sister approach in white pants with a matching, double-breasted jacket and a tall chef's hat. Morgan stood back as the two women embraced and the hostess disappeared behind two closed doors.

"What's going on, Hannah?" Kathleen asked her sister in French. Switching languages was an automatic reflex whenever Kathleen was around her family.

"Later. Right now, introduce me to this fine-ass handsome man staring at us like he's seen a two-headed naked lady," she replied.

Morgan laughed. "He understands French, Hannah. Morgan, this is my sister Hannah Winston," Kathleen introduced, switching back to English.

Morgan extended his hand. "Pleased to meet you, Miss Winston."

Hannah shook his hand and said, "Call me Hannah. We're almost family," she teased.

"Stop it, Hannah," Kathleen scolded.

"It's cool," Morgan replied, smiling at both women. "You have a nice place here, Hannah," he said, looking around the empty room.

"Thanks, but this is not my place. It's my friend Mark's, but he won't get in town until tomorrow."

"Hannah is the guest chef," Kathleen announced proudly.

"Nice."

"Where is everyone, Hannah?" Kathleen asked.

"You two are it. You have the whole place to yourselves...except for my staff, of course, and me. Don't worry, we'll stay out of your way. You won't see us unless you have to. You'll have plenty of privacy."

"How do you have any type of opening with just two people?" Kathleen frowned.

"Actually, the soft opening is tomorrow night. This is more like a soft...soft opening." Hannah gestured with her hands as she glanced around the empty room.

"What does that mean?" she asked, narrowing her eyes.

"That means you two are our guinea pigs to make sure we are ready for tomorrow. So let's get this drill started." Hannah waved the waiter forward. "This handsome gentleman is Carl, and he'll be your server this evening."

Kathleen sat down, and Morgan took the seat across from her. "Can I get you anything to drink?" Carl asked.

"I took the liberty of choosing a nice chardonnay to accompany the appetizers I made for you." Hannah sent Carl to the bar to collect the bottle, and when he returned he filled their glasses. Another young woman appeared with two large square plates. She placed the plates in the center of the table after Hannah had Carl remove the centerpiece.

"I prepared a baked brie with figs and walnuts. Oh, I hope you don't have a nut allergy," Hannah said to Morgan.

"No, I don't." Morgan's cell phone rang; he checked the screen and sent the caller to voice mail.

"Good, because it's divine. There're buttered Parmesan croissants, shrimp scampi dip and baked ham-and-cheese roll-ups. Try the roll-ups. They're ham, Swiss cheese and a poppy seed glaze. Everything's delicious, if I do say so myself." Hannah's whole face lit up.

Kathleen reached for a roll. "We better try one or she'll never leave us alone."

Morgan selected one and took a bite. "This is very good."

"Yes. Hannah, it's very good," Kathleen agreed.

"Great. We have a full menu, but if you trust me I can make you something fabulous," Hannah offered, smiling at both Morgan and her sister.

Morgan raised his right hand. "I'm game."

"That would be great. Thanks, sis."

"Excellent. You two enjoy and your dinner will be out shortly." Hannah exited the room.

Morgan reached for his glass of wine and raised it. "To a very interesting evening," he said, grinning.

Kathleen smiled, picked up her glass and clinked his with hers. "It's getting off to an interesting start, that's for sure."

Kathleen filled her plate with several appetizers and watched as Morgan did the same. "Your sister's pretty great and her cooking is amazing."

Kathleen wiped her mouth. "She really is…both my sisters are."

"What does your other sister do?" Morgan took a drink from his glass, and his phone rang again. He looked at the phone's screen; his smile disappeared and his face went blank.

"Anything wrong?" Kathleen took a sip of her wine. She wasn't sure if she really wanted to know the answer to that question, but she was happy she didn't have to answer his question about her other sister yet.

Morgan exhaled noisily. "I was engaged once. To a socialite named Bonnie Ford, and she's reaching out to me again."

"I see…" Kathleen's eyes dropped to her plate and her heart fell to the floor with the thought that this woman was back in his life. She set her mouth in a hard line, preventing all the emotional craziness in her head from escaping her mouth.

Morgan reached across the table and held Kathleen's hand. "Bonnie and I haven't been anything to each other in years."

"Then why is she calling you now?"

"I'm not sure. We haven't spoken yet."

"Engaged." Kathleen pulled her hand back and took another sip of her wine. *They must have had something pretty special if she still thinks it's okay to reach out to him. Maybe he still has feelings for her.*

Morgan sighed and sat back in his seat. He could almost see the wall coming back up between them, and Morgan knew he couldn't let that happen. Morgan hated talking about the circumstances behind his breakup with Bonnie but he figured if he didn't this might be his first and last date with Kathleen.

"The Ford family was part of the same social circle as mine. We met while in high school. She went to an all-girls boarding school, so we mostly saw each other on the weekends and holidays."

"So this was just a high school thing," Kathleen concluded incorrectly.

At that, her face had brightened like a light bulb, and he hated to disappoint her. *Damn. I wish I could just stop right here, but I will not start this relationship off on a lie.* "Not exactly. More wine?" He reached for the bottle.

"Yes, please."

Morgan topped off both their glasses and returned the bottle to the silver bucket where it had been resting on a bed of ice. They both took a drink before Morgan continued. "After high school, we went to the same college, and both majored in engineering. The Fords own a small refinery."

"Sounds like you two had a lot in common."

"I thought so. Even though Bonnie was pursuing her degree, all she wanted was to marry me, have kids and stay home."

"And you didn't like that." Kathleen nodded.

"Actually, that's exactly what I wanted."

Kathleen went poker-faced. "You did? Do you still feel like that?"

Here we go. I might as well ask for the check now. "If I'm honest, I love the idea of coming home and finding someone waiting for me. Not to wait on me hand and foot, if that's what you're thinking. I want a partner in every way. But—"

"But what?"

"I know this will be hard to believe but I grew up in a mostly traditional home. While my mother helped my dad out at the office a couple of days a week, for the most part, she was a stay-at-home mom when we were really young."

"Victoria Kingsley?" Doubt crossed her face.

"She wasn't always Victoria Kingsley. For a long time, she was Mrs. Alexander Kingsley and Mom. Then my dad and uncle died, and everything changed." Not knowing what Kathleen was thinking or feeling about these new revelations, their earlier conversations about his aunt and the emotions of his father's death rushing back overwhelmed him. He gripped the stem of his wineglass with more force than he realized, and it broke off in his hand, cutting him. "Ouch…"

They saw the waiter approaching, but Kathleen held up her right palm to stop his forward movement. She pushed her chair back and rose slowly and silently. Morgan sat still and closed his eyes. He was trying to bring himself back under control. Morgan felt the warmth of Kathleen's hands cupping his face. She turned his head and said, "Open your eyes, baby."

Her words and touch brought him instant relief. The emotional hurricane swirling inside him subsided. Morgan opened his eyes and stared down into the warmth of hers. She had knelt down right next to him. "What's developing between us, Kathleen, has already surpassed what I thought she and I had," he said, hoping she could see the conviction in his eyes.

Kathleen smiled, rose up and gently kissed him on the lips. "That's all I wanted to hear. Let's get your hand cleaned up. Does it hurt?"

Morgan sighed. "A little. But I want you to know everything about me. I don't ever want any lies or mis-understandings to come between us. My parents and brothers have great relationships and I want that too… with you."

Kathleen was fighting back tears at the sight of Morgan's pain and sweet declaration at the same time trying to slow her racing heart. His words wrapped around her like a warm sweater she had that once belonged to her mother. The idea that she'd been lying to him and his family about who she was and her motives for being there was making her ill.

"Carl, my man," Morgan called, waving him over. He wrapped his bleeding hand in his napkin. Kathleen stood and stepped aside.

"Yes, sir," Carl answered as he made his way over to the table.

"Do you have a first-aid kit?"

"Yes, sir, I'll get it right away."

"I think we should get you to a doctor," Kathleen suggested.

"No, it's not that bad. A couple of butterfly stitches should be fine."

Carl returned with the kit, and Hannah was on his heels. "Here you go, sir."

"What happened?" Confusion and concern were written all over Hannah's face.

"Just a small mishap. I'll pay for the glass," Morgan promised.

"Don't be ridiculous." Hannah waved off his offer. "Carl, please get this mess cleaned up."

"Yes, ma'am."

"Excuse me while I go take care of this." Morgan glanced down at his hand. "Where's the men's room?"

"This way, sir." Morgan kissed Kathleen on the cheek before following Carl to the other side of the restaurant.

Kathleen gazed after him.

"Wow, you really are into him, aren't you?" Hannah observed.

Kathleen stared down at her feet and slowly nodded. She raised her head and turned to face her sister. "Yes, I am. Too bad nothing will ever come of it." Tears began streaming down her face.

Chapter 13

Hannah took Kathleen's hand, grabbed her purse and led her to the ladies' powder room. The lounge area was large with mirrored walls; two white leather sofas and two white circle chairs sat in the middle of the room facing each other. Both women sat down on the first sofa they reached. "What are you talking about?" Hannah asked, wiping away Kathleen's tears.

"Morgan still has no idea who I am and that I've been lying to him. To his whole family."

Hannah frowned. "I don't understand."

"I just couldn't do it," Kathleen said, her voice barely above a whisper.

"Yes, you can. Let me help you."

"How?" Kathleen held her sister's gaze. "How can you help me with this? The Kingsleys thought I was there to train their staff on some new regulations. Not investigate them. I looked Morgan and his mother in the eyes and lied to them."

"Answer me this. Why do you do what you do?"

"What are you talking about?"

"Your job, why do you do it?" Hannah clarified.

"You know why. I don't want other families to go through what we did," she explained, reaching in her purse for a Kleenex.

"Right. Did you initially think you had a case against the Kingsleys? That they could be putting their employees in danger?"

Kathleen took a deep breath and released it slowly before replying, "Yes."

"If you found out that the Kingsleys had done something wrong, would you have let them get away with it?"

"No."

"I didn't think so. You were doing your job, Kathleen. Your investigation is over, right?"

"Yes."

"With a positive outcome, right?" Hannah's eyebrows rose. Unable to speak, Kathleen gave a quick nod. "So the case is closed."

"It is," Kathleen confirmed, swiping at her tears. "But I have to wrap up a few things still related to the policy writing aspect of things."

"Okay, how long will that take?"

"Not long. A week…maybe."

Hannah took her sister's hand. "So just tell him the truth then. It will be fine. I saw the way he was looking at you. He'll understand that you had a job to do. At least he won't have to worry about you being some gold digger."

Kathleen smirked. "There is that. But—"

"No buts. Just enjoy spending the weekend getting to know him better and let him get to know you too. There's more to Kathleen Winston than her net worth and job."

"Thank you, Hannah."

Hannah stood, grabbed her sister's hands and pulled

her off the sofa. "Now get up and fix your makeup. You have a handsome guy waiting for you, and I have a great meal to serve." Hannah kissed Kathleen on the cheek and left her to pull herself together.

Kathleen stood in front of the mirror and took a deep breath. She pulled her compact out of her purse and blotted her face. "Hannah was right—we're getting to know each other. This will be over soon, and I know Morgan will understand," she said to her reflection. She gave herself one last look and went back to join Morgan.

"There you are," Morgan said, standing next to the table.

"Just thought I'd freshen up. How's your hand?"

He held up his bandaged right palm. "It's fine."

"So is our table, I see." Kathleen noticed that the table had been redressed with fresh linen, new crystal glasses and dishes.

"Yes, it is. Shall we continue where we left off?" Morgan held out Kathleen's chair.

Kathleen took a seat. "Absolutely."

Morgan returned to his chair, but before he could even start their conversation, Carl returned, rolling out a two-level cart. "Your dinner is served," he announced.

"Thank you, Carl," Hannah said, coming up behind him. "Morgan, since you were such a good sport about trying my appetizers, I figured I should make you something special." Hannah raised the lids on the plates. "I hope you like your prime cut filet mignon medium rare. I know my sister certainly does."

Hannah handed them each a plate. The corners of Morgan's mouth quirked up. "I most certainly do," he replied with a broad smile.

Hannah placed a plate of asparagus and potatoes on

the table. "I'll send over a bottle of Vérité La Joie. It's an excellent red blend I hope you enjoy with your meal."

"I'm sure it will be great. Thanks, Hannah, for everything." Kathleen knew her sister was aware she wasn't just thanking her for the meal. She hated having such big lies between her and Morgan but she hoped he'd understand the circumstances.

Morgan cut into his steak and took a bite. "This is so good. It melts in your mouth."

"I'm sure it does, just like the asparagus. You should try some," Kathleen said, laughing at Morgan's plate, which was stacked with meat and potatoes, only before taking another bite of her asparagus.

Carl returned with a bottle of wine and presented it to Morgan. "Shall I open and pour?"

"Sure, and thank you," Kathleen replied as Morgan had his mouth full again. Carl offered the initial taste to Kathleen. "Excellent." Kathleen cut into her steak, tried her sister's potatoes, which she knew would be good, and smiled.

Carl filled both glasses before he returned to the kitchen. Kathleen took a sip of her wine and said, "So, a stay-at-home wife. That's what you're looking for."

Morgan held up his right index finger, swallowed his food and took a drink from his glass. "Wow, that is good. Your sister has excellent taste in wine."

"Yes, she does. She's a chef." Kathleen smiled. "Stay-at-home wife, that's what you're looking for?"

"Not necessarily. I just don't romance someone who is so driven that she forgets about what's important."

"Is that what your mother did?"

"Not intentionally. After my father and uncle died, she had to step up and lead our family and run the business. It consumed her."

"That couldn't have been easy." Kathleen reached for more asparagus. "You sure you won't try any?"

"The steak and potatoes are fine."

Kathleen smiled and shook her head at the look on his face. "You don't like green vegetables?"

"Not one that looks like it's a stem of a tree," he stated, adding more potatoes to his plate.

"So is that what happened to Bonnie? She became too consumed with her career? Changed the plan on you or something?"

"Not exactly." Morgan finished off his wine and picked up the bottle. "Would you like some more?"

"Sure. And if you don't want to talk about it, that's fine." Kathleen was a pro at dodging uncomfortable questions. She'd certainly had enough practice after her mother's death and whenever she was at any social function with her family.

Morgan refilled their glasses. "No, it's fine. I want you to know me."

Kathleen felt good about his statement and willingness to open up to her, but bad because she wasn't doing the same. She told herself that Morgan would understand why she held back on him and he'd soon know everything about her as well.

"While in college Bonnie embraced her privileged life."

"What does that mean?"

"She joined what we used to call league clubs. Clubs geared to trust fund babies who liked to believe they were doing good works for others, but in reality, all they did was write checks. Nothing real was ever for anyone but themselves. It was all just for show. Bonnie insisted that we follow members of our social circle to charity events that meant nothing."

"Like what?"

"Teas, fashion shows, and we even went to the Kentucky Derby. Although that was pretty cool."

Kathleen smiled and wished she could tell him that her family went to the Derby every year: one of the perks of her wealth. Attending the race was one of the many things her mother enjoyed and one of the last they'd done together. "Because of the horses, right?"

"Right."

"So she started changing?" Kathleen concluded as she continued to eat.

Morgan held Kathleen's gaze. "Yes, her wealth became everything to her. So much so that she was no longer my Bonnie."

His Bonnie. The words stung, even though she was part of his past. "Is that why things ended?" Kathleen reached for her wineglass.

"No. Things ended because I found out that she was not only cheating on me, but she'd only agreed to marry me to ensure her family would be able to do business with my mother, which is ridiculous. Victoria Kingsley only does business with people she wants to, regardless of the relationship."

"What?" Kathleen coughed, having nearly choked on her wine.

"Are you okay?" His face twisted with concern.

"Yes, I'm fine," she assured, reaching for her water glass.

Morgan waited for Kathleen to stop coughing before he continued his story. "She'd met someone more into her, and she wanted to end things with me, but her father told her she couldn't. For the sake of the family's business and for her to be able to maintain her lifestyle, Bonnie had to marry me in order for their family to be set financially. He even told her that she could keep her old boyfriend as her lover if necessary."

Kathleen's eyes widened, and her mouth fell open. Morgan threw his head back and laughed so hard he nearly fell out of his chair.

"Oh my goodness. How did you find out about all this?"

"Bonnie told me."

"She did?"

"If nothing else, Bonnie was honest." Kathleen's heart sank at his words. "For the most part. She didn't tell me about the affair until after it started, but at least she told me herself. Bonnie even told me about her father's suggestion. She thought we should go along with it. She even went so far as to assure me that I could take a lover too."

"Wow…"

"But we'd have to abstain from those relationships when we decided to start a family. Only not right away. She was thinking five or six years from the time we married."

Kathleen's nose crinkled. "She had it all planned out."

"That she did. That was the end of things between us. That experience left a bad taste in my mouth for relationships." Morgan reached for Kathleen's hand. "Until now."

Kathleen bit her bottom lip and smiled. "Thank goodness."

"What about you?"

"I told you. I haven't dated anyone since college. I've gone out with groups of friends and coworkers to celebrate the end of a…a training session," she stuttered.

Morgan tilted his head slightly to the right and his

forehead creased. "You celebrate the end of training sessions? Those must be some difficult students you had to deal with every day. Hopefully, that will not be the case when you leave us."

"Not at all. I can honestly say that you, your company and your whole team have been a pleasant surprise."

"Even after our bumpy start?" he teased.

Kathleen laughed. "Even after that."

Morgan leaned forward, brought Kathleen's hand to his mouth and kissed her palm, sending a warm feeling throughout her body and straight south. Kathleen squirmed in her chair, trying to ease the sensation between her thighs. Kathleen held his passion-filled eyes, and without thinking, she said, "Dance with me."

Without responding, Morgan held her gaze, pulled out his phone and slid his hand across the screen. After several seconds the perfect slow song began to play. Morgan rose from his seat, came around the table and offered Kathleen his hand. Kathleen exhaled slowly, trying to calm herself. She'd never been one for slow dancing, but in that moment she found herself needing to be close to him. Kathleen placed her right hand in his, hoping he didn't notice the slight tremor. Morgan pulled Kathleen into his arms, and she instantly felt a warmth and connection unlike anything else she'd ever felt before.

Morgan felt the tremor that Kathleen tried to hide subside the moment he placed his arms around her waist. Kathleen wrapped her left hand around his neck and her right around his waist. They swayed to the sweet sound of Anita Baker's "You Bring Me Joy." Morgan felt his body respond in a way it shouldn't in a public place, but he didn't care. He looked down into Kathleen's beautiful eyes and saw his own desires reflected back at him. She raised her chin, and Morgan lowered his head and gently kissed her on the lips.

Kathleen pressed her body into Morgan and moaned into his mouth. The sound ignited a passion inside Morgan that he'd never experienced. Morgan's sex was hard as steel, and he shifted his hips in a way that ensured Kathleen could feel what she had done to him. Cupping Kathleen's face, he devoured her mouth. They kissed each other as if this would be their only opportunity, and they were both determined to make it last. When their lungs demanded air, Morgan slid his lips from Kathleen's mouth to her cheek, jaw and finally to her neck.

"Yes," Kathleen whispered, running her hand slowly across his behind.

"Damn, baby," he whispered in her ear. They were so engulfed in their passion that they didn't hear Hannah enter the room until she called out, "Excuse me."

Morgan froze and returned to his full height as Kathleen buried her face in his chest. "It's okay, baby, but I'm going to need you to stand in front of me," he whispered.

Kathleen looked up at him and uttered, "Why?"

Morgan discreetly pushed his hips against her so she could feel why for herself. Kathleen giggled and replied, "Yes, of course."

"I think it's time for the check," he said.

Kathleen smiled up at him and replied, "It most certainly is."

Chapter 14

Kathleen turned and stood in front of an expressionless Morgan. "Hannah…"

"I apologize for the interruption, but I figured you'd be taking your dessert to go," Hannah explained, giving her sister a knowing look.

"Thank you. That…that would be great. I mean, that's great," Kathleen nervously replied. She couldn't believe how out of control she'd been with Morgan in such a public venue, in spite of the privacy her sister had promised. Morgan ran both hands down the sides of her arms. She figured it was his way of calming her down.

Hannah handed Kathleen a rectangular white box with a red ribbon wrapped around it. "There are three small Bundt cakes inside. One red velvet, one chocolate mousse and one lemon." She looked up at Morgan. "Lemon's Kathleen's favorite, so you should keep it safe. I'd hate for anything to happen to it. The consequences of such a thing could be quite surprising."

"I'll keep that in mind," Morgan replied.

Kathleen knew the message Hannah was sending, and by the way Morgan responded and held on to her, she figured her threat came through loud and clear. Hannah was the baby of the bunch, but she was such a powerful force that no one messed with her.

"Can you have someone bring us the check?" Morgan requested.

Hannah shook her head. "Tonight's on me."

"I can't let you do that," Morgan insisted, pulling out his wallet and handing Hannah a black credit card. "And please, include a generous tip for yourself and everyone working tonight too."

Hannah glanced at her sister before accepting the card. Kathleen tried to keep her face expressionless and response discreet. She gave a quick nod, knowing that if she didn't Hannah would put up a fight and potentially let something slip about their identities.

"I'll be right back."

Kathleen turned and faced Morgan. "That was very kind of you."

"Don't be silly. I'd never stick your sister with such a bill, even though she was the chef. This whole night had to cost a pretty penny."

Kathleen was sure it did, and he had no idea that they could cover whatever the cost a million times over. Hannah returned with his card and receipt for Morgan to sign. He put his card away, didn't even look at the receipt and simply signed it. Morgan handed it back to Hannah and said, "Thanks again for everything. It was really great meeting you."

"It was great meeting you too." Hannah hugged her sister and walked them to the door. "Enjoy the rest of your evening. It's starting to rain, so drive carefully."

"We will. Love you, sis."

"Love you too. Stay safe." Hannah gave Kathleen a cheesy smile.

Kathleen knew precisely what her sister was referring to. She was just hoping her face didn't reflect how warm other parts of her body were. Kathleen stepped out from under the umbrella the valet held for her and into the waiting vehicle. Morgan walked around the front of the car, tipped the valet and got behind wheel. They flirted and teased each other and kissed at every red light they hit.

Before Kathleen knew it, they were back at her house, sitting on the sofa on her third floor watching the rain. They opened the bottle of wine Morgan brought Kathleen earlier and shared the delicious, decadent desserts her sister made them while discussing the latest antics of the president. "Those were really good." Morgan placed his fork on the plate.

"Hannah's an amazing chef." Kathleen took a sip from her glass and held it to her lips.

"You're pretty amazing yourself." Morgan checked his Piaget Polo watch and said, "It's getting late. I should go."

Kathleen wasn't sure where she found the courage, but she placed her glass on the table, climbed onto Morgan's lap and kissed him passionately on the lips, leaving no doubt about her intentions. Kathleen slid her lips across his again before she whispered, "Or you could stay." Her heart was racing, and she felt lightheaded. It wasn't the wine either. It was all Morgan. Kathleen had never been so bold when it came to men, and she didn't care if it made her look bad. All she wanted was for Morgan to say yes.

Morgan cupped Kathleen's face with his right hand and ran his thumb across her lips. He stared up into her dilated pupils and asked, "Are you sure that's what you want?"

Kathleen licked her lips. "I've recently realized that I've never really been sure of anything until now. I want you."

Morgan released a breath he didn't realize he'd been holding. He reached behind Kathleen and freed her hair from its bindings, the silky strands falling across his hands as he gazed into her desire-filled eyes. He knew her need was a mere reflection of his own.

"Where is your bedroom?"

Kathleen stood, took his hand in hers and said, "Follow me."

Morgan let Kathleen lead him downstairs to the second floor and into her dimly lit bedroom. The room wasn't what he expected. He recognized the expensive contemporary works of art that graced her bedroom walls. They were as unique in style as their owner. The king-size bed with its floor-to-ceiling wooden headboard was clearly the room's focal point. The balcony off the bedroom offered a stunning view of the city's skyline and was a nice secondary player to the room.

"Excuse the mess." Morgan knew that Kathleen was a little nervous, especially since there wasn't one thing out of place, and he found her anxiousness endearing.

"Everything's fine, baby," he reassured her, running the back of his hand down the side of her face. "We don't have to do this tonight if you're not ready," he offered, in spite of the fact that his body was screaming for relief.

"We most certainly do."

"I just don't want you to have any regrets in the morning," he admitted.

"I won't. I just hope you don't," Kathleen said, dropping her eyes.

Morgan frowned. He raised her chin, forcing her to look at him. "Why would you say that?"

"I told you. I've only been with two men, and I can count on one hand how many encounters there were."

"I know what I'm about to say is a bit chauvinistic, but you have no idea how much that pleases me. I know my number's a bit higher."

"A bit?" Her brows came to attention.

"I'm healthy, and I have protection. I've never wanted anyone as much as I want you and I'll swear that on anything."

Kathleen slid her hands around his neck, rose up on her toes and kissed him. Morgan deepened the contact, and when Kathleen gripped his shoulders and pressed her hips against his erection, he nearly exploded. Morgan murmured, "Turn around." She did as she was told.

Morgan swept her hair aside and slowly unzipped her dress. As the zipper descended and her skin was exposed, Morgan leaned down and kissed it. Kathleen's dress landed on the floor, offering him a beautiful view of her smooth, soft back and a perfectly rounded rear end in a pair of red lace panties. Morgan assumed Kathleen wasn't wearing a bra. He soon saw how both wrong and right he was.

Kathleen turned to face Morgan, and he was right she wasn't wearing a bra. Instead, he was gifted with the sight of perfectly full breasts wearing a pair of nipple pasties, designed to keep them from making inappropriate appearances. It was a battle they were losing. Morgan's insides were raging like a volcano ready to explode. He had never seen anything more beautiful. "Damn..."

"I assume you like what you see?" she asked timidly as she began to unbutton his shirt.

"You know I do." His voice was husky.

Kathleen pushed the shirt off his shoulders, and it joined her dress on the floor. She unbuckled his belt, lowered his zipper and slipped her hand inside. "Oh… my…goodness," she stammered. Kathleen wrapped her hand around his erection, and Morgan closed his eyes. The softness of her touch, the warmth of her hand and the motions she began making created a fog in his mind, and he struggled to stay upright.

"Baby, I think…you should…stop," he stuttered.

"Why?" she questioned in a soft voice while her thumb focused on his tip.

Morgan took a quick breath and grabbed her wrist. He tried to remove her hand, only she didn't release him. "Because if you don't, you're going to reduce me to a fifteen-year-old boy again."

Kathleen giggled and pulled out her hand. "We wouldn't want that, now, would we?"

"No, we wouldn't." Morgan scooped her up into his arms and carried Kathleen the short distance to the bed.

"Keep the shoes on," he ordered in an authoritative tone as he laid her down.

Kathleen smiled up at him like a Cheshire cat. "Anything you say."

"You remember that." Morgan quickly divested himself of all his clothes and shoes and Kathleen of her lace panties.

Morgan stood naked before Kathleen, standing between her legs admiring the stunning creature laid out before him. Only for him, and he had every intention of keeping it that way. Morgan knelt down and began kissing and licking his way up her body. The closer he got to Kathleen's core, the more she squirmed. Morgan gripped her thighs with both hands, hovered over her and looked into Kathleen's eyes. "I'm going to make you mine."

"Please…"

Morgan lowered his head and kissed her sex. He used his lips, tongue and teeth to devour Kathleen. Her moans of pleasure, her scent and the taste egged him on. Morgan didn't let up until he felt Kathleen's hands burrow in his hair; her body began to buck and she screamed his name. He rose up and captured her lips, offering Kathleen a taste of her exquisite delicacy.

"Hmm…"

"Delicious, isn't it?"

"Yes," she said in a low voice between breaths.

Morgan tried to move away from her, but Kathleen wrapped her arms around his neck and legs around his waist and began to swivel her hips. "Don't move!"

He knew she could feel his shaft at her entrance. It was as if the lower half of his body had taken on a life of its own. "Baby, I have to go get the condoms out of my pocket."

"No, you don't." Her head turned, and he followed her line of sight. "Gift bag."

"What about it?"

"Get it." She dropped her arms but kept her legs around him like a vise grip. Morgan knew he could break her hold but the fact that she didn't want him to and the desperate way he wanted her had his heart beating fast and relenting to her will.

Morgan reached for the bag. He removed the tissue paper, looked inside and burst into laughter. "There's, like, thirty condoms in here."

"I know, all sizes and styles too. My sister Hannah

and her friend got them for me in case things developed between us. I'd say they have." Kathleen thrust her hips forward, allowing his tip to slip inside her. "Yes," she moaned.

Morgan felt her wetness and immediately pulled back. Her unfamiliarity with this level of desire clearly had Kathleen feeling reckless. He would know because he felt it too, but one of them had to retain some sense of sanity.

"Wait, baby." Morgan emptied the bag on the bed and picked out the appropriate one for him. He rose up off Kathleen, gently breaking her hold, opened the condom package and rolled the fine level of protection on as he watched Kathleen's hands play with her breasts. When Kathleen started to remove the pasties, he uttered, "Stop. Allow me."

Morgan kissed and sucked each breast, leaving her nipples for last. After leaving his mark on the inside of each breast, something he hadn't done in years, he slowly removed each covering as if he was opening a fragile gift. Morgan tossed them aside and held Kathleen's gaze. He could see the tears forming in her eyes. Morgan's sex was throbbing at her entrance, but he knew he needed a few more seconds of sanity to get the words that had to be said past his lips.

"You are mine," Morgan declared. Kathleen nodded as she wrapped her legs around him again, raising her hips up to him. "Exclusively. I won't share you."

"Neither will I," she replied.

"You won't have to. I'm yours." Morgan thrust his hips forward, burying himself deep in her warm wetness. Her walls engulfed him like a tight shirt, and he heard her take a quick breath. He looked down at her and held still, allowing her body to adjust to his size. "Are you okay, baby?"

"Yes. You're just…big." Morgan tried to pull back, only Kathleen tightened her hold. "No. I'm already adjusting."

Morgan knew just how to help that process along. He took her nipples in his mouth and sucked, licked and pulled, fighting every male instinct in him not to immediately take what was now his. Morgan needed Kathleen to have that first sweet release before they went on a journey that would have them reaching ecstasy together. He held still and consumed her breasts, neck and lips as Kathleen started slowly rolling her hips beneath him. Her movements increased, and Morgan's thrusts supported her efforts. When Kathleen exploded and dropped her trembling legs, Morgan's control snapped.

He rose up off her, took Kathleen by the ankles and introduced the heels of her designer shoes to the ceiling. Morgan set a marathon pace that allowed them to savor every moment in each position he introduced her to. The more Morgan showed Kathleen, the more she told him she wanted to try. Morgan released something inside them both that each knew only the other could satisfy.

After reaching the pinnacle of satisfaction, they fell asleep in each other's arms, listening to the sound of the rain and their heartbeats. Morgan knew he would never let Kathleen go and that made him sleep easy.

Chapter 15

Kathleen woke to the smell of freshly brewed coffee which told her that the fancy coffee maker that Hannah insisted she get was doing its job. Kathleen was naked and lying across Morgan's body; he was still sound asleep. They'd made love several times throughout the night and again in the early hours of the morning. She kissed him gently on his bare chest and eased off him, then slowly walked to the bathroom; her satisfied but sore body reminded her how badly she needed to get back in the gym.

She stood in front of the mirror and barely recognized herself. Yes, she looked the same, except for a few passion bites Morgan had left all over her body. They were strategically placed so that they could be admired by only the two of them. She didn't mind because the sensation of the act of receiving them had been such a turn-on. Morgan told her it was his way of reminding her that she was his. He even encouraged her to give him a few, which she had. Kathleen figured out the difference; what she saw was happiness, real happiness. It was written all over her face. The spark in her eyes, her rosy cheeks and the wide smile that wouldn't go away said it all. She was in love, and nothing else mattered. Well, almost nothing else. Kathleen knew she had to tell Morgan the truth about everything. She just had to find the right moment.

Kathleen quickly freshened up and decided to forgo her shower. She knew how much more fun it would be if she waited for Morgan. She giggled at the thought, and she reached for her robe, wrapping her body in it. Kathleen walked down the stairs, passed through her living and dining rooms to get to the kitchen where she found her sister Hannah pouring herself a cup of coffee.

"What are you doing here, Hannah?" Kathleen glanced over her shoulder to ensure that they were alone.

"I thought we'd ride together," she stated as she poured sugar into her black coffee.

Kathleen gave her sister the once over. She wore blue jeans, a white T-shirt with a blue jean button-down covering it and running shoes. *Oh crap, I forgot.* "The Ward project."

"Yes. Was your date so good that you forgot all about our Houston Third Ward service project? We're painting and doing whatever else they need us to do today?" Hannah took a seat at the island and took a sip from her cup.

"It was, and I did." Kathleen nervously tightened her robe.

"No worries, we have plenty of time. I'll make you a breakfast burrito while you change. You can give me all the details on the way over." Hannah hopped off the chair and walked over to the refrigerator.

"Oh…okay," she stuttered, not moving. Kathleen ran a number of excuses through her mind she could use to put off her sister at least a few more hours. The idea of leaving Morgan right now was the last thing she wanted.

"How late did he stay last night?"

"Pretty late," she said, knowing her face was probably in full blush mode.

Hannah peeped around the refrigerator door. "You want cheese, right? I always get confused if it's you or Kennedy who doesn't like cheese on their burritos."

"Yes, I like cheese but—"

"Good. Why are you so flushed?" Hannah returned her focus to the contents of Kathleen's refrigerator.

Before Kathleen could respond to her sister a pair of large arms engulfed her body. His natural smell, along with her vanilla body wash, was an intoxicating scent. Her body automatically leaned back into him and she closed her eyes. Kathleen felt at home in Morgan's arms. She hated they didn't have the chance to share the shower.

Morgan kissed her cheek and softly said, "Good morning," in her ear.

Hannah closed the refrigerator door, and Kathleen's eyes popped open.

"I see." Hannah gave a lopsided grin.

"Good morning, Hannah," Morgan greeted her, keeping his hold on Kathleen.

"Well, good morning," Hannah replied, placing the contents in her hands on the island. "I'm guessing everyone had a good night." Her eyes were bouncing between Morgan and her sister, who had suddenly gone mute.

"We did, and thanks again for the wonderful meal last night," Morgan said.

"You're welcome. I'm about to make another one.

I hope you like breakfast burritos. With or without cheese?"

"With cheese, of course. Can I help?" he offered.

"You sure can."

Morgan kissed Kathleen's hair, walked around and stood next to Hannah. Kathleen stood, still unable to speak, and watched them making breakfast together. She couldn't get over how handsome Morgan looked wearing last night's clothes. Kathleen watched in awe at how easily Morgan got along with her sister. Hannah was an easy person to like, but their wealth and her celebrity status made her guarded around others, something she and her sister shared, only Kathleen had kept people at a distance for the sake of her career. At least that was what she told herself.

"Don't just stand there. Get the plates ready and pour us some glasses of OJ," Hannah commanded.

"Sure." Kathleen went to her cabinets and pulled down three plates and three glasses and set them on the island. Kathleen could feel Morgan's eyes on her as she walked over to the coffeepot, selected two mugs that hung from the wall and turned to face her guest. The smile that Morgan gifted her was breathtaking; she'd never seen him so relaxed and she found it very attractive. Kathleen held up a cup and said, "Want some?"

Morgan's smile widened. "I most certainly do."

"Coffee… I mean coffee," she nervously clarified, trying not to blush. It was a feat she failed miserably at, by the smirk her sister sent her way. All the Winston women tended to turn crimson whenever they got embarrassed, nervous or really angry.

"I take mine with cream and—" he held up two fingers "—two sugars."

Kathleen poured coffee in both cups, pulled the

cream out of the refrigerator and added the appropriate amount to both cups, added the sugar and handed him his coffee.

"Thanks, baby." He held her gaze, and Kathleen smiled. She loved the term of endearment he'd begun to use.

"I'm good. Thanks for asking," Hannah said sarcastically.

"I was going to top off your cup too, sis."

"Let's eat before our masterpiece gets cold," Hannah stated, handing Kathleen her plate.

Kathleen looked down at the perfectly rolled stuffed burrito and took a whiff. "This smells divine, Hannah." She always admired the many masterfully compiled dishes her sister created in her kitchen.

"It was a team effort," she said.

"Not really," he countered. "But thanks for sharing the credit."

They sat at the island and ate. Morgan questioned Hannah about her training as a chef while Kathleen kept quiet. She loved how easily he seemed to fit in, which made her happy and sad all at the same time. Happy because she could see a real future with Morgan and sad because her lies could ruin it all.

"Baby, you okay?" Morgan asked as he rubbed her back.

"Yes, I'm fine. Why do you ask?" Kathleen frowned.

"Because you've barely touched even half your food."

"I'm full. I don't usually eat such a heavy breakfast. It's delicious, though."

Having finished off his burrito, Morgan reached for Kathleen's plate. "We can't let this excellent food go to waste." Both women laughed. "So what are you two lovely ladies doing today?"

Kathleen half shrugged. "Nothing—"

"Actually, we're helping to rehab the community center not too far from here," Hannah interjected.

Morgan wiped his mouth with his napkin. "Oh yeah, what kind of rehab?"

"Painting, refurbishing some of the wood furniture, tile work in the bathroom, stuff like that. Did my sister tell you—"

"Hannah—"

"That she refurbished all the floors in her house?"

"She most certainly did." Morgan gave Kathleen a proud smile before leaning over and kissing her on the cheek. Kathleen released an audible breath, which didn't go unnoticed by her sister. Hannah's brows snapped together, and she mouthed the words, "What's wrong?"

Kathleen set her face straight. "Could you use another set of hands?" Morgan asked.

"Really?" Kathleen's whole face lit up, in spite of the fact that her lies were making her sick. She knew she had to tell him the truth as soon as possible, but the idea of spending more time with Morgan made her very happy.

"Sure. I love doing service projects. Plus, I get to spend more time with my girl." He ran the back of his hand down the side of her face.

Kathleen loved the idea of them working together on such a worthy cause, but she wasn't sure this particular project was the right one. "That would be great but—"

"Yes, it would. We need all the help we can get if we're going to meet next weekend's grand opening."

Kathleen was trying to think of a counterargument, but she couldn't think clearly with the way Morgan was looking at her, and his constant touches clouded her mind. "You don't have anything to wear and didn't you mention something about going to see your brother and nephew?"

"Nephew?" Hannah asked.

"Yes, I have two. My older brother and his wife just had their first baby a few weeks ago. And my brother KJ—"

"The NBA player? I guess former NBA player is a little more accurate of a description," Hannah interrupted.

Morgan nodded. "Yes. He and his wife have a four-year-old son and will have another baby soon."

"That's great, Morgan." Kathleen could see the pride in his eyes.

"Yes, it is. I just saw Alexander's son, but I haven't gotten to spend much time with Colby since KJ had them out on the road with him. Now that he's retired, I'll get to see a lot more of him. He's a cool little dude too. I can't wait for you to meet him, Kathleen," Morgan said.

"So you want kids? Do you have any?" Hannah asked, back in protective sister mode.

"Hannah," Kathleen chastised, giving her sister the evil eye.

The corners of Morgan's mouth rose. "It's fine." He reached for Kathleen's hand and intertwined their fingers. "Yes, I want kids...with the right woman." Morgan squeezed Kathleen's hand but kept his eyes on Hannah. "And no, I don't have any children yet."

"Good answers," Hannah replied as she started cleaning the kitchen.

Kathleen rolled her eyes skyward. "Sorry about my nosy sister's question."

"No worries. Your sister's just looking out for you."

"What about your plans?" Kathleen asked, handing her and Morgan's plates to Hannah.

"I'll just call KJ and tell him we'll see them to-morrow."

Kathleen's heart stopped. Yes, he'd said he wanted her to meet his nephew, but she didn't think he meant now. As if she read Kathleen's mind, Hannah turned and faced her sister. "We?"

"Yes, of course, unless you have other plans."

Kathleen stared at Morgan in disbelief. He was open-ing up to her in ways she never expected. Everyone knew how fiercely private the Kingsleys were and yet Morgan wanted to share his life with her while she kept hiding hers.

"No, she has no plans," Hannah stated for a shell-shocked Kathleen.

One of the many daggers Hannah was shooting Kathleen with her eyes hit its target and snapped her out of it. "I have no plans."

"Good, you had me worried there for a second."

Kathleen frowned. "Worried?"

"I thought maybe my mother had you scared. Look, I know my family's wealth and power can be over-whelming and the media can be intrusive. I try to fly under the radar, so hopefully, they'll leave us alone. I promise I'll keep you safe."

Kathleen fought back tears, and her mouth was sud-denly very dry. She knew about trying to hide from her family's wealth and influence. Kathleen reached for her orange juice and finished it off. "Yes, your mother is scary, but it's fine. I can handle it."

"That's my girl," he said, bringing their hands to his mouth and kissing the backs of them. "I keep clothes at KJ's apartment. I'll go change and be back in less than an hour."

"You keep clothes at your brother's house?" Hannah

questioned, wiping down the island, having loaded the dishwasher. Kathleen was curious about that herself.

"Yes, at his old apartment downtown. He and his family are staying in his wife's old house until their new one is built. They've been having so many construction issues—maybe he should hire Kathleen," he teased.

"Maybe he should," Hannah said, smiling.

"Don't be ridiculous." Kathleen's eyes narrowed at her sister. "I'll walk you out."

Morgan held Kathleen's hand as they walked to the front door. As soon as they'd cleared Hannah's view, Morgan pulled Kathleen into his arms and kissed her in a way that left no doubt about how much he wanted her. Kathleen knew she was falling for him and only hoped he felt the same way about her. When he finally let them both breathe again, he asked, "Should I bring an overnight bag back?"

He looked like he didn't know the answer to that question. Kathleen rose up on her bare feet, wrapped her arms around his neck, gently kissed him on the lips and whispered, "Yes."

Chapter 16

Morgan made his way to his brother's apartment feeling like he was on top of the world. He'd finally met someone he believed was perfect for him. Someone he felt he could trust. He knew she didn't come from a wealthy background like his own, but hers must be somewhat privileged. Her artwork, furnishings and home told him that much; even if she'd bought her house at auction, it would have cost her a pretty penny. None of that mattered to him. He'd seen firsthand how his world could affect people like Bonnie and her family when they weren't used to it, and Morgan was determined not to let such differences come between him and Kathleen. He wanted a future with her.

After parking in front of his brother's apartment building, Morgan spent a few minutes speaking to the security guard before making his way up to KJ's penthouse. When he opened the door he was met with a big smile and a loud shout of "Uncle Morgan."

Morgan knelt down and scooped up Colby, swinging him in the air. "Hey, Colby. How's my favorite four-year-old nephew?"

Colby frowned. "I'm not four anymore. I'm five." He held up his right hand to support his assertion.

"That's right. You did have a birthday. Sorry I was out of town and missed it. You did get my gift, right?"

"Yep, you want to see it?" He squirmed until Morgan placed him on his feet and he went running to the back of the apartment.

KJ came out of the kitchen, saying, "Slow down, son."

"Okay, Daddy." Colby slowed his pace.

"Good morning," KJ greeted him.

"Morning." The two men bumped fists. "What you two doing here? Is Mia here too?"

"No, she's getting a haircut or trim…something, hell I never know. Want some breakfast?" KJ asked, leading Morgan into the kitchen.

"No, thanks."

"You sure?" He held up a kids-targeted cereal box. "Breakfast of champions."

"I'm sure," Morgan said, laughing at the funny expression on his brother's face. He found himself wondering if one day he'd be making that same offer to someone, only it would be his and Kathleen's kid's cereal. That thought didn't scare him in the least bit either.

Colby ran back into the kitchen but slowed down when he saw his dad's face. He held a fire truck nearly as big as he was. "Here it is, Uncle Morgan."

"Let me see that. Man, this is cooler than it looked online."

"It makes noise too," Colby informed him.

"Yes, it does," his brother agreed, giving Morgan the evil eye. "Remind me to return the favor one day."

"You might be able to sooner than you think."

KJ went expressionless. "Colby, you done eating?"

"Yes, Daddy."

"Then take your truck back to your room and watch cartoons while I talk to your uncle."

"Okay."

"Here you go, little man." Morgan handed Colby back his truck. "See you later."

"See you later, Uncle Morgan."

Both men stood and watched Colby leave the room. Morgan looked at his brother and smiled. "That's one great kid you got there."

"I know, and I'm blessed to be able to claim him as my own," KJ admitted.

"How's he doing…healthwise?"

"He's great. We're extra cautious when his asthma acts up. It can cause so many other issues in kids with Down syndrome, but we've been really lucky," he explained.

"That's good."

KJ leveled a look at Morgan, and he knew the turn the conversation was about to take. "Now, what's this about me being able to return the favor? Want to tell me something, brother?"

Morgan shook his head. "No, not yet."

"Sit," KJ ordered, taking a seat at the island. "Now you got me curious."

Morgan sat and rubbed his hands together. "I met someone."

"Seriously?"

"Seriously, and man, she's something special." Morgan's heart started beating so fast he felt like the sound might drown out the words he was trying to express. "I've never met anyone like her before. If you take Mom's strength, Aunt Elizabeth's kind heart and the beauty of all my sisters-in-law, you'll have my Kathleen."

KJ's eyebrows stood at attention. "Your Kathleen."

"She's family-oriented, knows the oil and gas business and she doesn't take my crap." Morgan was so engrossed in his description he nearly missed his brother's comment.

"She really must be something special. How long have you known this woman and where did you meet her?"

"I only met her a few weeks ago. She's the trainer that OSHA sent to update our systems and training program based on some new regulations that just went into effect," Morgan explained.

"Don't you think that's fast?"

"You know me—"

"I do, which is why I am asking. You don't get involved. At least not long-term," KJ stated with a worried look on his face.

"Neither did you until you met Mia," he reminded KJ.

"True. Even then I fought it."

Morgan nodded in agreement. "So did I but I couldn't seem to help myself."

"I know the feeling. Congratulations, man." KJ offered his hand, and the two men shook. "So when do I get to meet her?"

"I was going to bring her with me when I came to your house tomorrow, if that's cool."

"Tomorrow? What happened to tonight?"

"We have this other thing we need to do and I'm not sure when we'll be done or what shape we'll be in by this evening. Will tomorrow work?" he asked, hoping for a positive response.

"Of course. There will be plenty of BBQ."

"Great."

"Yep, you got it bad."

Morgan laughed. "I know."

"So what brings you to town anyway? Don't say it's just to see us," KJ questioned.

"I took Kathleen to dinner last night."

"Last night. Well, I know you didn't spend the night here, so I assume you two…"

"I should go change," he said, ignoring his brother's conclusion. "Kathleen and I are meeting her sister at a community center for a service project."

Morgan figured KJ got the hint that he didn't want to go there with him when he changed topics and said, "So she has a sister."

"Yes, and she's an amazing chef."

"A chef?"

"Yes, she has some popular show," Morgan offered, his forehead creased as he tried to remember the name of her show.

"That's cool. What's her name?"

"Hannah Winston. You know it?"

"No, but Mia might. She's really into cooking networks," KJ explained.

"She has two other siblings too. Her brother's in finance, I think, and her older sister is an executive. At least I think that's what she told me. I honestly don't remember what she said," he admitted. "I do know they all seem to do well for themselves."

"Well, I'm happy for you, man." Colby's laughter rang throughout the house.

"Me too, for you, as well. What time tomorrow?"

KJ shrugged. "How's one?"

"Sounds good to me. I'm going to change. I can't keep my lady waiting." It was a declaration that Morgan was beginning to enjoy making.

Kathleen sat on one of the chaise longues in her closet with her body and hair wrapped in towels. She looked up at her frustrated sister, and she knew she couldn't keep this conversation at bay any longer.

Hannah stood in front of Kathleen with her arms folded across her chest. "Now that you've had your shower, do you want to tell me what's going on? Why are you in such a frenzy about Morgan coming to help us today? The man is obviously crazy about you. He couldn't seem to keep his hands off you."

Her sister's words broke through the dam Kathleen built to hold back her tears; the truth of Hannah's statement was too much to bear. Kathleen burst into tears. Hannah sat down next to her sister and put her arms around Kathleen. "What's wrong?"

"I'm falling in…love with… Morgan," she said between sniffles as she tried to catch her breath.

"Oh, sweetie, that's okay. It's pretty clear to me he's fallen for you too."

"I know…" A fresh set of tears fell.

Hannah released her sister, left the dressing room, returning quickly with a box of tissues in hand. "Here you go." Kathleen took a tissue and blew her nose. She wiped her tears and took several deep breaths trying to calm herself. "Talk to me, Kat."

Kathleen offered her sister a weak smile at her childhood nickname. "I still haven't told Morgan the truth about everything."

"What?"

"I know, I should have told him." Kathleen dropped her face in the palms of her hands.

"Yes, you should have."

"I—"

"Kathleen, you had sex with the man without clearing the air about everything." Kathleen nodded, keeping her hands on her face. Hannah put her arm around her shoulders. "It's okay."

Kathleen dropped her hands. "No, it's not."

"No, it's not, and I shouldn't have encouraged you. I forgot how emotionally inexperienced you are and I don't want you to get hurt," Hannah stated. "But you *are* going to tell him, right?"

"Yes, of course. I was waiting for the assignment to end, but now, I'm going to tell Morgan as soon as my boss officially closes the case."

"I thought you did that already?"

Kathleen saw the confusion in her sister's eyes. "I did, but I don't have the final say."

"Well, when will that be?"

"Hopefully Monday, and I'll tell Morgan everything as soon as I know."

"Why does that even matter? I mean, you said they were innocent. Why not just tell Morgan now?"

"Because my deception was about business that I let turn personal—"

"But only after you'd determined that they were already innocent."

Kathleen shook her head. She stood and walked over to the dresser. "That doesn't matter. I still deceived him…them, and I put my reputation and job in jeopardy."

"How did you do that?"

"I got involved with the target of an investigation,

Hannah. That crosses all types of ethical boundaries," she explained, throwing her hands up in disgust.

Hannah heaved a sigh. "So what are you going to do?"

"I'm going to get this case closed, come clean to my boss and tell the Kingsleys the truth. I'm hoping when I explain things and give them the good news about the outcome of the investigation they might find a way to forgive me," she rationalized.

"And if they don't?"

"I don't know," Kathleen admitted.

"Well, if Morgan cares for you like I think he does, he'll find a way to move past it. I'm sure of it," Hannah stated with confidence.

"It's not just that."

Hannah stare fixed. "What else is there?"

"He doesn't realize we come from an equally wealthy background."

Hannah gave a nonchalant wave. "Oh that, that's nothing."

"It's something to him."

"I can't believe he hasn't figured it out." Hannah ignored her buzzing phone. "All he has to do is search the internet for you or me, for that matter."

Kathleen exhaled. "Thankfully he's not into social media."

"All right, but what does all this have to do with the service project?"

The look of confusion had returned to her sister's face.

"Dad supplied all the materials for this job."

"So..." Hannah frowned.

"So? Don't you think he'll find it odd that we're

doing a service project with a bunch of Winston materials lying around the place?"

"First off, our donation was in the form of money and workforce. They could purchase the materials from many different places, and our name isn't on any of them." Hannah started walking around her sister's closet, checking out her wardrobe. "You've been out of the business too long."

"So have you," Kathleen countered.

"Yeah, but I know what's going on and that we don't make the materials we use," she snapped back.

"You're right. Sorry, sis. I guess my paranoia is getting to me."

"It's fine. Look, I think you're concerned over nothing, but I'll head over now and make sure there's nothing out there that says Winston Construction or that there's no one's around to blow your cover, okay?"

"Thank you."

"No problem." Hannah hugged her sister. "Keep the faith, and I'll let myself out. See you soon."

"Hannah's right. Just keep the faith. You can do that because Morgan's worth it. What we have is worth all the risk," Kathleen told herself.

Chapter 17

Kathleen moved in front of her full-body mirror. She loosened her robe and looked down at the evidence of her and Morgan's passion last night and that morning, and all of his words came rushing back into her mind. Kathleen took a deep breath and released it quickly. "Everything is going be fine. As soon as you get dressed," she said, pointing to her reflection.

She opened her dresser drawer, selected a black lace bra and underwear set and slipped them on. She pulled out a pair of blue jeans, a green V-neck shirt and a blue jean jacket. Kathleen put on a pair of blue running shoes, lightly made up her face and pulled her hair up into a high ponytail. She was gathering up the towels when her doorbell rang. Kathleen tossed everything into her hamper, picked up her phone and purse and went downstairs to open the door.

"Hi." Kathleen was taken aback at the sight of Morgan in black jeans, a tan short-sleeve shirt, black leather jacket and black oxfords; she loved his more casual look. He was holding a brown leather bag and her heart raced because she knew what that meant. Kathleen stepped aside to let Morgan inside. As soon as he crossed the threshold, he dropped the bag, pulled Kathleen into his arms and captured her lips in a mind-blowing kiss. "Oh, wow."

Morgan leaned his forehead against hers. "I missed you," he admitted. His voice sounded weak.

"I missed you too. I'm guessing those are a few of your things."

"They are. Should I take the bag upstairs?"

"Later. We have to get to the Ward Community Center. You look great, by the way," she complimented.

"So do you, like always. I love the jeans, although they'll make keeping my focus that much more difficult." Morgan opened the door. "After you, my lady."

As they made their way to the community center, Kathleen shared its eighty-year history in Houston's Third Ward with him. She explained how the residents came together and contacted several companies to get support in bringing their community center back to its former glory. She left out the fact that her family's company had been their largest benefactor.

When they finally arrived at the center, Kathleen quickly scanned the area for any Winston Construction signs that might've been posted. Kathleen breathed a sigh of relief when she saw none. They exited the vehicle and headed inside.

"There you are," the center's director said as she approached Kathleen.

"Good morning, Mrs. Benson." Kathleen kissed the slimly built gray-haired older woman wearing a long flowered dress with a white apron wrapped around her waist.

"Good morning." She brought the glasses that hung around her neck to her eyes and checked the clock on the wall. "I guess it's still morning…barely. Now, who is this handsome gentleman?"

"Mrs. Benson, this is a friend of mine, Morgan Kingsley." Kathleen turned and looked up at him. "Morgan, this is Mrs. Benson. She's an old family friend, and she spearheaded the campaign to get this center updated. As a way to thank her for all her hard work, the community voted to make her the center's director."

"That's what I get for opening my big mouth," she teased, extending her hand.

Morgan gave her hand a gentle shake. "Pleased to meet you."

"Morgan came to help us out today. I'm sure you can find something for him to do." Kathleen looked around the center's entrance and all the boxes, furniture and sporting equipment that littered the foyer and every hallway leading from it.

"Are you good with your hands?" Mrs. Benson asked.

"I most certainly am," he replied, briefly cutting his eyes to Kathleen.

Kathleen felt warm all over, and she only hoped she wasn't as scarlet as Mrs. Benson's nail polish. "Morgan's family owns an oil and gas company, so he's always working with his hands," she quickly explained.

"Good. Head down that hall," she pointed to the left of where they stood. "Knock on the last door to your right and ask for Danny. He has a couple of walls that need a coat of paint."

Morgan reached for Kathleen's hand. "I guess I'll see you later."

Kathleen squeezed his hand and smiled. "I'll come by and check on you in a little while." She watched as he walked away and her heart immediately started to ache. Kathleen was starting to feel like she was losing something important. *Get it together, girl. Everything's going to be fine.*

"Hello…" Mrs. Benson snapped her fingers in front Kathleen's face.

"Yes, ma'am," Kathleen replied, snapping out of her trance.

"Someone's smitten, I see. I say that young man is more than just a friend."

Kathleen didn't want to be disrespectful to Mrs. Benson, but she didn't want to discuss her personal life with her either. *Deflect.* "Where do you need me today?"

"The library, of course. We still have to fill all those beautiful bookshelves you refurbished for us. I still can't get over your father's generosity. First, he donates all the money we need to restore and upgrade this place, and then he sends us thousands of books to fill our library shelves, so we're ready the day we open. Or should I say the Irene Winston Memorial Library."

Kathleen smiled. She loved the idea of the library being named after her mother.

Kathleen's mother had been an avid reader, especially during the last year of her life. Irene had an eclectic taste when it came to books. She loved everything except romance novels. Kathleen's mother once told her that the reason she didn't read about other people's romances was because she was living one of her very own. Kathleen now knew exactly what her mother meant.

"It was his pleasure. My mom was a big fan of reading."

"I know she was, sweetie." Mrs. Benson ran her right hand down Kathleen's arm as if she was trying to warm her up. "We better get to work."

"I'm on it. Just one more thing."

"What's that?" Mrs. Benson placed her right hand on her hip.

"Morgan doesn't know anything about my family's wealth and I'd like to keep it that way."

"He won't hear about it from me," she promised.

Kathleen sighed. "Thank you. I'll get to work."

Morgan stood in the doorway of the room he'd been directed to. He saw an older brown-skinned man with a shaved head wearing a blue shirt and a pair of overalls and work boots painting a wall. "Excuse me, sir, are you Danny?"

"Yes, how can I help you?"

"Hi, I'm Morgan Kingsley." He offered his hand, walking into the room. "I'm here to volunteer, and Mrs. Benson sent me to you."

"Did she now? I can't shake your hand but welcome. Do you know anything about painting?"

"Yes, sir, I sure do."

"Good. As you can see all four walls have been primed and are ready to be painted."

"Yes, sir, I can see that. Where would you like for me to start?"

"You can start by losing that fancy jacket of yours and rolling up your sleeves."

Morgan smirked. "Yes, sir." He removed his jacket and laid it across the chair near the door. He held out his arms. "Short sleeves, which wall do you want me to do first?"

"You're a young and virile-looking man, so you get the back wall," Danny said, laughing. "Everything you need is in the corner."

Morgan poured paint in a tray, selected a roller and got to work. After toiling in silence for nearly an hour,

Danny asked, "So what brings you here? I didn't see Kingsley Oil and Gas on the list of donors."

"You know who I am?" Morgan studied the older man.

"Of course, I spent twenty years as a longshoreman. I know all the companies in the gulf," he declared proudly.

"I didn't know anything about this project," he stated as he continued to work.

"I see. I thought maybe you were here anonymously."

"No, I came with a friend," Morgan said, silencing his ringing phone.

"Who, if I may ask?" Danny stilled his brush and looked over at Morgan.

"Kathleen Winston," he said proudly as his heart skipped a beat when he just mentioned her name.

"Kathleen's a good girl from a great family." Danny returned to his work.

"Yes, she is. Kathleen's something special."

"Did I hear my name?" Kathleen asked, walking into the room.

Danny put his brush down and hugged Kathleen. "Yes, you did, beautiful one. How are you?"

"I'm good. How have you been?" She gave Danny a quick kiss on the cheek.

"Fit as a fiddle."

Kathleen laughed. "I see you put this one to work." She gestured with her head toward Morgan.

"I sure did. Excuse me a minute." Danny left the room to answer his buzzing phone.

"Speaking of work, shouldn't you be doing some?" Morgan teased.

"As a matter of fact, I should. I just wanted to make sure you were handling your assignment okay."

Morgan laid down his roller, closed the distance between them in less than three strides and wrapped his arms around Kathleen's waist. "You sure that's all you wanted?" He gave her a wicked grin before leaning forward, kissing Kathleen passionately on the lips.

Sooner than either one of them wanted, Morgan ended their kiss, a move Kathleen clearly rejected by tightening her grip on his waist and back. Morgan took her hands and gently removed them from around him. His body was coming alive in a way he knew was inappropriate.

"Baby, we're in public," he whispered in her ear.

"It doesn't seem to matter where we are. I can't think when you kiss me like that," Kathleen admitted.

"Is that a bad thing?"

"I'm not sure. Bad things can happen when you don't think."

Morgan brushed a loose strand of hair from Kathleen's face. "Not if you're following your heart," he countered.

"Is that what we're doing...following our hearts?"

Morgan knew he was entering foreign territory and it unnerved him. He was determined not to let fear or his past ruin something that could be amazing between him and Kathleen. He stared into Kathleen's eyes, ran the tips of his fingers across her lips and said, "I am, and I hope you are too."

Kathleen rose up on her toes and snaked her arms around his neck. "I am too," she whispered gently, kissing him on the corner of his mouth and running her tongue across his lips before kissing him again.

Morgan was so lost in the gentleness of her touch, her kiss, that he hadn't heard Danny return. "You two keep that up, we'll never get this room finished, and I'd like to get home before the storm hits," he said, returning to his wall and paintbrush.

Kathleen turned in Morgan's arms and faced Danny. "There's a storm coming?" Morgan heard her tone rise an octave.

"Yep, and it is supposed to hit sometime tonight," Danny stated nonchalantly.

"You can't be afraid of a little rain. You certainly weren't afraid last night," he whispered in her ear.

Kathleen nudged him with her elbow and looked over her shoulder. "No, I'm not afraid of a little rain. It's the rapidly rising water that scares the hell out of me."

"It will be fine. My brother's house sits off the road, anyway."

"About that." She turned to face him, pulling out of his hold. "Can we step in the hall for a second?"

"Sure. I'll be right back, Danny." Morgan followed Kathleen out the door.

"What's going on?"

"Don't be disappointed, but I don't want to go with you to your brother's house tomorrow."

"Why, because of the rain?" His forehead creased.

"No. I just think things are moving a little fast. Maybe we should slow things down a little."

Morgan's frown deepened as he folded his arms and cocked his head to the side "Do you? You just said—"

Kathleen bit her bottom lip and dropped her shoulders. "What I meant…*mean*, is that we need to figure out what this thing is between us before we share it with others. It should be our secret. At least for a little while."

"You mean *you* need to figure out what this thing is, because I'm crystal clear." His annoyance was on full display. He couldn't believe this was happening…again.

Morgan ignored the goo-goo eyes two young volunteers sent his way as they passed them in the hall. His eyes bored into Kathleen.

"I just think it's a little soon to go public and start sharing it with more people."

"People…"

"Yes. Our whole family, friends…people we work with," she explained.

"Don't you think it's a little late? The secret is out."

"No, it's not. Just because *some* people know or maybe suspect we went out doesn't mean we're in a relationship. It's no one's business," Kathleen declared emphatically.

"It seems you don't know what this is, do you?" Morgan felt like he'd just been hit in the gut. He wanted a committed relationship with Kathleen and all that entailed, but it seemed she wasn't quite there yet. Morgan might not have been in a relationship for a while, certainly not one like he wanted with Kathleen, but he knew doubt in or about relationships never worked.

"I just think—"

"Don't worry about it. Take all the time you need." They stood silently staring at each other for several moments. "I should get back in there."

"Okay. I'll get a ride home from Hannah so you don't have to change your original plan and can go over to your brother's house tonight from here. I'd hate for you to get caught in the storm."

"If that's what you want." He dropped his arms. Morgan was choking on his hurt and anger. Hurt because he thought they were falling for each other and now he realized it was only just him, and anger because he'd sworn he'd never let this happen to him again. But he let his guard down, had given his heart to Kathleen, and she'd shoved it back in his face after stomping on it.

"I'll see you later?" She reached for his hand.

"Later." He gave her hand a small shake and walked away.

Kathleen stood and watched Morgan walk back into the room to join Danny. She'd felt sick throughout that conversation. Kathleen knew exactly how she felt about Morgan and she'd love nothing more than to shout it to the world. Unfortunately, she couldn't do that until she told him the truth about everything. The idea of expanding her lie to more of his family was something she couldn't handle and wasn't willing to do. The hurt she saw in his eyes pained her heart. The only thing she held on to was the idea that this would be over soon and everyone would know they were together and in love. She just had to stay strong and hope Morgan would too.

Chapter 18

Kathleen returned to the library and buried herself in work. That was what she always did whenever things in her life got hard. It didn't matter if it was her day job or hobby distracting her; she gave whatever it was her undivided attention. Working hard was her safe haven. She only stopped long enough to eat the contents of the lunchbox her sister had provided; something that was supposed to be a simple ham-and-cheese sandwich with a bag of chips ended up being a gourmet creation on a croissant with sweet potato fries. Hannah had even added a small version of one of the Bundt cakes she'd made her and Morgan the night before, bringing tears to her eyes.

After Kathleen placed the last set of books on the shelf, she stretched her arms out at her sides and rolled her neck. The hours of sitting, reaching and bending had taken their toll on her body. Much like Morgan had the night before. Kathleen had managed to push her concerns over Morgan out of her mind long enough to get her project done, and she was quite pleased with the outcome.

She looked around the room. "What do you think, Mom?" Kathleen felt a sense of warmth come over her and while she was pretty certain it was her imagination, she said, "Yeah, I like it too."

"You ready to go?" Kathleen turned to find Hannah standing in the doorway holding her bag in one hand and checking her cell phone in the other.

"What?"

"Morgan told me to be sure that I got you home safe."

"He did?" Kathleen frowned. She had hoped Morgan would have insisted on taking her home himself. It would have given her time to explain herself better.

"Yep. I thought you two would be inseparable all weekend, based on what I saw this morning," Hannah replied, keeping her eyes on her phone.

"That was before I put my foot in my mouth," she murmured.

"You two meeting up later?"

Hannah hadn't heard a word Kathleen had said, which was fine with her. "I'm sure."

"Where did he go?"

"He's hanging out with his younger brother," she explained. Kathleen decided to let her sister believe everything was fine between her and Morgan. She didn't want Hannah worrying about her. This was her problem to fix.

"Boys' night out," Hannah concluded. "You two starting to do couple stuff already? That's cool, just make sure he doesn't have too many boys' nights out. But by the look of things, I'm sure that won't be a problem."

"Yeah, keep them at a minimum. Got it."

"Well, let's go, I want to take off before the weather changes. You know how much I hate flying in the rain."

"Flying? Where are you going?" Kathleen picked up her purse, pulled out her phone and checked for a message from Morgan. She hid her disappointment at having found none as they left the center, only stopping long enough to say their goodbyes to Ms. Benson.

"I'm heading back to LA."

Kathleen frowned. "I thought you had the restaurant opening tonight."

"Yeah, about that, I kind of stretched the truth a bit."

"What do you mean you *stretched* the truth a bit?"

Hannah shrugged. "Last night was the soft...soft opening but real soft opening isn't for another couple weeks."

Kathleen's face contorted. "Do I even want to know what you had to do to make last night happen?"

"Nope." Hannah winked at her sister.

Kathleen gave her head a slow shake. "Thank you."

"Trust me, it was my pleasure making that happen for you two." Hannah's eyebrows started to dance. "Duty calls. This visit was fun, but between the show and my social commitments, I can't take any more time off."

"You work too hard," Kathleen observed.

"Hello, pot, pleased to meet you," Hannah replied with her left eyebrow raised.

"I know... I know, just call me kettle," Kathleen admitted, and they both laughed.

Hannah dropped her sister off at home, and after a tearful goodbye, Kathleen let herself in the house, nearly tripping over Morgan's bag. Kathleen closed and locked the door, dropped her keys and purse on the entry table and made her way to the kitchen where she pulled out a bottle of Stella Rosa Rosso from the wine refrigerator. She selected a glass from the cabinet, poured enough to ease her frayed nerves and finished off the contents, barely letting the taste settle on her tongue. After eating such a big lunch, she wasn't hungry. Kathleen topped off her glass, grabbed the bottle and headed back to the foyer.

Holding the glass and bottle in one hand, she picked up her purse and stared down at Morgan's bag. "Stop tempting me. I'm not calling him," she declared, picking it up. "I'm taking you upstairs just to get you out of the way," she explained as if she was talking to someone.

Kathleen placed her purse and the wine bottle on the dresser while she set Morgan's bag on the steamer trunk that sat at the foot of her bed. She stared at it while she took several more sips from her glass. "Stop it!" Kathleen topped off her glass, walked into her bathroom, started the water filling up her Jacuzzi tub and stripped. She lit several candles and dropped two bath beads in the water.

She finished off her drink and set the empty glass on the counter, slid into the warm water and let the tub and wine relax her. Kathleen's mind flashed back to the bath she'd shared with Morgan last night. He'd insisted on bathing her after the second time they'd made love. The way his large, masculine hands roamed her body sent sensations throughout her the likes of which she had never experienced before. Kathleen laid her head back against the tub's built-in pillow, and her hands followed the path Morgan's had. She touched her neck, breast and stomach as she closed her eyes and pictured Morgan's face. She let her legs fall open, slid both hands over the wet, soapy hairs that covered her sex, inserting the index finger of both hands inside her.

Between the rush of the water and the rapid movement of her hips, Kathleen soon brought herself to an orgasm, moaning Morgan's name. She opened her eyes and waited for her rapidly beating heart to slow its pace. As soon as she could move, Kathleen got out of the water, drained and cleaned the tub. She stepped into her shower and let the warm water and body spray finish what she'd only just started.

Clean and completely relaxed, Kathleen wrapped her hair in a towel and dried her body with another. She slipped into a robe, collected her wineglass, stood in front of the dresser and began drying her hair. Kathleen stared at Morgan's bag through the mirror, wondering what all he might have packed. Before her curiosity could get the best of her, Kathleen heard her iPad ringing. She was receiving an incoming video call.

"Well, hello, stranger," Gilbert stated, waving.

"Stranger? I talk to you every day," she reminded him, pouring the last of her wine into her glass.

"No, you send me work to do every day," Gilbert stressed, frowning. "When was the last time we actually sat down and shared some good tea?"

"I don't have time to sit around gossiping with you during the day. And neither do you, given all the work I send your way."

"I'm an excellent delegator."

Kathleen glared at Gilbert. "You're not overworking our intern, are you?"

"What do you mean by 'overwork'?" he asked, using air quotes.

"She better not quit, Gilbert," Kathleen warned him, feeling somewhat annoyed but not surprised and trying not to laugh.

"Calm down. Hard work builds character. Isn't that the BS line you always use on me when I complain about being overworked?" he reminded her.

"Yes, but she already has character," Kathleen said, laughing.

"I'll let you have that one. Hey, whose Prada bag?" His eyes widened.

Kathleen glanced over her shoulder before returning her attention to Gilbert. "It's nothing. Nothing to worry about. You aren't driving, are you?"

"Of course not. I'm in a car service heading downtown for drinks and maybe even a little dancing. You want to join me? I'm not far from your place. I can be there in no time."

"No thanks. Go have fun," Kathleen replied, brushing her hair. "I'll talk—"

"Oh no, you don't, nice try. You can either tell me right now what's going on or in twenty minutes when I'll be at your place."

"I hate you." Kathleen sighed. "CliffsNotes version." She picked up her iPad and sat on her bed where she explained just how complicated her life had gotten these past few weeks.

"Damn, girl." Gilbert shook his head. "Was he at least worth it?"

"Really? Is that all you have to say?" Kathleen lay across her bed, watching the rain hit the bedroom window. Her mind flashed back to the night before, when she had Morgan in her bed. Tears welled in her eyes and she reached for the pillow that Morgan used, gripping it as if it was a life buoy.

"You don't need me to say anything else. I'm sure you've already beat yourself up for crossing the line with the target of your investigation. And you're *really* kicking yourself for not going with Morgan to his brother's house tonight. So all there is left to ask is— was it worth it?" he reiterated.

Kathleen propped her head up with her left hand. "Yes, yes, it was."

"Then you know what you have to do," he said, raising his eyebrows.

"Refresh my memory."

"Call him and get him back there so you can enjoy the rest of your weekend. Come Monday morning, officially get the case closed and tell him the truth about everything."

"That's the plan, but I think I'll let him hang with his family. I'll see him Monday."

"Okay, if that's what you want, but before I go, open his bag and tell me what all he has in there," he said, making his eyebrows dance.

Kathleen laughed. "No, I'm not invading his privacy."

"I don't know why the hell not. He invaded all your privacy last night." Gilbert screamed in laughter.

Kathleen covered her face and mouth, laughing. "Boy, you are a mess."

"You sure you don't want to come out? I'm here, but I can be at your place in no time. It's barely nine."

"I'm sure." Kathleen was in no mood to socialize, despite having her spirits lifted. She'd made her decision and now all she had to do was wait.

"How about I run inside for a quick drink, and I'll come hang out with you after?"

"That's sweet, but I'm fine, really, I promise. Once the truth is out and I have a chance to talk to Morgan, I'm sure everything will be fine. I hope so, anyway. You just be careful."

"I will. Later." Gilbert ended the call.

Kathleen set her music to play before closing her iPad, sat up and placed it on her nightstand. She stared at Morgan's bag. "No, don't even think about it." She jumped when she heard a clap of thunder. *Chill.* Kathleen got up, grabbed her glass, walked downstairs and into her kitchen. She selected another bottle from her wine refrigerator and filled her glass. Kathleen stood in her kitchen, drinking her wine, staring down at her unpolished toes. "We need a pedicure bad," she said, wiggling her toes.

Heading back upstairs, she stood in the doorway of her bedroom, staring at Morgan's bag. *Don't do it.* "What the hell. A little peek won't hurt," she justified. Kathleen placed her glass on the dresser, stood in front of the bag and slowly unzipped it. The moment she opened the bag, the scent of Morgan's cologne filled the room. It wasn't an overpowering smell like it had spilled from its container. It was more of an aroma that wrapped around her like a warm blanket.

You've had your peek. Now close it. Kathleen's heart, body and mind were at odds. She ran her hands over the clothes at the top of the bag, savoring the feel of his black silk pajama top. Before she could stop herself, Kathleen untied her robe and let it drop to the floor. She pulled out the silk pajama top and slipped her body inside. The arms were too long and it fit her like a dress, but to Kathleen, it was perfect. The silky-smooth feel of the fabric against her skin and the combination of Morgan's natural scent mixed with his cologne made her feel safe. It was the next best thing to being in his arms.

Kathleen closed her eyes, wrapped her arms around herself and began swaying to the Teddy Pendergrass song "You're My Latest, My Greatest Inspiration." It was one of her parents' favorites. She and her siblings had watched them dance to it many times. Kathleen seriously missed both Morgan and her mother in that moment. Just as the song was coming to an end, she heard her doorbell ring, and she knew it was Gilbert. He never believed her whenever she said she was fine and he knew she was upset and sad about something. Gilbert was a great friend, but he couldn't fix everything, no matter how hard he tried.

"I'm coming, Gilbert." Kathleen picked up her glass, taking a drink from it as she went to greet her persistent friend. "I'm fine," she said, opening the door.

"That you are." Morgan's eyes roamed Kathleen's body. "Who's Gilbert?"

Kathleen's heart raced. She just knew Morgan could hear the rapid flow of her blood in her veins. Kathleen was so happy to see him she couldn't speak. The shock of his presence made her forget that she was wearing his clothes.

The corners of Morgan's mouth rose. "May I come in?" Kathleen nodded, and she took two steps backward.

Morgan had spent the last few hours brooding at his brother's apartment after canceling his plans for the evening and tomorrow; he knew he'd be terrible company. All Morgan could think about was Kathleen and how badly things had turned so quickly. He realized she might not be feeling the same way he was about her and he had to respect her request.

Intellectually, he knew that was the right thing to do. Unfortunately, his heart and body had another idea, which was what led him to her home. Morgan wasn't letting Kathleen go, even if he had to keep their relationship a secret. Kathleen was his. But first...

Chapter 19

Morgan crossed the threshold, closing and locking the door behind them. He leaned back against the door, placing his hands in his pockets so he wouldn't reach for her. Not yet, anyway. Morgan needed answers. He crossed his feet at the ankles. "Who's Gilbert, Kathleen?"

"We work together," she replied, speaking softly.

"So you're expecting a coworker…dressed like that, in my nightshirt. My favorite nightshirt, at that." Morgan was fighting to keep his emotions in check. He didn't want to jump to the wrong conclusions. Only he prayed that they would, in fact, be wrong. Morgan couldn't imagine his Kathleen doing such a thing, even if she was angry at him.

Kathleen's face reddened, and her free hand flew to her throat. She glanced down at herself. "I'm sorry. I shouldn't have…"

"It's fine. You look beautiful and sexy as hell. I just hope it's not for someone else."

"I'd never do such a thing." Kathleen lowered her

head, dropped her shoulders and said, "Morgan, you're the only man I want."

Morgan released a deep sigh that prompted Kathleen to raise her head and capture his gaze. He thought his heart would burst through his chest any second. Morgan pushed off the wall and closed in on Kathleen like an animal after his prey. He removed the glass from her hand, placed it on the nearby table and picked her up. Kathleen threw her arms around his neck, and her legs wrapped around his waist. They kissed as if their lives depended on the connection. Morgan walked them to Kathleen's bedroom where he tried to place her on the bed, but Kathleen refused to release him.

"No," she whispered between kisses.

Morgan cupped her face with both hands. "Baby, just give me two minutes, and we'll make love all night," he promised.

Kathleen dropped her arms and legs and watched as Morgan quickly undressed and rolled on a condom. She unbuttoned his nightshirt and opened it, putting her body on full display. Morgan stood, staring down into her gorgeous face. His eyes dropped to her breasts and erect nipples. He leaned forward and slid both hands slowly up her thighs. Kathleen shivered, and Morgan smiled, knowing he caused that response. Morgan hovered over Kathleen with his erection playing at her entry.

"Please," Kathleen begged with her eyes closed, raising her hips to meet his shaft.

Morgan stared into Kathleen's face, his heart pounding in his ears, as he tried to keep his caveman instincts under control. He had to get the words he'd been dying to say out. "Kathleen, look at me," he demanded. When she complied, he saw more than desire, which was all the encouragement he needed. "I'm in love with you."

Kathleen blinked twice before the first of many tears fell. "I...I love...you too," she stuttered.

Morgan lost control and his inner caveman took over. He made love to every inch of Kathleen's body. It was like all the years of love he'd stored away for the perfect woman, a woman he never expected to meet—his perfect woman—were released into Kathleen. Morgan had every intention of leaving his mark on Kathleen, body and soul, just as she'd left on his.

Morgan and Kathleen spent the rest of the night and all day Sunday making love and plans for a future they both wanted. They shared a few household chores: laundry, making food and cleaning the kitchen. They even made time to catch a few of their favorite political shows. Morgan noticed that Kathleen didn't seem too concerned about the nasty weather outside and he hoped that had everything to do with his presence. Morgan even tried to convince Kathleen to move in with him and come work for his family as a full-time trainer. However, he was willing to make the daily three-hour commute by car or hour and half by helicopter if she didn't want to leave OSHA or Houston. Morgan really didn't care what she did as long as they were together. He knew things had developed quickly, but Kathleen didn't seem to mind and even agreed to think about his every request, which was all he needed.

Monday morning arrived before Morgan knew it. Kathleen had explained that she needed to go into her Houston office for a few hours but would be at the plant as soon as possible. Waking up with Kathleen in his arms, making love, getting dressed together and having her send him off with a big kiss and a travel mug full of coffee, knowing he'd see her again soon, was a scene he was happy with and ready to replay again and again.

Morgan walked into the office to find Adrian pacing, holding a manila envelope. "Good morning." Morgan took a sip from his mug.

"You're late," Adrian snapped.

"Last time I checked, I was the boss. What's got you so riled up this morning?"

"This." Adrian handed him the envelope.

"What's that?" he questioned before taking the envelope in his hands.

"That's something you need to see for yourself."

Morgan pushed out a breath. "Fine. I'm in too good of a mood, and nothing in this envelope is going to ruin it." He placed his mug on the desk.

"Sorry, man…"

Morgan frowned as he saw the distress on his friend's face. He opened the envelope and scanned the contents. His jaw clenched. "Where did you get this?" His tone was hard and he was trying to keep his anger under control.

"It was under my door when I got in this morning along with a note."

Morgan's frown deepened. "Where's the note?"

Adrian pulled it out of his pocket and handed it to Morgan. *Your boy is being played.* "Thanks, I'll take care of it."

"You sure?"

"I'll talk to you later."

Adrian left the room, closing the door behind them.

Morgan took a seat behind the desk. He gripped the arms of his chair as he felt his rage building. He picked up the desk phone, threw it across the room and watched it hit the wall, shattering into pieces. It was exactly the way his heart felt: shattered. "Damn you, Kathleen."

Kathleen approached her office door and found Simpson with his back to her, talking to someone she couldn't see. "Good morning," she greeted him as she entered the room wearing her blue power suit. She had to have a hard conversation with her boss today, and she needed the added confidence this particular outfit provided.

"Good morning," he replied, turning his body and allowing his guest to be seen.

Kathleen froze as she met the intense glare of the woman sitting at her desk. The scowl on her face told Kathleen everything she needed to know. Victoria knew the truth. "Your timing is perfect. I was just telling Mrs. Kingsley the good news."

Kathleen shifted her focus to Simpson, but she could feel Victoria's eyes boring into her. If looks could kill, she would have been incinerated the moment she stepped into the office. "Good news?"

"Yes. I was just explaining that the investigation into her company has closed and that our top investigator had cleared Kingsley Oil and Gas of any wrongdoing personally," Simpson explained proudly.

"An investigation I knew nothing about until I received a call from one of my many helpful friends, telling me about a complaint that had been filed against my company weeks ago. I came by to discuss the situation with Mr. Simpson when he informed me that the case had already been closed. While I appreciate your findings—" she tilted her head slightly to the right "—I don't appreciate your methods."

"I apologize, Mrs. Kingsley, but we felt that was

the best way to keep the press out of it until we knew for sure there was nothing to the complaint. Kathleen was following our directives," Simpson stated, excessively blinking. It was a nervous habit he had whenever he was around powerful people he feared, and he had every right to fear Victoria Kingsley. They both did. Kathleen could see Simpson literally and figuratively sweating as he tried to appease Victoria but Kathleen knew Victoria's anger was directed more at her than the agency itself.

"Do you think I can have a moment alone with your top investigator?" Victoria pointed to Kathleen.

"Of course." Simpson happily left the two women alone.

"I love your artwork. Máximo Laura's tapestries are exquisite. I have a few of his works myself. In fact, I believe I sent someone to purchase yours for me but was told someone beat me to it. I guess now I know who that person was. Having just found out about all this, obviously, I haven't had time to look into your background. I have to ask myself how a woman working for a government agency affords such expensive artwork." Victoria gave Kathleen the evil eye. "What are you selling, positive investigative reports? Or maybe you're threatening companies with false investigations. What's your game, Miss Winston?" Victoria demanded, sitting forward in the chair.

Kathleen couldn't blame Victoria for being suspicious of her. After all, she had lied to both her and Morgan. "I'm not playing any games, Victoria." Victoria shot Kathleen a look that sent a chill down her spine. "Mrs. Kingsley, please let me explain."

Victoria intertwined her hands, rested them on the desk and gave Kathleen her undivided attention as if she was expecting to be dazzled by some tall tale. "Please…"

Kathleen took a seat in one of the guest chairs. She took a deep breath and released it slowly. "First off, I'm Kathleen Winston from New Orleans, Louisiana, and I'm one of four heirs to the Winston construction empire." Kathleen figured that was the fastest way to clear up any concern she had about her financial ability to purchase her artwork.

Victoria's brows stood at attention. "*You're* Jonathan Winston's daughter?"

"Yes, ma'am, one of them. Do you know my father?"

"Yes. We have a few friends in common. However, it's your sister Kennedy Winston that I'm most familiar with."

Kathleen nodded. That wasn't a surprise. Her family did a lot of business in Texas, and Kennedy was a formidable businesswoman. Of course Victoria knew her. "Kennedy is brilliant."

"She must be, to hold her own in such a male-dominated field like construction," Victoria said with what sounded like admiration in her voice.

"Much like you, Mrs. Kingsley."

Victoria's eyes softened a bit. "Why aren't you working in your family's business and why did you think you had to lie to my son and me?"

Kathleen's heart sank as she fought back her tears. She dropped her head and said a silent prayer for strength and Victoria's understanding. Kathleen knew she had to get through this without breaking down, but she wasn't sure she could. Now all she could do was wait for her prayer to be answered. Kathleen sighed, pushed back her shoulders and began to explain how this whole mess started.

After laying out the origin of the complaint, finding that it wasn't based on facts and Kathleen's reasons why they felt they had to deceive them, Victoria raised her right hand. "So in spite of your superior's initial objection to investigating my company you convinced them they needed to move forward."

"Yes, ma'am, I did." Kathleen knew it was the right thing then and she stood by her decision even now, although she was second-guessing her methods.

"Why?"

Instead of offering the argument she'd used to convince her bosses to move forward, Kathleen decided to share a truth she only recently realized, thanks to Victoria's son. Kathleen cupped her hands and set them in her lap. She began to explain how what had happened to her mother affected her. Her mother's death triggered a need to seek justice for her loss. The company responsible for her mother's death had long since been closed, thanks to her father.

Kathleen directed her anger at other organizations accused of doing the same or similar acts. She admitted that she had been single-mindedly focused when it came to her investigative role and it served her well professionally. "I had been right about every single company we went after until now. The moment I realized that fact, I closed the case. I'm sorry I lied to you, but I was doing my job, regardless of my driving factors."

Victoria sat expressionless. "Just doing your job?"

"Yes, ma'am." Kathleen pressed her lips together and raised her chin almost defiantly. She had laid out her case, and now she waited for the judgment.

Victoria reached for her ringing phone, read the caller's name and sent the call to voice mail. "Was part of your job getting my son to fall in love with you?"

Kathleen gasped, and her lips parted slightly.

Victoria rose from her chair, came around the desk and stood in front of Kathleen. She leaned back against the desk; her hands gripped its edge and she stared into Kathleen's eyes. "Was it your job to take a man who didn't trust his women romantically and make him not only trust you but love you? Was it your job to break my son? Because if he can't find a way to forgive you it will break him. Where exactly is *that* in your job description?"

Kathleen felt as if the air had suddenly been sucked out of the room. The idea of doing that to Morgan was breaking her heart, and she was having trouble moving what little oxygen she had through her lungs. Kathleen's tears began to flow faster than she could wipe them away. Victoria heaved a sigh and stood. She pulled Kathleen out of her chair and into her arms. Kathleen surrendered to her tears, and Victoria held her until she was all cried out.

Kathleen stepped out of Victoria's arms and said, "I'm so sorry. I would never intentionally hurt Morgan."

Victoria kissed Kathleen on the cheek. "You love my son, right?"

"Yes, very much."

"Then you know what you have to do. Morgan's going to be angry, and he'll try to push you away. Don't let him," Victoria advised, picking up her purse and phone.

"I couldn't if I wanted to."

"I get why you did what you did and I'm praying things will work out for both of you. But know this— if you ever hurt my son again, you'll have me to deal with me. Understand?"

"I do, but that won't be necessary," Kathleen promised.

"That's my girl," she said before exiting the office.

Kathleen brought herself under control, found her purse and touched up her makeup. "I'm not going to lose you, Morgan. But first things first," she vowed, reaching for her office phone. She called her boss. "Simpson, we need to talk."

Chapter 20

Morgan had managed to pull himself together because he had more pressing things to attend to than his shattering love life. The plant just received a warning that a hurricane in the gulf had shifted and was now headed in their direction. Morgan and his team had fewer than ten hours to get the plant ready and evacuate all but essential personnel. He was standing behind his desk looking over the final plans when Kathleen walked into his office and closed the door behind her. His body and heart instantly responded to the sight of her until his mind stamped them down.

"We need to talk. It's important," Kathleen said, holding her purse at her side.

Morgan dropped his pen on the desk and crossed his arms at his chest. "I don't think so." He reached into his drawer and pulled out the documents he'd received and tossed them on the desk in front of her. "Someone beat you to it. I know everything." Morgan was fighting hard to keep his anger under control. She had made a fool out of him. She had been investigating him while he was falling in love with her.

Kathleen placed her purse on the desk, picked up the pictures and press clippings and started flipping through them. "I—"

"I especially like the article about OSHA agent Kathleen Winston receiving a special award for her bravery and hard work taking on a plastics company. I *personally* like the picture of you and your sister leaving some charity event a few weeks ago with your father, construction mogul and billionaire Jonathan Winston. This must have been a rough duty for you, compared to your charity events."

"It was an event in honor of my mother," Kathleen whispered.

"Like I said, there's nothing left to talk about." He returned his attention to his plans. "You should go. The hurricane is heading in our direction. You need to get back to Houston while you can. Whatever you're investigating will just have to wait."

"My investigation is already closed. Please, baby, let me explain," Kathleen begged.

There was a knock on the door before it opened. "Excuse me, boss." Adrian entered the office holding a clipboard. "Oh...hi, Kathleen."

"Hi, Adrian," she replied in a hushed tone.

Morgan dropped his hands. "Where are we?"

"We shut down all the oil heating units and locked down the fuel storage tanks. We're in the process of storing the diesel heaters, drilling equipment and everything else on the checklist," Adrian assured him.

"Make sure the mobile gas pumping systems are drained," Kathleen advised.

"Yes, of course," Adrian replied, smiling.

A smart and beautiful liar. Bonnie 2.0. "Good. What about the staff?" Morgan asked, trying to keep his focus on Adrian, but in his peripheral vision, he could see sadness cloud Kathleen's face. While there was a part of him that wanted to hear Kathleen out, his hurt and anger wouldn't let him.

"All nonessential staff are being evacuated now." Adrian checked his ringing phone.

"And the bunker?"

"It's ready. Excuse me. I got to take this, boss." Adrian stepped out of the room.

"What's the bunker?" Kathleen asked timidly.

Morgan went poker-faced. "It's a ten-thousand-square-foot steel underground storm and bomb shelter."

"Do you really think it'll be necessary to send everyone down there?" Her forehead creased.

"It depends on the category of the storm when it hits land and whether or not we'll take a direct hit. See how that works. You ask me a direct question, I answer it." Morgan checked his watch. "You really should leave now. Get back on the road before the weather turns too bad."

Kathleen remembered Victoria's words. She loved Morgan, and there was no way she was going to walk away from him without a fight. Kathleen stood with her right hand on her hip. "I'm not going anywhere."

"Excuse me." Morgan came from around his desk, placed his hands in his pockets and stared down at Kathleen.

Kathleen could see how angry and hurt he was, but she also saw something else. She saw love and desire, and that gave her the additional courage she needed to get through the next few moments. "You heard me. I'm not leaving. I love you, and you love me. We're going to talk about this. Maybe not right now, but we will discuss everything. You say you know everything, or at least you think you do? Then you know what I'm capable of doing. Now put me to work. How can I help?"

"Fine. Stay. You can help Ms. Monica from the cafeteria. We sent most of her support staff home."

Kathleen felt hopeful when Morgan didn't dispute the fact that he loved her. "If that's where you want me." They stood staring at each other in silence. With a racing heartbeat, Kathleen conjured up a bit more courage and reached for Morgan's hand. She placed it over her heart and her hand over his heart. "I know you can feel my heart beating just as I feel yours. For as long as our hearts pump blood throughout our bodies, we will love each other. I know I have a lot to explain and account for and I will. Just know that I'm still yours and you're still mine."

Thunder roared, and Kathleen jumped. Morgan lowered his hands and snaked them around her waist. "It's okay. You're safe."

Kathleen buried her face in his chest and cried. Not out of fear but sadness for what she could have lost. Morgan held her and rubbed her back but gave Kathleen no assurances that they would be fine. He was comforting her as he would anyone else, and that just made things worse.

"Excuse me...again," Adrian announced.

Kathleen stepped out of Morgan's arms and turned her back on both men. She needed to pull herself together. She reached in her purse, pulled out a Kleenex and wiped her face.

"What's up?" Morgan asked.

"Everyone's in place. I'm headed to the watch center."

"Good, but first I need you to take Kathleen to the lounge," he ordered.

Kathleen swirled around so fast it made her dizzy. "What? I thought I was helping Ms. Monica in the cafeteria."

"You are, only the cafeteria is closed. We moved everything we need to another location. It's an enclosed area where we'll wait out the storm while we decide if it's necessary to move into the bunker," Morgan explained, his tone flat.

"Oh." Kathleen appreciated Morgan's explanation, only she wished it wasn't so professional.

"Where will you be?" Adrian asked Morgan.

"I'll make rounds and meet you at the watch center after."

"Cool. You ready, Kathleen?"

"Give me a minute please." Kathleen was talking to Adrian but looking up at Morgan. Morgan gave Adrian a quick nod and stepped out the door. Kathleen closed the distance between them, cupped his face with shaking hands, rose up on tippy toes, hoping he wouldn't push her away and kissed him gently on the lips. While Morgan didn't stop Kathleen and even returned her kiss, it wasn't quite the response she was hoping for either.

"You should go," Morgan murmured, his tone having softened.

Kathleen picked up her purse and walked to the door. She placed her hand on the knob, looked over her shoulder and said, "We're not over. We love each other too much."

Kathleen spent the next several hours reminding herself of that fact as she helped Ms. Monica prepare the lounge for what could potentially be a long stay. The large room with cocoa-colored walls and gray Berber-carpeted floors was warm and inviting. Half the room offered leather-style sofas, lounge chairs, a dining table that seated fifteen and an entertainment center with a 262-inch TV in its center. The other half of the space was being set up for sleeping; thirty cots were actively being assembled.

"Wow, this place is something else," Kathleen stated as she helped unpack boxes of prepackaged meals.

"Victoria Kingsley doesn't believe in doing anything halfway, trust me," Ms. Monica confirmed.

"I'm beginning to see that." Kathleen nodded in agreement.

"So how are things going with you and Morgan?"

"Umm…excuse me?"

"Child, please. Ray Charles and Stevie Wonder are still arguing over who saw the feelings developing between you two first."

Kathleen laughed, something she hadn't done since before she walked into her office that morning. *So much for keeping our relationship a secret.* "It's fine. I guess."

"You guess. What did you do?" Ms. Monica questioned, giving her the side-eye.

"What makes you think *I* did something wrong?"

Ms. Monica took Kathleen's empty box and slid her another one to unpack. "Because I've watched the Kingsleys' boys grow into men. I know everything about every one of them. The one thing I know for certain about Morgan is that if he decides to entrust his heart to someone else again, that's it. She's it. Once he makes that decision, that woman can count on two things." She held up two fingers. "He'll never hurt her, and he'll love her forever. If I have to guess if everything is all right between you two, it's not. So I'll ask again, what did you do?"

Kathleen knew Ms. Monica was just trying to help, but she didn't feel right about sharing so much with a virtual stranger to her. "Everything is fine...at least it will be. I hope."

Monica offered a supportive smile. "If it's meant to be, it sometimes might take a lot of work to make it so."

The corners of Kathleen's mouth rose. "I don't think that's how the saying goes."

"That's because it's not a saying. It's a fact. Now get busy. We'll have several people piling in here soon and we need to be ready."

"Yes, ma'am."

Later that afternoon, Morgan was sitting in the office watching weather reports on three different TVs, monitoring his production boards and gauges while reading production reports when Adrian jumped up and said, "That's enough. Put your shoes on and let's go to the lounge and hang out with everyone else."

"You go right ahead," Morgan replied, keeping his eyes on the center TV.

"There's a TV in the lounge, several in fact, if you must keep watching, but we both know the storm is going to miss us. We'll get hit with a lot of hard rain for several hours, but as long as our pumps hold up we'll be just fine. Just like always."

"What's your point?" Morgan asked, his annoyance taking a stand.

"My point is, you need to go find Kathleen and work this thing out."

Morgan scowled at his friend. "Aren't you the one who busted her in the first place?"

"No, that would be whoever sent me that information on her. I just thought you needed to know so you could find out what was going on. Not just end things with her. That woman loves you, and we both know she doesn't need your money. Hell, I think she may be richer than you are."

"Do you have any idea who sent it to you?"

"No. Maybe someone's upset that she picked you over them, but does it really matter? The truth is out and the question is, what are you going to do now that you know?"

Morgan tossed his pen on the table and sat back in his chair. "I don't know who I'm having a relationship with, a down-to-earth OSHA trainer or a rich OSHA investigator trying to... I don't even know. I don't know who the hell she is, man."

"She's the only woman I've ever seen you fall for in years. She's the real deal, and you know it."

Morgan heaved a big sigh. "How can I trust anything she says?"

Adrian shrugged. "Just follow your heart, man."

"I did. I asked Kathleen to move in with me before this."

Adrian's eyes got wide as saucers. "That's big for you, dude. What did she say?"

"That she'd think about it." Morgan reached for his ringing phone, half hoping it was Kathleen. Recognizing the number, he rolled his eyes skyward.

"She didn't say no. What's up?"

"I'm not sure. Bonnie Ford's been calling lately."

"Dude, don't do it," Adrian said, shaking his head.

"Don't what?"

"Go backward."

"Hell, no. I wouldn't do that to Kathleen or myself," Morgan declared.

"Good. Did Kathleen tell you she loves you?"

"Yes." Morgan's heart skipped a beat just remembering the moment.

"Do you believe her?"

"Absolutely," Morgan murmured. The emotions that he'd been keeping at bay started hovering around the edge of his sanity.

A sudden loud crash that sounded like thunder startled both men. "What the hell was that?" Adrian asked, looking around the room.

Kathleen. "What the…" Morgan stood and stared out the window before checking the board. "A transformer blew."

Adrian joined Morgan at the window. "Looks like there's a live wire dangling too."

Morgan grabbed his jacket and pulled on his rubber boots. "Call the on-site fire department, and I'll radio Jim and his team. They're in the area."

Morgan called Jim, one of their longtime production managers, as he quickly made it out of the building and into his truck. His first instinct was to go and check on Kathleen, but he knew she was in a safe place and he needed to check on his people and the situation. He drove through a treacherous downpour and flooded streets to get to the other side of the plant. The rain made a trip that would have normally only taken him five minutes take him nearly ten, during which his mind kept wandering to Kathleen. Morgan knew she'd heard what he had and was probably scared to death. Morgan's first thought was her, and that scared the hell out of him too. What if the woman he'd fallen in love with really wasn't the woman he fell in love with? He knew he couldn't go through that pain again.

When Morgan arrived on-site, everything was under control. He pulled his vehicle next to several others as well as a small fire truck. The transformer was dead, and the loose wire was being removed. "Jim, is everything all right?" Morgan called out, exiting the truck as he walked to where Jim stood in a nearby covered area with several of his men nearby.

"Yeah, that damn transformer was brand-new too. It looks like it got hit by lightning."

"You got the wire down pretty quick," Morgan said, looking up at the pole.

"We were already over here when it blew."

"Here?" Morgan pointed at the ground.

"Yep, we came to check this storage unit." He used his thumb to point at the structure they were standing in front of. "We heard it pop, and before I knew it, Bubba was dressed, up that pole and had ripped that sucker down in no time."

Morgan looked over to Bubba, who was smiling so wide Morgan could see all the teeth in his head. He walked over to the young man. "Good job. I assume you took all the safety precautions."

"Yes, sir, especially the ones Ms. Kathleen taught us."

Morgan frowned. "Kathleen?" He looked at Jim.

"Yeah, she taught the team how to control the adrenaline they were sure to feel in moments like these. It helped them stay calm so they could think. She also showed them the safest and fastest way to deal with live wires."

"I must have missed that class," he murmured to himself, scratching his beard.

"She added it to the computer-based program you already had in place," Jim explained.

"That's good," Morgan acknowledged.

"Now, David, your other fearless leader over there, jumped in the back of the truck like a cat," Jim teased, laughing.

"And Jim nearly peed his pants," David replied as he approached both men.

"Sure did," Jim admitted, laughing.

"Anyway, Ms. Kathleen told us to be aware of our surroundings. I didn't know where I was standing."

Kathleen…

David shook Morgan's hand as he put his phone away. "I have to check on the wife. She hates this weather, and she worries if she doesn't hear from me every five seconds."

Morgan knew how much David and his wife adored each other. He thought about Kathleen, and his heart sank because his love and anger were at an impasse. Morgan thanked everyone and ordered his men to the lounge and their firemen back to their station. He reminded everyone to stay vigilant but to get some much-needed rest. Morgan needed to follow his own advice, but before he could do that he needed answers. Other than Kathleen, Morgan figured he knew the one person who just might have a few.

Chapter 21

Morgan returned to the office and pulled out his cell phone. "Damn," he said as he noticed his battery was low and placed it on the quick charger. Morgan placed his iPad on its cradle as he sat, dialed the number and nervously waited for his video call to connect.

"Morgan, darling, you look stressed. Is everything all right?" Victoria asked, frowning.

"Not even a little bit."

Victoria nodded slowly and sat back in her chair. "So Kathleen told you."

"Wait, what?" Morgan sat forward and stared into the screen. "You knew?"

"That Kathleen Winston, heiress to the Winston Construction fortune, is an investigator for OSHA? Yes, I just found out."

"Why the hell didn't you tell me?" he yelled.

Victoria tilted her head to the right but remained quiet. Morgan took a deep breath and released it slowly. "My apologies, Mother. Why didn't you tell me what was going on?" he asked, his voice calmer.

"Remember when you came to me all excited and said that you were marrying Bonnie?"

"What does that—"

Victoria presented her right palm to the screen, stopping Morgan in his tracks. "Do you remember?"

"Yes, ma'am, I do."

"Do you remember what I told you?"

Morgan went blank-faced. He was in no mood for games, but he knew if he didn't go along he would never get the answers he needed. Morgan nodded. "That Bonnie was my mistake to make."

"Do you know why I said that?"

Morgan shrugged, not interested in the past but knowing he had to listen if he wanted her help. "Not really."

"Because you're just like me. I know everyone seems to think Alexander takes after me the most but in reality, it's you. If I told you what a silly little thing I thought Bonnie Ford was, you would've ignored me and married her that much faster. Fortunately, she showed her true colors before I had to intervene."

"So you let me fall for someone out to destroy our family instead?" he asked, feeling his anger rising.

"I didn't let you do anything, son, and you started falling for Kathleen before I even met her."

Morgan ran his hands down his face and shook his head. "I don't understand what you're talking about, Mother."

"I knew something special was happening between you two the day I walked in, and you were arguing over the training programs. The way she held her own with you, I knew she was something special."

"She was something special, all right…she's a liar." The words stung his throat as he spat them out and he felt like he was betraying Kathleen even thinking such a thing.

"Morgan, she was doing her job."

"And you're okay with how she went about it?" His brows snapped together.

"No, but I understand now why she did it."

"This coming from a woman who would threaten to banish us from the house if she ever caught us lying to her." Morgan threw up his hands in frustration. "You'll need to explain that one to me, Mother."

Victoria spent the next thirty minutes explaining to Morgan everything she knew about Kathleen and her situation, from the specifics of the complaint against the Kingsleys, her motivations and zeal to seek justice for those she believed were being mistreated, to the remorse she felt for being wrong after confirming that the accusations were baseless and hurting people, specifically the man she loved.

"Her mother? She did all of this because of her mother?" His tone was flat. Morgan wasn't sure how he felt in that moment.

"Yes, son, she did. You remember how that felt, don't you? How the loss of someone so important in your life makes you change how you view the world and the people around you?" Victoria's expression closed up, and she reached for a glass with red wine in it. "Do you remember, son?"

Morgan's mind flashed back to the day, several months after his father's death, when he'd written a hateful letter to his mother accusing her of loving her company and freedom more than her family because all she seemed to want to do was work. He'd lost his father, and their world was turned upside down. Victoria moved the family to a secluded ranch to ensure their safety. Only, in Morgan's young mind, this was a bitter betrayal. He thought it was his mother's way of getting them out of the way so she could focus on her business.

His father's loss, the sudden move and his mother's disappearance into work changed his idea of how wives and mothers should act. Morgan recalled vividly the night he'd left her the note. She came into his bedroom while he pretended to be asleep, kissed him on the forehead, returned the note to him and whispered, "I love and forgive you, son." They'd never spoken of the incident until now.

"Mother, I was a young, dumb kid when I wrote that note," he said, lowering his head and feeling ashamed.

"Look at me, son."

Morgan slowly raised his head and held his mother's loving gaze. "You were a child who lost his father and thought he was losing his mother too. I understood. You went from having the mother you wanted to getting the mother you needed. A mother who had to lead and protect her family and couldn't be there every day."

"Everything just changed so quickly."

"I know it did and I'm sorry that had to happen. However, it shaped you into the man you are today. A man I'm very proud of too," she said, smiling before taking another sip of her wine.

"So you think the death of Kathleen's mother did the same for her."

"Of course it did."

Morgan took a deep breath and released it slowly. "What should I do?"

"You don't need me to tell you what to do, sweetheart."

"Oh, you'll interfere in everyone else's love life but

not mine," he said, feeling happy now that the mood had lightened.

"I didn't interfere with—"

"Mother, please, stop it. Alexander and China?"

"That's been simmering for years." She gave a nonchalant wave.

"True. Okay, Mia and KJ?"

"Your brother met Mia because he had to do community service," Victoria defended herself, sipping her wine.

"Community service that you initiated with your friend the NBA commissioner," he accused, raising his left eyebrow.

"I don't know what you're talking about."

"Okay. But we all know you brought Brooke back into the company so she and Brice would stay together."

Victoria nodded her head slowly and held up her near-empty wineglass. "All I did was show a little kindness to two people who needed it. If my bringing Brooke home helped make it easy for your brother to decide something he'd already decided on, so be it." Victoria finished off her wine as if she'd just made a toast to herself.

"So why not do the same for me?"

A wide smile crawled across Victoria's face. "I have," she said, ending the call.

Morgan sat back in his chair and smiled. *Okay, Mother. I'll show a little kindness.* He picked up his cell phone and dialed the number he'd been avoiding too long. When he heard the call connect, he said, "Hello, Bonnie, it's Morgan. I'm returning your calls."

"Morgan, thank you for getting back to me."

"Is everything okay?" He could hear fear and relief in her voice.

"Well, that depends on you."

"Me?"

"Yes, first let me do something that I should've done years ago."

"What's that?" Morgan's interest was piqued.

"I want to apologize and thank you."

"For what?"

"I was terrible to you. I had no idea what real love was or what I had—"

"Bonnie, that was a lifetime ago. You don't need to—"

"Yes, I do. The love we had was special, Morgan, and I blew it over nothing…for nothing."

"Yes, it was, but it was also a young love…a kid's love. Neither one of us really understood that at the time."

"I agree, and I'm sorry we didn't have the chance to figure that out the right way and in the right amount of time too. I hope you can forgive me."

"Of course, Bonnie. Everything worked out for the best."

"Yes, it did, which leads me to my thank-you."

"Thank-you?"

"Yes, if you had gone through with my harebrained idea, who knows where we'd be right now?"

Morgan laughed. "Who knows?"

"Certainly not as happy as I am now and I only pray you have or will find someone who makes you that happy too. So thank you."

Kathleen's face, her laugh, her smell and even her recent words of love and commitment to him filled his mind. *I have.* "You're welcome. Now what else is going on? I know you didn't just call me for closure."

"You're right. I didn't call just for closure."

"What's up?"

"When we broke up, and after graduation, I went to work for my father. I dated a few of Daddy's picks before I came to my senses. A couple of years ago I met a computer whiz named Bill Wright, and we eloped."

Morgan wasn't exactly sure why he was so shocked, but he was. "I hadn't heard. Congratulations."

"Thank you. Bill's a private geek and we live a very full but low-key life now."

"As long as you're happy, that's all that matters." Morgan realized he really believed that too. Being happy with the one you loved really was all that mattered.

"I am. Well, I was."

"What's going on, Bonnie?"

"Dad's sick, Morgan. He has heart issues, and he needs to retire."

"I'm sorry to hear that."

"Me too. You know how much Dad loves working. As long as he follows the doctor's orders, he should still live a full and happy life. Me and Mom aim to make sure of it too."

Morgan smirked. "With you two in his corner, he doesn't stand a chance. He's going to be just fine."

"Here's the problem. Dad's trying to convince my husband to run the company. He doesn't want to, but Bill's like you. He'll do anything for family, especially since he lost his at such a young age."

"I'm so sorry you're having to deal with all this, but I'm not sure what any of it has to do with me."

"You know how cutthroat this business can be. Even for a small oil refinery like ours. Bill won't be able to handle it, and he'll kill himself trying. We're pregnant, and I don't want my husband to lose who he is, trying to do something he can't and doesn't even want to do in the first place," she explained.

"Why don't you run the company? It sounds like you've been doing it anyway."

"I am, but I'm having a baby, and I want to stay home. I'm done with working. I want to be a wife and mom now."

"I get that, and I'm happy for you, but again, what does—"

"I want…no, I *need*, for you to buy our company."

"What?" Morgan sat up in the chair and looked at his cell phone as if he were on a video conference call with her.

"Our company is small compared to some of the others, but it's profitable and has been for the last few years. I made sure of it. We own just about everything. We have minimal debt on the books, and we have cash in the bank."

"Your father wants to sell?"

"Not really, but none of us have much of a choice anymore."

Morgan ran the back of his left hand under his chin. "Why sell it to us?"

"Not us, you. I've done my due diligence. Every company that you've personally brought into your family's portfolio has been midsize and fetched a good price. You kept the majority of the staff—even the executive teams—and you've combined the company's names with the Kingsley brand. What was the last one? A drilling parts and service company, I believe. I heard you made the Shield brothers one hell of an offer and Shield Parts became Kingsley-Shield Parts and Service. That's a much better name, by the way. Yours is the only company my father would ever consider selling to. The Kingsleys are the only real good guys in this business."

Too bad Kathleen didn't know any of this before she pushed for her investigation to move forward. Focus, man; this isn't about Kathleen.

"Thanks, but I can't take credit for that. My cousin Kristen is the queen of branding."

Bonnie laughed. "I remember. So, will you consider it?"

Morgan sat back quietly as he tried to consider her request and what it could mean for their company but his mind kept going back to his mother's and now Bonnie's words about love and happiness, and all he wanted to do was find Kathleen.

"Send me the proposal."

"Really?" He heard pure joy in her voice, and that made him smile. Morgan was happy for her, and it was nice to know the old Bonnie was back.

"Yes, really. If everything is as you say, we'll meet your price."

"Thank you, Morgan, and whoever it is who's managed to steal your heart...your adult heart...is a very lucky woman."

Chapter 22

Kathleen sat nervously in a large leather reclining chair wrapped in a blanket, watching news reports on her iPad while listening to the rain. Everyone was standing around as if nothing was happening. It was like they were all just hanging out at a friend's house. It was after midnight, and everyone had just enjoyed a huge barbecue dinner that Ms. Monica and a few guys prepared under the back patio. A number of the staff had called it a night. Others were playing card games and watching movies. Even though Adrian and others assured her that Morgan was okay, Kathleen needed to see it for herself.

Her phone beeped. She was receiving yet more calls and texts from her family. Kathleen had told everyone that she was safe and fine, but like her, they wouldn't be satisfied until they saw it for themselves. Kathleen promised to call everyone in the morning. She was too tired, physically and mentally, to deal with anyone right now. All she wanted to do was find Morgan so they could talk. However, Kathleen knew she wouldn't make it out the door without someone stopping her.

Plus, she had no idea where he was, so she played what she would say to him over and over in her mind until she fell asleep.

It was after eight the next morning when Kathleen woke to the sound of laughter and the smell of freshly brewed coffee. She scanned the room, but there was still no sign of Morgan. "You can run, but you can't hide from me for long, Mr. Kingsley," she murmured to herself. Kathleen picked up her bag and made her way to the ladies' room, where she freshened up and put on a new set of clothes. After changing into a clean pair of jeans and a white T-shirt, she slipped her feet back into her boots and returned to the lounge.

"There you are," Adrian said, walking up to Kathleen.

"Here I am. Good morning."

"Good morning to you too. I came to tell you that we just got the all clear."

"All clear?" Kathleen's brows knitted together.

"Yes, the freeway is open, so you can go home."

Kathleen shook her head. "Did Morgan send you to tell me to go home?"

"Yes…no. I mean, he told me to tell everyone."

Kathleen turned her back to him. "Sure he did," she replied, fighting back tears.

"Look, you can ask him yourself. He just walked in."

"What?" Kathleen turned in time to see Morgan walking across the room with purpose toward her. Her heart rate increased with every step he took. He looked tired, and his beard was way past its five-o'clock expiration. The black jeans, white company T-shirt and work boots he wore screamed *sexy*.

"Good morning, Kathleen," Morgan greeted her.

"Good morning," she replied, searching his face for any signs of anger but finding none.

"That's my cue," Adrian said, walking away.

"Did Adrian tell you—"

"That it was safe for me to go home? Yes, he delivered your message." Her voice was curt.

"I'm sure you'd like to sleep in your own bed."

"Yes, I would. Care to join me?" She held his gaze.

Morgan held his hands at his sides, dropped his shoulders and exhaled noisily. "Actually I—"

"Morgan," Adrian yelled from across the room. "Morgan, you need to hear this."

They both turned toward Adrian, who had a worried look on his face. Kathleen followed Morgan over to where Adrian stood. "What's going on?"

"The hurricane missed us but Port Arthur got hit pretty bad, and Main Street is impassable. There's debris everywhere. They're opening an emergency shelter in the old meatpacking warehouse outside town."

"Let's pack up all the excess supplies we have here and get them over to the warehouse," Morgan ordered. "We can set this place up as a rest station for the first responders. We can open the kitchen here and if anyone can make it in to help out, great."

"They also need access to our heavy-duty vehicles for a few rescues. Some communities got flooded, and they don't have a way to get to the people who need help."

"Of course, whatever they need," Morgan assured him.

"Here." Adrian handed him a pink piece of paper. "The mayor wants you to give him a call."

"Thanks." Morgan turned and faced Kathleen. "You should probably go home."

Kathleen reached for his hand. "I can stay and help."

"You need to go home and get some rest. It'll be safer for you too. I don't know how long I'll be, but I'll call you as soon as I can." Morgan leaned down and gave her a quick kiss on the lips before turning to leave.

Kathleen wiped away a lone tear that fell as she watched Morgan walk away. She walked over to where she'd left her purse and pulled out her phone. "You have no idea who you're in love with. I'm not going anywhere without you, Mr. Kingsley," she said as she dialed and waited for her call to connect. Kathleen knew that there was a way she could help the town and its people who had been so wonderful to her whenever she was in town.

"Kathleen, thank God you're all right. I've been worried sick." His accent was thick and his voice full of fear.

"I'm fine, Daddy, but I need your help."

Morgan and his team spent the rest of the day and most of the evening helping the small town start to recover, from aiding with rescue operations to setting up smaller shelters. No matter how hard he tried to fight it, Morgan wanted Kathleen by his side. He knew they had a lot to work out and he certainly had a lot of questions, but Morgan loved Kathleen, and he wasn't letting her go. Morgan prayed he hadn't blown it by pushing her away, trying to keep her safe. He knew she thought the worst of him because he hadn't had time to explain. Morgan only hoped she wasn't too upset. He wanted to call Kathleen and ask her to come back but how could he after insisting that she leave?

As they drove through the town on their way back to the plant, Morgan noticed a path down Main Street had been cleared, allowing easier access from one side of town to the other. Several lights had been set up, illuminating the way. Large Dumpsters, cranes and trucks were parked on the outskirts of town. The name on the side of each vehicle—Winston Construction—caught his attention. Several black SUVs were parked in the parking lot of the largest hotel still in full operation.

"Pull over," Morgan ordered.

"What's up?"

"That's what I want to find out," Morgan stated, his curiosity aroused. He knew this had to be Kathleen's doing.

Adrian pulled into the lot, parked near the door and cut the engine. "Now what?"

"Now you go inside and have a beer at the bar."

"There's beer and food back at the plant, you know. Are you buying?"

"Don't I always?" he reminded Adrian as he exited the truck.

Both men entered the quiet lobby, waved at the familiar faces behind the desk and walked into the bar. Several men unfamiliar to him were drinking, eating and watching different sports games and the news coverage of the storm on the different TVs.

"How about that beer?" Adrian asked as he took a seat at the bar.

"Sure." Morgan sat on the stool next to Adrian and took in the environment.

"Now what?" Adrian asked, trying to get the bartender's attention. "Two long-neck Budweisers."

"Coming right up," the bartender replied.

Morgan scanned the room and noticed an older brown skinned, gray-haired gentleman wearing a gray suit sitting at a corner table alone near the bar's front window, nursing what appeared to be a glass of whiskey.

"Here you go." The bartender handed both beers.

"Thanks," they chorused.

"Can I get you anything else?"

"How about a little information?" Adrian asked.

"Information is my specialty," he replied, leaning across the bar.

"You know anything about these cats in here to-night?" Adrian asked.

"They're from out of town, and they all work for the dude in the corner," he said.

"How do you know that?" Morgan asked.

"A couple of the guys told me. They're in town to help the town recover from the storm."

"That's cool," Adrian said, reaching for the peanut bowl and pulling out several packages.

"Thanks," Morgan replied, turning to face the room.

"No problem."

"What are you looking for?" Adrian asked.

"I'll know when I see them," he replied, taking a long pull from his bottle.

"Wow, who is that?" Morgan followed his friend's line of sight."

"Wait, is that Kathleen? No…but she looks like her," Adrian said.

"Yes, she does," Morgan agreed, knowing who she had to be.

A beautiful woman wearing a red pantsuit and heels had joined the older man at the table. Before Morgan could react, Kathleen entered the bar, wearing an off-the-shoulder blue denim dress that came to just above her knee and heels that made her legs look longer than normal. Her exposed skin was like a siren's call to him. Kathleen headed for the table, offering a smile that didn't reach her eyes.

"There's Kathleen," Adrian said, pointing with his beer bottle.

"I see." Morgan stood, pulled out a hundred-dollar bill and dropped it on the bar. "You can take off if you want. I'll get a ride."

Adrian laughed. "I bet you will."

Morgan made his way over to the table. As he approached, he heard Kathleen and her guest conversing in French. Before he could introduce himself, Kathleen whipped her head around and caught sight of him. She flew out of her chair and into Morgan's arms.

"You're okay. I was so worried," Kathleen confessed.

Morgan felt whole again. He tightened his hold on Kathleen and replied, "I'm fine, baby. I'm also sorry. I should have never tried to send you away," he whispered.

Kathleen leaned back and looked up into his eyes. "I'm the one who owes you an apology and anything else that will make things right between us again," she insisted, raising her head to meet Morgan's kiss. The moment their lips touched, Morgan's body responded, and he had to force himself to remain in control.

"Kathleen Winston," a stern baritone voice called out.

"Before you two embarrass us any further, Kathleen, why don't you introduce us to the reason we had to pull our team off a multimillion-dollar job and get here so fast?" The other woman's annoyance was coming through loud and clear.

Kathleen turned in Morgan's arms. "Sorry. Daddy... Kennedy, I'd like you to meet Morgan Kingsley." Kathleen looked up at Morgan, and the look of love and happiness on her face made him weak. It was a feeling he was beginning to relish. How could he have ever doubted her?

She directed his attention toward her family. "Morgan, this is my father, Jonathan Winston, and the one with the sour look on her face is my older sister, Kennedy."

Morgan held on to Kathleen with one hand and reached to shake Kathleen's sister's and father's hands with the other. "Pleased to meet you both."

"Join us," Kathleen's father ordered, his voice stern.

Morgan recognized the tone in her father's voice and he felt Kathleen squeeze his hand. He knew she was assuring him that she was with him, no matter what, which made him relax.

"Be nice...please. He's extremely important to me," Kathleen told her family in French, taking the seat she'd abandoned that Morgan now held out for her.

After helping Kathleen into her chair, Morgan took the seat to her right. Kathleen's father tossed back his drink and waved over the waitress. "Young lady, bring me another and bring him more of whatever he's having."

"Yes, sir. Will you be having your usual, Mr. Kingsley—whiskey neat—or would you like another beer?"

"My usual, Susan, thank you," Morgan replied.

Kathleen's sister gave Morgan the once-over before saying, "Mr. Kingsley—"

"Please, call me Morgan."

"Morgan, I recently had the chance to see your mother in action. She's quite formidable," Kennedy complimented him.

Morgan's eyes cut to Kathleen. *Oh no.* Kathleen had

to make sure Morgan knew their relationship had nothing to do with her family's business. "You had the opportunity to work with Victoria. When did we get in the oil and gas business, Kennedy?" Kathleen frowned at her sister.

Kennedy matched her sister's confused look. "We aren't. I know you've been away from the business for a minute and that I'm the company's CEO, but you should know that too, Kathleen," she said before reaching for her wineglass and taking a sip. "We were at Sotheby's for an auction a few months ago. I saw her decimate the other bidders in pursuit of a stunning painting that she just had to have. It was impressive."

Morgan reached for Kathleen's hand and intertwined their fingers. "That sounds like my mother."

Kathleen breathed a sigh of relief when Morgan squeezed her hand. "I asked my father to send help for the town, and fortunately we had a crew nearby," she explained to Morgan.

"Yes, it is. I saw the equipment parked at the edge of town, not to mention all the lights illuminating the town square and Main Street." Morgan turned to Kathleen's father. "Thank you, sir."

"Here you go." The waitress returned with both men's drinks.

"Thank you and please add their drinks to my tab," Morgan instructed.

"Yes, sir." The young woman smiled and walked away.

"That wasn't necessary but thank you," Jonathan said, reaching for his glass.

"It's the least I can do."

"Actually it's not," Kennedy stated.

"Kennedy," Kathleen admonished.

"It's okay, sweetheart. What else can I do?" Morgan asked Kennedy, reaching for his drink.

"You can convince my sister to come work with her family where she belongs now that she's left OSHA."

Morgan's head snapped to Kathleen. "You quit OSHA?"

Thanks, Kennedy. "Yes. That's one of many things I needed to talk to you about."

"What is there to talk about? You're a Winston with engineering and architectural degrees going to waste. We could use you at the company we will inherit someday," Kennedy said.

Kathleen loved her sister, but right now she wanted to strangle her. Kennedy's practical side annoyed the hell out of her. "Kennedy, I have plans of my own."

"Looks like I have a lot to learn about you still," he whispered. "And I'm looking forward to it."

Kathleen giggled. "Kennedy, I—"

"Kathleen, you can't seriously be considering taking another government or low-paying job. Not that you need the money, but most places can't pay you nearly what you're worth." Kennedy's mouth was set in a hard line.

"Why is everything about money and status with you, Kennedy?" She scrutinized her sister.

"Because you're a Winston." Kennedy turned to their father. "Aren't you going to say anything?"

"Kathleen, are you in love with this young man?" their father asked in his preferred language.

She held her father's gaze as she felt Morgan's eyes on her face. Kathleen raised her chin, turned her attention away from her father to Morgan and replied in English, "Yes, Daddy. I love him very much."

Morgan released an audible sigh, brought Kathleen's

hands to his lips and kissed them. He turned to her father. "I love your daughter too, sir…very much."

"Well, that's that." Jonathan Winston turned his attention to Morgan and in English said, "When you two decide to marry, Kathleen—"

"Daddy—"

"—there will be a proper wedding. There will be no elopement. Is that understood?" he stated, ignoring Kathleen, who was shaking her head.

"Yes, sir," Morgan replied with a wide smile.

Chapter 23

"Now that that's settled, we should leave these two to do whatever. We have a plane to catch," Kennedy stated sarcastically, rising from her seat.

Jonathan Winston got to his feet and finished off his drink. "We should go."

"What... Where are you going?" Kathleen's eyes jumped between her sister and father.

"Thanks to this grand gesture of yours, we have to go smooth things out with a pretty pissed-off client," Kennedy informed her sister.

"Sorry, Daddy." Kathleen and Morgan got to their feet.

"Sir, please allow me to cover the cost for the inconvenience," Morgan offered.

Jonathan set his glass on the table. "I'm an extremely wealthy man, and I'm not talking about my ridiculously large bank accounts. I have the love of four children who mean more to me than any amount of money. Satisfying their needs and often their wants is my pleasure, regardless of the cost. Not to mention the people of this town we get to help too. I can't begin to give you a number to repay that particular pleasure."

"I can," Kennedy said, winking at Kathleen, who burst into laughter.

"Do you have to leave now? We could have dinner," Kathleen suggested, feeling overwhelmed with happiness.

"Next time. Kennedy's right. We need to go smooth Old Man Beckman's feathers. Reassure him that his building will get built on time and within budget." He extended his hand to Morgan. "Take care of my girl."

"Yes, sir." The two men shook hands.

Kathleen hugged and kissed her father and sister before walking them to their car. As he stood and watched the car pull off, Morgan leaned over and asked, "Is that invitation still open?"

Kathleen looked up, frowning, feeling perplexed. "What invitation?"

"To join you in bed."

Kathleen giggled and turned red. She pulled a key card out of her pocket and handed it to him. Kathleen hid her face in Morgan's chest as he picked her up and carried her through the lobby, down the hallway to the elevator for the short ride up three flights to her hotel room. Morgan opened her door, crossed the threshold and placed Kathleen on her feet. He backed her against the door and kissed her as if it was his last opportunity.

Kathleen gently pulled back and said, "We should talk."

"It's not necessary. I know everything," Morgan explained, then devoured Kathleen's mouth and raised her dress.

"Wait…what do you mean it's not necessary?" Kathleen asked between kisses. She could see the love and passion in Morgan's eyes, and she wanted nothing more than to satisfy the need that they both shared, but Kathleen was determined to clear the air before they went any further.

Morgan sighed, dropped his hands and took a step back. "I talked to my mother."

Kathleen's forehead creased. "Victoria talked to you. What did she say?"

Morgan took Kathleen's hand and walked over to the sofa. He sat down and pulled Kathleen onto his lap. "When I found out who you were and what you really did for OSHA, I called her. I felt she had a right to know if someone was coming for us."

Kathleen bowed her head. "I was...at first."

Morgan used the index finger of his right hand, slid it under her chin and raised her face. "I know. I also know why you felt you had to."

"I'm—"

Morgan placed two fingers over her lips. "Let me finish. Yes, I was angry when I found out the truth. Well, most of it, anyway. But in spite of my anger, I couldn't deny how much I love you. I knew there had to be more to the story. There was no way the woman... my woman...would do anything to hurt me intentionally. Not my future."

Kathleen was so overwhelmed by the sincerity in Morgan's voice and love in his eyes she could no longer hold back her tears. "I wouldn't."

"After my mother explained what happened to your mother, it all made sense."

Kathleen cupped his face. "I'm so sorry I lied to you."

"It's over." He gently kissed her on the lips.

Kathleen shifted her body and straddled him. "Yes,

it is." She rose up slightly and pulled her dress over her head and tossed it. "Now, where were we?"

Morgan smiled. "One more thing."

Kathleen swerved her hips, leaned forward and kissed him. "Just one." She pulled his shirt over his head and dropped it to the floor.

He smirked. "Why did you quit your job?"

"I was hoping you'd forgive me and make me a better offer," she explained as she unbuckled his belt and unzipped his pants.

Overwhelmed with love and need, Kathleen freed his erection, slid the fine cloth covering her sex to the side and lowered herself onto him. "Yes," she whispered, circling her hips. "Damn, no condom."

When Kathleen rose up off Morgan, he held his tip at her entrance. "We're both healthy and in love, right?"

"Yes," she moaned as his tip slipped back inside her.

"Your future's with me and you want my babies, right?" He thrust his hips upward slightly.

"Yes...oh yes," she cried out with her eyes closed.

"Then we're fine," he insisted.

Kathleen gripped Morgan's shoulders with both hands and slowly but deliberately circled her hips, engulfing his shaft. Morgan removed Kathleen's bra, caressed, kissed and sucked her breasts. They moaned their satisfaction in unison. As Kathleen's need increased, she took more control and Morgan grabbed her hips with both hands to assist in her effort. The manic pace he set had them sweating, breathing hard and then falling into sweet bliss together.

After, Morgan wrapped his arms around Kathleen and whispered, "Marry me," in her ear. She leaned back and stared into his eyes. The lump in Kathleen's throat wouldn't let the words come forward. She nodded and kissed Morgan with a great deal of passion.

After surrendering to the need for air, Morgan wiped away Kathleen's tears and asked, "How's that for a better offer?"

Finding her voice, Kathleen replied. "One I couldn't possibly refuse."

* * * * *

MILLS & BOON

THE HEART OF ROMANCE

A ROMANCE FOR EVERY READER

MODERN

Prepare to be swept off your feet by sophisticated, sexy and seductive heroes, in some of the world's most glamourous and romantic locations, where power and passion collide.

HISTORICAL

Escape with historical heroes from time gone by. Whether your passion for wicked Regency Rakes, muscled Vikings or rugged Highlanders, awa the romance of the past.

MEDICAL

Set your pulse racing with dedicated, delectable doctors in the high-pressure world of medicine, where emotions run high and passion, comfort love are the best medicine.

True Love

Celebrate true love with tender stories of heartfelt romance, from the rush of falling in love to the joy a new baby can bring, and a focus on t emotional heart of a relationship.

Desire

Indulge in secrets and scandal, intense drama and plenty of sizzling hot action with powerful and passionate heroes who have it all: wealth, statu good looks…everything but the right woman.

HEROES

Experience all the excitement of a gripping thriller, with an intense romance at its heart. Resourceful, true-to-life women and strong, fearless face danger and desire - a killer combination!

To see which titles are coming soon, please visit

millsandboon.co.uk/nextmonth

MILLS & BOON
True Love
Romance from the Heart

Celebrate true love with tender stories of heartfelt romance, from the rush of falling in love to the joy a new baby can bring, and a focus on the emotional heart of a relationship.